JOYCE MARLOW

Hodder & Stoughton
LONDON SYDNEY AUCKLAND TORONTO

FOR JOY ROWE
with my love

British Library Cataloguing in Publication Data

Marlow, Joyce, *1929–*
    Anne
    I. Title
    823'.914[F]

    ISBN 0-340-40665-8

Published by Hodder and Stoughton,
a division of Hodder and Stoughton Ltd,
Mill Road, Dunton Green, Sevenoaks, Kent TN13 2YE.
Editorial Office: 47 Bedford Square, London WC1B 3DP.

Photoset by Rowland Phototypesetting Ltd,
Bury St Edmunds, Suffolk.

Printed in Great Britain by St Edmundsbury Press Ltd,
Bury St Edmunds, Suffolk.

PART I

I

Childishly excited, but doing her best to appear maturely composed, Anne stood on the terrace at Chenneys with her mother and Philip, to welcome the guests to her coming-of-age ball. The weather usually behaved for her birthday and for the great occasion of her twenty-first it had excelled itself. A heavenly day had darkened into a perfect evening.

Beyond the terrace the rose gardens and the trees along the sweep of the drive were looped with fairy lights, coloured spotlights shone in the herbaceous borders, across the parkland and the ornamental lake, highlighting the mass of water lilies, turning the marquees that had been erected on the main lawn into rainbow-hued visions from outer space. Behind Anne, white spotlights illuminated the Tudor manor house, glistening on the mullioned windows, silhouetting its elegant lines.

It was Philip who had organised the delightful spectacle. Privately, Anne always thought of him as 'Philip' and publicly, according to how she was feeling, she addressed him as 'stepfather', very occasionally as 'stepdaddy' like her siblings, or, when she was really furious, as 'Sir Philip'. That he adored her mother, simply worshipping the ground his darling Kessie walked upon, behaving as if he were her divinely appointed guardian angel, truly husbanding her fragile strength, were undeniable facts. Over the years Anne had more or less come to terms with Philip's presence in her life, though her mother's remarriage, to him of all people, had devastated her almost as much as her father's death.

'Julian!' she cried, delighted that he was among the earliest arrivals.

Evening cloak draped over his shoulders, top hat in hand, in his white tie and tails Julian presented a picture of masculine elegance. The presents were being piled on the oak table in the entrance hall, to be opened later, but Anne deserted her post on the terrace to open his. Inside the elaborately gift-wrapped package, decorated with a pink bow and an orchid in a stiff cellophane box, was a jewel case and inside that lay the loveliest pearl necklace.

'I h-hope it's all right, Anne. It's f-fearfully difficult choosing jewellery for a lady and I've arranged that you m-may change the necklace if you wish. But I know you like p-pearls.'

'It's beautiful. Thank you a million times, Julian. And if somebody can find me a pin, I'm going to wear your orchid. Will you fix it for me?'

There was always somebody on hand at Chenneys to provide virtually anything and while she waited for a pin to be produced, Anne thought Julian's stammer was its worst when he was nervous or emotional. There was no reason for him to be nervous – socially he did not lack confidence and anyway he knew both her mother and Philip – so Anne attributed the stammering to an innate shyness entangled with his feelings towards her. They had met as children during the war, his father, Guy Kendle, having become one of her father's closest friends, but Mummy had not kept in touch with Mrs Kendle. With a mother like her, it was no wonder Julian stammered in the first place. Anne and he had remet at a party just over a year ago and they'd found they had much in common, including a love of literature, he having read English at Cambridge, she at Oxford, and perhaps because both their fathers had been killed in the Great War, a commitment to world disarmament and pacifism. Deep as their friendship had grown, it had not yet progressed beyond that point.

When the pin arrived, slightly embarrassed but giving her his charmingly deprecatory smile, Julian fixed the orchid to the left strap of Anne's ball gown. As his long fingers brushed her exposed skin she felt her blood heating. Perhaps tonight he would make a move in a romantic direction.

After Julian's arrival it was as if a seaside excursion train had suddenly disgorged its passengers at Chenneys, droves of people trooping up the steps to the terrace. Anne felt a bit like royalty, shaking hands, kissing her closer friends, repeating, 'Yes, isn't it the most glorious evening?', 'Lovely to see you', 'So glad you could come', which last statements held true for virtually all the guests. The exceptions were the local county snobs whom Mummy had said they should invite as a matter of courtesy and the ghastly Marchal family who were even more snobbish. To be fair to Philip, which Anne freely admitted she seldom was, he liked his relations no more than she did and they were, thank heaven, seldom invited to Chenneys; and the stupid spelling of a name pronounced 'Marshall', derived from Norman ancestors who had landed with William the Conqueror in 1066.

After the hordes had arrived, Philip said he thought Kessie should have a brief rest. In a pleated silk, mushroom-coloured evening gown, the fur collar of the matching jacket framing her lovely chestnut hair, Anne's mother was at her most radiant. With a smile she said to her husband, 'Yes, I will in a minute, darling. But it's time Anne enjoyed herself and I want to watch her start the dancing.'

Julian was still on the terrace, talking to a group of friends. Holding out her hand towards him, Anne called, 'Are you going to be my partner for the first waltz?'

Momentarily he looked startled but, recovering his composure, flashing his sweet smile, Julian stammered, 'Oh y-yes. I'll b-be honoured, Anne.'

Holding Mummy's arm, Philip limped down the steps with Anne and Julian. It was Philip's good fortune that a childhood accident had maimed his right leg, rendering him unfit for active service in the Great War. A tidal wave of guests followed them towards the marquee, in which the floor had been laid for dancing. On Anne and Julian's entrance the orchestra stopped playing bland background music and the band leader smiled at them as they took their places in the middle of the floor. After Julian had bowed ceremoniously to Anne, to the strains of 'The Blue Danube' they glided across the floor. Apart from the pleasure of floating in Julian's arms – he was an excellent ballroom dancer – Anne enjoyed being the centre of attention.

When the waltz finished, she kept the focus on herself by grabbing Peter Tomkins' hand – he being one of the under-gardeners – and having the next dance with him. It was not a big success because Peter's face was beetroot red and he kept falling over both their feet. Temporarily Anne declined the requests for dances from a cluster of male friends and went outside, for on her way to the marquee she had noticed estate workers and villagers from Marshall Minnis sprinkling the lawn like disconsolate daisies. They were all in their best bibs and tuckers, the men mostly looking self-conscious in their hired evening suits, the women wearing artificial silk and imitation satin gowns, with cheap artificial flowers pinned to their bodices. Everybody was relaxed enough with her, assuring Miss Anne they were having the time of their lives, but her efforts to introduce them to her other friends were no more successful than the dance with Peter Tomkins had been. After stilted conversations, nearly everybody shot back into their class-conscious boxes and with a slight sigh, deciding the night of her twenty-first was perhaps not the best time to change the world, Anne gave up.

'Having a social conscience must be the most frightful bore.'

'How would you know? You're an absolute wart.'

'May the wart have a tango with his big sister on her big night?'

At the age of sixteen, Mark was already nearly six feet tall. With the same loose-limbed frame, black hair, dark skin and dark eyes, physically his resemblance to their father was at times heart-stopping but he had already announced, 'I'm fed up with being told how like dear dead Daddy I am, particularly when I can barely remember him. I'm not Tom Whitworth, mark two. I'm Mark one.' The pursuit of his own personality had led Mark to be as unlike Daddy as he possibly could be, flippantly uninterested in Socialism or social problems. He fancied himself as a dancer and, maddening as he was, Anne was enormously fond of her young brother. Graciously, she said he could have a tango with her.

On their way back to the dance marquee, Anne saw Julian in conversation with Theo Marvell. Theo was the couturier Philip delighted in bringing to Chenneys for his darling Kessie's sake and over the years he had become a family friend. Claiming descent from Andrew Marvell, proclaiming that his genius lay in dress designing rather than poetry, he was an outrageous character and, Anne presumed, a homosexual. Practically her sexual experience was limited, but theoretically she was well-informed, her mother and Philip having given her a free run of Chenneys' splendid library which contained some *fascinating* books.

Theo spotted her and with his arms outstretched, he minced towards them calling out, 'Dearest heart, I've said it before but I'll say it again, your darling Mama's ensemble and your gown are among my most ravishing creations. You look utterly divine. Doesn't she look too dazzling for words? From *devant* and *derrière*.' Theo swung Anne round so that Julian could admire the daring backlessness of the softly clinging, lime-green chiffon gown he had designed for her coming-of-age. The sibilant voice that emphasised every other word then informed them, 'Backs are on their way in. Legs on their way out.'

Simultaneously Mark said, 'Where are they going?' and Anne said, 'What do you mean? Legs are on their way out?'

Theo explained that the pendulum of fashion was about to be swung by such as he, towards the reintroduction of long skirts. Anne said neither she nor any modern young woman had the slightest intention of obeying the dictates of fashion and swathing themselves in long skirts. Theo said, 'Darling heart, with sinuous, shapely legs like yours, I sympathise but . . .'

'It's nothing to do with the shape of my legs,' Anne interrupted loftily, though actually she took pleasure in displaying their contours in the current knee-length skirts. 'And it has everything to do with freedom of movement and the emancipation of women and . . .'

'You're not going to be tiresome tonight and give us tedious lectures about women's rights. I am simply not going to allow it. You're all madly emancipated now anyway, and there's nothing more to be said.'

'Ha!' Anne always enjoyed an argument and the teasing verbal skirmishes with Theo were fun. 'That's what you think.'

'Yes it is, sweetie-pie, and the subject's closed. By order of Marvell.' With his head on one side, Theo said, 'I care for the chunks of the Marchal family jewels. They do things for you. And for my gown. But isn't this . . .' lightly he touched Julian's orchid, '. . . a teensy-weensy bit much?'

'No. It was a present from Mr Kendle.'

'Have we put our tiny feet into it?' Tilting his head again,

Theo smiled toothily at Julian who was looking distinctly embarrassed, but with only a slight stutter he managed to say, 'May I have another d-dance with you, Anne?'

'Of course you may.' To Mark she said, 'You can have one later.'

'Ta ever so,' her brother replied.

'Who's the big fat Jewess?'

'The family's in trade. Naturally. Aren't they all? Lawson's Doilys, I gather. Anne found her at Oxford. You know what la Whitworth's like about lame dogs and lost causes.'

The tribal gaggle of those Anne designated 'the county snobs', drifted past Rebecca who was sitting on one of the rustic benches that had been placed round the lake. They knew she was in earshot, Rebecca thought furiously, or did they imagine big fat Jewesses had no ears? As a guest at Chenneys, with difficulty she held her tongue and thought it was a good job 'la Whitworth' hadn't heard them.

Her paternal grandfather had been born Chaim Lewental in Frankfurt and he'd had a hard time in England until he'd hit upon the idea of designing and manufacturing paper, rather than linen, doilys. Once Lawson's Dainty Decorative Doilys – he'd anglicised his name – were covering plates and cake-stands the length and breadth of the British Isles, grandpa had married, sired a large brood and brought them up to be good English Jews. Until she was seventeen Rebecca herself had felt as much English as Jewish and regarded England as her home. Then, in the sixth form at Manchester High School, she had become friendly with a pretty, seemingly nice girl called Doreen Shawcross who had invited everybody to her seventeenth birthday party, except Rebecca. For several days, baffled as much as hurt, she said nothing, before deciding to solve the mystery by observing, 'You haven't invited me.'

'Oh, I thought you'd understand.' Doreen looked annoyed that the subject had been brought up. 'I can't invite you into my house.'

Slowly absorbing the implications of the remark, Rebecca remembered blinking at Doreen as she tossed her head and the blonde curls bounced on her cheeks. She said, 'If your party were being held in a field, would you have invited me?'

Before she walked away, feeling more desolate than she ever had in her life, Rebecca had the satisfaction of seeing a discomfited expression steal over Doreen Shawcross's pretty pink features and of realising that by speaking her mind briefly and to the point, she had found a useful weapon. It was one she had since cultivated. Later, after anguished, then angry, internal debate, she had decided the Zionists were right. Until the Jews had a National Home of their own, which way back in 1917 Mr Balfour had promised them in Palestine, the periodic persecution and the continual humiliation of her race would not cease. Rebecca was now a convinced and committed Zionist.

Glancing across the lawn, she saw Anne about to enter the marquee that had been erected for the dancing, arm-in-arm with her charming young devil of a brother and Julian Kendle. The first time Anne had introduced her to Julian during one of his visits to Oxford, Rebecca had fallen hopelessly in love with him and 'hopeless' was the right word. She had no false modesty about her intellectual abilities – she had gained the First Anne had muffed – but physically Rebecca was convinced she was unattractive, and she knew herself to be calamitously clumsy. Julian was a bred-in-the-bone Roman Catholic and Rebecca sensed the slight, almost unconscious, aversion to her Jewishness. Finally, perhaps most importantly, she would do nothing that might come between a friendship that was immensely precious to her, like trying to steal Anne's boy friend, in the unlikely event that she could.

Or one of her boy friends. Sandy Dalziel was striding across the lawn, though him Anne could keep. Crossly he said, 'There you are, Lawson. I thought you were supposed to be helping us.'

'I am.' Good old Communist Sandy could be as casually anti-Semitic as most of 'em. Only last week he'd talked gaily about getting the Israelite moneylender off his back, after he'd shown Rebecca the expensive present he'd bought for Anne's twenty-first.

'Come on then,' he urged. 'It'll be midnight before we know where we are.'

Just before midnight, before the final minutes of the twenty-first anniversary of Anne's natal day, though not her party, ticked away, everybody crowded into the refreshment marquee. She mounted the rostrum with her family, champagne glasses were charged and in his splintered, upper-class tones Philip proposed the toast: 'Pray lift your glasses to drink to the coming-of-age of my dear stepdaughter Anne. May she be blessed with good health and happiness throughout a long, successful life.'

Everybody lifted their champagne glasses on high and drank to her future, and in her ear Philip murmured, 'My own special toast to you, my very dear and difficult stepdaughter.'

In the circumstances Anne replied, 'Thank you, stepdaddy.'

She felt chokey as her nearest and dearest toasted her. Apart from Kate. What was the little madam up to that she couldn't be bothered to drink to her sister's coming-of-age?

The rendition of 'Happy birthday, dear Anne' almost lifted the canvas off the marquee and to a storm of clapping and cheering and an explosion of the press photographers' flashguns, Anne then cut the seven-tiered, fantastically iced birthday cake. Philip wasn't keen on invasions of his privacy but he accepted that the Whitworth–Marchal family was newsworthy – himself the most successful of playwrights, his wife the renowned suffragette and widow of Tom Whitworth, his eldest stepdaughter voted 'Oxford's favourite undergraduette' – and his wife's contention that within limits, co-operation with the press was preferable to harassment.

Then, in Anne's other ear Mummy whispered, 'Your father would have been so proud of you.'

Coming-of-age was a watershed, an occasion for looking backwards as well as forwards and the memory that had haunted Anne for twelve years, that she knew would haunt her until her dying day, flashed into her mind.

It was of the very last time she had seen her father, just before he returned to France after his brief, unexpected visit home in October 1918. They were standing in the hall at The Grove, the house in London where she had been born, and Daddy bent down to kiss her. She took his officer's cap from his hand and placed it firmly on the thick black hair, cut short in army style. With a grin he stood up and saluted her. Then he said, '"Be good, sweet maid, and let who will be clever." That's what the poem says. I want you to go on being good, but take no notice of the last bit. You cultivate that bright little mind of yours, Anny-Panny.'

Calling her by her infant nickname, he ruffled her hair which had still been hanging down her back, caught in a bow. The taxi had been waiting to take him and Mummy to the station, Daddy told them he'd soon be home, this time it would be for good, and he'd take them out for tea and they could eat as many cream buns as they wanted. Then she and Con, the twins Kate and Mark, had stood at the front gate with their devoted housekeeper, waving goodbye to Daddy as the taxi disappeared down the hill. Within the month her adored father had been killed and Anne's secure, stable childhood world had collapsed.

On the whole, even if things had not turned out exactly as she had planned – only getting a good second class degree had been a bitter disappointment, though it was her own fault for not working hard enough for Schools – Anne felt she had not let her father down. And her Oxford friends were thumping the tables and shouting, 'Speech, speech!'

She had inherited some of her parents' oratorical powers but on this occasion she was going to surprise everybody by the brevity of her speech. Holding out her hands for silence, eventually gaining it, Anne said, 'I want to thank everybody for making this the most fantastic day of my life. I hope you're all enjoying it as much as I am.' After the roar of assent had subsided she went on, 'And I'm going to be serious for a couple of minutes.'

A posse of her friends called out, 'Shame!'

'In these surroundings, it's all too easy to forget the fearful economic problems enveloping our country and the world. I don't expect you to dwell on them tonight . . .'

'Good-oh!'

'Nor do I expect to be heckled at my own coming-of-age party!' That got a laugh. 'But personally I'm going to do my darnedest to make the nineteen-thirties a more just and, above all, peaceful decade. And here endeth the first, and last, lesson of the evening.'

When the cheers had died away, to Anne's surprise Sandy Dalziel, who had been amazingly conspicuous by his absence all evening, jumped on to a chair. Sandy was actually the

Honourable Alexander James Iain Dalziel which surname, for reasons best known to the Scots, was pronounced 'Daleel'. His ginger hair and freckled face were the reasons for the diminutive, 'Sandy'. They'd met at Oxford and shortly after their introduction, in the middle of the Cloister Quadrangle at Magdalen, he'd gone down on one knee, put his hand on his heart and said, 'Will you do me the honour of soon becoming my wife, oh beautiful Anne Whitworth?' At regular intervals ever since, usually in some equally inappropriate or ridiculous place, Sandy had popped the question. It was fun having a devoted cavalier, they were both political animals (which Julian was not), sharing the view that it was their duty to rectify the world's injustices, if not the best way to achieve the millennium, Sandy being as dedicated a Communist as Anne a Socialist.

She presumed he was about to announce the firework display, though she didn't see why Sandy should do the honours, but what he actually said came as a complete surprise. 'Before the fireworks that have been laid on for your delight, we have devised a short entertainment. We are presenting the final scene from *Comus*. Don't worry if you don't know the story. Few people do. Milton's masque is rarely performed. Or read. Other than by intellectual types from Somerville.' That got a laugh from the male contingent of Oxford friends. 'Just step outside and enjoy the show.'

Everybody streamed outside and Anne realised how secretly busy her friends and the Chenneys staff had been. Close by the lake, a piano had been trundled into position. As Con started towards it, Anne said, 'Are you in on this?'

Her favourite sister smiled and nodded. When Con seated herself at a piano, something akin to the transformation scene at the end of a Christmas pantomime occurred. Gone was the gentle creature who wanted everybody to be happy, in its place was a young woman whose intense concentration drew the subtlest and most passionate sounds from the keyboard. Con was already studying at the Royal College of Music in London and Anne knew she was destined to be a famous concert pianist.

Once everybody was settled, Con launched into the opening bars of *The Moonlight Sonata* which were perfect for the final scene from *Comus*, Anne thought, because the lulling sounds always made her think of lapping water rather than moonlit reaches. When Kate as Sabrina fair apparently rose from the lake, doubling for 'the smooth Severn stream', there was a gasp of pure pleasure from the audience. Her elaborate green make-up glittering, her water-lily-garlanded hair and the drapes of her costume flowing behind her slight figure, Kate sped down Sandy's path of artificial emerald light to the darker green spotlights in the centre of the playing area. There, accompanied by Con on the piano, in her sweet soprano voice she sang Sabrina's song, 'By the rushy-fringed bank, Where grows the willow and the osier dank.'

They were enchanted moments, for Kate had a magical ethereal quality that caught at the throat. Her sister's failure to appear for the toast was now explained. How could she, in costume and make-up, without spoiling the surprise? Anne felt an absolute heel for harbouring unkind thoughts. When the entertainment was finished and the applause had died away, she headed the congratulations to producer and players. Looking immensely pleased with himself Sandy accepted them as his due, but anxiously Kate said, 'Was I really all right?'

'You were delightful, the personification of Sabrina fair.'

From childhood days Kate had announced her intention of being a famous actress and at the praise she almost purred with pleasure. With delicate features in an oval face, slanting green eyes, and the silky black hair she had inherited from Daddy, Kate's charms were kittenishly feline, and their relationship was, Anne acknowledged, a scratchy one. Kate had long seemed determined to prove that anything big sister could do, she could do better, yet Anne was the big sister whose approval she apparently needed.

The firework display was another enchanting spectacle but after the last rockets had spumed into the sky, Philip said he thought it was time Kessie retired. She didn't argue, which meant she was exhausted. After Anne had kissed her mother goodnight, she saw Julian coming towards her. Sandy was busily discussing his production of *Comus* with a group of admirers, which would keep him engaged for the next half-hour and perhaps allow her to slip away with Julian. But then Rebecca appeared and, infuriatingly, she stayed chatting

17

to Julian about the difficulties of keeping *Comus* a secret and their fears that Anne had guessed something was afoot. Fortunately, one of their Oxford friends called out, 'Lawson, you're the expert on Restoration drama. We need you to settle an argument.'

After Rebecca had reluctantly left them, Anne decided boldness had better be her friend if she wanted to end a perfect day in the way she had dreamed. Smiling at Julian she said, 'Do you feel like a short stroll far from the madding crowd? The birthday girl does!'

'I was about to m-make the same suggestion.'

Damn, Anne thought, why hadn't she given him the opportunity, instead of leaping in, though she was elated to hear the suggestion had been in his mind.

Side by side they wandered across the moonlit parkland. Since coming down from Cambridge a few years ago, Julian had been working as a publisher's editor and Anne asked how life at Stoddard and Simpson's was. He said, 'Actually, I'm growing a bit frustrated. My sympathies are with the authors. Most of them really are rather badly treated and, unlike your stepfather, most of them are very bad at business. But if I say anything to old Josiah Stoddard about better terms, he bites my head off and insists we're all one big happy family in which nobody's happier than his authors.'

Not for the first time Anne marvelled at the way Julian discussed publishing affairs without a single stammer or stutter. Yet if she mentioned personal matters, which she wanted to, his words would start falling over themselves. Was he aware, she wondered, of the dichotomy between his business and personal self? Would it be helpful to mention it? At the moment, Anne decided, it might send him back into his shell of shyness which was the last thing she wanted.

'Do you know what I'd like to do?' he said.

Anne thought, Make love to me, I hope. She said, 'No. But do tell.'

'I'd like to set myself up as a literary agent, to give my authors more personal encouragement and support, and to help them handle their business affairs.'

'Julian, what a spiffing idea! Why don't you? You're not short of the money to set yourself up, are you? I'm sure Philip

18

would lend you some if you are. You know what he thinks about publishers!'

They both smiled because Philip's glacial rows with the publishers of his plays were notorious in the book trade. Julian said, 'No, no, it's not that. It's, well, I d-don't think m-my . . .'

Ah, enter the dragon woman centre stage, Anne thought. His mother had to be connected with Julian's emotional problems. As anticipated, he went on to say he didn't think his Mama would be pleased at the idea, particularly as she hadn't been well recently. In her attempts to get him back to the Kendle family estate, Ryby Hall, which was in the detached, lakeland part of north Lancashire, Julian's mother was always dying, or if she wasn't she said his grandfather was.

'Honestly, Julian, your mother and your grandfather are as strong as oxes. When they do finally pop off, they'll both be made into Oxo cubes.'

'Anne!' Julian laughed. 'You do say the most d-dreadful things!'

During this conversation she had been steering him in the direction of the summer house, in whose secluded purlieus Anne hoped romantic things might happen. As they approached the chalet-type building, from the gigglings and whisperings floating through the open window, other people had been smitten by the same idea, so there was no option but to continue walking. Beyond the summer house, the path led through a copse towards the stream and still talking about Julian setting up as a literary agent and Anne being one of his clients after she'd written the novel that was shaping in her mind, they proceeded along the path. At one point a fallen branch lay in their way; solicitously Julian took her arm in his and helped her over.

Once they had passed the obstacle, however, to Anne's disappointment his hand dropped to his side. When they reached the rustic bridge that spanned the stream, she halted. For all her general self-confidence and theoretical sexual knowledge, in matters of the heart she found herself as shy as Julian appeared to be, but they were in one of the prettiest parts of the estate and on such a night as this, with the strains of a Viennese waltz echoing faintly, it was the romantic setting *par excellence*. Julian had wanted to escape from the throng, he was five years her senior, he must be more experienced, he must know how she felt about him, so surely he must now take the initiative.

To prod him into action, breathily Anne said, 'Just look at the moon.'

Julian looked at the eager, upturned face shining in the moonlight, rather than at the moon itself. Anne wasn't pretty like her sister Con or potentially beautiful like Kate; her features were too sharp, but she had that unusual copper-coloured hair cut into a softly waved, shingled style and those beautiful eyes, dark and challenging. At the moment they were gazing at him with expectant desire and he knew she was waiting for, wanting him, to kiss her. He liked her immensely, her mixture of boyishness and girlishness appealed to him, the slim hips, long legs, small breasts, and he had felt the urge to be alone with her, yet . . . averting his gaze, Julian stared into the darkness of the surrounding woods. There were those memories pushed to the back of his mind and he was only too aware how tangled and deep-rooted his emotional difficulties were. Perhaps if his father had survived the war things would have been different, but as it was he had constantly to balance his mother's need for him, his dislike of hurting her, his feelings of guilt when he did, with his own desires and ambitions.

'Oh, there goes a flashing argent fish. It looks as if it's escaped from the lake.'

The incisiveness of Anne's voice refocused his attention on her. While the confused thoughts had been racing through Julian's mind, she had walked on to the rustic bridge and she was now leaning over one side, staring down into the platinum ribbon of the water flowing gently underneath. The shawl had slipped from round her shoulders and in the daringly backless evening gown, her skin from shoulders to waist was a silvered expanse of flawless flesh. Having presented him with this erotic sight, slowly Anne turned round. She had taken off her long gloves and was leaning against the side of the bridge, her left arm stretched across the wooden struts, arching her body so that the soft chiffon folds of her lime-green gown outlined her figure and the swell of her neat breasts was emphasised. With her right hand, she started to swing her gloves, and she was looking straight at him, those dark eyes glinting in the moonlight. Part of Julian wanted to accept the provocative invitation but . . . the earlier determination deserted him and he knew he was going to stammer appallingly.

'Should w-we n-not be g-getting back? Everybody w-will be w-wondering w-where the birthday g-girl is.'

2

Just before Christmas Anne was sitting at the typewriter in the living room of the third-floor flat in Gower Street. In their Somerville days she and Rebecca had frequently discussed being bachelor girls together in London, once they came down from Oxford, and the lease of this Bloomsbury flat which had two bedrooms, bathroom, kitchen and living room, had been her mother and Philip's splendid twenty-first birthday present. Apart from a few early alarms and excursions such as Lawson managing to fuse all the lights late one night and neither of them having the faintest idea what to do, they had settled in beautifully.

With her First tucked under her belt several good jobs had been dangled in front of Rebecca but she had chosen to work for the Jewish Agency for Palestine. This was no surprise because the Agency had been set up by Chaim Weizmann who had founded the British Zionist movement when he was living and lecturing in Manchester and, as an adopted Mancunian, Mr Weizmann was a particular hero of Rebecca's. Until Anne published her first novel and the shekels started to roll in, she aimed to keep herself by freelance writing. During the day, apart from the activities of Mrs Guppy, the cleaning lady who came in to 'do' for them, Sundays excepted, Anne had the flat to herself, to bang away on the Underwood portable typewriter Con and the twins had given her for her twenty-first, or to pad around smoking furiously when she was stuck.

At the moment she was thinking about Julian. She'd stopped blushing at the memory of the way she'd flaunted herself on the night of her twenty-first but she found the situation baffling and frustrating. Still, if he wanted to behave as if the incident on the rustic bridge had never happened, she didn't see what she could do about it other than continue to be friendly and hopeful. With a sigh Anne returned her attention to drafting a review of a blandly boring book by the wife of an Empire-builder who couldn't write for toffee. Having read through the lines she'd just typed, she tore the paper from the machine and threw her efforts into the wastepaper basket. Then the telephone rang. Only too glad of the interruption, she put her cigarette in the ashtray, lifted the receiver from the hook and said, 'Museum 2305, Anne Whitworth speaking.'

'Good morning, Miss Whitworth. Jack Parry-Jones here.'

'Oh hello.'

Somewhat to Anne's surprise, because she'd imagined Sandy involved in epic stage productions, he had accepted a job as a trainee radio drama producer with the BBC. Jack Parry-Jones was a 'talks' producer she'd met recently when Sandy had invited her to lunch at Savoy Hill. After they had lunched the three of them had enjoyed themselves 'testing' her voice in an empty studio. The men had stood her in front of a big round microphone perched on a long narrow stand, wheeling the sound-boards into position so that she was virtually enclosed in a little cell, giving her earphones so that she could hear how her voice sounded. Alarmingly sharp, it seemed to Anne, but they'd said she had a good microphone voice for a woman. Indignantly, she had demanded to know what they meant, *for a woman*. They'd said they regretted to inform her that microphones and most women's voices did not agree, other than trained actresses and not all of them. They thought it had to do with the higher female pitch.

Over the telephone Jack Parry-Jones's own lilting Welsh voice went on, 'Look, I'll be frank with you, Miss Whitworth, I've been badly let down at the last minute. I have a books programme going out this afternoon. What people might like to read for Christmas. I know you're well read and *au fait* with the current literary scene and I was wondering if you'd be interested in taking part? Give the young woman's choice. That is, if you're available.'

'I am and I'd love to.' And I know one book I shan't be recommending, Anne thought.

'Good-oh. We're actually on the air from four to four-thirty, so if you'll be at the studios by three o'clock, please, I'll fill you in.'

Anne said she would be there on the dot and after he had rung off, she jumped up from her chair and shouted, 'Yippee!'

They hadn't discussed money but she presumed she would be paid something. Thus far editors were proving less eager than Anne had anticipated to commission her to write articles or review books for them, so the broadcast was extra welcome. Having telephoned her mother and other friends to give them the great news, she was jotting down the titles of some books she'd enjoyed reading recently and the reasons why, when she heard the roar of Sandy's Bugatti snorting to a halt outside in Gower Street. While they had a snack lunch he proffered his professional advice for her broadcast, 'Speak directly into the microphone, but treat it as a friend. Keep your voice as level as possible and whatever you do, don't shout. Otherwise you'll overload the works and put us temporarily off the air. Some silly bitch did that only last week.'

For her first broadcast Anne selected her blue rep dress and jacket with the red trimmings and the matching hat with the snugly turned up brim. When she pirouetted round the living room in her outfit, Sandy said, 'That'll keep up the tone of the BBC.' He himself was looking artistically scruffy in an old pair of Oxford bags, with a coloured shirt, a four-in-hand tie and a brightly patterned pullover. He had however plunged into his job with enthusiasm, declaring, 'Radio is Shakespeare's muse of fire that can and will ascend the brightest heaven of invention', and if outsiders attacked the BBC he leapt to the defence of the best, most independent broadcasting corporation anybody had set up anywhere.

It was a fine winter's day, blessedly free from fog, and Sandy insisted on driving Anne to Savoy Hill in the Bugatti so that she could relax, though the way he drove, swerving round corners, cutting across oncoming trams, tearing down Kingsway at what seemed like ninety miles per hour, as if he were on the race-track at Brooklands, was not calculated to relax anybody. In the hospitality room Anne was given a cup of tea and Jack Parry-Jones introduced her to the chairman and her fellow broadcasters. The elderly literary gentleman, P. H. Carew, said to her, 'Ah, I remember your mother in her suffragette days, Miss Whitworth. What a game young lady she was and what a good speaker. In the space of thirty minutes, without moving from your chair, you will address more people than your mother reached in seven years of travelling the length and breadth of the British Isles.'

Anne presumed the observations were well intended but they did nothing to calm her mounting tension and by the time they were conducted into the studio, one in which they sat round rather than stood in front of the microphone, her stomach was churning with nerves. She had been a leading light of the Somerville Debating Society—it was at an inter-college debate with Magdalen that she had first met Sandy – but this was something entirely different. Anne watched the second hand of the studio clock jerk towards four o'clock and from behind the glass partition where he had joined Jack Parry-Jones, she saw Sandy giving her the thumbs-up sign. Then the studio manager signalled to the chairman who said smoothly into the microphone, 'Good afternoon, ladies and gentlemen. May I introduce our guests . . .' Frantically, Anne tried to recall Sandy's instructions and prayed she was not about to make a fool of herself.

Once she started speaking, she thoroughly enjoyed giving her views about books and on three occasions she begged to differ with Mr Carew's, though politely of course because he was an old man and naturally the tone of the broadcast was highly civilised and urbane. Then all too soon, before Anne had time to say a half of what she wanted to, the chairman was winding up, thanking his guests for a spirited and interesting discussion which had given him food for Christmas reading, as he hoped it had the listeners. Excitedly, Anne stayed talking with Sandy and Jack Parry-Jones who both congratulated her and when the pubs opened they took her round the corner for a drink. Sandy said, 'I told you she was a rare orchid who'd turn up trumps, if you'll excuse the mixed metaphors. One of our Anne's strengths is that she thinks about the consequences of her actions *afterwards*.'

That was an untrue statement but for the first time it occurred to Anne that Jack Parry-Jones had taken a chance on her. Several BBC people in the pub said they'd heard the broadcast and how well Miss Whitworth had come over, and, feeling justifiably pleased with herself, Anne accepted another gin and It, and another. A noisily excited argument then developed about women's role in the new society and as the one woman in the group Anne found herself heavily outvoted. Sandy was the most vociferous in his assertions that the battle of the sexes was finished and it was now the task of all right-minded people to overcome the menace of Fascism and fight for the brave new world, or somebody's version thereof, preferably his Communist one, in which there would be equity and justice for all, irrespective of sex, race or creed.

'There's neither room nor need for separate women's groups now,' he said loudly. 'They're merely divisive.'

'That's what men have always said,' Anne retorted equally loudly. 'I'm certain we have a special contribution to make to world disarmament and a permanent peace, which is why I'm active in the Women's Peace Party. For one thing, we had no political power whatsoever when the war broke out, therefore we cannot be held responsible for . . .'

'Women joined in the war-effort eagerly enough,' Jack Parry-Jones observed. 'You can say it was because of the way you proved yourselves during the war that you got the vote and other rights.'

'You can if you want,' said Anne. 'It's not true. If the suffragettes hadn't raised the consciousness of women as a whole, they wouldn't have been able to leap into the breach and do the things they did.'

They stayed until closing time and Anne thought she kept her sex's end up pretty well, though she wasn't herself entirely sure whether having got their feet under the table, as it were, it was now a question of women extending their leg-room, while they fought for the future side by side with men; or whether they still had specific problems as a sex that justified separate groups, other than in the pacifist field. When they left the pub Anne certainly felt she was the equal of any man and as they roared back to Gower Street in the Bugatti, she found Sandy's driving so exhilarating she sang *The March of the Women* at the top of her voice.

Once they were in the flat the exhilaration spread into a feeling of delicious abandonment. Anne had left a message with Mrs Guppy to bank up the fire and while Sandy put some more coal on, she threw off her hat, dropped her fur coat on to the sofa, collapsed backwards into the high-winged armchair and kicked off her shoes. Her euphoric mood was, she appreciated, probably slightly heightened by the unaccustomed amount of alcohol she had drunk but she was completely, joyously, in control of herself and the situation. Stretching her arms above her head, Anne came to her decision. She was a modern, emancipated young woman, she was of age and it was high time she satisfied her mind's urgent curiosity and her body's increasingly urgent demands. For whatever reasons, Julian had declined the covert invitation to induct her, but good old Sandy was sure to be willing.

'Do you want to make love to me? Rebecca's up north, Jewish Agency business, so we have the flat to ourselves.'

As she threw out the overt invitation, she heard Sandy's intake of breath before he whooped, 'Do I not, divinest honey-bunny.'

Then he fell on top of her, and as he kissed her Anne was fearfully conscious of his bulging hardness pressing against her, though that was what she wanted. Wasn't it? The preliminaries failed to rouse her in the way she'd imagined but Sandy was excited enough and she expected things would improve once they really got going. They decided to make love on the rug in front of the fire and while he stoked up the blaze, Anne checked that the front door of the flat was bolted, just in case Rebecca returned unexpectedly. Doing a Rebecca, she almost fell over the carpet as she came back into the living room.

There she saw that Sandy was already down to his vest and underpants, so nonchalantly she took off her blue rep jacket and dress, though she had slight trouble with the buttons, followed by her cami-knickers. She undid her suspenders and hoped Sandy was watching as she unrolled her silk stockings by placing each long leg in turn on the chair. Having chucked the stockings and suspender belt on top of the fur coat on the sofa, naked she turned round to look at Sandy. In the buff he was very lanky and bony and she wouldn't know whether or not, comparatively speaking, he was well-endowed. The only other male organs she'd ever seen had belonged to the village boys in the bushes behind the church in Marshall Minnis, dating back to the days when Mummy and Philip had first married and Anne had hoped that if she were discovered in such disgusting activities, her hated stepfather's reputation would be ruined. Actually, of course, he would have been sardonically amused, and she'd soon become embarrassed and bored, playing games of literal strip-poker.

'Gosh, you're beautiful,' Sandy whispered as he stared at her.

'Oh, before we start probably,' Anne corrected herself, 'properly, you do know what you're doing, don't you? I don't want to have a baby or anything.'

'I should hate you to have anything other than a baby.' At this observation Anne giggled, partly because she was suddenly feeling nervous, but also because Sandy did make her laugh. He went on, 'But I absolutely agree, we don't want an infant at the moment, so fear not, honey-bunny, your Sandy will protect you.'

They lay together on the rug and he kissed her breasts and massaged her crotch, though Anne did not find the latter experience as erotically stimulating as when she did it herself. But with the fire warming her limbs and the reflection of the flames casting a golden glow over Sandy's pale skin, she felt expectantly excited. When Sandy eventually tried to thrust himself into her body, Anne's hymen proved to be as securely bolted as the front door. When he pushed harder, she yelled, 'Stop it, you're hurting me.'

After what seemed like hours of his thrusting and desisting when commanded to do so, of Anne's shrieking and finally bursting into tears, he subsided completely and they gave up. While she sobbed disconsolately in his arms, complaining that her head was aching too, Sandy did his best to comfort her. He said, 'Some girls are ever so tight, I gather, honey-bunny. Unless the man behaves like a brute, you have to take it ever so gently.'

Snuffling back her tears, Anne said, 'I'm hungry. I haven't had anything since lunchtime. Do you want something to eat?'

'I wouldn't mind.'

At twenty-five past two in the morning—from her prone position on the rug, over Sandy's shoulder Anne glanced at the clock on the mantelpiece—she finally lost her virginity. The following moments, however, were even more shattering than the earlier part of the evening for by then Anne was sober, whereas earlier on, she now realised, she had been drunk. In those following moments nothing in particular happened as Sandy panted and snorted and banged away on top of her, except her thinking she'd never expected the induction to be such a rupturing process and there had to be more to making love than this.

At half past seven in the morning Rebecca fitted her key into the lock of their flat. When she found the door would not open, she took out the key, dropped it, and tried several more times before finally realising that for once her cackhandedness was not to blame and the door was bolted on the inside. Damn and blast it! They rarely bothered but perhaps being by herself Anne had decided to make doubly sure.

Wearily, Rebecca pressed the bell. There was no response so she kept ringing. All manner of politicking was bedevilling the Jewish Agency and she'd had a particularly exhausting week on what had been an information-cum-fund-raising tour. Rebecca had spoken to dozens of Jewish women's groups all over the north of England, trying not to lose patience with those who still bleated that Zionism undermined their assimilated positions in their own countries, asking in how many countries Jews were truly assimilated, with particular reference to the success of Adolf Hitler's anti-Semitic campaigns in Germany.

The trying week had culminated yesterday at home in Manchester.

Anne didn't know how lucky she was to have a mother like hers, nor, whatever she said about Sir Philip Marchal, in having so understanding, long-suffering a stepfather. Rebecca's parents were proud of their clever daughter but her mother now thought she should 'settle down'. When

Mummy made up her mind about anything, Daddy was no match for her. Yesterday Rebecca had arrived at the Lawson house in West Didsbury to find that the relations had been summoned to a tribal tea-party. During the course of this grisly ritual, Rebecca's filial duty to marry Daniel Robisch – such a nice Jewish boy he was and so devoted to her – had been washed, ironed and thoroughly aired. Daniel Robisch was a *schlemiel* and what they actually meant was the Robisch and Lawson families were interested in a business merger which the marriage would help cement. By nine o'clock Rebecca could stand no more. She had announced that she was returning on the overnight train to London, but it had been a wearisome journey, the weather had turned freezingly cold and all she wanted to do now was to fall into bed.

Keeping her finger pressed on the bell, she also thumped on the knocker and eventually she heard the bolt being scraped back, the door opened and Anne's bleary-eyed, pyjama-clad figure stood revealed. As Rebecca entered the hall and shut the door behind her, Anne went into seemingly unnecessary explanations about doing a broadcast yesterday, trying to let Rebecca know, and Sandy coming back with her and before he left saying she should bolt the door. Taking off her coat and hat, preparing to hang them on one of the protruding 'antlers' of the hall-stand, Rebecca saw Sandy's motoring coat. She gazed steadily from it, to Anne, and back again to the heavy leather coat. The blood flushed into Anne's cheeks and with a theatricality her sister Kate would have been ashamed to adopt, she made a startled surprised movement and said loudly, 'Oh goodness, Sandy's forgotten his coat.'

'He must have been cold,' Rebecca observed dryly. 'It's been sleeting on and off for hours.'

Her tired mind realised why Anne had been so fulsome with her explanations and fully registered what it had only half-noted as she'd descended from the taxi in the snow flurry. Sandy's Bugatti parked in Gower Street. Obviously he was in the flat and from Anne's reaction, presumably in her bed. In theory she and Anne frequently discussed sexual matters, agreeing that while they did not approve of promiscuity, emancipated women were as entitled as men to experience and enjoy pre-marital relationships with those they cared for.

In practice, their emancipated attitudes did not extend to speaking of their own sexual needs, dreams or desires. When Rebecca woke there was no sign of Sandy Dalziel and neither she nor Anne mentioned his overcoat.

The Dalziels had already invited the Whitworth–Marchal family to celebrate Hogmanay at Melkeith, their baronial mansion outside Edinburgh, an invitation Anne's mother and Philip had declined, it being a long way for her to travel in midwinter. Anne spent much of the Christmas holidays chewing over the question why the long anticipated experience of losing her virginity had proved such a hideous disappointment. She had no desire to see Sandy at the moment, but she couldn't think of a good reason for crying off at the last minute. She and Con, Kate and Mark duly travelled north on the *Royal Scot*. The Dalziels' house-party was in fact great fun.

The New Year's Eve ball was spectacular, Sandy and his fellow Scotsmen resplendent in kilts and sporrans, silk shirts and lace ruffles, tartan kneesocks and buckled shoes, everybody whooping their way through reels and strathspeys, and on the stroke of midnight linking hands to sing *Auld Lang Syne* in its proper Scottish setting, accompanied by the bagpipes. The Whitworths then put through a pre-booked telephone call to Chenneys to wish their mother not only a happy New Year, all the very best for 1931, but a happy forty-sixth birthday and after that everybody piled into traps and motor cars to go first-footing round the estate and the dour granite town of Melkeith.

Anne had finally fallen into bed and was drifting into sleep when Sandy came padding into her room and slid under the bedclothes beside her. They made love and at the precise moment Anne thought passion was about to overwhelm her, he finished. After he had lit two cigarettes, he said, 'How about starting the New Year by announcing our engagement, honey-bunny?'

Having drunkenly invited him to be her lover, sober Anne found she had neither the further confidence to say, 'It's not working for me', nor the heart to shatter his happiness. Lamely she replied, 'Not yet, Sandy. I want to establish myself first, to prove I'm not just Tom Whitworth's daughter and Sir Philip Marchal's stepdaughter, or the wife of the Honourable Alexander James Iain Dalziel.'

That last bit placated him and made Anne cross with him and herself. He should realise he was not satisfying her, and if he didn't she should in all honesty tell him.

On her return to London Anne was invited to take part in several more broadcasts which meant she was always bumping into Sandy. She enjoyed her modicum of fame as 'a lady broadcaster, the spirited voice of young English womanhood' which was how the *News Chronicle* described her. She also now agreed with Sandy that broadcasting was an exciting medium and Savoy Hill a power-house where you could almost scent the ideas blooming, and it was he who had provided the entrée so Anne didn't want to seem churlishly ungrateful. She just kept hoping things would improve on the physical side. Or that Julian would show an interest in that area.

Not long after Easter Julian invited her to have lunch at a swish French restaurant situated round the corner from Stoddard and Simpson's offices in Covent Garden. When Anne arrived to find a bottle of champagne in an ice bucket on their table, she realised it was a special occasion. As he greeted her Julian said, 'May I s-say how very attractive you look?'

'You may,' Anne smiled. 'I hope you noticed I'm wearing your pearls.'

Julian nodded but his eyes were on her outfit—she had chosen her emerald green, fine wool, loose jacket and matching dress with the v-neckline and smart side-pleats—not its accessories. Teasingly he said, 'I recall you being uppity with Mr Marvell and I read your article in the *Manchester Guardian*'s women's page about not following the absurd dictates of fashion, but I see you've succumbed to the lengthening s-skirt.'

Looking down at her calf-length dress Anne said gloomily, 'I just began to feel nakedly exposed with my skirt above my knees. Perhaps one day we'll stop being slaves to the whims of Theo Marvell and his ilk and wear what we like.' The waiter was preparing to uncork the bottle, so she asked, 'Why the champagne?'

The cork popped, the best bubbly liquid whooshed from the bottle but with deft speed the waiter filled their glasses.

Julian then said, 'I am about to leave Stoddard and Simpson. Without acrimony I'm glad to say, though Josiah Stoddard thinks I'm mad. Why does the old boy think I'm mad? Because I'm in the process of setting up the J. C. Kendle Literary Agency. That's what we're celebrating.'

Julian held up his champagne glass, Anne raised hers and after they had drunk a toast to the stupendous success of J. C. Kendle Ltd, she asked what the 'C' stood for? Julian replied, 'Christopher. It was one of my father's names.'

'Ah. I'm sure he'd have been pleased at the idea of you being a literary agent and helping authors.' Even if your mother isn't, Anne thought.

While they were waiting for their *boeuf bourguignon* to arrive, casually she said, 'I've mapped out the characters and the plot for my novel. And I have the title. It's *Whatever Happened to Wordsworth?* During a tutorial in my last year at Somerville, Miss Rendall was criticising an essay I'd done on the Lake poets and she said, "Whatever happened to Wordsworth? may be an interesting question, but thus phrased it is unlikely to appeal to your examiners." I remember thinking, But it'd make a good title for a book. Don't you agree?'

At this question Julian employed his unconscious habit of lowering his eyelids before looking up at her. For a man he had particularly thick lashes, his eyes were a velvety brown, the habit focused attention on them, and without doubt he was a most attractive creature. His inviting her to share this celebration lunch made it obvious how much he liked her and Anne simply did not understand his sexual reticence. He said, 'What sort of novel do you have in mind?'

'Ah. Actually, it's going to be a detective story. I like the idea of working out complicated plots – I have that sort of mind, good at jigsaws and crossword puzzles – and I want to reach a wide public. Wordsworth will be the corpse.' That made Julian laugh and Anne went on, 'My hero's name is Seth Pollard and he hails from a working-class background which will make him completely different from anybody else's Detective-Inspector from Scotland Yard. And I think I'll be able to get quite a lot of mileage out of the social differences and some subtle comments on our class-ridden society and . . .'

'Make sure they are subtle,' Julian interrupted firmly. 'Readers of detective stories do not want Socialist polemics. But it all sounds most intriguing, and you will give me first chance to read the finished typescript, won't you?'

That was the invitation for which Anne had been angling. She said, 'Who else would I want as my literary agent but J. C. Kendle?'

Julian gave her his charmingly deprecatory smile but made no further comment. Their *boeuf bourguignon* arrived and it was simply delicious. They went on talking, Anne did enjoy being in his company, and the only time he again stuttered was when his mother's name was briefly mentioned. Then he said, 'Are you definitely going to Moscow this summer to see your Aunt Sarah?'

Anne nodded. In those terrible months after her father's death and her mother's heart attack, Aunty Sarah, Daddy's favourite sister, had been the rock to which she had clung like a piece of storm-tossed flotsam. The sudden secret decision to uproot herself and her little daughter Tamara who had been born in England, to rejoin her husband, the Bolshevik politician Mikhail Muranov whom she'd met whilst serving as a nurse in Russia during the war, had been another traumatic event in Anne's young life. Since then she had seen Aunty Sarah and Tamara and met Uncle Misha—a splendid larger-than-life character—twice only. Anne's plan to visit the Muranovs in Moscow had Sandy's wholehearted approval. With adult eyes, he said, she could see what a splendid new society the Communists were building.

Perhaps because Julian knew she was going with a group that included Sandy Dalziel, he made no further comment other than observing she should gather interesting material for a book.

The proposed visit collapsed at the eleventh hour in the most unexpected manner. Anne was suddenly advised to be vaccinated for smallpox before she left for Russia but the day after the vaccination her arm started to swell agonisingly and her temperature to rise alarmingly. Rebecca put her to bed and telephoned her GP, Doctor Serena Abbott who was an ex-suffragette friend of Anne's mother, though, unlike most of their parents' friends, never called 'Aunty' Serena by the Whitworth children, for the good reason that she was known as 'Stephen'.

Having examined her, Stephen said, 'I regret to inform you, Anne old thing, you're among the small percentage who react badly to the vaccine. In effect, you're suffering from an attack of the cowpox dear old Doctor Jenner rightly recognised as being preferable to smallpox.'

Anne groaned, 'I hope I never get smallpox.'

After Stephen had left, Rebecca said, 'She's a marvellous character, isn't she? Now I've met Doctor Abbott and seen her striding around the place, I can just imagine her making that priceless remark.'

'Which one in particular?' Anne groaned again.

'You know, the one you told me about at Mrs Pankhurst's funeral. When she pushed her way through the reverential crowds at the graveside, and bellowed at Miss Pankhurst, "Sad day, what! Still your mother went out with a bang, Christabel, life's work accomplished. Votes for all women one week. Dead the next."'

Anne felt too ghastly for even that treasured epitaph to bring a smile to her lips. For several days she was quite ill and Mummy was on the point of arranging for a private ambulance to convey her to Chenneys, when she began to feel better. By that time the group she should have travelled with had departed for Moscow. Sandy went with declared reluctance but realising he wanted to be let off the hook of gallantry, Anne insisted he go. After a couple of weeks' recuperation at Chenneys, her plans for the summer totally disrupted, she decided to go north to Lancashire.

3

Outside, the moors were barely visible through the dank mist and the rain was slanting across the soggy grass, but inside the kitchen was warm and cosy, the fire banked high on this

34

chill summer's day. On one side of the kitchen range Madge Kearsley was relaxed in her rocking chair, puffing away on her cigarette, on the other side Anne was sitting bolt upright in the armchair. Excitedly she said, 'Oxford and Chenneys and even Bloomsbury are privileged islands in a sea of misery and injustice. This is where real life is being endured, here in The Dales. I hadn't realised things were so bad up north. I feel so guilty about being so privileged. And people keep saying to me, "Ee, if only your Dad had lived, Miss Anne, he'd have done summat." Well, I'm alive and I'm furiously angry and I feel I should do "summat".'

'Put your anger to best use and wear your hairshirt on Sundays.'

Anne laughed; Madge was one of her very favourite people. She was a contemporary of Daddy's, they'd grown up in the back streets down by the River Mellor, they'd gone to the same elementary school, and they'd remained friends until his death. Madge herself had been married three times. Her first husband had been killed in an accident and she'd had his body *cremated* which had caused a sensation in The Dales. When she'd put some of his ashes into an egg-timer, saying 'The bugger never did any work while he was alive, so he can do some now he's dead', that had created an even greater sensation. Her second husband had been killed at Neuve Chapelle in 1915 but Madge had announced, 'You needn't sympathise. I'm sorry for his sake but I made another rotten choice, so personally I'm glad to be shot of him.' Two years later, to most people's astonishment, she'd married Frank Kearsley, a highly respected figure in Lancashire Socialist circles and a man twenty years her senior. When Frank had suffered a severe stroke, Madge had partially redeemed herself in local opinion by nursing him devotedly until he died a couple of years ago. She said three husbands was more than enough for anybody and now she lived by herself in this little terraced house clinging to the hillside above Mellordale.

Madge took another cigarette from the packet and lit it from the dog-end of the one she'd been smoking. Throwing the butt into the fire, she leaned forward in the rocking chair and her hennaed hair shone a garish red in the reflection of the flames. 'Now listen to me, Anne Whitworth, you're a daft ha'porth at times, for all your university education. Life's allus been hard and harsh for most folks up here, though I don't know whether or not that makes it more "real". Your Dad wanted to make it better. So do you. But he belonged here and he never lost contact with his roots. You don't know where yours are, do you? If you want my opinion, you'll do more good going back where you belong and carrying on with your writing and talking on that there wireless, than by messing about up here trying to turn yourself into a combination of lady superintendent, shop steward and district nurse.'

'That there wireless' had pride of place in the middle of the dresser in the far from tidy kitchen. Madge always refused to take money when Anne visited, so on the strength of her recent earnings she had bought a handsome radio with a polished oak frame which, after loud protests, Madge had finally, delightedly, accepted. Anne considered the description of her would-be endeavours to alleviate the fearful hardship created by the devastating unemployment in The Dales, a trifle unjust. Would not chucking everything up and coming north to help the dispossessed be the proper thing to do? Madge had, however, made a good point about her being unsure where her roots were.

Having disposed of Anne's worries to her satisfaction, Madge decided they could do with a cup of tea and she went through the ritual of warming the teapot on the hob on the kitchen range, while the black kettle boiled on the fire-plate. Carefully, she then put in one heaped teaspoonful of tea for Anne, one for herself, and one for the pot, pouring on the water the minute the kettle lid started to bounce. Several brisk stirs of the liquid in the pot, the milk poured into the cups first, and what Madge called a decent cup of tea was nicely mashed. After she'd lit another cigarette, while they drank the strong brew, Madge launched into her stories of the old days which Anne loved hearing as much as she enjoyed the recounting, particularly as most of them involved the young Tom Whitworth.

Madge told one tale which Anne found poignant evidence of their sex's only too pitiful and recent ignorance, though the way she related it was funny enough. It concerned a naïve young ha'porth in The Dales who'd bestowed her favours on a lad killed at Arras and then found herself in the pudding club. When she went into labour, Madge said, the girl kept yelling about the knife and nobody could understand what she meant until Madge herself realised the lass thought they'd have to slit her open to let the baby out. While Madge paused to light yet another cigarette, Anne lit one too and thought this might be an opportune moment to discuss her problems with somebody who was assuredly vastly experienced and unlikely to be shocked by anything. For even if she settled in The Dales and broke off the relationship with Sandy, it would still be helpful to have the matter sorted out for the future.

'Madge, I want to ask your advice. It's a rather delicate subject and . . .'

'Sex has reared its head in your young life, has it? I can't say I'm surprised.' Madge gave her full-throated laugh and Anne smiled before clearing her throat and announcing, 'I'm having an affair. Only it's not working for me on the physical side. And I've been wondering, well, we don't . . . um . . . use a proper contraceptive . . .'

'He withdraws,' Madge said helpfully.

Anne cleared her throat again and said, 'Yes. I've been wondering if that might be part of the problem. And if I were um . . .'

'Fixed up, things might be better. I can't guarantee that, Anne luv, and I don't keep a stock in the larder, but Madge does know how to help you. And given a day or two, she will.'

'Oh Madge, I wasn't expecting you to do that, honestly, but thank you!' Anne jumped up and smacked a kiss on her cheek.

'That's enough of that. You'll have me accused of corrupting the young next.'

A couple of days later, on another chill summer's evening with the rain driving down from the moors, after they'd had their high tea Madge drew the curtains in the kitchen and said, 'We'll do it in front of the fire. We might as well be cosy.'

For a few seconds Anne couldn't think what she meant, until Madge said, 'Well come on, you'll have to undress if you want me to fix you up.'

Standing in front of the leaping flames, her eyeline level with the clutter of objects on the mantelshelf that jutted above the kitchen range, Anne saw the famous egg-timer containing husband number one's ashes and she had a desperate urge to giggle. But her embarrassment soon disappeared. Madge's attitude was cheerfully clinical and she obviously knew exactly what she was doing. Was she the Marie Stopes for the advanced spirits in Mellordale? While she was being fitted with a contraceptive cap, Anne's only worry was that the cigarette stuck between Madge's lips might burn her in an unfortunate place.

Before she left The Dales, Anne decided she needed some facts and figures to balance the first-hand personal stories, for the hard-hitting article, or maybe series of articles, she intended to write, to do her bit to bring home to fat, well-fed citizens the extent and depth of the deprivations so many of their fellow Britons were suffering.

It was another dank, chill day as she walked down the steep lane from Madge's house and the pervasive stench of the gas-works at the end of Jubilee Street soon hit her nostrils. Responding to the cries of ''ow do, Miss Anne' and 'Do you reckon we're going to 'ave any summer this year?', she proceeded along the grimy cobbled streets to the town square, where even the trams waiting at the terminus looked disconsolate in the murky drizzle. Turning into Hulton Street, Anne passed the Tom Whitworth Memorial Hall and the queue of pinched-faced women, children in reach-me-down clothes, and one-legged men hopping on their crutches, was already winding through the memorial gardens. At her mother's instigation, funded by her and Philip, a soup kitchen had been set up for the most desperately needy families, but the anger again surged through Anne that such charity should be needed thirteen years after the end of the Great War for Civilisation. Some civilisation! Which couldn't even provide decent artificial limbs for those who had lost theirs, serving their country in the fields of Picardy and Flanders.

Today, however, Anne was not on duty at the soup kitchen, though Madge was. She walked further along Hulton Street, up the steps and into the soot-ingrained red-brickness of the Mellordale Municipal Library. Waiting until the young woman at the counter had date-stamped the books of an elderly man, Anne smiled and said, 'Hello, I'm Anne Whitworth. I'm writing some articles about The Dales and I wonder if you can help . . .'

The librarian pointed to the printed notice which read SILENCE and said, 'Could you keep your voice down, please?'

The tone was not rude, but neither was it friendly. Accustomed either to being recognised, or greeted with open arms once she'd announced who she was, Anne looked sharply at the young woman. She was in her early twenties and she wasn't unattractive, her hair a prettily waving brown, her features neat, her figure trim in an unstylish white blouse, grey skirt and grey cardigan. Although it wasn't as developed, she had the same sour, disapproving air as Julian's mother, displayed to the full as she listened to Anne explaining what she was looking for.

Then the librarian said, 'I hope you don't intend to depict us as unemployed savages, starting every sentence with "Ee, by gum", and speaking a quaintly unintelligible dialect.' Her own accent was posh Lancashire, the flat 'a' and the other broad north country vowel sounds ironed to the point of over-enunciation and Anne wondered how many elocution lessons she'd had.

In response to the question, Anne said loudly, 'I don't intend to do anything of the sort.' Dropping her voice and trying to control her temper she added, 'I've been coming to The Dales since I was a child. My father was the Labour MP, you know. I myself am a Socialist.'

'Many of us are good Socialists,' the young woman said primly. 'Hard-working, civilised, God-fearing folk.'

Having got that information off her chest, she directed Anne to a stack of pamphlets in the reference section, and in a neat handwriting which went with her neat person, she jotted down the name of a man in the Town Hall who could be of further assistance. Before she left the library en route for the Town Hall, Anne walked over to the counter and with another smile said to the young woman, 'Thank you very much for your help. I've found lots of useful material.'

There was no answering smile, merely the response, 'It's one of the reasons I'm here. To help the general public.'

To most members of the general public Anne had no doubt the young librarian was politely correct, sour only with those who overstepped her self-imposed boundaries, and she had the strong feeling there was an element of personal resentment against her. Why there should be, she couldn't imagine, and it wasn't a matter she intended to let bother her.

Anne scrambled over the last stretch of tussocky grass and rocky outcrop towards the summit of Netherstone Edge, a pilgrimage she always made before she left The Dales. The weather gods had decided to be kinder today and though there were dark clouds in the sky, they were fast-moving and the moorlands were a mosaic of sunlight and shade.

Just below the highest crags of the Edge, on a plateau worn smooth by wind and rain and clambering feet, the cairn had been built. Before the serried rows of white headstones had filled the British war cemeteries in France and Flanders, various makeshift headstones had existed. Anne's father's had been a Celtic cross with the hand-painted inscription: 'Major "Tom" Whitworth DSO, MC and bar, MP. 18th (Pals) Battalion Manchester Regiment. Killed in action on the Sambre Canal, November 7th 1918. R.I.P.'

The cross had been brought back home and embedded into the cairn, at the bottom of which were the words: 'This monument was erected by public subscription in honour of the Member of Parliament for The Dales 1907–1918, a Lancashire man who loved this place on the Pennine moors.'

Erecting a monument up here on Netherstone Edge had been Madge and Frank Kearsley's idea and Anne thought it was a beautiful one. The only drawback was that it had turned a spot previously frequented only by enthusiastic ramblers or the likes of Tom Whitworth, into a popular landmark. Ignoring the shouts of the children who were clambering near the cairn and the antics of a courting couple in one of the rocky crevices, for several minutes Anne stood looking down on the three towns of Upperdale, Mellordale and Lowtondale that were collectively known as The Dales. The mill chimneys rose from the slate roofs like dirty candles and though only half of them were now lit, their smoke still hung over the length of the valley. Up here by the black rocks of the Edge the clear wind always blew and as it ruffled her short hair and fanned her cheeks, Anne came to her decision.

Madge was right. She should follow her own star, using her anger in the best way she could. She would therefore return south where maybe Madge's ministrations would improve her love-life, to continue her campaigning for a better world and to complete *Whatever Happened to Wordsworth?*

4

On the top of Magdalen Tower the white-robed choristers embarked on the Latin hymn that traditionally at sunrise on the first of May, announced that spring had arrived in Oxford. If the fickle English sun failed to put in an appearance they sang all the same but today, blissfully, the dawn light was spreading fast. The last notes of the treble voices shivered into the still air, the dawn hymn of welcome was over, spring had officially arrived in Oxford, and the choristers trooped down the stairs. The fortunate ones who had packed the roof of the tower – the less favoured had listened from Magdalen Bridge or from punts on the River Cherwell – started to follow, but Anne had forgotten the heart-stopping beauty of the sleeping city of Oxford and was in no hurry to descend.

The colleges and their quadrangles lay beneath her like models, their stones seeming fresh-scrubbed, their lawns new-mown, the dome of the Radcliffe Camera and the spire of St Mary the Virgin were carmine-tinged and the long graceful curve of the High was wrapped in mauve shadows. Beyond the toytown spires and domes, the sun's rays were glinting on the dew of Christ Church meadow and the waters of the Isis, and the distant undulations of field and wood were emerging from the early morning mist.

''Tis lovely on a morning like this, isn't it?' Sandy said.

'Yes,' Anne replied shortly.

Sandy had been given a couple of tickets for the tower and invited her to spend a few days with him in their *alma mater*, saying it would be good for her to have a break, which was true. Anne had just returned from an exciting but exhausting week in Geneva, where she had been the youngest delegate to an international women's disarmament conference and lobby of the League of Nations. Other than her involvement with the Women's Peace Party, events in the last nine months had not turned out as she had hoped.

Anne had worked extremely hard writing *Whatever Happened to Wordsworth?* but when she had completed the book, the J. C. Kendle Literary Agency was still not a reality. The initial reason for the delay was Julian's mother being taken ill – Anne suspected it was a strictly psychosomatic illness aimed at preventing her darling son becoming a literary agent – but he had shown the backbone Anne knew he possessed, gently but firmly refusing to abandon the project. However, by the time Mrs Kendle had decided to recover, Julian had lost the chance of ideal offices. He had not yet found suitable premises. Having no desire to join another literary agency, liking the idea of standing on her own feet and getting her first detective novel accepted by her own effort, Anne had submitted the typescript directly to George Garland who once upon a time had played croquet with her at Chenneys. Mr Garland's rejection letter had been courteous and, she supposed, encouraging – he was sure she would soon find the right publisher and be extremely successful.

Whatever Happened to Wordsworth? had nonetheless been rejected.

When Ernest Lamont had similarly rejected the book, Anne's disbelief and desolation had been boundless. She had consoled herself with her mother's comment that submitting the typescript to Philip's ex-publishers might not be the best of ideas and taken her advice to let Julian read it, even though he was not yet in business as a literary agent.

'Do you want to stay up here a while longer?' Sandy enquired in a tone that suggested he did not.

'Yes.' To convey her mood to thick-skinned Sandy, Anne

leaned further over the parapet and stared soulfully down at a milk-cart and horse trundling along the High.

Their personal relationship hadn't blossomed either. 'What an enterprising honey-bunny you are,' had been his enthusiastic comment after she had first used the contraceptive cap Madge had fitted. It had done more to improve his enjoyment than hers. Since Sandy's return from Russia, with the news of how greatly her Aunt Sarah longed to see her, his political views had hardened. His attitude to the débâcle of the General Election – Ramsay MacDonald betraying the entire Labour movement by agreeing to lead a so-called National Government – had not pleased Anne, for Sandy had snorted, 'What can you expect of Socialists? They're Liberals in new clothes. Communism is the only hope for humanity.'

For today, Anne decided, she would forget about the world's problems and about her own weediness in not telling Sandy they were less than ideally suited. As she turned away from the parapet, among the figures moving towards the stairs she suddenly saw Julian's unmistakable swan-like neck. Astonished but delighted, she called out, 'Julian! What are you doing here on an Oxford May morn, you Cambridge interloper?'

Sandy murmured, 'Not the most tactful of cries. Look who he's with. Or to be pedantic, as befits his companion, with whom he is.'

Anne looked and said, 'Oh. Well. I suppose we'd better go over.'

Julian's companion was Doctor H. V. X. Martindale, renowned Fellow and Tutor of Magdalen College. His classicist father had burdened him with the forenames Hector Victor Xerxes and to the postwar generations of Oxford undergraduates he was known as H.V.X. Now in his late thirties, he had a good war record but had since become a dedicated pacifist, as Anne was sure her father would have done, had he survived the holocaust. There was no need to introduce Sandy to H.V.X. because he'd read history at Magdalen and been tutored by him. Politely, they said 'Good morning', as did Julian and Sandy, though Anne didn't think they liked each other.

'M-may I introduce M-miss Anne Whitworth to you,

Doctor Martindale?' Julian stammered which meant he was nervous.

H.V.X. extended his hand and in his suavely precise voice said, 'I am delighted to meet you, Miss Whitworth. It was a pleasure denied me when you were Oxford's favourite undergraduette.'

Taking his hand which was soft and beautifully manicured, irked by a feeling of being patronised, with a sweet smile Anne said, 'Ah, but I had the pleasure of attending a couple of your lectures.' Then, consumed by curiosity as to what Julian was doing here, she turned to him and said, 'Fancy us meeting like this. I'm taking a few days off. What brought you to Oxford for May morn?'

Julian glanced at H.V.X. who steepled his fingers in the slightly precious gesture Anne recalled from his lectures, before saying, 'Pray do enlighten Miss Whitworth.'

'I didn't actually come for the May morning festivities. I stayed on at Doctor Martindale's invitation. You see, Anne, I've now signed the lease for offices in Clarges Street, the J. C. Kendle Literary Agency is officially in being and Doctor Martindale has become my first client.'

Momentarily, despite Julian's obvious delight, Anne felt furiously hurt. He should have given her the news first, she should have been his first client, not Doctor Martindale. But she hid her chagrin as Julian went on to tell her, 'I've negotiated a contract for Doctor Martindale to write a new full-scale biography of Queen Elizabeth which I feel sure, with the depth of his knowledge and the clarity and lucidity of his prose, will enjoy a wide readership.'

'How splendid,' said Anne, and how prettily phrased, she thought.

On their way down the stairs Julian elucidated, though with the bells of Magdalen Tower clanging out for May morn it was a little difficult to hear all he said. Anne gathered that he had long admired Doctor Martindale's academic books and felt he could and should reach a wider public. Recently therefore he had written inviting H.V.X. to lunch when he was next in Town. To his surprise the invitation had been swiftly accepted, perhaps partly because Doctor Martindale had met his father in the trenches. Over lunch they'd got on

44

frightfully well and he'd been more than interested in Julian's proposals. Anne waited until they were down the stairs and out into the open air before she asked, 'Have you managed to read *Whatever Happened to Wordsworth?* yet?'

'Yes. In fact I was going to telephone you tomorrow.'

'And?'

Julian was teasing her because he said, 'If I am not mistaken, you will in time achieve the same sort of success as a detective authoress as your distinguished predecessor from Somerville College, Miss Dorothy L. Sayers.'

'Oh Julian!' Ignoring the qualification 'in time', impulsively Anne hugged him.

Drawing swiftly back from the embrace, he glanced over his shoulder towards Doctor Martindale who was regarding them, or perhaps more precisely Anne, with an amused expression that riled her. But her elation returned when Julian said, 'May I handle the book for you as your literary agent?'

'Of course you may! Why do you think I sent it to you?'

Anne decided she'd better let Julian know that *Whatever Happened to Wordsworth?* had already been twice rejected. He merely asked what on earth she'd sent it to George Garland and Ernest Lamont for? Detective stories weren't their line; it was a Stoddard and Simpson book. Then he said, 'Shall we have lunch next week to solemnise our union and discuss things?'

Julian gave her his charming smile which sent a quiver through Anne's stomach muscles, and she couldn't help thinking what an ideal union theirs would be in every way. She said she would be delighted to lunch with him next week. Then Sandy, who had been looking bored ever since she'd called out to Julian on the top of the tower, said, 'Isn't it about time we pushed off?'

After they had bade farewell to H.V.X. and Julian, as prearranged Sandy punted her up the River Cherwell to Parson's Pleasure for the traditional egg and bacon breakfast. Then, as it was such a lovely day, they punted further along the Cher. Having risen before dawn, with the blue sky above, the sun on her face, lulled by the movement of the craft, Anne fell asleep. When she woke Sandy had moored the punt in the shade of weeping willows, and settled himself into the other seat so that their outstretched legs were touching. While he puffed smoke through his long cigarette-holder, he gazed at her intently.

Anne yawned, ran her tongue round her sleep-furred teeth, and said, 'What time is it?'

'A quarter past one. Do you want to eat?'

'Not particularly.' Stretching her arms above her head she said, 'I feel deliciously lazy.'

'You look as delicious as you feel, honey-bunny.' The intensity of Sandy's gaze was making Anne feel uncomfortable so she sat up, but as she did he grasped her shoulders. She was wearing a sleeveless muslin dress and she felt the heat of his hands on her bare skin. He said, 'I think it's time we got married. The gloss has gone from having an affair. I'm frankly bored with Mr and Mrs Howlingale and Mr and Mrs Portwine.' On the occasions they had stayed in hotels, Sandy had delighted in registering with ridiculous names. 'You've established quite a reputation as a broadcaster. You've written your book. So what are we waiting for?'

Anne gazed at the sunlight splintering into diamond fragments on the green water beyond the shade of the willows, at the shiver of their feathery fronds in the gentle breeze, at anything except Sandy. Perhaps this was the crunch moment in their relationship but she couldn't think what to say except, 'I don't want to marry you.' If he were more aware of other people's emotions he would have some inkling of her true feelings, but then if he were aware he wouldn't be Sandy. She had done nothing to blight his expectations of marriage so her announcement would come as a fearful shock.

'You're not still riding your romantic high horse, are you? You don't still see it as another of your noble duties to save him from himself, do you?'

The sharpness of Sandy's tone made Anne turn her head to look at him. She knew he was referring to Julian but with a puzzled frown she said, 'I haven't the slightest idea what you're talking about.'

In the same sharp tone, his freckled face flushed, Sandy said, 'Oh come on, honey-bunny, we're not playing games. This is serious. It's our future we're discussing. You're a sophisticated young woman. You've read your Havelock-

Ellis. You know damn well what Julian Kendle's sexual proclivities are, even if he's not sure himself. Which is, I suppose, why you imagine you might rescue him. Why do you think H.V.X. and he have hit it off so well? It's not Kendle's clever mind he's attracted to, it's his beautiful body. And it's past time you . . .'

Anne stared wide-eyed at Sandy, not wholly grasping what he was saying. Abruptly, he stopped and said, 'Oh sweet Jesu! You really don't know about H.V.X. being a closet queen, as queer as the proverbial coot. I thought it was common knowledge. And you hadn't . . . oh, honey-bunny, I'm sorry.'

'Julian Kendle's sex-u-al pro-cliv-ities. Julian Kendle's sex-u-al pro-cliv-ities.'

The words hammered in Anne's head to the rhythmic clack of the trains' wheels on the journey from Oxford to Marshall Minnis Halt. They were still thundering in her brain as she entered her mother and Philip's bedroom at Chenneys, the loveliest of rooms with an ornate ceiling, exposed beams, latticed windows, and a genuine Tudor four-poster bed. Her mother was propped against the pillows but as Anne kissed her and worriedly enquired how she was feeling, she said much better. It was her own fault for overdoing things — among other activities she was involved with Madge Kearsley in setting up a self-help centre in Mellordale — and she'd merely accepted Doctor Stuart's advice that a few days' rest would be a good idea.

'A very good idea,' Anne said, for her mother's skin had its waxen pallor and her veins were blue-ridged.

Drawing one of the basketwork chairs to the bedside, fleetingly Anne wondered what it would be like to make love in the vastness of the four-poster with somebody you really cared for. Did Mummy and Philip ever . . .? It was unlikely at their ages and with her heart condition, and their sexual relationship was certainly not one she cared to dwell upon. After she'd settled herself in the chair, Anne said, 'My stepfather says I'm not to upset you and I wouldn't have come if I'd known you were . . . but Rebecca's out of town and anyway, it's you I want to talk to . . . and . . . oh Mummy . . .'

Despite her determination not to break down, particularly in view of the state of her mother's health, Anne burst into tears. When she'd stopped crying, wiped the stains from her face and blown her nose furiously, her mother said, 'I should be much more upset if you didn't want to talk to me and I found out whatever it is by devious means. So have a cigarette, take a deep breath, and tell me all.'

Puffing away on her cigarette Anne started to relate the day's events as coherently as possible. '. . . and once I'd realised what Sandy meant, I leapt from the punt and it capsized and I left him in the water. I ran along the towpath and my dress was sopping wet and my shoes were squelching water, but I just kept running and my brain felt like an electric washing machine with all the thoughts whirling around. I had ridiculous ideas, like contacting Theo Marvell because I thought he'd know whether Julian is what Sandy says he is. And I felt so stupid, too. I mean, I pride myself on my powers of observation and perception and I hadn't the vaguest idea Doctor Martindale is a . . . but I suppose he must be because I can't see why Sandy should make that up. And I think I'd better tell you I've been having an affair with Sandy and he wants to marry me. So do you think he was simply being jealous about Julian? Latching on to the fact that he isn't aggressively masculine? Julian hasn't ever kissed me or anything and I know he likes me, but it doesn't mean he's a . . . does it, Mummy?'

Kessie watched her daughter stubbing her cigarette into Philip's ashtray and thought, oh poor Anne, she wasn't having much luck with her love-life in this emancipated era. Her affair with Sandy Dalziel – damn and blast him for his unthinking tactlessness – had obviously proved unsatisfactory, and how sweet of her to imagine her mother was unaware of it! Kessie's main worry had been how much Anne knew about contraceptive matters but with her daughter keeping resolutely silent, she herself hadn't felt able to mention the subject and she could now only presume that the necessary precautions had been taken.

In any circumstances, even if he sorted himself out, Kessie doubted Julian Kendle would prove the right man for Anne and in her innermost heart perhaps she did too. Maybe that was part of the reason why Seth Pollard, her Detective-Inspector in *Whatever Happened to Wordsworth?*, had emerged the way he had. Until Philip had finished his reading of the original typescript, Kessie had with difficulty remained silent but then, with a mixture of pride and worry, she'd burst out, 'It's very good, isn't it? Intelligent, highly readable, and fiendishly well plotted. The twist at the end took me completely by surprise. Didn't it you? But you realise what Anne's done, don't you? Seth Pollard's her idealised, romanticised version of Tom. When I commented that he was rather like her father, she said, "Oh not really. I've used Daddy's passion for justice as Seth's mainspring as a detective, and his Lancashire background for authenticity, but that's all." It isn't all, is it? Has Anne indulged in a dangerous fantasy, creating a father-as-lover figure?'

Philip had begged Kessie to calm down. He'd then said it wasn't unusual for novelists to create fantasy lovers, consciously or unconsciously, particularly if they were writing for a popular market and their own love-life was less than satisfactory. He did not consider Anne's having based Seth on her romantic conception of her father necessarily to be dangerous. It could provide a safety valve or be a method of working Tom out of her system.

'Or it could stoke up her obsession with his memory,' Kessie had said.

It was the dilemma of the real-life Julian Kendle, not the imaginary Seth Pollard, that was currently causing her daughter so much anguish. Having stubbed out her cigarette, Anne was gazing anxiously at Kessie, the tears again incipient in the dark eyes that were the only feature she had inherited from her beloved Daddy. Kessie's voice was at its huskiest as she spoke slowly and carefully. 'I think Sandy was right when he observed that Julian is sexually mixed-up. His problems go way back. He was only thirteen when Uncle Guy was killed and even before the war he hardly knew his father.'

'Didn't he?' Anne looked surprised. 'Why not?'

'I doubt Uncle Guy and Mrs Kendle ever had much in common, apart from their upper-class Catholicism, and the marriage disintegrated soon after Julian was born. They kept up appearances but Mrs Kendle appropriated Julian and Uncle

Guy spent much of his time travelling round the world.'

Anne looked even more surprised and Kessie could almost see her daughter's sharp mind working. She correctly anticipated the next question. 'Why did he write *Poppies* for her then?'

Kessie decided she might as well tell Anne the truth, or part of it anyway. 'He didn't. He wrote the poem for Aunty Alice.'

'What!' Anne exclaimed with inelegant amazement.

'You remember coming down to see Daddy here at Chenneys, when part of the house was a wartime convalescent hospital?' Anne nodded. She had the clearest memories of her first visit to the house that was to become her home. 'Well, do you remember Uncle Guy was here recuperating from his wounds too, and Aunty Alice turning up out of the blue?' Anne nodded again. 'It was love at first sight for them and they embarked on a passionate affair. Guy had only just written the poem for Alice when he was killed, so it was among the effects returned to Mrs Kendle and she had it published.'

'Even though she knew it hadn't been written for her?' Anne queried. Kessie said yes and her daughter said, 'Typical!'

'Aunty Alice went berserk but after she was killed in the air-raid, there didn't seem any point raking over the embers of a dead love-affair, so most people have continued to believe *Poppies* was written for Captain Guy Kendle's beloved wife.'

At least one thing now made sense to Anne. It had long baffled her how Uncle Guy could have loved his ghastly wife so much that in the Armageddon of Passchendaele, he'd found the time to pen the lines that had caught the mood of the wartime hour and made *Poppies* such a phenomenal success. Her attention riveted by this astonishing information, Anne listened as her mother continued.

'The point about all this, insofar as it concerns Julian, is that he hardly knew his father and from infancy he's been smothered by jealous, over-possessive mother-love which Uncle Guy's affair with Aunty Alice only heightened. The combination can, I gather, make sensitive men less masculine than they might otherwise be.'

'You mean Julian is queer and I'm wasting my time having romantic ideas about him,' Anne said flatly.

With a slight sigh, her mother replied, 'I don't know whether you'd be wasting your time or not, but I think you'd be well advised to forget Julian, romantically speaking. Apart from anything else, Anne, he's the heir to Ryby Hall and the Kendles are an old and proud Roman Catholic family. You have no conception of the problems that would entail for somebody brought up as a Unitarian who now professes to be an agnostic!'

Her mother smiled wryly but Anne did not smile back. It was all far too serious for her. She said, 'I have to go on seeing Julian. He's just become my literary agent.'

'I'm delighted to hear that. And of course you have to go on seeing him!' Kessie expostulated. 'Once you've recovered from your shock, and I do appreciate how you must feel . . .' She held out her hand which Anne clasped. 'But once you've recovered, just behave normally. If Julian wants to discuss his problems with you, he will. Otherwise my advice is to do nothing . . .'

'Except tell Sandy to go to hell.'

Kessie laughed, gladdened by the evidence of her daughter's youthful resilience. She said, 'You can do that if you want.'

Telling Sandy to go to hell was more easily said than done. He telephoned constantly and the huge bouquets of flowers arrived at the Gower Street flat with the regularity of April showers, until Rebecca said, 'For heaven's sake, Whitworth, whatever he's done, put him out of his misery.'

So Anne invited Sandy for a drink. He arrived clad in a suit of sackcloth that he'd had specially made, his face smeared with ash, clutching another huge bouquet which he went down on his knees to present to Anne. After she'd told him he was an idiot and to wash his face, she said she forgave him but she didn't wish to discuss the matter further. 'And of course you realise we're just good friends now.'

'Oh, are we?' Sandy said. 'I happen to love you, honey-bunny. I know you're the only woman for me. So I'm prepared to wait until you change your mind again.'

'You're going to have a very long wait,' Anne said.

Sandy just grinned at her.

Anne's next action was based on the premise that when you were feeling blue, the best way of reviving your spirits was to take positive, slightly mad, action. She informed Rebecca, 'I'm going to buy myself a car. Could you possibly forget Zionism and Palestine for a few hours and come with me?'

Rebecca who insisted on monthly accounting and settling of the flat expenses down to the last farthing, said, 'Can you yet afford to buy and run a car?'

'Not really,' Anne said cheerfully.

After a brisk homily about the dangers of living beyond one's means, Rebecca agreed to accompany Anne to a show-room in Mayfair where she had in fact already fallen in love with the bright red, latest model, sporty MG displayed on a revolving stage in the main window. She adored the car's low-slung body, the shining white spokes of its wheels, the headlights perched either side of the neat radiator, and the sleek lines of the mudguards-cum-running-board that swept in one connected piece from the headlamps to the trim rear.

When they climbed into the MG for a test run, Rebecca said, 'I don't think this was made for ladies of my size.' But after Anne had nipped through the London streets, whizzed on to the Great West Road and back to the sale-room in Mayfair, she announced, 'It's terrific! Will you teach me to drive?'

Anne said she would. Her mother having been a pioneer woman motorist, she herself had learned to drive on the Chenneys estate when she was sixteen.

After she had inspected the necessary documents, taken a deep breath, and written out the largest cheque she'd ever signed – it was for £175! – proudly, exhilaratedly, Anne drove Rebecca back to Gower Street. There, as it stood parked outside the flat, they christened the MG 'Bill' in honour of William Wordsworth.

Behaving normally with Julian proved not to be difficult. When Anne next saw him it was a business occasion which meant he was at his most confident, and she arrived at his Clarges Street offices in Bill which put her in a good humour.

Julian appeared to be doing very nicely, thank you, already employing a personal assistant as well as his secretary and the clerk-telephonist. The offices had been redecorated and were all very stylish with white-painted walls, tubular chairs and desks, and shining aluminium bookshelves. In the corner of Julian's room there was a huge tank, full of tropical fish, which he said he found most relaxing to watch when he was under pressure.

To begin with Anne found herself watching him like a hawk for traces of effeteness, but none was apparent, and she came to the conclusion that whatever Julian's emotional, family problems were, they had doubtfully turned him into a homosexual. Reluctantly, she also concluded that her mother had been right in saying it was up to Julian, not her, to change the boundaries of their relationship.

While they were having a cup of tea, served in bone-china cups, his father's name came into the conversation and Anne couldn't resist the temptation to mention *Poppies*. Almost immediately, without any trace of a stammer, Julian said, 'I know it was written for Alice Conway, not my mother, if that's what you're wondering.'

'Oh.' Anne was nonplussed by the unaccustomed forthrightness and the asperity of his tone, though these presumably were among the qualities he drew upon when dealing with publishers. She found herself stuttering slightly, 'W-well y-yes. I've only just found out about *Poppies*, you see.'

'Some kind soul in the know told me some time ago. I gather my father was having a passionate affair with Mrs Conway when he was killed. It must have wounded my mother terribly. I imagine the reason why she allowed the poem to be published as if it had been written for her, was because she didn't want the family name, or my father's memory, publicly besmirched. Had Mrs Conway and my father survived the war, nothing would have come of their affair, you know. My father was a Catholic too, if not apparently a particularly good or devout one. Mrs Conway was American by birth, wasn't she?'

'Yes.'

'She was married to Jonathon Conway, the actor?' Anne nodded and, his voice at its most incisive, Julian said, 'Then

I have no doubt she'd have gone to Hollywood with her husband and baby daughter and wallowed in being a film star's wife.'

Anne thought, ouch, in future I keep off *Poppies* because on that subject Julian's loyalty obviously lies with his mother.

They then got down to the reason for Anne's visit, her signature on the contract Julian had negotiated with Stoddard and Simpson for *Whatever Happened to Wordsworth?* After she had signed her name with a flourish, duly witnessed by Julian's secretary, Anne informed her agent, 'Philip says he couldn't have negotiated a better contract for a first book. Greater praise cometh not from him!'

Julian looked pleased and they then discussed the outline Anne had drafted for her second Seth Pollard detective story. She had given it the title *Poisonous Matters* and Julian made one or two suggestions before saying, 'And you will bring up the Lady Helena Brockenhurst–Seth Pollard romantic interest, won't you?'

Lady Helena was a character from *Whatever Happened to Wordsworth?* whom Anne had not intended to keep, but everybody who had so far read the book, including her publishers, insisted the incipient, across-the-class barriers romance with Seth must not be jettisoned. As Anne said yes, she'd keep the love interest running behind the main murderous plot, she thought it was the only romance she was likely to enjoy for some time. Still she could make Helena and Seth do what she wanted and the prospect of being a full-time bachelor girl did not at the moment dismay her. She wasn't twenty-three until September and she'd never intended to marry until she was twenty-five. Professionally things were looking bright. Apart from writing *Poisonous Matters* she must devote as much time as possible to speaking out against the continuingly dreadful unemployment situation and the interlocking questions of disarmament, world peace and the menace of Fascism.

PART II

5

'Sieg Heil! Sieg Heil!'
It was the most astonishing sound Anne had ever heard, thousands of voices chanting in unison, reverberating across the Römerberg, hitting the surrounding buildings like the waves of a stormy sea crashing against the rocks. In the centre of Frankfurt's historic square, the brownshirted storm-troopers of the *Sturmabteilung* ringed the huge bonfire and, fanned by a slight wind, the flames were leaping high into the night sky. Their reflection was bloodying the waters of the Justice Fountain and casting a lurid glow over the faces of the crowds.

The date was 10 May, 1933, just over the year since she had been in another university city, standing on the top of Magdalen Tower listening to the sweet voices of the choristers tremble in the dawn air. The contrast between that occasion and this one was mind-numbing and Anne found it extremely difficult to believe that in towns and cities throughout civilised Germany, from Berlin to Düsseldorf, from Hamburg to Dresden, the public burning of books declared by Herr Hitler and his recently elected Nazi Government to be culturally non-German, was taking place.

When Rebecca had announced that she was going on a holiday-cum-business-trip to Frankfurt, to visit her German relations and to assess the situation on behalf of the Jewish Agency, eager to find out for herself what was happening in the new Germany, Anne had asked if Rebecca's relations could possibly put her up? Herr Doktor and Frau Wolff had been only too delighted to do so. Having taken it in turns to drive Bill from London, Anne and Rebecca had arrived a couple of days ago at the Wolffs' spacious house off the Bockenheimer Landstrasse.

The chant of *'Sieg Heil'* ebbed to a swishing sound. The

works of Thomas Mann, Stefan Zweig, Bertolt Brecht, Lion Feuchtwanger and Sigmund Freud had already been cast into the fiery furnace and in the comparative silence the voice of an SA man bellowed through the loudhailer, 'Heinrich Heine.' With fervid enthusiasm the students hurled Heine's poems into the burning mass and as they landed, a spiral of auburn sparks shot upwards before cascading prettily on to the cobblestones. The incineration of Heine's life-work was driving the crowd to a high pitch of baying enthusiasm and above the brutish roar Anne heard the chant, '*Jud, sau Jud.*'

By her side Kurt Wolff murmured, 'Alas, poor Heinrich! And to think he became a Christian convert!'

Kurt was the Wolffs' son. The same age as Julian, in his twenty-ninth year, he had just been dismissed from his post as a university lecturer for no other reason than his being Jewish, an action Anne found incomprehensibly monstrous. Temporarily he had returned to Frankfurt to live with his parents. Assisted by his fluency in her native tongue – Kurt had spent a year at Cambridge and spoke delightful English – Anne and he had already established a rapport.

When the last of the culturally undesirable works had been thrown into the bonfire, with the wind whipping the flames into a speckled orange wall and showering sparks over the Römerberg, their right arms upraised in the Nazi salute, full-throatedly, lustily, the crowds sang *Deutschland über Alles*. As they started to disperse, Kurt gave Anne his wry smile and said, 'That was an exciting evening's entertainment. Better than Guy Fawkes night in England.'

'If you've nothing better to say, shut up,' Rebecca snapped at her distant cousin and Anne shared her friend's reaction. Much as she liked Kurt, his sardonic comments seemed horribly inappropriate.

In a mass surge the three of them were swept towards the alleyway that led from the Römerberg square under the bridge linking the old houses of the Rapunzelgässchen. Then they heard the woman's voice shouting in English, 'Anne, Anne. Over here, over here.'

With some difficulty, they forced their way against the outgoing tide towards the young woman who was jumping up and down, waving her arms. Anne asked Rebecca, 'Do you know who she is?'

'Not the foggiest. She's your friend apparently. Not mine.'

When they finally reached the young woman she held out her hand to Anne and said, 'This is the top-hole surprise. How long would it be since the jolly days in Oxford?'

The mention of Oxford and the use of the English slang jogged Anne's memory and she realised it was Wanda Ohlendorf who had attended a women students' peace conference as a delegate from Frankfurt University. Her failure to recognise the German girl was unsurprising as her hairstyle had changed dramatically in the intervening years, from a smart shingle to flaxen plaits coiled round her head in Rhine-maiden fashion.

'Anne, I have the honour to present to you my dear brother Helmut.' Wanda smiled at the shadowy figure silhouetted against the glow of the burning pyre. 'Helmut, I have the honour to present to you my dear friend from the University of Oxford, Miss Anne Whitworth.' She took great care pronouncing Anne's surname, a difficult one for native German speakers. 'My brother speaks the English better than I. He work for the year in your country.'

Helmut Ohlendorf stepped forward, greeting Anne with excessive politeness, clicking the heels of his boots, kissing her hand, and his English was fluent. With only the slightest of accents he said, 'It is indeed an honour to make your acquaintance.'

Despite the politeness and the warmth of the fire blazing behind them, a shiver ran down Anne's spine. Helmut Ohlendorf was an SS officer. Was her frisson caused by the uniform itself, designed to inspire fear, black from peaked cap to boots, the only colour the silver of the death's head cap badge, the runic double-S flash, and the red and white of the swastika armband? Or had she shivered because of the stories she'd heard about the SS activities? Helmut Ohlendorf himself was a fine figure of a man, as the saying went, tall, broadshouldered, fair-haired and fair-skinned like his sister, with the same regular, if heavy, features.

Concealing her astonishment that Wanda's brother should be in the SS, Anne said briskly, 'This is my friend Rebecca

Lawson, whom I don't think you met at Oxford, Wanda.'
After the Ohlendorfs had shaken Rebecca's hand, Anne turned
towards Kurt who was standing impassively behind them.
'And may I introduce a relative of Miss Lawson's – Herr Kurt
Wolff.'

The light from the flames was glinting on Kurt's neat
spectacles but Anne couldn't see the expression in his eyes as
he shook Wanda's hand, before inclining his head towards
her brother and to her amazement saying, '*SS-Obersturmführer*
Ohlendorf and I are old acquaintances. We were at university
together.'

Oh God, Anne thought, is he another well-educated van-
dal?

Wanda said, 'Did you enjoy the *Frankfurter Nachtlichten*,
Anne?'

Enjoy! What an extraordinary verb to choose. Staring
straight at the German girl, she said, 'No, I did not. It was
sheer cultural barbarism. As a writer myself, I should be
honoured to have my books burnt alongside such illustrious
authors.'

Wanda squealed in horror, 'We would not dream of burning
your books, dear Anne. I have read *Votever Happent to
Vordsvurt?*. It is the ripping story. It should be translated into
the German.'

Anne was glad to hear Wanda had read her detective novel
which had been published just before last Christmas. After
this evening's spectacle, should she be offered a German
translation (which to date she hadn't been), she wasn't at all
sure she would accept.

'What was your opinion of the *Nachtlichten*, Wolff?' Helmut
Ohlendorf enquired.

'Surely my opinion has no value for you,' Kurt replied
politely.

''I do not personally dislike all Jews.'

'Ah.' In an even politer tone Kurt said, 'Perhaps you recall
some words of Heinrich Heine's then? *Das war ein vorspiel
nur, dort, wo man Bücher/Verbrennt, verbrennt man auch am Ende
Menschen.*'

Anne did not speak German but Rebecca, who had learned
the language from her paternal grandfather, did. She heard

the sharp intake of her friend's breath and she saw the frowns cross both the Ohlendorfs' faces. Helmut then said stiffly, 'That is a statement of exaggeration which typifies the Jewish mind, Wolff. It endorses the necessity to purify the German mind through fire.'

'What did Heine actually say?' Anne asked.

With an apologetic smile Kurt said, 'Sorry. Roughly translated, his words mean: "That was only a beginning, for those who burn books, end up by burning mankind."'

'Oh.' Anne appreciated why the quotation had produced such reactions and despite the heat of the flames she shivered again. The warning contained in Heinrich Heine's words she endorsed as fervently as the Ohlendorfs did the barbarity of the *Nachtlichten*, even if it did seem a trifle extreme.

SS-Obersturmführer Ohlendorf cast a contemptuous glance towards a group of Brownshirts who were laughing raucously as they prodded the bonfire. His gaze returned to Anne and with the utmost earnestness he said, 'We in the *Schutzstaffel* are not anti-Semitic pigs. But we have studied the works of your great scientist Charles Darwin. By select breeding we shall purify and strengthen the Aryan race, in the process cutting out the cankerous and diseased parts. Thus we shall rid the Fatherland of the decadent filth that has enveloped it since the end of the Great War. You will readily comprehend, Fraulein Whitworth, that Jews have no place in the New Order of the Third Reich. But we should have no objection to their establishing themselves elsewhere. We should support the Zionist aim of the Jewish National Home.'

Helmut Ohlendorf had a light, high-pitched voice. The contrast with his manly frame gave him a curiously sinister air. Or was she being fanciful, Anne wondered, unduly affected by the atmosphere in the Römerberg? Having had his words addressed directly to her, she decided she had better make a response but she was so astonished by their content, all she could think of saying was, 'Miss Lawson's a Zionist. She works for the Jewish Agency for Palestine.'

Turning his head stiffly towards her, Helmut Ohlendorf favoured Rebecca with an appraising inspection and in the glare of the flames his eyes shone like two pale-blue marbles. Anne watched while Rebecca held his gaze unblinkingly, until eventually he said, 'I am greatly concerned with finding the correct solution to the Jewish problem. I would be interested in meeting you for a preliminary discussion of the situation, Fraulein Lawson.'

Anything beyond the preliminary stage, his inflection implied, would be dealt with by men. Coolly Rebecca replied, 'If you wish to contact me, I'm staying with the Wolffs.'

'Would you also be staying with Fraulein Lawson's relations, Anne?' When Anne said she would, Wanda went on, 'You would be most welcome to stay with us, would she not?'

As Helmut Ohlendorf nodded, Anne said furiously, 'I'm more than happy where I am, thank you very much.'

Apparently unaware of Anne's anger, Wanda said she must take tea with her in one of Frankfurt's top-hole tea-houses and she must come to dine with the Ohlendorfs. 'Must' appeared to be a key word for the Nazis. Anne's mother asserted that people didn't basically change. What occurred was a strengthening or weakening of their innate characteristics, according to how life treated them and they reacted. Yet how could the girl who had been a modern-minded pacifist during those summer days in Oxford, have turned into this creature with the flaxen plaits who apparently approved of the 'Nightlight', supported her brother's racial garbage and didn't think one should stay with a Jewish family?

When they returned to the house off the Bockenheimer Landstrasse, Herr Doktor and Frau Wolff had already retired for the night. Lavish as their hospitality was, Anne wasn't altogether sorry because her hosts' English was on a par with her German, which limited or lengthened conversation, as either Rebecca or Kurt had to translate. In addition, the older Wolffs had politely made it clear they had no wish to discuss the current difficulties of German Jewry. Their daughter Luise was however in the lounge, though that was perhaps a rather modern term for the large, high-ceilinged, ornately corniced room, cluttered with solid oak furniture, hung with nineteenth-century oil paintings and, when the heavy brocade curtains were drawn, lit by wrought-iron wall brackets and a central candelabra.

Anne found Luise an intriguing character. Rake-thin, elegantly stylish, according to Rebecca, at the age of eighteen – she was now twenty-six – Luise had caused a scandal by eloping to Berlin with her equally young boy friend. He was of the Jewish faith and they had married but the romance had not continued in fairy-tale fashion. Apparently he had behaved very badly. 'What did he do?' Anne had enquired curiously. 'Dunno,' Rebecca had replied. 'My German relations don't wash their dirty linen in public or private.'

Two years ago Luise had returned from Berlin with her twin girls to live with her parents. Whatever her husband had done she refused to forgive him, even when he'd recently come to Frankfurt with the proposal that his wife and now four-year-old daughters accompany him to the United States where they could make a fresh start. Rebecca gathered he hadn't been too upset when his offer was turned down. He was now in New York and with the backing of her eminently respectable parents, which spoke volumes for their dislike of her husband, Luise was preparing to divorce him. Anne's curiosity about people longed to know more, but she doubted even Kurt would air this family secret.

As the three of them entered the room, Luise said, 'What was the *Nachtlichten* like? Was it so very awful?'

'Yes.' Anne flopped into one of the leather armchairs. 'And to make matters worse, we met this ghastly SS officer.' She explained to Luise who Helmut Ohlendorf was. 'He's like a robot from *RUR*, behaving as if he's human but programmed with the most terrifying rubbish.' From the depths of the armchair into which he'd sunk, Kurt laughed at the comparison. 'From what I can make out, he seems to think all German Jews should be shipped to Palestine.'

Luise waved her arm and the sleeve of her shot-silk evening jacket shimmered in the light of the candelabra. The Wolffs of course dressed for dinner but having decided not to accompany them to the Römerberg, she had not changed her clothes. She said, 'I would not be shipped to Palestine. Why would I be? Our family, you see, Anne, lives in Frankfurt since the seventeenth century. So who should say we are not the good Germans and do not love our country?' Our robotic SS officer for one, Anne thought, as Luise continued, 'My parents would believe that the moment's troubles for us would be temporary.'

'You've been believing that for a considerable time,' Rebecca said sharply.

Unperturbed by the sharpness, in her charming, German-structured English Luise said, 'Now that the Nazis have the power, my parents would believe that they would . . .' she lifted her shoulders and spread out her hands in an elegant gesture '. . . how would you say it?'

'Exercise restraint?' Rebecca suggested, though the irony of her tone appeared lost on Luise.

It was not lost on Kurt who shifted his weight in the armchair, stretched out his legs and gave Anne his wry smile. She had the distinct impression that in other circumstances the rapport between them might have bloomed into something more intimate, which could have been interesting. As it was, he was a Jewish gentleman, she a Christian lady, and the shadow of Adolf Hitler lay between them.

Luise was saying, 'If we would behave with the calm and the dignity, my parents believe the life would soon return to the normal.' Somewhat unnecessarily, seeing she had rejected her husband's offer to leave Germany, she added, 'I would believe my parents would be correct. And now, if you would excuse please, I would retreat for the night.'

'Me too,' said Rebecca.

'Oh.' Anne herself didn't feel in the least bit sleepy. On the contrary, there were dozens of questions she wanted to ask and she was dying to continue the conversation.

Her disappointment must have shown because Rebecca said, 'Sorry, but I've a meeting early tomorrow morning with the Frankfurt Zionists. All three of them. That's an exaggeration but one of the many problems facing *SS-Obersturmführer* Ohlendorf and myself is that Zionists in Germany are as thick on the ground as butterflies at the North Pole. Luise and cousin Sophia and Aaron . . .' Rebecca addressed the older Wolffs in this manner '. . . are not alone in their optimism. Most Jews here seem to regard us Zionists, not the Nazis, as the main threat to their comfortable existence.'

With that declaration, rather abruptly and just managing

to stop herself from slipping on the parquet flooring, Rebecca said goodnight and they went up to their respective bedrooms. With so many unasked questions and confused emotions racing round her head, Anne found it impossible to sleep. She followed her normal practice in such circumstances, pouring her confusion into a long letter to her mother, thereby trying to clarify her thoughts. It was half past three in the morning before she switched off the bedside light and slipped into an uneasy sleep.

6

When Anne woke it was only six-thirty and try as she would to stop them, the thoughts about anti-Semitism, book-burnings and the Nazis continued to race round her head like an animal chasing its tail. Abandoning any hope of getting back to sleep, Anne climbed out of bed, padded across the cavernous room and hauled back the heavy damask curtains to reveal the sunlight spreading across the sky, giving promise of a fine day.

The Westend district of Frankfurt was the abode of many well-to-do Jewish families and the 'liberal' synagogue the Wolffs attended, a vast edifice with a huge chandelier in the entrance and a fountain playing in the inner courtyard, was just around the corner. The streets were tree-lined; many of the houses were detached with their own gardens, which was uncommon in Frankfurt, but their red and ochre brickwork, intricately decorated towers and gables, projecting attic windows and balconies with little portals, were equally uncommon in London. Enjoying the German atmosphere in the tranquillity of the early morning sunshine, it was several minutes before Anne's gaze focused on Bill, parked outside the tall iron gates of the Wolffs' house. With a disbelieving frown, she pushed up the lower window frame and leaned out to have a clearer view of her beloved car. Then she started to scream.

'Oh no, no, no, no.'

Without pausing to don her dressing-gown or slippers, wearing only her green silk pyjamas, Anne rushed out of the bedroom and across the landing, almost knocking over one of the maids carrying hot water towards Doctor Wolff's bedroom. Down the staircase she leapt and the marble tiles of the entrance hall were cold to her bare feet. As she struggled to open the front door which was still bolted, Anne was conscious of somebody making a fearful racket before she realised it was her own voice.

Once outside on the pavement she stopped shouting but as she walked slowly, silently, round Bill, the tears started to trickle down her face. The headlamps were smashed and the piles of broken glass glittered in the sunlight filtering through the trees, though that was a minor calamity in comparison to what the Nazi vandals had done to the beautiful red bodywork. Along the running boards and across the doors they had daubed black swastikas or *Hakenkreuz*, as the ancient symbol that until recently had denoted fertility and good luck, was known in Germany. The *pièce de résistance* was reserved for the sleek expanse of the bonnet on which, in thick white paint, there was a crude cartoon of a Jewess with a huge hooked nose, above a large Star of David and the word *Dreckjüdin*.

Anne started to sob uncontrollably and then Rebecca's arm was round her shoulder and her friend was saying, 'Don't, Anne, don't. Come inside.'

'Look what they've done to Bill,' Anne bawled. 'They're direct descendants of Attila the Hun.'

'I know, I know, but there's nothing we can do at the moment. So come back inside. There's a good girl.' Rebecca was trying to propel her towards the wrought-iron gates. 'Don't let them see they've got you down.'

'I don't care,' Anne shouted at the faces that had appeared at windows and the small crowd that was collecting.

'My parents do though.' Through the blur of her tears she saw Kurt who said softly, 'And you'll upset them even more if you stay here, sobbing your heart out in your bare feet and pyjamas.'

66

At this plea, registering that Kurt had thrown on a pair of trousers and a raincoat, and that although Rebecca was stockingless she was wearing a dress, Anne allowed herself to be shepherded into the Wolffs' house. At the bottom of the stairs Luise's twin daughters, Helga and Herta, were standing in their long white nightdresses, wide-eyed and wondering. As Anne crossed the marble hall Helga ran towards her, holding out her little hand in sympathy. Giving the child a watery smile, gently Anne squeezed her fingers. It would be Helga who had made the gesture for she was a bright, curious, sensitive, not always obedient little girl, whereas her sister Herta was placidly, smugly, well behaved. Then Luise herself appeared at the top of the stairs, immaculately groomed as always, and a few sharp words in German sent her daughters scurrying back up the stairs.

Rebecca and Kurt led Anne into the breakfast room where within minutes she was wrapped in her dressing-gown, drinking a cup of strong sweet tea and smoking a cigarette. The entire adult household appeared to be fluttering around her, except 'flutter' was an inappropriate verb to describe Herr Doktor Wolff's soothing bedside manner and the measured movements of his portly figure.

Kurt said, 'My parents cannot adequately convey their sense of horror and shame at the vandalising of your car.'

Inhaling on her cigarette, gaining comfort from the nicotine, Anne said, 'It wasn't their fault.'

'My father wants me to assure you he'll find the best garage in Frankfurt to repair it and you won't know that it was ever . . .'

'What do you mean, *he* will? I am insured and won't the police . . .'

Quickly, Kurt interrupted. 'We're not notifying the police.' As Anne opened her mouth to convey her astonishment, quietly he begged, 'Don't say anything, please, Anne. Just accept that for all his apparent calm and optimism, my father is a frightened and bewildered man. His world has turned upside down, including his belief in an impartial police force and judiciary. The last thing he wants at the moment is to draw official attention to the Wolff family.'

While Kurt was talking to her, Doctor Wolff had obviously

been giving instructions to Rebecca who said, 'Cousin Aaron suggests you have a hot bath which will help you to relax. Then you can have breakfast in bed and he'll give you a sedative. When you've had a good sleep, some of the shock will have worn off.'

One of the maids was apparently already running the bath, a monster porcelain affair with wide claw feet. When Anne was lying in the hot scented water she felt some of the tension draining from her, but she longed to be in the familiar surroundings of her favourite bathroom at Chenneys, gazing at the mosaic spread of the peacock's turquoise tail that had so fascinated her on her first childhood visit to the Marchal family home. Looking at Rebecca who was sitting at the end of the porcelain bath, she said, 'I'm sorry I made such a scene. Are your relations shocked by an *Engländer* being so emotional?'

'Kurt isn't. He insists we're a romantic, emotional race. I think the others probably are. But then they don't know Anne Whitworth, do they? They think the vandalism was probably caused as much by anti-feminism as anti-Semitism. There haven't been any attacks on Jewish property in the Westend district and women who own and drive cars are still a pretty rare species. Not to mention dead against the Nazis' *Kinder, Küche, Kirke* policy. You know, children, kitchen, church as our God- or Adolf Hitler-given priorities. Obviously the yahoos who did it thought Bill belongs to me.' The cast of Rebecca's features, including her somewhat hooked nose, spoke of her Jewish blood, she had driven the MG into Frankfurt and since their arrival she had used the car as much as Anne. 'Sorry about that.'

'Don't mention it.' Through the steam Anne gazed at Rebecca. 'I want to apologise for once accusing you of sniffing like a bloodhound on the trail of anti-Semitism, scenting insults where none existed.'

'No, no.' Vehemently Rebecca shook her head and the glossy black hair that was her crowning glory, fell damply across her forehead. 'I'm the one who should apologise. What happens in England, Daddy being refused membership of the golf club, that sort of thing, pales into insignificance besides what's happening here.' Even Doreen Shawcross's inbred

68

prejudice, Rebecca thought, though she'd never told anybody that. 'I'm worried, Anne, I really am.'

'So, according to Kurt, is his father.'

'Well, I wish he'd behave as if he were. I wish they all would, instead of doing their deeply patriotic, long-suffering Jewish act.'

While she soaked herself and listened to Rebecca venting her feelings, Anne knew she didn't want to be sedated. Despite her ardent pacifism and desire for friendship between nations, her feelings towards Germany had long been ambivalent. After all, it was a German sniper's bullet that had killed her father. At the moment, though it was an irrational and unfair impulse; what she wanted was to escape from this house and the smothering sympathy of its German occupants.

After she had dried herself, feeling slightly guilty at deceiving her friend, Anne told Rebecca she would go straight to bed to await her breakfast and the sedative. The minute Rebecca disappeared down the stairs, she shot into the bedroom where she dressed like greased lightning. She then scrawled a note, 'Have gone for a walk. Don't worry if I'm away for an hour or so. Need to clear my head. Love Anne', which she left on the pillow. Slipping into her most comfortable shoes, the white kid court ones with the medium heel, she grabbed her handbag and, her heart thumping from the exertion and the sensation of being a naughty girl, she crept out of the room.

Oh hell's bells!

Standing in the open doorway at the far end of the landing was Helga, now dressed in long white socks, blue dress and blue-and-white checked pinafore. Anne put her finger to her lips and said, 'Shush.' Bless her little heart, Helga got the message. Placing her own finger to her lips, she smiled at Anne and retired into the bedroom where she kept somebody engaged in conversation. Tiptoeing down the stairs Anne heard the murmur of voices from the breakfast room, and the slam of a door from the direction of the kitchen froze her against the wall. Nobody emerged and she was safely out of the front door, through the wrought-iron gates, and into the street. Keeping her eyes averted from the desecrated Bill, she walked quickly away from the house.

★   ★   ★

By midday Anne was sitting at a café table set out in the Römerberg. Gaudy in the sunlight, the red flags with the black swastikas in their white circles draped the balcony of the Römer, Frankfurt's medieval town hall, and they hung from the windows of the six- and seven-storeyed gabled houses surrounding the square, proclaiming the city's ardent support for the Nazis. Anne felt like a criminal returning to the scene of the crime, though the only evidence of last night's bonfire was the large brown patch on the cobblestones near the Justice Fountain. Had it happened last night? It seemed to her like half a century ago.

'*Der Kaffee, bitte,*' she said carefully to the young waiter who smiled at her and said, '*Sie sind Engländerin?*'

Unsmilingly she replied, '*Ja, ich bin Engländerin,*' before studiously returning her attention to the continental edition of the *Daily Mail*. Whether Fred Perry would win the men's singles title at Wimbledon this year wasn't a subject that greatly interested Anne but it was about all her tired brain felt capable of absorbing.

The intense concentration of the young man sketching at a nearby table drew her attention to him. Apart from the sketchpad and the movements of his right shoulder, all she could see was the back of his head with the thick brown hair curling untidily into his neck. His jacket was on the seat and Anne noticed that the collar of his check shirt was frayed. There was something about him . . . she'd seen him somewhere before . . . a couple of Brownshirts strutted past and he turned his head to look at them. The profile that appeared to have been carved from the rocks of Netherstone Edge, slotted itself into place in Anne's memory.

'*Danke,*' she thanked the waiter for the coffee.

Part of the huge sum raised by the Tom Whitworth Memorial appeal had gone to build the Memorial Hall and gardens in Mellordale, while the remainder had been used to endow an annual scholarship for a working-class lad to study at Ruskin College, Oxford. While she was at Somerville, Anne had made a point of welcoming the recipients. The first two had been most grateful for her personal attention but the last beneficiary had not. To start with, B. D. Broughton had refused the invitation to tea, so Anne had gone out of her way to meet him in the common room at Ruskin College where he'd been sitting sketching when she'd been shown in. After a few surly grunts in answer to her attempts at conversation, he'd said he hadn't realised winning the Tom Whitworth scholarship entailed being patronised by his daughter. Furiously, Anne had said she wasn't patronising him, she was merely trying to be friendly, and he'd said she could have fooled him. Controlling her temper, she'd said they didn't appear to have much to say to each other, which she'd thought would give him the opportunity to apologise, or something, but he'd replied, no. After she'd swept from the common room she'd still expected to hear from him, but the rest had been silence. His loutish behaviour had been a pity because B. D. Broughton came from The Dales, he had a deep voice with Lancashire inflections similar to her father's, and Anne had found him potentially by far the most interesting of the scholarship holders.

It was nearly four years since their unfortunate encounter but in her present state she longed to talk to a compatriot. Draining her coffee, Anne stood up and walked over to his table where he was still busily sketching, and said, 'Hello, you're Mr Broughton, aren't you? I'm Anne Whitworth.'

He glanced up at her. She had forgotten about his eyes. Julian had those thick lashes fringing his velvety brown orbs, but B. D. Broughton's lashes – she didn't think she'd ever known his Christian names – looked as if they'd been brushed with mascara, riveting attention on his large, clear, slate-grey eyes.

'Oh yes,' he said after he'd gazed at her with disconcerting steadiness. 'I remember you.'

'May I join you, if I promise not to patronise you? Which is what you accused me of last time we met. I'm feeling rather blue.'

'Please do.' Belatedly, he rose to his feet and pulled out a chair for her to sit down. When she had settled herself he said, 'What's up?'

Anne had retained an impression of his chunky solidity, broad face, broad shoulders, rugged features, but the startlingly attractive, watchful eyes went with an extraordinary quality of self-containment that she had similarly forgotten. As she started to relate her recent experiences, a thought struck Anne. She said, 'I presume you are still a Socialist? And you don't approve of the Nazis?'

'The Socialist lad I stayed with in Munich has just been released from three months in Dachau which is what the Nazis call a *Konzentrationslager*. They say they've pinched the idea from the concentration camps we set up in the Boer War. Herding their opponents together, sealing them off from the rest of society. I presume you've heard of Dachau?'

Both Rebecca and Kurt had relayed some horrific, barely believable stories about the way the SS men who ran the camp were treating their mostly political prisoners. As Anne nodded – who was being patronising now? – he said, 'Your questions are answered then.'

Other than that response, Mr Broughton listened attentively but impassively to her story. Slightly defensively Anne finished by saying, 'I suppose in the context of what's happening in Dachau and Oranienberg . . .' To emphasise her awareness she thought she'd mention another concentration camp the SS had set up. '. . . having your car vandalised is small beer. And I expect you'd say I'm lucky to own an MG. I did buy it myself. From the proceeds of *Whatever Happened to Wordsworth?*'

'Whatever happened to who?' he said.

Anne started to laugh. Then she wasn't laughing any more, she was crying. She folded her arms on the table and buried her face in them, gasping, 'Oh hell. I'm sorry.'

She heard him saying, 'I'd buy you a drink. Except I'm skint. I can provide a clean hanky.'

After she'd wiped the tears from her face and blown her nose on his handkerchief, Anne turned towards him and asked, 'Do I look awful?'

'I've seen worse.'

Then, for the first time, he smiled and the effect was like a sunburst in a stormy sky, transfiguring his features. Anne said, 'While I find a ladies' room, will you order us both a drink, please? I'd like a glass of wine. And something to eat. I'll have some of the delicious German cold meats and a salad. And one of their luscious cakes. You choose what you want. Please don't argue with me about paying, otherwise I shall only start crying again.'

'Your servant, Miss Whitworth.'

Taking a deep breath, throwing the conventions of polite society to the winds, she said, 'Seeing we've remet in peculiar circumstances, would you like to call me Anne? I only know you as B. D. Broughton. What do the "B" and "D" stand for.'

'Benjamin Daniel, but I'm known as Ben.'

She gave him a tremulous smile and Ben watched her disappear inside the café. He couldn't say Anne Whitworth had stayed in the forefront of his mind but he certainly remembered her. If anything, she was now classier and more confident than the condescending madam who'd so riled him at Oxford; driving across Europe with her pal, traipsing about Frankfurt by herself, and 'Please don't argue about paying' – he wasn't going to because he hadn't eaten a square meal for days – and 'Would you like to call me Anne?' But somehow today, right from the start, even before she'd shown her tearful vulnerability, she hadn't irritated him.

During the last few weeks in Germany, Ben had picked up enough of the lingo to get by. The waiter was bringing the spread he'd ordered – soup, rolls, a mound of frankfurters, a slice of Black Forest cake and a glass of beer for himself – when Ben saw Anne returning to the table. She appeared to have recovered her composure. She'd told him she'd simply thrown her clothes on to escape from her friends' house and he wondered what she looked like when she took trouble with her attire. With her slender height, in a buttercup-yellow and white silk polka-dot dress with a skirt that swished round her silk-stockinged calves, white court shoes, a snazzy pageboy hat on her shining copper-coloured hair, she could have stepped straight from the pages of *Vogue* magazine. Ben recalled finding her attractive that day in Oxford, which was maybe one of the reasons he'd been so rude to her. Silently he said, 'Down, boy' to the stirring in his loins because becoming involved with Miss Anne Whitworth was a complication he could afford even less now than four years ago.

While they were eating their food, she asked what he was doing in Germany. When he informed her he was hitch-hiking round Europe, mostly looking at the art galleries, she said,

'How do you live if you haven't any money? Are you particularly interested in pictures? Is drawing your hobby?'

She was a nosey parker, with this habit of firing off personal questions. Ben did not believe in wasting words, nor in letting folk know what was going on in his head, and normally he'd have told her to mind her own business but he felt surprisingly indulgent towards her. She'd obviously been deeply affected by the book-burning last night and the poor kid had suffered one hell of shock this morning. He said, 'I've lived by doing odd jobs when I can get them. Or by doing sketches, if anybody wants to buy them. And drawing isn't my hobby. I've always wanted to paint for my living.'

'Really?' Her eyes opened wide and, typically, she asked more questions. 'What were you doing at Ruskin College then? Why did you enter for my father's memorial scholarship?'

'In my folks' opinion, your Dad walked on water.'

Delightedly she laughed and she had lovely pearly teeth which denoted good food and good health. That remark had obviously gone down a treat. To his astonishment, or maybe it was those big brown eyes gazing at him so eagerly, Ben found himself elucidating.

'My folks are longtime Socialists. And my Dad served in your Dad's company on the Somme. He had the good luck to be invalided out, if you can call it that. His leg was blown off at Contalmaison. It was Dad who badgered me into entering for the Tom second-only-to-God Whitworth scholarship.' She laughed again as Ben added, 'The last thing I expected was to win it. I wrote a right bolshie essay.'

'My mother thought it was most original. She was one of the judges.'

Ben's parents had a high opinion of Tom Whitworth's widow too. They'd even forgiven her for marrying that playwright with the handle to his name. 'Any road, when I did win Dad was like a tomcat with two bowls of cream, so I couldn't not accept.'

'Didn't you enjoy your year at Oxford?'

'Not much.' Anne Whitworth looked surprised. Then she offered him a cigarette which, to her equally obvious surprise, he refused, informing her, 'I've given up. They get in the way when I'm painting.'

74

'Oh.' She craned her neck towards his sketchpad and said, 'May I see your drawings?'

Why not? Ben thought. He'd always had a facility for drawing people, capturing a good likeness of facial structure and body shape, but portraiture wasn't his scene, he was after something entirely different. Handing the book to Anne, he watched her slowly turning over the stiff white pages – Ben preferred to go without food rather than use poor-quality paper – intently examining the pencil drawings. There were smart Frankfurters in the Opernplatz; a group of Nazi kids in shirts and shorts and kneesocks, saluting the flag in the Palmengarten; sinister SS officers staring at the Rothschild-haus in the Börnestrasse; and several pages of the Jewish market traders in the Börneplatz, including a couple of ortho-dox Jews in kaftans and broad-brimmed hats, deep in conver-sation outside the synagogue. Ben's interest in Jews was not great – the only one he knew personally kept the pawnshop in Upperdale – but the faces in the Börneplatz had fascinated him and he always pencilled in the background, to give his figures a context. The final drawings were of a uniformed nursemaid wheeling a pram across the Römerberg, and the SA men strutting past the Justice Fountain and to emphasise this ironic juxtaposition, Ben had shaded in the statue of Justice holding her scales.

After she had finished her silent examination – Ben appreciated her *not* making the customary yelps of appreci-ation – Anne Whitworth looked up at him and said, 'May I buy the drawings?'

'What? All of them?'

'Yes.'

'What for?' Ben asked suspiciously. He didn't mind her paying for a meal but he damned well didn't want her charity.

'Because I think they're brilliant. On a practical level, you say you're skint. You also say you want to earn your living as an artist. Well, I'm offering to buy what I'm sure will be a damned good investment. How much do you want for the whole sketchbook?'

Although Ben disliked women swearing, the briskness of her tone made him smile. He replied, 'No idea.'

'Oh.' At this announcement her businesslike air evaporated,

she looked deflated and touchingly girlish. Then she said 'Oh' again, rummaged in her handbag, extracted her purse, opened it and grimaced. 'I haven't enough money on me, anyway. Look, if you're not frantically busy this afternoon, why don't you come with me to the Wolffs? We can discuss the price then. I'm sure they'd love to meet you. And I think I should be getting back, anyway.'

To Anne's delight, Ben said he wasn't busy this afternoon and he'd happily escort her to wherever she was staying. In fact, he thought she needed a bodyguard. Pulling a face at this comment, she slipped him the money for the bill so he wouldn't be embarrassed by her actually paying. After he had settled the account, he slung his jacket over his shoulders, stuck the sketchpad under his arm and they walked together towards the Rapunzelgässchen. He wasn't as tall as Sandy or Julian or even dear Kurt, no more than five feet ten, but his body was beautifully compact, he moved with an easy stride, and what did his comparative lack of inches matter?

Anne herself felt as if she were walking on air, intoxicated not by one glass of wine, but because it had happened. Here in the Römerberg, the historic heart of a city and a country about which she had highly ambivalent emotions, she had been struck by the lightning of love. Without a shadow of a doubt, their re-encounter had been ordained and Ben Broughton was the man for her.

7

It was Rebecca who discovered Anne's note and, shock or no shock, she was annoyed with her friend for disappearing without a word. When Anne had not returned by lunchtime, cousins Aaron and Sophia were in a terrible state so Rebecca and Kurt widened the area of their search from the leafy streets and parks of Westend to the centre of Frankfurt.

Rebecca had the notion that Anne would be somewhere in the vicinity of last night's book-burning, therefore she and her cousin decided to comb the maze of old streets leading into the Römerberg. They had arranged to rendezvous in an hour's time outside the cathedral, hoping that one of them would have found Anne.

When Rebecca turned the corner into yet another alleyway, she saw three SA men in the shaft of sunlight penetrating the shadows cast by the tall houses on either side. The light glinted on the peaks of their postman-style caps, on the straps across their brown shirts, on the leather of their boots. There was nobody else in the street and through the shadows the stormtroopers swaggered towards her.

'*Kück mal wie die dicke Jüdin füllt die Ganzegasse?*' one of them bawled.

Everybody assured Rebecca there had been few physical attacks on Jews, at least not in public, but they said there had been no outrages in the Westend district. Yet Bill had been vandalised. The Brownshirts were advancing on her, loudly discussing the best way of teaching the big fat cow of a Jewess the lesson that filling the whole pavement was an insult to pure-blooded Aryans. What should she do? Cut and run? With her clumsiness she was bound to fall over. Rebecca's fear was atavistic but she decided to keep walking as if the stormtroopers did not exist.

Within a few steps she had reached the stormtroopers and they were blocking her path. They were quite young and they had the faces of pink porkers, though that was an insult to pigs. They started to circle round her, mouthing their obscenities, and Rebecca smelled their stale breath which made her feel sick. The walls of the houses seemed to be closing in on her, instinctively she shut her eyes and she felt their fingers prodding her breasts and buttocks as if she were a lump of meat. Her hat was pulled off and she was being shoved backwards and forwards like a punch-ball. All the time they were making filthy gibes about Jewish whores. Suddenly the anger overcame Rebecca's fear; she wasn't a Jew from the *stettl*; they couldn't treat her like this. Opening her eyes, she spoke commandingly and clearly in English.

'Would you mind getting out of my way.'

77

It wasn't a question, it was an order. Imperiously, Rebecca stared into their flushed, sweaty faces. Although they were still encircling her and doubtfully had any knowledge of English, they stopped shoving her and glanced uncertainly at each other. Rebecca was thinking the use of her native tongue and her authoritative manner had done the trick and they might let her through, when she heard the shouts from the Römerberg end of the alleyway.

Anne and Ben turned into the street at the precise moment the SA men started to hustle and jostle Rebecca. Peering from the shade, through the shaft of sunlight into the further shadows, for several seconds Anne could not make out what was going on. Then her eyes found their focus and the uniforms told her three beastly Brownshirts were harassing some poor soul. With a raucous cry, one of them held the pink straw hat in the air and it was just like the hat she'd talked Rebecca into buying from Derry and Toms. It took several more seconds before Anne realised it was actually Rebecca's hat and it was her friend who was being molested. Shouting at the top of her voice, she raced down the narrow street and grabbed the swastika-banded arm of the nearest stormtrooper.
'What do you think you're doing? How dare you? Leave my friend alone!'
Startled and astounded at being thus assailed by a young woman, the SA man gave Anne a hefty push which caused her to lose her footing.
When Anne suddenly yelled and set off down the street at a gallop, naturally Ben followed her. He reckoned he'd learned to control his aggressive temper, but as the storm-trooper shoved Anne and she fell to the cobblestones, instinctively he strode towards the bugger and hit him. Ben had been a northern area schoolboy boxing champion and the blow landed on the SA man's chin, knocking him out cold. He was flexing the knuckles of his left hand – he was a south paw and it was a long time since he'd hit anybody so hard and without gloves – when the other two buggers jumped him. Ben's detestation of Fascism in general and Nazi bully-boys in particular, mixed with his fury that one of them had

manhandled Anne, overcame prudence or restraint and he returned their blows with all the native aggression and half-forgotten expertise at his command.

The Brownshirts' attention being otherwise engaged, Rebecca was left standing on the edge of the mêlée and for a few seconds she was so stunned by what was occurring she stayed immobile, her mouth wide open. Who on earth was this man who'd come charging after Anne and was laying into the stormtroopers like Georges Carpentier, except he wasn't French, he was English because he was shouting, 'You sodding bullies, you half-baked buggers!'

With detached interest Rebecca noted that he had a Lanca-shire accent, before her wits returned. Scrambling round the Brownshirt who was lying on the cobblestones with his legs spreadeagled, she knelt down beside Anne who was sitting on the edge of the pavement, looking somewhat dazed. Anxiously Rebecca asked, 'Are you all right?'

'I think so,' Anne said. 'Where's Ben?'

Rebecca turned her head as another of the Brownshirts fell to the ground, clutching his crotch (Ben had abandoned the Queensberry Rules). Struggling to stand up but obviously feeling giddy, Anne said, 'Oh, oh heavens. Shouldn't we help him?'

'I don't think he needs our help.'

Whoever Ben might be, Rebecca thought, he was a belliger-ent so-and-so. Not that she altogether objected to his ag-gression for in this world, alas, whatever Anne hoped and preached, there were moments when you had to answer force with force. Whether this was one of them, Rebecca had her doubts, but if Ben could knock out the other Brownshirt, they could make their escape and rendezvous with Kurt by the cathedral. Otherwise they were in trouble, tangling with Herr Hitler's boys. At the Römerberg end of the street Rebecca saw the people gathering, she heard the shouts and the blast of the police whistle, and they were in trouble.

As the policemen pounded towards them, Anne said, 'Help me up. I'm not grovelling to them.'

Having assisted Anne to her feet, seeing she herself spoke good German, Rebecca tried to explain to the most senior police officer what had happened but she was rudely pushed aside. By now quite a crowd had gathered, there was a lot of noise, which in the narrowness of the street reverberated against the high walls of the houses, Anne was adding to the tumult by shouting in English, but attention was focused on the stormtrooper who remained upright, and on Ben. His nose was bleeding and his shirt torn, otherwise he looked considerably less the worse for wear than the SA men. Ben's hands were swiftly handcuffed behind his back, which made Anne shout again, 'What are you doing?'

It was obvious what they were doing. They were arresting him. Having redrawn attention to herself, Anne was promptly flanked by two policemen in the coal-scuttle hats which to Rebecca's English eyes made them look like characters from a musical comedy. Then an ambulance arrived at the nearer end of the alleyway, to cart the injured stormtroopers off to hospital. Rebecca didn't think they were badly hurt, the first one had recovered consciousness and become extremely voluble, pointing at Anne and baring his rotten teeth at Ben, and the second one was merely limping and looking evil-tempered. All three were having a whale of a time, giving their version of 'the incident' which consisted of their having been walking peaceably along, when this arrogant young woman tried to push them off the pavement. When they politely remonstrated, this maniac of a man attacked them.

The curious distortion of what had actually happened made Rebecca realise that in their fury at being worsted by Ben, the stormtroopers had completely forgotten her. She had become one of the crowd, some of whom were gazing not unsympathetically at Anne and Ben, though others were loudly condemning the unprovoked attack on good German citizens in broad daylight in the streets of Frankfurt. Then, at the Römerberg end of the alleyway, a police car screeched to a halt, followed by a police van.

'*Schnell, mach schnell!*' the remaining Brownshirt shouted at Anne and Ben.

In an agony of indecision, Rebecca watched as they were marched towards the van, Anne with reasonable courtesy, Ben roughly. Her personal pride and courage, her loyalty and love for Anne, said she should have stuck like a leech to her friend's side. Seeing she hadn't, she should now run after her and share whatever lay in store. Atavistic instinct, coupled with the experience gained during the years of lobbying and negotiating for the Jewish Agency, learning when to press the advantage and when to shut up and count ten, told Rebecca to be cool and practical and forget the heroics.

Ben was bundled inside the police van and, with his wrists handcuffed behind his back, he lost his balance and the storm-trooper kicked him as he lay on the floor. Anne longed to kick the Brownshirt. Apart from that lout, two policemen also climbed into the van and the younger one helped Ben to his feet. He was then pushed on to the narrow bench that ran along one side of the vehicle, and the policemen flanked him. It was indicated to Anne that she should sit down, which she did, as close as possible to Ben. The rear doors clanged, the engine snorted, and the vehicle set off. With the doors shut it was gloomy inside the van and there was an unpleasant smell of stale sick and sweaty bodies. Anne had a sudden extraordinary sensation that she'd been in this situation before which, in im-agination, she had, listening avidly to the stories of her mother's suffragette days, to her graphic descriptions of the first time she'd been arrested and the terrifying journey through the streets of Edwardian London in the horse-driven Black Maria.

This experience couldn't be worse than that, Anne told herself. Holding her nose to lessen the stench, accustoming her eyes to the dim light, she leaned outwards so that she could vaguely see Ben. She said, 'Sorry to have got you into this mess. Are you all right?'

'Could be worse. Most folks'd say I got you into it. How are you?'

'Could be worse!'

Actually, Anne's right arm was bruised, every time she moved her right shoulder there was a stab of pain – she had fallen on this side – the back of her head ached, while the rest of it felt as if it were stuffed with cotton wool. This sensation of seeing and hearing everything through a wodgy softness was heightened by everybody's speaking German. Apart from Ben and . . . As if he could read her thoughts, he said, 'Where's your pal?'

Where was Rebecca?

'I don't know,' Anne admitted. 'But I expect she's gone to get help.'

'Good. I reckon we're going to need it.'

At that moment the vehicle swung sharply round a corner and they were all flung to the left. Once they were sitting upright again, Anne was thinking this experience had assuredly bound the two of them together, when the SA man suddenly yelled at Ben, leaned over and hit him in the face. Through the gloom Anne could see the policeman who'd helped him to his feet looking discomfited by the action, though the other one was grinning, and that the blow had made Ben's nose start to bleed again. She felt the fury boiling in her veins and she spat at the Brownshirt, 'You . . . you . . . *schweinhund*.'

Ben said softly, 'Calm down, luv. That was an order to stop talking! Don't provoke them any more than I already have.'

What an unpredictable lot the Nazis were. Why had they been allowed to talk at all? Even in her fury Anne was delighted that Ben had called her 'luv'. At the police station, where they were marched up the steps, through an entrance hall and into what she presumed was a charge room, she tried to keep his advice in mind. The stormtrooper who was sticking to them like a limpet, subjected the policeman sitting behind the high wooden desk to a long harangue.

'What's he saying?' Anne whispered to Ben.

'Dunno. My German isn't up to it. Doubt it's a favourable report, though.'

The sergeant or whoever he was, peered down at Anne and started to question her. Excitedly she said, '*Ich bin Engländerin. Ich sprechen nicht Deutsch.*' When he was questioned, Ben responded impassively but intimated that he too was English and didn't speak German.

The sergeant was a middle-aged man with a drooping, Kaiser-type moustache, and he looked nonplussed because he obviously didn't *sprechen* English. The Brownshirt stamped up and down the room shouting and it was apparent he was demanding that they be charged nonetheless. The contents of Anne's handbag and Ben's pockets were then laid out on the desk, together with his sketchpad which one of the policemen must have picked up from the pavement. The sergeant began to leaf through the sketchpad but the SA man snatched it from him which did not please the older man, though he made no protest. A sign of the times and of the SA's power, Anne thought. She watched while the stormtrooper's expression changed from one of surprised approval as he inspected the drawings of the posh Frankfurters and the Nazi youngsters, to a veritable curling of his fat lips as he regarded the many sketches of the Jewish market traders, to one of positive venom as he reached the last drawing of the Brownshirts by the Justice Fountain. For Ben had caricatured their strutting arrogance and lumpen faces in the same way as the vandals had daubed the Jewess on Bill, but with infinitely more talent.

Looking at the stormtrooper's livid expression, Anne experienced a seismic tremor of fear for Ben. '*Er ist* . . .' Oh hell, how did you say 'mine' in German? Frantically, she pointed from the sketchbook to herself, shouting, '*Er ist* . . . mine, mine.'

The SA man appeared to understand what she meant, but with a nasty smirk he picked up the pencils and india rubber that had come from Ben's pockets, prodding him in the chest with the former, rubbing the caked blood from his nose with the latter. Then he said something to the sergeant in German, the sergeant nodded reluctantly, Anne thought, and issued instructions to the two policemen who grabbed Ben's shoulders and propelled him towards the doorway.

'Where are you taking him?' Anne started to run after him but the SA man grabbed her bruised right arm. She winced from the pain and gasped, 'Let me go.'

He duly did, but not before Ben had disappeared, followed by the stormtrooper.

Even when she was led along corridors where the thump of the policeman's boots and the tap of her court shoes echoed resoundingly, and locked into this room, Anne felt no fear for herself, only for Ben. It was a bleak little room, windowless, lit by an unshaded electric bulb hanging from the ceiling, the furniture consisting of two wooden chairs and a desk.

Her diamond wristwatch, an eighteenth-birthday present from her mother, had been taken from her and it seemed to Anne as if twenty-four hours had elapsed since she'd been arrested, though it was probably two hours at most.

As she heard the key turning in the lock, she stopped pacing round the room and sat down as composedly as she could in one of the chairs. Perhaps it was Rebecca with the British consul, or a lawyer, or somebody who spoke English, or . . . it was the policeman who'd helped Ben and looked sheepish when the SA man had hit him. In his hand was a tin mug which he gave to Anne, saying, '*Hier ist eine Tasse Tee für Sie.*'

'*Danke,*' Anne said.

Watching her sip the weak tepid tea – dear old Madge would have spat it out in disgust – he enquired, '*Gut? Gut?*'

He spoke very slowly and loudly as if she were mentally deficient, though talking thus to people who didn't understand your language was a common habit. Then confidentially he said, '*Bald kommt jemand der Englisch spricht.*'

Anne understood the bit about an English speaker and smiled faintly at the policeman because he was trying to be nice, though her head no longer felt as if it were stuffed with cotton wool, but rather as if it had been invaded by a detachment of miniature Brownshirts, stamping backwards and forwards in their boots. In fact her whole body was now aching fearfully. It was only after the policeman had gone, with an ominous rasping of the key in the lock, that the fear and guilt started to creep into Anne's brain like the mist rolling down from the Pennine moors.

It was her fault that she was imprisoned here and Ben was . . . please, dear God, don't let anything awful happen to him. If she'd stayed put in the Wolffs' house . . . if she had, she'd never have remet Ben Broughton . . . but she shouldn't have dashed so impulsively to Rebecca's aid . . . and she and Ben were technically guilty of assaulting the Brownshirts, well Ben more than technically, the reason why would be immaterial to a Nazi judge, and the other kind of German judges had already shut up or been dismissed. Then she was shivering convulsively from the chill of the room and the thinness of her silk dress, her teeth were chattering like castanets, and she was weeping wildly. Her mother always said a good cry did you good and Mummy knew what she was talking about. If, as a well-brought-up Miss born in late Victorian days, she could survive the experiences she'd been through . . . Out loud Anne said, 'I can survive this.'

Having gulped back her tears, she decided that there was no point dwelling on what might be happening to Ben; better to think of pleasant things; such as Con's wedding.

Initially, her darling sister's announcement that she was becoming engaged to Gavin Campbell-Ross had been the most devastating shock. Gavin was a friend of Sandy's, a regular at the Dalziels' New Year house parties, and on coming down from Oxford he'd gone into the Diplomatic Service. Anne considered him a typical Foreign Office bod, medium height, medium build, medium good-looking, medium everything, incapable of giving a straight answer or clear opinion about anything. His saving grace was a genuine love of music which, Anne had carelessly presumed as he trotted devotedly after Con, formed some sort of bond between them.

After she had recovered from the shock of the engagement, she'd said furiously to her sister, 'What about your music? Your career as a concert pianist?'

Gently but firmly Con had replied, 'That was your plan for me, Anne. Not mine. I'm not personally ambitious like you and Kate. You're both determined to win every race you enter but I don't mind coming second, or third, though I wouldn't want to be last. What I want, what I've always wanted, is to marry and have lots of children. So does Gavin. I shall go on playing the piano of course, for myself and for them, and for anybody who cares to listen.'

Which put her in her place, Anne had thought, and zero marks for observation and understanding. She'd still rushed off to her mother and said, 'You can't let Con marry *him* and throw away her talent and ruin her life. She's only twenty.'

But Mummy had said, 'Con can be just as stubborn and determined as any of you, if more sweetly so, once she's made up her mind about something. She's made up her mind about Gavin. I brought you all up to be emancipated and stand on your own feet, so I can't complain when you are and do.'

'I don't consider marrying Gavin Campbell-Ross being emancipated,' Anne had said crossly.

Philip's contribution had been the comment, 'Con has the talent, but not the temperament, to be a concert pianist.'

Which was more or less what Con herself had said.

When Gavin had learned that he was being posted to the Berlin Embassy at the end of last year, Con and he had decided to marry on her twenty-first birthday which, as Con said, would save Mummy and stepdaddy the expense of two celebrations! It had been a beautiful day, the sky a soft blue with puffs of white cloud, Chenneys cloaked in the russets and auburns of late autumn. In a billowing lace wedding gown designed by Theo Marvell, Con had looked simply lovely and as they exchanged their wedding vows in the Norman church in Marshall Minnis – at least Con had omitted the word 'obey' – she and Gavin had gazed at each other so lovingly, Anne had thought perhaps her favourite sister knew what she was doing, though the waste of her talent still rankled.

The memory of the wedding made the tears prick again in Anne's eyes. How she longed to be safe and secure at Chenneys. Or up in The Dales with Ben. She was so tired, so very, very tired . . . she felt herself drifting into the blessed oblivion of sleep . . . With a start Anne sat up in the chair.

The door had opened and framed in the aperture she saw the tall figure clad in black. The peak of his cap was shading his face but the light was shining on the death's head skull. Oh God, she had been handed over to the SS for interrogation.

Once the police van had snorted away, Rebecca decided to find Kurt as quickly as possible. He knew Frankfurt and he had a cool head which could view the situation dispassionately. Thank the Lord, he was waiting by the cathedral. He listened without interruption to her lucid resumé of the facts which was one of Rebecca's talents. She finished by saying, 'I think the best thing I can do is to contact the British consul and impress on him the possible gravity and definite urgency of the situation. Yes?'

'No. I think the best thing you can do is to get hold of Helmut Ohlendorf.' When Rebecca raised her eyebrows, Kurt went on, 'All consulates have to move through diplomatic channels which are not noted for their speed. Anne and her friend have mixed it with the SA. The SA are involved in a fight for supremacy with the SS. Nothing will give *SS-Obersturmführer* Ohlendorf more pleasure than to do the SA down. There's also the personal element, or as much of a personal element as the SS allow themselves in their dedication to serving their Führer. I took Ohlendorf to be smitten by Fraulein Whitworth, which shows he has a remnant of humanity and good taste.'

Kurt gave Rebecca his wry smile and she thought, You're a bit smitten too, aren't you, dear cousin? He said, 'Do you know who this man Ben is?'

'Not the foggiest,' Rebecca replied. 'Anne can't know him well because I've never met or heard of him.'

Fortune was with them. A friend of Kurt's lived in a house close by the cathedral, he possessed a telephone and he was at home, if for the rotten reason that as a Jew he had been dismissed from his consultancy at the hospital. He said he appreciated the irony of the SS being contacted from his apartment and Rebecca was soon connected by the operator. Helmut Ohlendorf was in his office and after she had spelled out her name to a secretary, she was put through to him. He presumed she was telephoning to make an appointment to discuss 'the Jewish problem' which showed how much store he set by that, but Rebecca said another, more urgent problem had precipitated her call.

They spoke in German and Rebecca drew on unexpected reserves of her grandfather Lewental's language, answering the *SS-Obersturmführer*'s barked questions with polite lucidity, though with his surprisingly high-pitched voice, particularly over the telephone it sounded more like petulant yapping. Rebecca emphasised that it was the SA who were involved, she appealed for his assistance, and she laid the flattery and the snobbery on with a trowel. She had observed that many Nazis were appalling snobs, only too willing to ape the worst characteristics of the old Junker class they allegedly despised, and that they had a considerable respect for their Anglo-Saxon cousins in England.

'If you can possibly sort out the difficulties for both Fraulein Whitworth and her friend, I know she will be most grateful.' Please don't ask me what the friend's surname is, Rebecca thought, having done her best to intimate there was no romantic interest between Ben and Anne and his actions had been prompted by chivalry towards the weaker sex. She decided to finish her recital by plugging the snob angle. In her most dulcet tones – she knew she had a pleasantly modulated voice – she said, 'I'm sure Fraulein Whitworth's stepfather will be grateful, too. Sir Philip Marchal's plays are so popular in Germany, aren't they? If the problem can be resolved without publicity, I think that would be best, don't you?'

There was a pause before Helmut Ohlendorf replied, and Rebecca held her breath. Then he said, 'You may leave matters in my hands, Fraulein Lawson.'

8

'Good morning, may I come in?'

'Yeah, do.' Propped against the pillows, Ben smiled as Anne put her head round the bedroom door.

'And how's the patient today?'

'Beginning to feel faintly human again. The old Jew's a good doctor.'

'Yes.' She wished he hadn't thus referred to Doctor Wolff but she had no intention of upbraiding him at the moment. 'I see you've had your breakfast.'

Anne knew perfectly well Ben had had his breakfast because she'd been monitoring the comings and goings in the Wolffs' house for the last hour. Apart from the servants, everybody had gone out. Anne herself was still being molly-coddled, having her own breakfast in bed, rising when she chose, though frankly her aches and pains had vanished and she'd recovered her spirits several days ago. Since the evening of that terrible day when Ben had been brought to the house in an unmarked ambulance and carried inside on a stretcher – Doctor Wolff's subsequent examinations and X-rays had revealed that though he had been badly beaten up, nothing actually appeared to be broken or irreparably damaged – this was the first opportunity she'd had to speak to Ben alone.

The clarity had returned to his slate-grey eyes and they followed Anne's movements as she walked into the room, with an expression that made her skin tingle and her heart thud. To produce such a reaction was why she had plotted to visit Ben on his sick-bed, clad in her favourite peignoir, a powder-blue silk garment, lace frills at neck and wrists, cut on the bias so that it clung to her figure, with a tight waistband that accentuated her slender shapeliness. Anne's problem was that though her love and desire for him had been intensified by the ordeal he had suffered on her account, and she wanted Ben to know that it had; though she was capable of being seductively provocative, as she had been with Julian and was now being with Ben, unless she was drunk, as with Sandy, certain inhibitions and proprieties stopped her being completely brazen and openly stating her emotions.

So decorously, Anne seated herself in the armchair placed near the bottom of the bed. Having surveyed Ben from afar, she announced, 'You do look heaps better, though still a bit like a . . .' she searched her mind for a suitable simile '. . . a panda.'

'Ta,' he said.

'Do you realise we have an *SS-Obersturmführer* named Ohlendorf to thank for our release?' Ben said he'd gathered as much and Anne told him how cleverly Rebecca had behaved. 'But he was typically beastly about her. He said, "Naturally, your Jewish friend ran away. You will appreciate, Fraulein Whitworth, that all Jews are cowards, interested only in saving their own skins."'

'I could have hit him but I said, "Fraulein Lawson's father won the Military Cross for his bravery at Vimy Ridge. And

Herr Doktor Wolff was awarded the Iron Cross for medical services under fire at Verdun." Do you know what Helmut Ohlendorf said? Dead seriously he said, "The Iron Cross, first or second class?" When I said I hadn't the faintest idea, he became thoughtful and said Herr Doktor Wolff could be relied upon to keep his mouth shut. That was when he told me Herr Broughton had, due to an unfortunate administrative error, been handed over to the SA and *SS-Obersturmführer* Ohlendorf had galloped to the rescue in the nick of time. He then showed his own fangs, by saying he was sure neither I nor Herr Broughton, if released unconditionally, would wish to contact the newspapers or press any counter-charges. Because any such actions could have unfortunate repercussions on the Wolff family. So I agreed we would not. I hope you think I did the right thing.'

At Anne's somewhat breathless recital Ben laughed and said, 'I think you did marvellously, you and your pal Rebecca. At that moment, I'd have agreed to more or less anything to get out of the clutches of the SA. All I want to do now is get out of Germany as fast as I can.'

'Yes, Helmut Ohlendorf suggested that would be a good idea, once you were recovered. Oh, just before we parted company at the police station, he suddenly produced your sketchbook and became playful – which was a painful sight – about Herr Broughton having talent as an artist but being wayward and decadent in his choice of subjects. But I have the drawings safe and sound, and I haven't paid you for them.'

'Accept them as a gift.' Anne started to protest that she couldn't possibly but Ben said, 'Just take them, luv.'

Again absorbing the Lancashire use of 'luv', she said, 'Thank you.'

He was now lying back against the pillows, gazing at her with the sultry stillness that in other circumstances betokens a thunderstorm. Anne crossed and recrossed her legs, and the silk of her peignoir rustled softly as she burbled, 'You'll never guess what *SS-Obersturmführer* Ohlendorf's parting shot was! It absolutely took the biscuit! He begged to be allowed to take me to dinner and the opera before I left Frankfurt!' Anne then noticed the copy of *Whatever Happened to Wordsworth?*

that she'd given Ben, lying open on the bedside table. Waving her arm towards the book, she asked, 'Are you enjoying it? Do you like . . .'

'Are you ever going to stop talking?' Anne stopped and he said, 'Does the door lock?'

'I don't know.'

'Find out.'

Her slippered feet ran across the brown and orange lozenge-shaped pattern of the carpet, over the parquet flooring, towards the door. Had she anticipated going the whole hog? Not really, but her body was positively trembling with desire. Having reached the door Anne said breathily, 'Yes, there is a key. Are you sure you're well enough to . . .?'

'Shut up,' Ben said. 'Lock the door and come here.'

Anne obeyed his instructions, kicked off her slippers and walked towards the bed. Throwing back the bedclothes, he drew her down on to the sheet. His hands were cupping her face, holding it tightly, his lips were on hers, their tongues entwining, Anne's fingers were digging into his neck and his were trying to undo the row of tiny silk-covered buttons on her peignoir. Lifting his head, he said hoarsely, 'Take the damned thing off.'

Anne slid from the bed, stood up, unslotted the silk loops from the buttons, pulled the peignoir over her head and holding it at arm's length, dropped it on to one of the carpet's orange lozenges. Naked she stood, looking down at Ben who had thrown off his pyjamas. His body was compact and muscular, his arms spattered with fine brown hairs from wrists to elbows, there was a line of hairs from his throat to his navel and curving under his breastbone. The beating the Brownshirts had given him was still evident and, desperately as she wanted him, the bruising of his skin made Anne frown slightly.

'Are you quite sure you're . . .?'

In response he grasped her round the waist and pulled Anne on to the bed. As Ben licked and kissed her breasts, she pressed his head against her nipples, crying out in unaccustomed ecstasy, until he levered himself on to his hands and arching his back, gazed down into her face. She smiled up at him and said breathlessly, 'Oh Ben, I love you, I love you.'

As breathlessly, he said, 'Put me in.'

His full weight fell on her, Anne's hands eagerly sought and found, and though it was a year since she'd had sexual intercourse, she was so wet with desire that he entered her easily. He was thrusting inside her in a way she'd never experienced with Sandy, penetrating deeper and deeper, and she forgot about Sandy, she forgot about everything except the sensations of their sweat-soaked bodies moving in complementary ravishment. Then Ben was holding her so fiercely she could hardly breathe and, his voice throbbing, he said, 'Tell me when you want me. God, you're sensational. Tell me, tell me . . .'

'Now, Ben, now, now . . .'

Nothing like the climax had ever happened to Anne, even if it was slightly marred by Ben's having to withdraw. For quite a while they lay silently in each other's arms, until eventually Anne said, 'I'm a sticky mess.'

'That's the female lot.'

'It's not so bad when I use my "thing". I do have one.'

'Good.'

Hauling herself upright, Anne espied the china jug and basin on the marble-topped wash-stand. Having padded across the room and cleaned herself, she skipped back to the bed where she pulled a face at the recumbent Ben and said, 'The sheet's in a mess, too. Do you think I should do something about it?'

'No.'

He drew her back into his arms and slowly he ran his fingers along her cheekbone, down her neck to her breasts, circling her nipples which made her shiver with delight. His hands were remarkably smooth and well-kept, nothing of the hoary-handed son of toil about them, his fingers shortish and stubby, nothing of the taperingly artistic about them. They prodded her navel which made Anne giggle, and they stroked the furry triangle in her crotch. The renewed desire rippled through her and she felt his stirring as he said, 'I could take you all over again, you gorgeous hussy.'

'Yes please,' Anne said, twining her legs round his buttocks.

From downstairs in the hall there was the murmur of

voices, topped by Helga's childish tones arguing with her mother. Hastily untwining herself, Anne said, 'Heavens, they're back.'

Ben watched as she jumped from the bed and bent down to pick up her peignoir. He said, 'You're just what the doctor should have ordered. Come and see me again.'

'Thank you, kind sir. I will. And I'll make sure I have my "thing" in!'

During the next week Anne found it extremely difficult to keep her hands off Ben, and *vice versa*, but though he was now allowed up it wasn't easy for them to find the space or the moments to make love. Most days somebody was at home and most nights somebody seemed to be awake, a sign of how secretly disturbed the Wolffs were. Circumspectly, they managed to assuage their passion, though one day Anne walked straight into Kurt as she crept from Ben's bedroom, when he was supposedly having his afternoon rest. The particularly wry smile that flickered across Kurt's face made Anne blush furiously and blether about lending Ben a book to read.

Then Ben said he felt much better and ready to go home. Doctor Wolff was dubious but Rebecca was due to return to England, so it was agreed they could travel together. Before their departure, Frau Wolff suggested a picnic in the Taunus to enable Ben to enjoy the beautiful Hessian countryside and to leave with pleasant memories of Frankfurt. Early on the Sunday morning two cars drew up outside the house, Doctor Wolff's own Mercedes-Benz, a massive vehicle built like a tank, and an equally large if less tank-like Daimler borrowed from a friend. Watching the servants staggering in and out of the house, loading stuff into the boots of the cars, Ben said, 'Are we going on manoeuvres?'

'Sh,' Anne said. 'This is all for your benefit, or our benefit.'

They piled into the two cars, together with Helga and Herta's nursemaid, a pretty, fair-haired girl called Gretchen. With the respective chauffeurs at the wheels, they set off at a steady pace northward along the Bockenheimer Landstrasse. It was a beautiful morning and by the time they reached Kronberg the sun was high in the sky, shining on the picture-postcard white gables and red-tiled roofs of the town nestling among the trees. Seated in the leading Mercedes-Benz were Doctor and Frau Wolff, Rebecca, Kurt and Luise, all of whom to a lesser or greater degree looked Jewish. As the two vehicles swung right into the main street, a group of young Nazis came marching towards them and for one terrible moment Anne thought they were going to block the roadway, but they contented themselves with standing on the pavement, waving their swastika flags, hurling insults and bawling the Horst Wessel song.

Apart from the repeated cry of '*Juden*' Anne didn't understand the actual insults. In the narrow, steep street, the cars proceeded slowly and as the Daimler crawled past the members of the *Hitlerjugend*, their hands banged on the bodywork which was a terrifying experience. The normally placid Herta started to sob, then one blond-headed example of young Nazi manhood bent down and spat through the half-open window. The glob of spittle landed on Helga's cheek but as she screwed up her face and cried out in shocked disgust, Ben whipped a handkerchief from his pocket. Wiping the spittle from the child's face, he stuck out his tongue at the Nazi youths who were now fortunately out of vision. The gesture made both Herta and Helga laugh and Anne love him more than ever, if that were possible. Having comforted her charges, Gretchen suddenly burst into tears and Ben used the other end of his hanky to wipe the trickles from her face. The nursemaid gazed at him adoringly and Anne realised she wasn't the only female to find Mr Broughton highly attractive. With sideways glances at Helga and Herta, Gretchen started to whisper to him in German and when she'd finished imparting her confidences, Anne asked what she'd been saying.

'As a good Aryan, I gather the lass is under pressure to leave the Wolffs' employment. But she likes working for them, she loves Helga in particular, so she doesn't want to.'

'The whole situation is simply appalling,' Anne said. 'And the way those youngsters are being indoctrinated is fearful. We have to do something about it.'

'Mm,' Ben said.

They followed the Mercedes-Benz which continued to climb slowly upwards and although she was shaken by the incident, Anne was glad the Wolffs had not turned back. To their right the turrets of Kronberg's medieval castle rose from the trees, to their left the land dropped away to a distant view of smoky Frankfurt, then they were in the foothills of the wooded Taunus and the cars were drawing off the road into a sunlit glade. Ben had his sketchpad with him and as he sat down on a log and began to draw, Helga danced behind him clapping her hands and saying, 'Clever Ben. Draw me. Please. Please.'

Anne and he had been teaching her English and, bright child that she was, Helga was learning fast. Ben said if she behaved naturally, he would. To Anne, he observed, 'Some picnic!'

Apart from Ben, who was wearing one of the two checked shirts and pairs of baggy trousers he possessed, everybody else was smartly attired, three-piece suits and homburg hats for the men, afternoon gowns for the women. Anne had donned the green and white flowered dress Theo Marvell had designed for her, which had short 'butterfly' sleeves and a 'butterfly' bow on one shoulder. With the chauffeurs acting as manservants, folding tables and chairs were set out in the shade of the trees, lawn tablecloths and napkins, silver cutlery, bone china and cut glass produced. When all was organised they sat down in style to a sumptuous repast; mounds of cold meats, bowls of salads and fruits, platefuls of plump rolls and luscious cakes, and bottles of Rhenish wines.

In a mixture of English and German, with laughing translations, the conversation flowed as freely as the wine, and the atmosphere was so happily civilised that Anne found it difficult to imagine there had been an incident in Kronberg. Until, that was, they heard the rustling in the undergrowth and the sound of a dog barking loudly. Everybody then sat absolutely still, even the ebullient Helga. Anne glanced at Ben and his eyes were watchful, his body tense. Her own heart was pounding and she thought, Oh God, have they followed us up here? Are they going to smash everything to pieces?

Then the enormous Great Dane bounded from the trees, woofing joyfully, wagging its tail, rushing boisterously round the table. A few seconds later its perspiring young owner, a lad of about eighteen, panted after the dog. He wasn't in Nazi uniform and he apologised profusely for interrupting their picnic and the dog's name turned out to be 'Wolf' which everybody agreed was a charming coincidence. After this incident, although the underlying tension didn't completely disappear, the atmosphere became more relaxed, the sun shone through the trees and their faces warmed by its rays, their stomachs replete, conversation waned. Doctor Wolff's double chin nodded on to his chest, but Helga remained full of life, and Luise suggested that Gretchen take both girls for a walk. Stretching his arms, Ben said, 'That's a good idea. Feel like a stroll, Anne?'

Nodding, Anne rose from the table and she saw both Rebecca and Kurt eyeing her quizzically. Had her eagerness shown? Had Rebecca guessed what was going on, too? Preserving a decorous distance, Anne and Ben wandered into the woods but once they were well out of sight of the picnic party, they were in each other's arms. Ben broke the embrace and said, 'First of all I want a good piss. Then I want you, me luv.'

'Do you have to be so vulgar?' Anne said, though actually she wanted to spend a penny, too.

After they had attended to one of nature's demands, they found a shaded thicket and lay together in the undergrowth to indulge another. Their desire was so urgent, they undid and removed only essential garments, and it was so overwhelming as to be swiftly sated. With a long, satisfied sigh Anne laid her head on Ben's chest, he stroked her hair and after a while she said, 'I do love you, Ben. I wish I didn't have to go to Berlin. Well, I want to see my sister Con but I wish you could come, too. I don't know how I'll survive without you, Ben. Do you think we can get married as soon as I'm back in England? It doesn't have to be a posh wedding like Con's. We can marry in a register office, if you want, and . . .'

'I'm married, Anne.'

'. . . and we can decide later where we're going to live and . . .' For a couple of seconds Anne continued to throw out her proposals. Then his words penetrated her brain, she shot up and stared at him. 'What do you mean, you're married? Oh, that's a bloody stupid question. Why didn't you tell me? Why, why?'

Ben looked at Anne silently as she went on shouting. 'Why didn't you tell me? What do you think I am? Some sort of tart who jumps into bed with any man who takes her fancy?' She was pummelling his chest and shaking his shoulders hard and, outside the confines of passion, such treatment still affected his bruised body. Wincing, he sat up and grasped her wrists whereupon she yelled, 'Let me go. You're hurting me.'

Slowly he released his grip, her hands dropped to her sides, and she sat back on her heels staring at him. The frilly white bow on her shoulder was creased from their recent love-making, her lower lip was trembling as she struggled not to cry, and her dark eyes were wide with angry hurt. What the hell did he say to her? Ben thought. Anne had never asked him whether or not he was married and he'd had no intention of getting involved with her until she'd come into his bedroom the other week. He'd never thought she was a tart but he'd reckoned having affairs, no strings attached, was par for the course for high-class pieces who flaunted their emancipated status, and maybe bedding a working-class lad provided an extra kick. He had been surprised when Anne had told him she'd only had one lover. Ben had never known anyone like her and she'd got right under his skin, maddening, randy bundle of entrancing femininity that she was.

Unleashing her anger and her hurt, she started to fire her questions at him. 'How long have you been married? Were you married at Oxford? Where is your wife? What's she doing while you traipse round Europe? Or do you have a family, too? Is she looking after the kiddiwinks while you gallivant round the art galleries and have affairs with any woman who takes *your* fancy?'

In the circumstances Ben hardly felt he could tell Anne to mind her own business. While he was considering what to say and how much of his personal, intimate relations to reveal, she snapped, 'If you really don't feel you owe me any explanations, I'm going back to join the others. You can do what you want.'

Her tone remained angry but there was a decided tremor in her voice and as she made to rise to her feet, gently Ben held her hands. He said, 'Sit still a minute, luv.'

'And don't call me "luv".'

'I think I do love you, Anne. That's the trouble.'

At that her face crumpled, she buried her head on his chest, and her shoulders were heaving. After he'd soothed away her tears, they sat with their arms round each other and then typically, she asked the crunch questions. 'Are you one of those men who profess to be able to love lots of women at the same time? Do you love your wife?'

'No.'

'Did you ever? I mean you can't have been married very long. You're only twenty-six.'

'I've been married three years. No, I don't think I ever loved her.'

'Why did you marry her then? I suppose that's a stupid question, too.'

'Yes,' said Ben.

Why had he married Irene? Because his parents had a marriage which had survived poverty and hardship, disappointed dreams and the trauma of Dad losing his leg, so he'd grown up believing in marital monogamy? And though he liked the company of women and had a healthy sex drive, he wasn't by nature promiscuous? Because Irene was the first person who'd appreciated his paintings and seemed to understand what he was trying to do? Or because she'd decided she wanted to marry him and when she set her mind to owt, Irene was a cussedly determined madam?

'Where is your wife now?' Insistently Anne repeated the question. That challenging look had returned to her eyes and a slant of sunlight was burnishing the copper colour of her hair, as she fired a fresh salvo. 'Do you live together? Do you have a child? Or have you already realised you made a mistake and agreed to go your own ways?'

Ben sighed. He owed Irene summat, but he owed Anne too. Slowly he said, 'My wife had a baby eighteen months after we were married. It was a little girl. Still-born. Irene nearly died and she can't have any more kids.'

'Oh Ben, I'm sorry.' Anne looked up at him. 'For making those remarks about kiddiwinks, I mean.'

'Yeah, well I won't pretend the tragedy brought us closer together. I suppose you can say we've reached an unspoken agreement. We have a house in Upperdale and we live together but anything I want to do in the cause of art is okay by Irene. She's in regular employment, she pays the rent and most of the bills.

'I see,' said Anne. 'What does she do?'

'She's a librarian.'

With a sudden movement Anne shot up and said, 'Does your wife work in Mellordale Central Library?' Surprised, Ben nodded and she announced, 'I've met her. She didn't appear to like me. Would that be because you'd mentioned your encounter with me at Oxford and your feelings about the Tom Whitworth memorial scholarship?'

'Could be,' Ben admitted.

'That solves a minor puzzle. I wondered what she had against me. *Then.*' Anne emphasised the word 'then', before looking straight at him and saying, 'Will you marry me if she'll divorce you?'

'She'll never divorce me, Anne.'

Only too clearly Anne recalled the young librarian with her woolly cardigan and disapproving air. She appreciated that she could have a fight on her hands. In a way she felt sorry for Irene but the marriage had been a mistake. 'Never' was not a word to daunt a member of the Whitworth family, and she intended to take Benjamin Daniel Broughton as her lawful wedded husband.

9

'Isn't this fun!' Kate exclaimed.

They had just arrived at Hermann Göring's residence in Berlin, to be greeted with unctuous ceremony by Nazi minions. The invitation, extended to select members of the British Embassy staff including Gavin Campbell-Ross and family, was to an informal reception. Anne wondered what the Nazis' idea of a formal one would be. The vast entrance hall and the adjoining rooms were already packed with guests, the men in stuffed shirts or Nazi uniforms, the women in lavish evening gowns, dripping with jewellery. The hallway and rooms were massed with flowers stiffly arranged in large baskets, the walls hung with enormous paintings. An orchestra was playing sickly music, waiters and waitresses laden with trays of drinks and canapés were moving deferentially among the guests and through open French windows – it was a balmy summer evening – Anne could see the garden festooned with fairy lights.

She looked towards the people lining up to be presented to Hermann Göring. Standing with his legs apart, his potbelly protruding, the Great War air ace, recently appointed Nazi Air Minister, was wearing a dark-blue uniform with white facings. Around his neck, across his broad chest, there were enough decorations to shoot down an aeroplane. Anne said, 'Are we expected to join the queue and make our obeisances to that overdressed oaf?'

'Some time during the evening Gavin and I are. It's part of the job,' Con said mildly. 'You don't have to if you don't want to.'

Anne wasn't sure whether or not she wanted to because she hadn't yet made up her mind whether or not to make her dramatic intervention.

Wrinkling her dainty nose Kate said, 'Don't be such a grouchy snob. Honestly, I've never had such a marvellous time. London's so tame compared to Berlin. You have to admit, darling, the Nazis do make life exciting.'

Unfortunately, Anne had.

Since her arrival in the German capital a month ago, swiftly followed by the twins' on a summer holiday visit to Con and Gavin, they had all been plied with invitations to this, that and the other dinner party, function or event. Last night from the vantage point of the British Embassy on the Wilhelmstrasse, they had watched a mile-long procession of German youth marching through the heart of Berlin, bands playing lustily, flaming torches held aloft, swastika banners swirling. As a spectacle it had been impressive and without doubt, Anne thought, part of the Nazis' appeal was their understanding that circuses are as important as bread, though she couldn't see the vulgar, slightly sinister theatricality typified by Hermann Göring, going down in England. Or at least she hoped she couldn't.

People they'd already met were calling out to the 'so delightful, so handsome, so popular Whitworth family', as Count von Krannhals described them. Allowing for the Teutonic exaggeration, Anne did see what the Count meant and why the Whitworths were so much in demand. Con's prettiness and the sweetness of her nature made her effortlessly attractive and at the moment she was positively radiant. The reason for her radiance was because she was expecting. Mark was now a very good-looking nineteen-year-old, with a casual charm that had the girls swarming around him like bees round the proverbial honeypot, though her brother's flippant attitude to life continued to worry Anne. As for Kate, she was blossoming into a real beauty. This evening, in a flouncy blush-pink evening gown with a draped shoulderline gathered by silk roses at her bosom, she looked like an exquisite china figurine.

Con and Gavin were drawn into a posse of diplomats, Anne, Kate and Mark into Count von Krannhals' group. From previous uninhibited conversations, it did not surprise Anne that the upper-crust German guests were being bitchily rude about Hermann Göring. In a similar English accent to her husband's, which made Philip's cut-glass variety sound plebeian, the Countess said, 'Do you think our Hermann has a manservant locked away in a cupboard, polishing his medals night and day?'

After the laughter had subsided, Anne said, 'Are you sure you're going to be able to *control* Herr Hitler and Göring and the rest of them?' She emphasised the word the Count and his friends used frequently. 'You don't seem to me to have had much success *controlling* them in the first months of the Third Reich's existence. What about the book-burnings and the way Jews are being treated? Or indeed anybody who crosses the Nazis' path.'

The fate of one opponent of the Nazis was imprinted at the forefront of Anne's mind. Was she going to make her public stand or not?

Still uncertain, she listened politely as the Count said everybody knew Adolf Hitler was a vulgar upstart and Hermann Göring a poltroon, but Germany had been in chaos and needed firm leadership. With the utmost confidence he could inform Anne that Hitler's useful demagogic appeal was being channelled and *controlled* by intelligent, civilised Germans; although he didn't say the words 'such as ourselves', they were implicit in his smug smile. The Count added, 'As for the Jews, personally we have several Jewish friends, but *en masse* they are a greedy, ostentatious, untrustworthy race. If they are discriminated against, they have only themselves to blame for insisting they are different from us ordinary mortals.'

Anne said she thought that was nonsense and a brisk argument developed. When that was finished, without anybody having changed their opinions, she turned to the Countess. Before she left Frankfurt she'd met Wanda Ohlendorf at a 'top-hole' tea-house. Volubly, if not over-coherently, Wanda had explained why she had become an ardent Nazi. Her reasons seemed quite extraordinary to Anne who wanted to know if they were shared by the Countess and her ilk.

'Do you feel it was German women who let their menfolk down in the Great War? Do you believe it was their inability to cope with their new-found emancipation and their clamouring for peace – rather than the British blockade or the fact that the German Army was actually on its knees – that brought about your defeat? Do you see that as part of the reason why Herr Hitler has such appeal for so many German women? Because they feel guilty and he preaches the old, old sermon. Big bold men going out into the world and weak little women staying at home?'

The svelte middle-aged lady standing next to the Countess said, 'Of course we don't. It's Herr Hitler's sex-appeal that attracts the young ones. And it was not we women who betrayed the men in the trenches. It was the Jews and Communists.'

Her last words took Anne's breath away. Out of the corner of her eye, she saw Kate, who must have slipped off, waving to an SS officer who strode up to her, clicked his heels and kissed her hand. Knowing that if she stayed put she was likely to lose her temper, worried about Kate's acquaintance, Anne said, 'Will you excuse us for a moment?'

Taking Mark by the arm she led him towards his twin sister, en route saying, 'Where did Kate meet him?'

'How should I know? Am I my sister's keeper?'

'Yes, to an extent you are. Or at least here in Berlin you should be.'

'Ha! It's not like you to be so old-fashioned, Annie.'

As they approached Kate, the SS officer clicked his heels again before striding away. Pretending she'd only just seen them, Kate said, 'Oh hello. Finished arguing?'

'And exactly who,' Anne demanded, 'is he?'

'His name's Ernst. I met him at that lakeside party. He's a sweetie.'

'A sweetie!' Anne exploded. 'Even you, Kate, must have some inkling what being in the SS means. They see themselves as the élite corps of the master race, they see women as sexual toys and breeding machines, they implement the Nazis' racial garbage, they run the concentration camps, they . . .'

Kate stopped listening to what 'they' did because when her sister became all excited and moral and virtuous she was the most fearful bore. She herself supposed the Nazis had done some awful things but she thought Anne and even darling Con grossly exaggerated their sins. Everybody said Herr Hitler had restored order and he was getting people back to work and surely Anne should be impressed by that because she was always going on about the unemployment situation at home. In their spooky black uniforms, Kate found the SS men frightfully attractive and she had enjoyed roaring around Berlin in Ernst's huge car with the swastika flags fluttering from the bonnet.

Anne was now saying, 'Con told me that Gavin told her they're very disturbed at the Embassy by the stupid English girls who've nothing better to do than to flock to Berlin and embark on affairs with SS officers. Then they expect the Embassy staff to extricate them from the messes they get themselves into. Some of the messes are very unpleasant, I gather.'

Kate loved gossip, particularly the spicy variety, and she longed to say, 'Oh, do tell.' In the circumstances she decided to say haughtily, 'I have no intention of having an affair with Ernst.' Swiftly, before her sister could give her another lecture she went on, 'If you must know, he has contacts with the film studios here in Berlin and he's introduced me to a producer who wants me to play a marvellous part in a new film. And I'm fed up with RADA.'

'Are you indeed?' said Anne. 'You made enough fuss about going there.'

Kate had been livid when Mummy had insisted she stay at school until she was eighteen, to take her Higher School Certificate before becoming a student at the Royal Academy of Dramatic Art last September. Pouting which she knew she did prettily, she said, 'Yes, well, how was I to know RADA's little better than a finishing school? I want to be an actress, not one of Gavin's stupid young women with nothing better to do. So I'm going to leave RADA and accept the film offer.'

Putting his arm round her shoulder Mark said, 'You'll be playing with fire if you do, Kate.'

'Chamber pots to you,' she snapped at her brother who normally backed her during family rows. Mark had just finished his first year at Christ Church and he had informed them that his had been the brilliant brain behind the Mystery of the Oxford Chamber Pots – one hundred had appeared overnight on buildings from the Martyrs' Memorial to Magdalen Tower – a title Anne had his permission to use for her next Seth Pollard novel.

Anne said, 'You're under age anyway. And if you imagine Mummy and Philip will let you take part in a piece of Nazi propaganda – if an SS officer has anything to do with it, that's what it'll be – you can think again.' The problem of her age had already occurred to Kate and she pouted but then Anne said, 'If you promise not to see that ghastly man again or have anything to do with the SS, I might help you talk to Mummy and Philip about leaving RADA.'

Kate brightened up. She wasn't as interested in Ernst as all that. For one thing he'd absolutely no sense of humour and he had been a bit nasty when she'd refused to let him kiss her. Darling stepdaddy was never a problem but Mummy could be one and Anne was very good at talking her round. Honestly what mattered to Kate was her career, which she'd prefer to take off in England. Licking her thumb and making horizontal and vertical gestures with it in the direction of her heart, which she thought was somewhere near the roses on her bosom, in her best RADA voice she said, 'After this evening – I can't be rude to Ernst, can I? He has gone to get me a drink – but after this evening I promise to ignore the entire SS. Cross my heart and hope to die.'

Still trying to make up her mind what she should do, Anne was surveying an enormous Nazi-style painting of Siegfried, who looked like an overgrown member of the *Hitlerjugend*, when Con came over. She said, 'We've received our summons. Do you want to be introduced to Göring?'

Dropping her cigarette into a *kitsch* ashtray on a tall stand entwined with nymphs, Anne nodded. At least she had made one decision. But her heart was thumping as she walked with Con into the vast, high-ceilinged room where their host was now holding court. And the scene last week, when Gavin had come into the drawing room of the delightful house the Campbell-Rosses had rented, to find Anne curled up in a chair reading, was as vivid in her mind as if it had happened a few minutes ago.

After his customary comments about nothing in particular, Gavin said, 'I made enquiries about your friend, Renate Meyer.' Startled by this statement, Anne looked at him blankly. 'You know, your Socialist friend from Frankfurt who was arrested.'

Yes, she knew who Renate was. They'd met at the international women's peace conference in Geneva last year and they'd found they had a similar sense of humour that made them giggle at some of their more solemn, earnest colleagues' pronouncements. They'd kept in touch and though Anne had received no reply to her last letter, while she was in Frankfurt naturally she had driven to Renate's house. But Renate had not been there. The conversation with her mother had been difficult, not only because neither spoke the other's language well, but because Frau Meyer was an obviously frightened woman.

Eventually, Anne gathered that soon after the Nazis had come to power, for the crimes of being a pacifist and a Socialist Renate had been taken into 'protective custody'. She was in a women's prison called Stadelheim which was outside

Munich. Anne had posted off a long letter and a large parcel but there had been no response, so when she'd arrived in Berlin she'd asked Gavin if he could make enquiries through his German contacts. Having recovered from her surprise that he should have done so, Anne put down her book and gave her brother-in-law her full attention.

'I regret to have to tell you, your friend apparently suffered a heart attack in Stadelheim prison and died there three weeks ago.'

'A heart attack!' Anne exclaimed. 'But Renate was only my age and she was bursting with good health when we met in Geneva.'

'She may have had an undetected heart weakness.'

Devastated by the news, Anne asked him point-blank, 'Do you think she had? Or do you think she died as a result of maltreatment in Stadelheim?'

'Obviously I cannot know, Anne.' After a pause, to her even greater surprise, Gavin actually gave an opinion. 'But I would think the latter explanation is the more likely.'

Choking back her tears Anne said, 'Thank you for making the enquiries, Gavin', to which he replied politely, 'Not at all. I'm only sorry they produced such unpleasant answers.'

She and Con were now nearing the group in front of Hermann Göring and almost as if she could read Anne's thoughts, her sister said, 'I know you think Gavin's a bit of a drip. By your standards, perhaps he is. But successful diplomats really do have to be discreet and he is ambitious. He wants to end up as one of His Britannic Majesty's top ambassadors.' Con gave the impish smile that was part of her charm, with its suggestion that she wasn't always an impossibly nice young lady. 'If you think about it, Gavin had to have something about him to marry me.'

'What on earth do you mean?' Anne exploded. 'To marry you!'

'To marry into the Whitworth family then. We may be having a big success in present-day Berlin but the Diplomatic Corps isn't mad about Socialist fathers, ex-gaolbird suffragette mothers, and aunts who're married to high-ranking Russian Bolsheviks.'

With a laugh Anne said, 'I don't think Gavin's a drip.'

Actually, she still considered him an extremely lucky young man, having Con as his wife, but she had somewhat revised her opinion of Mr Campbell-Ross.

Close to, Hermann Göring looked even more gross and overdressed than from a distance. Anne's stomach was now churning furiously and the question was thudding in her head. Should she follow in the footsteps of Aunty Alice who long before she'd fallen in love with Julian's father, had made her dramatically public stand for the suffragette cause when, at a swish London reception, she'd called on Mr Asquith to stop the abomination of forcible feeding? That had been in Liberal Edwardian England, this was 1930s Nazi Germany, and what had Aunty Alice's courageous action in any case achieved? Nothing. It had taken the outbreak of the war in 1914 to stop the forcible feeding of hunger-striking suffragettes. Possible failure, Anne told herself, was no excuse for not acting.

A Nazi aide was introducing Gavin, who spoke surprisingly good German, to Hermann Göring. In his turn Gavin presented his wife and unlike Anne, Con was learning the language fast. His fat face creasing into smiles, Göring had quite a long conversation with the Campbell-Rosses; the Nazis were only too eager to impress their Anglo-Saxon cousins. As he was presented, Mark merely nodded laconically. With overplayed gallantry Göring then kissed Kate's hand and while she gazed up at him with her fascinating green eyes, chattering confidently in her schoolgirl German, he regarded her fragile beauty appreciatively. Not that madam was in the least bit fragile, Anne thought, and in a few seconds it would be her turn to have her hand kissed. Should she snatch it away and for the sake of the murdered Renate and everything she had believed in, metaphorically seize the opportunity with both hands and shout loudly, 'Please, Herr Göring, in the name of justice and humanity, stop imprisoning the Nazis' opponents in concentration camps. And let German Jews live in peace.'?

He did not speak English and Anne had no idea how to say those words in German. Of itself, with the Whitworths' family connections and her own small fame as a writer and broadcaster, her intervention must have an impact. Perhaps the publicity would make the Nazis re-think their appalling policies. It could also ruin Gavin's career and what effect would that have on her beloved, pregnant sister?

Gavin was now presenting Anne. Hermann Göring lifted her hand to his lips and she was glad it was gloved so that she could not feel their touch on her skin. He was smiling at her, eyeing her as he had Kate. In a colourless voice Gavin translated what their host was saying. 'The Minister is delighted to meet you. He hopes you are enjoying your visit to the Third Reich. He says you are *auffallend* which means "tall and beautiful".'

Feeling small and ugly, Anne knew she was not going to say a word in reply. Or not any words that mattered. When their 'audience' was finished, unsure whether she had acted in cowardly or sensible fashion but certain she needed a breath of fresh air, she walked slowly away.

In a secluded corner of the garden Anne leaned against a tree, breathing deeply. Oh God, how she wanted Ben, how she wished she were in his arms, how her body ached to make love with him. It had been a fortnight after her arrival in Berlin before he'd written and a desperate Anne had been considering sending a cable to Rebecca, or to Madge Kearsley asking her to make discreet enquiries in The Dales.

From her evening purse Anne extracted the precious letter, for though Ben had since sent her a couple of postcards he hadn't written again. Moving into the glow cast by a particularly garish bunch of fairy lights, she reread his letter for the hundredth time. The first two pages contained an amusing description of his journey back to England with Rebecca, then in his beautiful script he had written:

'Nothing has changed in The Dales. The odour from the gas-works scents the air, the smoke sits in the valley, the factory whistles hoot, the workers clatter out, the unemployed hang forlornly round the street corners, drawing the last dregs of nicotine from their fags. They're anonymous ants, not yet to themselves maybe, but the great industrial society is devouring them. That's what I'm trying to paint, me luv, people in the process of losing their individuality, being overwhelmed by machinery. It all started here in Lancashire, the Industrial Revolution that's revolutionised our world. Coming from a long line of industrialised ants who've struggled to retain their identity and dignity, I want to give pictorial warning that if folks don't watch out, they'll be completely overwhelmed, not just by the machinery, but by the mass movements and corporate organisations industrialisation has spawned.'

For the hundredth time Anne knew why Ben had won the Tom Whitworth scholarship to Ruskin College. More than ever she couldn't wait to see his paintings and discuss what he was trying to do. It was halfway down page four that he became personal and the blood still rushed into Anne's cheeks as she again read his words.

'I miss you like hell, me luv. I long to see that hoity-toity expression on your face, the confident set of your head, the swing of your hips and the suppleness of your shapely legs. I long to have you in my arms, to straddle you, to thrust myself inside you, to ride you. My lips ache to kiss those beautiful breasts and those pink nipples in their brown, wrinkled-velvet rings. I want to smell the perfume of your body, to caress your satin smooth skin, to stroke your glossy hair. Your hair is the colour dreams are made of and if I were a portrait painter I'd create a new colour to rival Titian, copper with bronze tints, and I'd call it Annian.'

In the light of these lines, his final paragraph remained as disconcerting as the first time Anne had read it. For here Ben had written:

'I've been walking over the moors, clearing my head, but I've started a new painting and it's going well. I could be down south towards the end of August. I take it you'll be back in England by then? I'll contact you either in London or in Kent. Don't tangle with any more of Hitler's mob. I must assuredly love you and trust you, Anne Whitworth, to have put pen to paper in this fashion. Yours, Ben.'

There was no mention of Irene anywhere in the letter, though presumably Ben was living with her in Upperdale.

Or at least staying in the same house with her because from what Anne had inferred, their sexual relationship was at an end. Not wanting to push Ben too hard until he had sorted things out with his wife, Anne had decided that if he could wait until the end of August before he straddled her and kissed her pink nipples in their velvety-brown rings, etcetera, etcetera, so could she.

The waiting had been a greater agony than she had imagined possible. At times she had felt like screaming with the desire for Ben, the longing to touch him, to talk to him, just to be with him. She hadn't mentioned him to Kate who was an appalling gossip but even more fully than she had with Rebecca, she'd poured out her heart to Con. 'And when I told Rebecca that Ben's married, she said, "Oh gawd, Whitworth, lay off him then!"'

'She's quite right, Anne. You're just storing up heartache. It's all very well you saying you love him and he loves you, but what if his wife loves him too and that's why she won't ever divorce him?'

'Then I'm even more sorry for her. But it's not my fault Ben doesn't love her. And if she won't divorce him, I shall live with him in sin. Because I can't live without him.'

Anne remembered how she and Con had laughed at her defiantly dramatic statement.

Leaning against the tree, staring up at the fairy lights in its branches, she came to the decision she should have reached ages ago. She was driving Bill back to England tomorrow. Anne didn't trust the likes of Count and Countess von Krannhals to *control* the likes of Hermann Göring and Adolf Hitler, or even Helmut Ohlendorf. People at home needed to be told what was happening in Germany so that the Nazis could be halted in their tracks. And what she had said to Con was the truth. She couldn't live without Ben one minute longer.

PART III

10

It was gone seven o'clock in the evening before Anne and Ben returned to the cottage she had rented for the summer. From the top of the cliff there was a fabulous view of the Dorset coastline with the almost perfect circle of Lulworth Cove visible to the left, and on this most heavenly of July evenings the heat haze was still smudging the outlines of the cliffs and the golden light was reflecting on the mirror-like surface of the sea.

They had spent the day following David Lloyd George as the temperature soared into the 90s Fahrenheit and he stomped round south Dorset, commemorating the centenary of the trial and sentence of the six 'Tolpuddle Martyrs' for their trade union activities in 1834. As a good Socialist Anne had wanted to participate in the week-long festivities so she had chosen the day when their ex-Prime Minister was present. Mr Lloyd George had been delighted to see her and invited both of them to have tea with him.

During the course of the meal Herr Hitler's name came into the conversation, as it inevitably did these days. Anne said she and Ben had been in Germany last year and she was amazed at the number of people in England who seemed to think he and the Nazis were a joke, or actually applauded what they were doing. To her utter astonishment Mr Lloyd George replied, 'Ah, we must not judge too swiftly or harshly, Anne. There are vast problems to overcome in Germany. Speaking as one who has been known to huff and puff to impress the multitude and frighten the sacred cows, I suspect Herr Hitler may be doing the same. I look forward to the pleasure of meeting him soon.'

Ben made no comment and with difficulty Anne held her tongue. Then the old war-horse regaled them with stories of the days of power and glory when he'd known the young

Tom Whitworth. Patting Anne's hand, the Welsh intonations in his voice at their most liquid, he said, 'Your father's death was a tragic loss, not only to his family, Anne, but to the country. A tragic loss.'

Until his recent remarks Anne had thought Mr Lloyd George's long years in the wilderness a sad loss to the country but if he considered Herr Hitler to be a possibly good thing, she now had her doubts. As usual Ben had his sketchbook with him and the old boy asked if he might see the contents. The drawing of him giving an impromptu speech under the 'martyrs' tree' in Tolpuddle tickled his fancy, whereupon Ben tore it neatly from the sketchpad and said, 'Have it, sir, with my compliments.'

Although Anne now fully appreciated that Ben's paintings, as opposed to his drawings, were what mattered, she wished he wouldn't distribute the latter with quite such largesse because they too had a distinctive, original quality. What was more, people liked them and were willing to pay good money for them which did not, alas at the moment, hold true for his paintings.

As they said farewell Mr Lloyd George asked Ben whether his friendship with Anne – there was a mischievous glint in his eye as he'd uttered the word 'friendship' – was of recent origin or whether he'd known her father. Ben replied, 'No, I never met him. I feel as if I had though.'

Anne hadn't been sure what to make of that comment.

From the clifftop above Lulworth, a track barely wide enough to drive Bill along led to the rented cottage. As they bumped their way down she said, 'Do you know, when Mr Lloyd George kissed me goodbye, I had a distinct feeling it was more than grandfatherly. I gather he was quite a lad in his day. He made a pass at my mother once.'

'If he can gallop around the way he did today, I don't reckon his day's over,' Ben observed and Anne laughed. Then he said, 'Jeez, it's hot. Let's have a swim before supper.'

'What a lovely idea.'

The track stopped at the cottage and to reach the cove below you had to scramble across the precipitous slopes of tussocky grass and clamber over the rocks. This evening as usual Ben leapt from the last spur of rock to the beach, beckoning for Anne – daring her? – to follow. They were both strong swimmers and they forged their way through the calm sea which, in the evening light, was a translucent green. Way out, they floated on the slightest of swells, gazing at the sweep of the coastline until Ben said, 'Race you back.' He set off as he spoke which gave him the advantage but there was no nonsense with Mr Broughton about being gallant to the fair sex, or at least not to those who preached equality. By the time Anne reached the beach he was already towelling his naked body. In the seclusion of 'their' cove they usually swam in the nude. Ben's towelling of Anne's body stoked their ardour and he half-carried her to their secret place in the shelter of an overhanging rock, where they had already several times made love with passionate wildness.

The intensity of their desire was as fierce as ever. Sometimes Anne just wanted to twine herself around Ben which, unless he was deeply involved in his painting when he was liable to tell her to bugger off, she did. Sometimes she turned to see him looking at her and she watched the erection rising like a tent pole in his trousers. One of the reasons why they wanted each other so demandingly could be that they had not in the last fifteen months spent a great deal of time together. It was nearly fifteen months since they'd remet in the Römerberg and one day very soon Anne knew she must have a serious talk with Benjamin Daniel Broughton.

The next morning a large post, all of it for Anne, included a long letter from Con who was still in Berlin with Gavin. The letter contained several pages about baby Callum's activities – in the spring Con had given birth to a dear little boy – and said they would be home on leave in August. Would Anne please visit them in Scotland as soon as possible?

The letter from Kurt Wolff also hoped Anne would soon be visiting them again. It went on to inform her that the Nazis were amusing themselves renaming parts of Frankfurt. They now had the Adolf Hitler Brücke, the Hermann Göring Ufer and the Horst Wessel Platz, whilst the Mendelssohn-strasse had become the Joseph Haydn-strasse, the one composer being a *sau Jud*, the other a good Aryan. Anne did not consider that information the least bit amusing, though pretending it was perhaps helped Kurt to survive in Nazi Germany. Over the page his news was more cheering. Apart from the name-changing, life had returned to a sort of normality for Frankfurt's large Jewish population, to such an extent that neighbours who had emigrated last year to Switzerland had just returned to their beloved Fatherland.

Anne passed on this news to Ben. 'Perhaps those who like Mr Lloyd George believe Herr Hitler's really a lamb in wolf's clothing are right after all.' He replied, 'I doubt it. Has Kurt been reinstated as a university lecturer?'

Anne said no and took his point. The deeply dismaying letter was from Julian, concerning the typescript of her third Seth Pollard detective novel *And Hideous Things Were Done*. The plot concerned an act of vengeance dating back to an incident in the Great War, and part of the story was set in present-day Germany. Julian had written:

'The first half of the book is up to your usual high standards but, being brutally frank, which is one of the things a literary agent has at times to be, the second half is a turgid muddle. You ride your Nazi hobby-horse too hard, Anne, which won't do in a detective novel. Although I realise you have been urged to bring up the romance, you simply must tone down the later love scenes between Seth Pollard and Lady Helena Brockenhurst. Josiah Stoddard would have apoplexy if he read them! In its present state, I do not feel it would be wise to submit the typescript to Stoddard and Simpson. I must therefore ask you radically to rethink and rewrite the second part. I append my editorial comments. When you have digested them, I suggest we talk things over. I shall be only too delighted to take you out to lunch, or what you will. Do let me know if you are coming up to Town. With my best wishes, Ever yours, Julian.'

For the first time in her career as a detective authoress Anne had encountered real difficulties writing the second half of *And Hideous Things Were Done*. If Julian considered it 'turgid' in its present state, he should have read the countless pages she'd chucked into the wastepaper basket! She transmitted her literary agent's verdict to Ben who looked up from buttering the fresh rolls she'd driven into Lulworth to buy for breakfast. Laconically he said, 'Your agent's right. The third volume of a detective series ain't the right place to storm the citadels of Nazism. And your faithful fans won't thank you for descriptions of breasts and balls.'

That comment made Anne laugh, though she protested, 'I don't so much as mention Seth's balls! And I wanted to describe just a little of the rapture I know with you.'

'Ta!' Ben gave her the sudden smile that was as brilliant as the sunlight streaming into the kitchen. Gulping his tea, he said it was a splendid light and he was off into the garden to paint. Once having given his opinion, somewhat to Anne's chagrin he tended to terminate conversations. Personally she liked to examine subjects in more detail.

After she had cleared away and washed up the breakfast things, she retired into the front room where she read through Julian's comments, before typing a long letter to him. In this she said she objected strenuously to his describing her opposition to Nazism as 'a hobby-horse' and some of his editorial suggestions were nitpicking nonsense, though she admitted he was probably right about the need to dilute the more erotic scenes and the diatribes against Fascism. Having got that off her chest Anne did not start to wrestle with the problems of rewriting the second half of her book. For a long time she sat smoking and staring out of the window, watching the sunlight break on the sea and the gulls hovering immobile in the soft blue sky, before wheeling away with raucous shrieks.

Aged twenty-four years and – she counted on her fingers – nine months, by some people she was regarded as a success. For Anne, her success was small-scale and qualified. True, she was among the select band of 'lady broadcasters' but her enthusiasm for the BBC had waned. Perhaps it had something to do with the move from cosy old Savoy Hill to Broadcasting House, the vast, impersonal building in Portland Place. Or more likely, as she'd told an astonished Sandy the last time she'd seen him, it was because 'The BBC seems to think it's done its bit by having any women broadcasters at all. Do they employ us as announcers or to read the news or in any really serious adult capacity? No. They shunt us into children's programmes as "Aunty Mabel" and "Aunty Doris".'

'I didn't know you wanted to be a full-time broadcaster.'

'I don't,' Anne had replied loftily. 'But that's not the point.'

She didn't want to be a full-time journalist either. That didn't prevent her being furious when editors accepted her articles about women in The Dales or in Germany but rejected her serious efforts. Anne was convinced that was because they dealt with unemployment or Fascism as a whole, not with the so-called women's angle.

As for her detective novels, true she'd had two published but they hadn't been widely reviewed. The occasional articles about her harped on the facts that Sir Philip Marchal was her stepfather, war-hero Tom Whitworth her father. In such pieces Daddy was always the war-hero, not the crusading Socialist politician. Anne resented the implication that her detective stories had only been published because of her privileged background. They hadn't. Of that she was sure. For one thing she knew *Whatever Happened to Wordsworth?* had been twice rejected and for another, gentlemanly old Josiah Stoddard was about as sentimental as a python. Anne felt alternatively cross and depressed that the originality of her detective stories, the fact that she was extending the boundaries of the genre, had not been recognised.

As Ben had observed, she was slowly building up a following of 'faithful fans'. Everybody told her it took time to establish oneself and few people were in reality overnight successes. Anne wanted to be among the few because time was something that haunted her. Ever since her father had been killed, she'd had the feeling that at any moment fate was liable to kick her in the crotch. In case it did, it was vital to enjoy success while she was young, to establish her ground, to prevent herself again being knocked totally off-balance.

Early in the afternoon Ben called through the open window, whereupon Anne immediately and thankfully stopped typing because she wasn't getting anywhere with the editing of *And Hideous Things Were Done*. Ben's wanting her opinion of his work was always a matter requiring instant attention.

The recurrent theme of his paintings was as he'd described in his letter. Hundreds of ant-like human beings overshadowed by the blank eyes of many-windowed factories and belching mill chimneys, or lost in the maze of back alleys, with the sweep of the moors occasionally visible in the background. The colours were drawn from his native Lancashire landscape, the rain-sodden grey-greens of the moorland grass, the russets of decaying bracken, the grey-blacks of the smoky cotton valleys. Anne found his pictures rivetingly, ambitiously original and they spent a fruitful, if argumentative, couple of hours discussing the merits and demerits of his current canvas. While they were talking and arguing, at the back of her mind she was aware that part of the reason why she was feeling so frustrated and unsuccessful, lay in the unsatisfactory state of her relationship with Ben.

It was another beautiful evening and they had an alfresco supper in the cottage garden, sweet with the perfume of night-scented stocks and honeysuckle, while they watched the sun setting in spectacular crimson bands whose reflection bloodied the sea. After they'd eaten their meal, lighting a cigarette for comfort, Anne decided the moment of truth had arrived. She said, 'Ben, I want to talk to you.'

'I thought that was what you'd been doing most of the afternoon.'

'You know exactly what I mean and what about. Us. Is this how you expect things to continue? You living in Lancashire, me in London, meeting under false pretences such as you telling your wife somebody's loaned you a cottage for the summer and you're by yourself painting night and day. I hate lying and cheating and I love you, Ben. I want to spend the rest of my life with you. I've told you I don't mind being branded as a scarlet woman and living with you in sin . . .' Anne laughed slightly at the hackneyed phrases before rushing on. 'I know what it will entail but it'll be worse for me than for you. It always is worse for the woman because of all that primeval rubbish about Eve the temptress. Why succumbing to temptation should be judged less blameworthy than tempting, I don't know.'

Anne paused and inhaled deeply on her cigarette because Ben's touching concern about his wife's suffering with their still-born child made what she was about to say a delicate subject. Slowly she said, 'And, not right away, but one day before I'm past it, I'd like to have a baby, Ben, your child. I thought I'd better tell you. Calmly, I mean, not in the throes of passion. That's how I feel about things and I want to know how you feel and what you intend to do.'

After a few seconds' silence he said, 'Give me a fag, luv.' He had reverted to smoking occasionally, though not when he was painting. As Anne handed him a cigarette and flicked her lighter, he added, 'I'm not prevaricating. I'm assembling my thoughts.'

Frankly, she thought he should already have assembled them but she'd had her say and for the moment deemed it wiser to keep quiet.

Leaning back in his chair, puffing smoke into the mysterious mauve colour of the gathering twilight, Ben cogitated. Ideally, what he wanted to do was to paint and to live with Anne. At times she maddened him, the boundless energy and headstrong, self-willed idealism slopping in so many directions. For an intelligent woman who knew life could not be depicted in blacks and whites, she had this extraordinary need to be what she called honest which meant having everything clear-cut and bone-dry; though her need to be equally honest with herself rendered her vulnerable and aroused Ben's protective instincts. Above all Anne stimulated him, not merely sexually, but by heightening his senses she convinced him that he could translate his inner visions on to canvas.

Another problem of a different sort was the world Anne inhabited. Against his better judgement she'd persuaded him to visit Chenneys where, to Ben's surprise, he'd found he liked her mother who was definitely 'jannock', straight-down-the-line, with a habit of giggling that her charm made endearing, despite her middle-age. Once he'd recovered from the ice-splintering accent and haughty manner, Ben had even liked Sir Philip Marchal with his nice line in mordant wit and obvious devotion to Anne's mother. He'd been chuffed when Lady Marchal had bought one of his Lancashire paintings and Sir Philip the large canvas of the Nazi rally which Ben had done in four sections to form a swastika, using blacks, reds and whites. Although the world of Chenneys, of money and good taste, servants and space, artistic appreciation and influential friends, had proved less odious than anticipated, it remained one Ben had no desire to enter.

'Well?' Lighting another cigarette, Anne broke the silence.

Slowly Ben started to put some of his thoughts into the spoken word, a process of which he was chary. For once Anne listened intently, interrupting only three times. When he stopped she said, 'If it's merely a question of differing styles of life, I've already told you I'm more than happy to live up on the moors. I can write there just as well as, if not better than, in London. And I'm willing to curtail some of my activities, though not all because I think they're important. You think fighting Fascism's important, too. Are those really the difficulties? You haven't mentioned how you feel about Irene.'

What did he feel about his wife? Aloud Ben said, 'Guilty, I reckon.'

'I see. What about children? You haven't mentioned that subject either. Don't you want any?'

That was a question he and Irene had avoided discussing, other than a vague suggestion that maybe some time in the future they might consider adoption. Ben couldn't say the urge to reproduce himself was his strongest instinct but the thought of Anne bearing his child – their child – was pleasing and he admitted, 'Yeah, I'd like to have a kid one day.'

'Well then? Do you want to live with me, or do you not? Because you can't go on having me and Irene. I'm not made like that.'

Damn her mania for being honest and having showdowns! Forced into a corner, Ben knew there was only one answer. Stubbing out his cigarette, he took Anne's hands into his and said softly, 'You've bewitched me and I doubt I can live without you.' In the light of the rising moon he saw the tears glistening in her eyes and the unspoken question behind the tears. Because untypically she didn't ask it, he added, 'When I leave here, I'll go straight to Upperdale. I'll talk to Irene and tell her it's all over between us.'

'Be as nice as you can to her, won't you?'

Ben nodded.

★   ★   ★

It was pouring with rain when Ben got off the tram in Longden Lane and the water whooshed from the lines as the tram rattled away. Adjusting his rucksack on his back, making sure the waterproofing was secure, he tucked his portfolio under his arm, and climbed up Nether Brow towards Gladstone Terrace. The rain was sheeting across the brickwork of the houses, bouncing on the cobblestones, rushing down the gutters, and Ben could have wished for a less depressing return to Upperdale.

Gladstone Terrace consisted of nine redbrick houses built in the 1880s when Mr Gladstone was the Grand Old Man of British politics, the darling of the people (if not of Queen Victoria). The houses had small front gardens, reached by mounting the flight of stone steps from Nether Brow and walking along the path. Their position was really quite pleasant, above the smoke of the town, with the open moors only a few hundred yards further up the Brow. From the outside the Broughtons' house, number 7, looked like any of the others, only more so, the donkey-stoning of the front step and window ledges brighter, the paint shinier, the lace curtains frillier.

Irene was monitoring his arrival because she opened the front door as Ben turned into the front garden and in her restrained way she was pleased to see him. She even gave him a peck on the cheek before she said, 'What an awful day. I don't know what it's been like down south but we've had a beautiful summer. Mother and I had a perfect week in St Anne's.' Ben's stomach lurched as his wife said 'St Anne's', though her visit to that select Lancashire watering hole with her mother (whom Ben could not abide) was an annual event. 'And you'd better get out of those wet clothes. I'll run the bath for you.'

The bathroom was Irene's pride and joy, or one of them, the result of hard-nosed bargaining between her and the landlord, whereby the cost of the installation had been split fifty-fifty. While he was soaking in the hot water Ben thought of Anne in similar circumstances, sitting chatting away or firing crossword puzzle clues at him, or the two of them together in the huge tin bath that had been a particular feature of the Dorset cottage.

When he came downstairs Irene had high tea laid in the back room which was their main living room, the front parlour being reserved for high days and holidays. Over the meal she continued to be friendly, unusually loquacious about life at the library, and when she'd inspected the painting he'd completed in Dorset she had the judgement to appreciate it was his best yet, if not the reason why. After two and a half months' absence Ben felt he had to give his wife a breathing space before dropping his bombshell, so for several days he kept quiet.

Although not promiscuous by temperament, Ben was sexually experienced when he married and he'd taken it for granted that Irene would share his healthy instincts, but even before the trauma of their lost child which had put her right off sex for months, their love-life had never been exciting. When they had finally cohabited after the still-birth of their child, one night Ben had suddenly looked down at his wife who had been lying underneath him with her eyes tight closed and a pained expression on her face, so he'd withdrawn which had made her open her eyes and say, 'What's the matter? You haven't finished, have you?'

'No. But it's not meant to be a form of medieval torture. If you ever feel you'd actually like to make love with me again, as something pleasurable for us both, let me know.'

A fortnight later Irene had said coyly, 'I shan't mind if my hair gets mussed up tonight', and it had been a few seconds before Ben had grasped the implication of her words. They had made love in bed in the dark, the straight sandwich way she preferred, and since then the non-appearance of her lace sleeping cap had become the signal that she was in the mood to give him his oats. On the Friday night after his return home, when Irene climbed between the sheets with her wavy brown hair only too visible, Ben's heart sank just like any long-suffering wife's. He felt he couldn't *not* oblige but, having switched off the light and obliged, he knew he had to tell her the truth sooner rather than later.

Irene did not work at the library on Saturday afternoons. She cleaned the house. After she'd done his 'studio', in other words the back bedroom which had the best light, an operation Ben allowed her to carry out once a week on the strict understanding she touched nothing, he shut himself in to paint, while his wife indulged in her orgy of scrubbing, brushing, and polishing. They had their high tea in the immaculately clean kitchen, with the plates on the Welsh dresser positively gleaming, and seeing it was such a lovely evening she suggested they had a walk.

Why not? Ben thought. Maybe the fresh air would take some of the sting from what he had to tell her. They walked up Nether Brow towards the open moorland, where the banks of grey and white cloud were drifting slowly in a pale blue sky, and the sun was shining on the swell of the Pennine hills. As they approached a wooden stile wedged between the dry-stone walls that criss-crossed the landscape, his Lanca-shire accent broad, Ben said, 'Let's rest awhile, luv. I've summat to say to you.'

Having perched herself on the stile's horizontal ledge and arranged her black skirt neatly around her lisle-stockinged legs, shading her eyes from the dazzling light of the slowly dying sun, Irene looked at him queryingly. Ben couldn't think how to break the news gently, so in his flattest voice but now avoiding the dialect words she disliked, he said, 'I've met somebody. I've fallen in love with her. I want to live with her.'

After only a few seconds, without looking at him, but quite calmly his wife replied, 'I see. You know I can't divorce you. You're my husband. We were married in the sight of God.'

Irene managed to keep her voice calm but to use the sort of cliché she despised, her body felt as it had been turned to stone. Not her mind though, that was raging. Her dilemma was that she could no longer give rein to the emotions she possessed. Until she was seven years old, an only but not lonely child, Irene had lived with her parents in a semi-detached house with a nice garden in the new housing estate perched above the smoke of The Dales. Then had come the terrible day when Daddy had lost his job as a clerk with the District Bank, and it had been years before Irene had realised her vague, kindly father was an alcoholic. Although he was now dead, with her mother she still had to keep up the pretence that he'd suffered from poor health and the bank had treated him disgracefully.

Once her father's savings had gone, they had been forced to move into a terraced house in the worst area of Upperdale but Mummy had insisted they keep up standards, that Irene speak properly, not with the dreadful, slovenly accents of the local children, tasks which in the circumstances she had found difficult. Until she had won her scholarship to Mellordale High School and learned to control herself, Irene had spent many hours standing in the gloomy hall of their horrible house, or locked into her bedroom with the equally horrible view of dustbins and privies, as a punishment for her unruly behaviour.

Irene shivered slightly at the memory of those days and her husband said, 'Are you cold? Do you want to move on?'

Still without looking at him, she said, 'No, thank you.'

'Here, have my coat.' Solicitously he took off his jacket and draped it round her shoulders. Irene would have liked to have thrown the jacket to the ground and stamped on it, but unable to relieve her feelings she continued to stare at the tussocky grass.

Along the road of her Calvary, of being tormented by the local children as a stuck-up madam and terrified that her middle-class friends at Mellordale High School would discover where she lived, Irene had eventually found God and Socialism. Her mother approved of the former, but not the latter, and she was horrified when her daughter met that godless Socialist, Benjamin Broughton (she insisted on calling him 'Benjamin'). It was the residue of the original rage inside Irene that had been drawn to Ben whom most people in The Dales considered a proper nut-case, preferring to do weird paintings rather than develop the pugilistic talent that could have made him the world middleweight boxing champion.

Irene had given Ben everything she could, understanding, encouragement, a home, and the freedom to paint without undue financial worry, though when he had money Ben was generous with it; and upholding her own belief in his genius, the ex-Mrs Tom Whitworth and her present husband, Sir Philip Marchal, had recently bought two of his large canvases. Because she suspected she wasn't very good in bed, Irene had also obliquely indicated that Ben could have discreet affairs, not that he was a womaniser in the way artists were traditionally supposed to be. And it wasn't that she didn't want to love him physically, but throughout her childhood her mother had muttered darkly about the things you had to put up with in marriage, and one day in her teens, coming home late from a rehearsal of Mellordale High School's production of *Twelfth Night*, Irene had literally stumbled over a couple doing it in an alleyway. The spectacle had underlined her mother's gloomy warnings and the physical act of love had assumed a disgusting aspect Irene had never completely been able to cast from her mind.

As if from a great distance she heard Ben saying, 'No point being sorry, Irene, though I am. I didn't want things to turn out this way. I'll clear off as soon as I can.'

For the first time since his shattering announcement, Irene looked up at her husband. The clear grey eyes she loved so much, though she'd never been able to tell him she did, were gazing at her with . . . what? Compassion? Pity? Ben could keep his pity, so could the gossips in The Dales, so could her mother whom Irene could hear saying, 'I told you he was no good. I told you not to marry him.' If he, or they, imagined she would let him go just like that, without putting up a fight against the wiles of his floozie, he and they were sorely mistaken.

Aloud, in the same calm, dignified tone of voice with which she'd greeted his announcement, Irene said, 'If that's the way you feel, you may go whenever you wish. I don't wish to know who she is, or anything about her. But you will always be my husband, Ben, and if at any time you want to return to the house that will always be your home, you will be welcome.'

11

From the moment Anne introduced Ben and Julian on the terrace at Chenneys, it was obvious they did not like each other. Julian was looking particularly tall and slim in a latest-fashion, single-breasted, grey suit with wide pointed lapels on the jacket and neat turn-ups to the trousers. A striped silk tie, a handkerchief folded into the breast pocket, and a dapper bowler hat completed the picture of the well-groomed man. Ben was wearing his customary baggy trousers, checked shirt, and ill-fitting jacket with a sketchpad, pencils and accumulated rubbish bulging from the pockets. His grey eyes looked Julian impassively up and down, before he held out his hand and in a strong Lancashire accent said, 'How do.'

Julian winced slightly from the strength of the handshake and in response his voice had its most politely strangulated upper-class tones. Ben's gaze then travelled to the Rolls-Royce which was standing in the drive below the terrace, the beautiful 1905 Silver Ghost model which had been a wedding present from grandfather Thorpe to his pioneer lady motorist daughter and which, though Mummy's health had long since disbarred her from driving, had been kept in immaculate condition. With the same flat Lancashire intonations, Ben said, 'Are we going in that?'

'Yes,' Anne snapped, 'we are.'

While they had been in Dorset, she had asked Ben if he would care to accompany her and Rebecca on their pilgrimage to the Great War battlefields this September. In London, Rebecca had bumped into Julian and likewise invited him. Both men having accepted the coincidental invitations, the girls had laughingly decided a foursome would be pleasant. From the way Ben was doing his 'I'm only a Lancashire lad' act, Anne now had her doubts. As they walked inside

Chenneys she whispered to him, 'If you're going to behave like an oaf, we might as well call the whole thing off.'

'I shan't say another word.'

'That won't be helpful either.'

Fortunately, Ben liked Mummy – who did not? – and more surprisingly he appeared to like Philip too, so he was on his best behaviour at the dinner table.

The next morning when they sailed out of Folkestone harbour, the sun was shining on the white cliffs and Anne thought of her father, watching the coastline of his beloved England disappear that last time, convinced he would soon be home for good. After they had disembarked themselves and the Silver Ghost, with Anne at the wheel they drove through the prettily smiling, if rather boring countryside, from Boulogne to Étaples. There they stopped to view the desolate sandhills with their windswept pine trees overlooking the estuary of the River Canche, that had been the vast British wartime base camp.

Julian said, 'Goodness, it's a b-bleak place even in the s-sunshine.'

'Yeah,' Ben grunted, as he gazed at the rows of white headstones in the military cemetery.

Ben had stopped doing his Lancashire lad act but he was at his most silently watchful, which could be even more disconcerting. In the face of the unspoken hostility Julian was being impeccably good-mannered, though he was stammering a fair amount which indicated his discomposure. From Étaples they drove to Albert, the small Picardy town that had been another place only too well known to millions of British soldiers in the Great War.

Doing her best to pretend they were all the best of friends, Anne looked up at the golden statue of the Virgin Mary, high on the reconstructed basilica of the Catholic church. She said, 'Daddy used to send me postcards during the war. He sent me one of the church when it was a shell-shocked ruin and the Virgin was leaning rather drunkenly from the top of the dome. He told me the Tommies called her "The Lady with the Limp"! He also told me the Virgin had become a symbol to the local people who believed that if she fell, the Allies would lose the war. Of course, she was finally blown off during the German bombardment in 1918 and I remember being dreadfully upset when I heard the news.'

After breakfast in the *pension* in Albert, with the map of the Somme spread in front of them, Julian and Ben started to argue about the best route to take for the day's pilgrimage. Eventually Rebecca snatched the map from Ben and said, 'For heaven's sake, I'll do the navigating.'

With Rebecca making it only too apparent she considered it was Ben who was behaving badly, which actually it was, liking all three and loving one of them, Anne damned the accidental invitations that had brought the two men together. Upset, irritated, anxious, she could only pray Ben would stop being difficult and the tension would lessen.

Their first act of remembrance was at Thiepval. Staring at the ridge of low-lying hills dominated by the massive memorial arch, laconically Ben observed, 'If the top brass had thought from then till Domesday, they couldn't have found a worse position for the British Army to attack front-ally. The only stretch of high ground to be seen for miles and thickly wooded to boot.'

'And the Germans had h-had eighteen months to d-dig themselves in,' Julian added.

'Yeah,' Ben grunted his agreement, which was a welcome relief.

The tears pricked Anne's eyes, the lump thickened in her throat, as they examined the seventy-three thousand names inscribed on the huge columns of the memorial arch, of those who had been killed in the Battle of the Somme but had 'no known graves'. Chokily she said, 'The phrase the troops coined was more savagely accurate. I remember hearing Daddy talking about men being "blown to buggery".'

From Thiepval they drove to the village of Contalmaison, where Ben's father had had his leg blown off and where his son sat on a wall, impassively sketching a girl driving a gaggle of geese down the rebuilt main street. Leaving the Silver Ghost surrounded by admiring villagers, they walked across the fields to Mametz Wood. Anne informed her friends, 'Daddy won his first MC here.'

Then she shivered, imagining her father fighting inch by bloody inch through the wood, the machine-guns cackling, the 'whizz-bangs' exploding, men screaming in agony or lying silent in death. Today the trees were thick with autumn leaves and the only sounds were the crackle of twigs under their feet and the cawing of the rooks. The reminders of the carnage of the Somme lay all around them, however, fragments of water bottles, helmets and bayonets, coils of rusty barbed wire, stumps of shell-shattered trees, warnings of subsidence and sudden dips in the ground that marked the partially filled-in trenches. Clumsy as ever, Rebecca tripped over a rotting stump and from its dead roots, a skull rolled.

'Oh God!' Julian looked sick. He looked even sicker as Ben squatted on his haunches, produced his sketchpad from his jacket pocket and made a rapid pencil drawing of the skull, before gently pushing somebody's earthly remains back into the soft earth and covering it with leaves.

When they reached the small British military cemetery at Flat Iron Copse, they found Rebecca's uncle's grave easily and read the inscription: 'Second-Lieutenant Reuben Lawson. East Lancashire Regiment. 14 July 1916. At the going down of the sun and in the morning we will remember him.'

Among the Christian crosses, perhaps it was the sight of the lone Star of David on Reuben Lawson's grave and the knowledge of the Nazis' virulent anti-Semitism, that made the tears well fiercely in Anne's eyes and caused her to cry out, 'It can't happen again. They can't have died for nothing. We can't have another war. We can't. We must find another way of defeating the Fascists and their beastly policies.'

'We will, Anne, we will,' Julian said.

On the following day's drive from Albert to Ypres, Ben kept saying, 'Stop here a minute will you, luv?'

Although he phrased his words as a request, there was a strong element of command in his voice. At the first couple of sites – a cluster of British graves stuck in the middle of a ploughed field, a larger military cemetery semi-enclosed by a new housing estate – Rebecca and Julian obviously had no objections to Ben's sketching. Then the sun disappeared, the grey clouds gathered, which made their journey through the mining towns of the Lens plain even more depressing, and he continued to ask Anne to stop the Silver Ghost. She sensed her friends' growing irritation as he sketched whatever caught his eye, but apparently Ben did not. Or if he did, he didn't care.

As they entered Ypres Anne said, 'During the war Daddy gave me a map of the Western Front. I had it pinned to my bedroom wall and I moved little flags backwards and forwards to mark the British front lines. We've just travelled their whole length – less than the distance from London to Manchester. Doesn't it make you want to weep? To think hundreds of thousands of lives were sacrificed over so small an area of ground?'

'Yes,' Rebecca said. Neither Ben nor Julian disagreed.

They arrived in Ypres just in time to check into their hotel, have a wash and walk the shorter distance from the town square to the massive limestone arch of the Menin Gate memorial, erected to honour the armies of the British Empire who had stood here from 1914 to 1918 and the further fifty-five thousand of its soldiers who had no known graves. Just before eight o'clock the policeman on duty stopped the flow of traffic through the arch, the clocks struck the hour, and the bugler sounded the Last Post in the nightly tribute to the fallen. In the cavern of the arch, as the strains of the Last Post echoed with heart-aching plangency, Anne clutched Ben's hand and he returned the pressure of her grip. For several minutes after the bugler had departed and the traffic was once more speeding through, all four of them stood silently on the pavement, unable or unwilling to speak.

Eventually Rebecca said, 'I don't know about you lot but my withers have been wrung to shreds. I suggest we go and have a jolly good meal.'

They all agreed that was a good idea, though there was the problem of Ben's having no dinner jacket which hadn't mattered in unsophisticated Albert but in Ypres reduced the places in which they could eat; including, Anne had already noted with dismay, their hotel dining room. Why hadn't she thought about Ben's wardrobe before they left England? His answer would be: because rich folks like you take for granted such matters as having the right attire for all occasions. Looking at Julian, what Ben actually said was, 'Sorry to make you go slumming, Mr Kendle, but we don't have much call for evening dress in The Dales. Even less for white tie and tails.'

'Actually, there are quite a few people in The Dales who wear both,' Anne snapped, partly because she was cross with herself, but mainly because at times Ben was too tiresome and childish for words.

Fortunately, they found a pleasant restaurant which did not demand that its customers be 'properly' dressed. While they were waiting for their orders to arrive, diffidently Julian asked if he might see Mr Broughton's sketches. There was a silence, during which Anne thought she really would hit Ben if he said no, but then ungraciously he pulled his sketchbook from his jacket pocket and handed it to Julian. After Mr Kendle had made complimentary but knowledgeable comments, Ben appeared to accept that well-bred and effete Anne's literary agent might be, but a totally drooping upper-class twit he was not.

After that it turned into an enjoyably relaxing evening. Ben even told a story which made them all laugh, about an illicit still that had been set up in a row of privies in the back streets of Upperdale, thriving until the illegal brewers got uproariously drunk one night and roamed through the town, bawling bawdy songs at the tops of their voices. Rebecca became positively skittish with Julian and, if Anne hadn't known her friend better, she could have imagined she had a crush on him. She attributed the behaviour to the emotion of their pilgrimage and to the wine, of which they drank a fair amount. To round off a day which had, thank heaven, smoothed the edges of the two men's mutual dislike, Ben crept into Anne's bedroom. They made love passionately and she fell asleep in his arms, though he wasn't of course there when she woke up.

The following morning the sky was greyly overcast and as Anne washed and dressed, she felt the dragging pains in her stomach which meant her period was about to start early, dammit, and it might be a bad one. She would have preferred to stay in bed but they had arranged to visit the largest of all the British Empire Great War cemeteries, Tyne Cot. On the drive out of Ypres towards Passchendaele, Anne informed her friends, 'Daddy told me about the names the troops gave some of the worst places. You know like Flat Iron Copse and Rotten Row and Dud Corner and Hellfire Corner. Apparently, during Passchendaele, the Northumberland Fusiliers christened some heavily fortified German pill-boxes "Tyne Cottages", or "Cotts" in the vernacular. Did you know that's where the cemetery got its name?'

Her friends admitted they had not known. And it was another emotional occasion, the thousands of white head-stones standing like squat ghosts in the murky morning light, overshadowed by the huge circular wall inscribed with thousands more names of those who had disappeared without trace into the Passchendaele mud. Among the names on the Tyne Cot memorial wall was that of Captain A. G. C. Kendle, MC, Manchester Regiment. Having paid her silent homage to dear Uncle Guy – since she'd learned of his affair with Aunty Alice, Anne found his memory even more attractive – she walked away, followed by Ben and Rebecca, to allow Julian to pay his own respects to his father's memory.

By the time they returned to Ypres, the period pains were clawing at Anne's stomach like an iron ratchet. After she had parked the Rolls-Royce outside the hotel in the town square, where it attracted the usual attention, Ben frowned at her and said, 'You look lousy.'

Anne replied, 'How observant of you. I feel lousy and I'm going back to bed. You lot can do what you want.'

In the attempts to disperse the pain, she lay in bed clutching the hot water bottle and sipping the glass of hot peppermint Rebecca had obtained. When Ben came to see her she moaned, 'Go away.'

'I only came to comfort you, luv, and see if there's anything you want.' After Anne had said there wasn't and he'd stroked her hair, which was comforting, he observed, 'I'm glad I'm not a woman.'

Although the worst of the pains had passed by the next morning, Anne still felt mouldy and the most emotional time of all lay ahead, the visit to her father's grave. Over breakfast, Julian offered to drive the Silver Ghost to Le Cateau, an offer Anne accepted with some reluctance. For so polite and considerate a man, he was a surprisingly wild driver. Or did the wildness, like his occasional bursts of asperity, indicate

Julian's hidden depths? But it was pouring with rain, Anne herself had no desire to drive, Ben didn't know how to, Rebecca had never handled the Rolls-Royce, so Julian was the only option.

They had proceeded no more than a few miles towards Mons before Anne knew she had made a big mistake in letting him take the wheel. Julian was charging along regardless of the slashing rain, the state of the roads, other vehicles, or pedestrians. Both she and Rebecca shouted loudly as he appeared not to notice an elderly woman pushing a handcart towards them, and it was only by wrenching the wheel hard that he missed the old girl. When Julian almost crashed into an oncoming truck, in a deliberately broad Lancashire accent Ben said, 'For Pete's sake, slow down, Kendle. Do you need glasses or summat?'

Was Julian short-sighted? Anne wondered. She had occasionally seen him don glasses. Was his problem that he couldn't see properly and wouldn't admit it? When they stopped for coffee she decided she must take over the driving, so she said she was feeling much better, thank you. In the appalling conditions Anne didn't enjoy the rest of the drive to Le Cateau one little bit but there wasn't much traffic and they reached their destination safely. Once in the small French town, however, they were misdirected to their hotel. The mistake improved nobody's mood, notably Anne's own, for though the Silver Ghost was normally a pleasure to drive, its size made it difficult to turn round or reverse in Le Cateau's narrow, hilly, cobblestoned streets. By the time they had found the hotel and had a snack meal, it had stopped raining, though it remained the gloomiest of late afternoons. When Anne announced that she'd like to go to the cemetery, Rebecca said, 'Wouldn't it be better to leave it until tomorrow?'

'No, I'd like to go now. We have the Sambre Canal to visit tomorrow.'

The Sambre Canal was where her father had actually been killed in the dying days of the war. Anne remembered eavesdropping and hearing him saying to Mummy, 'And the weather's always so bloody awful over there' – he hadn't sworn in his children's presence but Daddy's language had on occasions been choice. She felt it would be appropriate to visit his grave in the sort of conditions the troops had endured for most of their four years in northern France and Flanders' fields.

The military cemetery was on high ground outside the town, and in the dank greyness of the afternoon there wasn't a soul to be seen among the ubiquitous rows of white headstones in the British section; uncommonly, there were German graves here too. But Anne had a plan of the lay-out and without difficulty they found her father's grave. For several seconds, barely conscious of Rebecca, Ben and Julian behind her, she stood on the soggy grass of the neat green paths that ran between the ranks of Portland stone, staring at her father's last resting place. Were the decomposing remains of the man she had loved so dearly actually here? Had thousands of bodies been disinterred and reinterred when the Imperial War Graves Commission had undertaken the melancholy task of organising the cemeteries? Anne went on staring at her father's regimental insignia, the coat of arms of the City of Manchester, and the words beneath them. Her mother had not chosen to add any lines to the standard inscription, as one had been permitted to do, and it read simply: 'Major E. T. F. Whitworth, DSO, MC and bar, MP. Manchester Regiment. November 7, 1918.'

Anne then bent down to lay her bouquet among the numerous posies and wreaths that already decorated the grave. Perhaps it was the stark simplicity of the inscription, or the touching number of floral tributes, or the fact that her father's was one among the hundreds of thousands of graves she had seen in the last few days, or perhaps more prosaically it was the action of bending down and straightening up, on top of the effects of a bad period and the awful drive, but like levitating bodies the white headstones started to float before Anne's eyes and momentarily she thought she was about to faint. Presumably she looked as if she might too, because Ben's arms steadied her. Although her head cleared, her vision did not. The tears were blurring her eyes and with a howl Anne buried her head on Ben's chest, giving full vent to her anguish.

12

The evening began quietly and pleasantly enough. Anne appeared to have recovered some sort of equilibrium, though much as Rebecca loved her the breakdown in the cemetery had been Anne's own damned fault, pushing herself beyond her emotional limits. Frankly, though she wouldn't have missed the experience for anything, Rebecca would now be glad when they were on their way home. Fortunately, because it had started to rain again and none of them felt like going out, the hotel in Le Cateau did not insist on dressing for dinner.

They had reached the dessert stage – Rebecca was enjoying her chocolate eclairs immensely although, with her weight problem, they were the last things she should have ordered – when Anne mentioned the Peace Pledge Union. Sir Philip and Lady Marchal as well as Anne herself had already joined the ranks of well-known sponsors, to encourage those who remained uncommitted or uncertain, to make their pledge: 'I renounce war, and never again directly or indirectly will I support or sanction another.' Glancing pleadingly from Ben to Rebecca, Anne said, 'After what we've seen in the last few days, can't I persuade you two to sign?'

In the act of finishing his lemon sorbet, Julian, who had been among the first to sign, looked up and in an astonished voice said, 'Haven't you already pledged your support?'

'No,' said Ben.

'Why not, if you d–don't mind my asking?'

From the lack of expression on his face, Rebecca knew he did mind, at least insofar as Mr Kendle was concerned. Ben Broughton was definitely not her cup of tea. Julian remained her ideal man, though the last few days had, alas, confirmed that his interest in Rebecca Lawson, other than as a friend of Anne Whitworth's, was nil. But Rebecca understood some of the reasons why Anne was so besotted by B. D. Broughton. If you liked the earthy type, which presumably she did, he was attractive; he had undoubted talent as an artist; he stood up to Anne; like her father he came from The Dales, and her continuing obsession with 'Daddy' was another thing that had been confirmed in the last few days. What Rebecca could neither understand, nor forgive, was Ben's boorish attitude towards Julian.

He was at it again, with barely concealed contempt informing a persistent Julian that those who believed the Peace Pledge Union would have any effect, were flying in the face of history. To be honest, Rebecca shared Ben's views. She could not see well-meaning pacifists halting the Nazis in their tracks and she had already told Anne, that as a Jew she was prepared to fight them if necessary and it would therefore be dishonest of her to say she renounced war. Rebecca had no intention of explaining this to Julian. Having been brought up by a devoutly anti-Semitic Catholic mother, he was not as sympathetic as he might be to the plight of her race. When pushed, as he had been on occasions by an indignant Anne, he tended to share the view that the Jews had brought their troubles on themselves.

Leaning back in his chair, Ben said, 'Let me ask you a question, Mr Kendle . . .'

'Not the one about what I would do if a Nazi, or some other thug, was about to rape or kill Anne.' Uncharacteristically, Julian interrupted and the hint of asperity had entered his voice. With wry sadness, Rebecca noted he hadn't mentioned anybody raping or killing her.

'What would you do?' Ben demanded. 'Let her be raped or killed from pacifist principle?'

'Ben, that's unfair!' Anne cried out.

Julian flushed and stuttered, 'Are you s-suggesting that by being a p-pacifist, I'm also a c-coward?'

'Nothing was further from my mind.' Ben looked at Julian with his impassively insolent gaze. 'It's currently fashionable to be a pacifist, but it can take guts to be one.'

'Really, Ben!' Anne said furiously. 'If you think we're pacifists because it's fashionable . . .'

'I don't think you are, luv.'

'B-but I am?' Julian was now as furious as Anne and in his emotion he stammered painfully. 'You've m-made your opinion of m-me only too c-clear from the m-moment we m-met, Mr B-broughton, and I c-can assure you I've had m-more than . . .'

'And I can assure you, Mr Kendle, if I'd known you were coming with us, I'd have stayed at home.'

Loudly Rebecca said, 'I suggest everybody shuts up and counts ten.'

At that moment the waiter approached their table and said to Julian whom he regarded as the obvious head of the party, '*Vous voulez du café, monsieur? Vous le prenez ici ou dans le . . .*'

Anne cut in, '*Non merci, pas à ce moment.*'

Why the hell hadn't Anne taken advantage of the proffered respite? Rebecca thought furiously, because within seconds they were all plunged into a blazing row. With angry incoherence it ranged over bad manners, lack of consideration and respect for others' feelings and beliefs, English class-consciousness and Socialism, as well as cowardice, principles, Fascism and pacifism. Then, simultaneously they all paused to draw breath. As he glared at Ben, the old cliché 'If looks could kill' was true of Julian's pacifist soul. He said, 'I d-don't think anything useful will be achieved, and c-considerably more harm c-could be done, by c-continuing this c-conversation.'

Pushing back his chair, Ben stood up and said, 'For once we're in complete agreement, Mr Kendle.'

Without a word of apology, without excusing himself, he walked towards the door and Rebecca's non-pacifist soul could have killed him. Every eye in the dining room followed Ben's strides – who said the English were an unemotional race? For a few seconds after his exit there was silence at the table. Anne put her face in her hands and Rebecca watched Julian stretching out his hand to touch her lightly on the shoulder. Softly, but his voice slightly hoarse from its unaccustomed anger, he said, 'F-forgive me, Anne. That was unforgivable. T-today of all days.'

Which was precisely what Rebecca was thinking, though her censure was directed against Ben, not Julian. Anne took her hands away from her face and stood up. Anxiously Rebecca enquired, 'Where are you going? Not after Ben?' As

Anne nodded, she said, 'Don't. Come and have coffee with us. Let him calm down.'

A few minutes later Anne banged on the door of Ben's bedroom, his voice responded ungraciously, 'Who is it?' and she marched in saying, 'Who do you think?'

Ben had kicked his shoes off and was lying on the counter-pane of the bed, and Anne noticed he had a hole in the toe of his left sock. He didn't get up as she entered but he turned his head and his eyes had their smouldering look, though it was not the gaze that denoted sexual passion. Upset and angry with him as she was, Anne remained confident that it was just a question of talking to her beloved, so pushing his feet out of the way she sat down on the end of the bed and said, 'You behaved abominably, Ben. Did you have to be so rude and objectionable?'

He countered with the question, 'Why didn't you tell me. you were bringing him?'

'I've already told you I didn't know Julian was coming when I invited you and . . .'

'You knew weeks before we left England.'

'All right, I did, but how was I to know you'd loathe each other's guts?' Struck by a sudden thought which might explain things, Anne asked, 'Are you jealous of Julian by any chance?'

'Jealous? Of him! You must be joking, luv. He's a pansy.'

'No, he's not,' she said quickly, too quickly, because Ben raised his eyebrows and smiled sardonically at her. 'And it doesn't excuse your behaviour, in any case.'

After another silence he said, 'I didn't leave my wife to traipse round Flanders' fields with you and your nancy-boy.'

Anne sat bolt upright and said the first thing that came into her head. 'If you must be so horrible about Julian, do stop using euphemisms. The words you want are "sodomite" or "homosexual".'

'Yes, ma'am.' Ben tugged a lock of his brown hair.

'And stop behaving like an overgrown schoolboy.' The implications of his remark penetrated her brain and she said, 'And we'd better get things straight. Are you saying you're already regretting leaving Irene?'

'Not really.'

'What do you mean?' Anne felt her heart thumping because this conversation was taking a completely unexpected turn. 'Not really?'

The thick fringe of his lashes heightened his speculative gaze but Anne felt she was regarding a stranger, as slowly he said, 'The last few days have made me wonder whether it's me you want, or whether what you're looking for is a reincarnation of your father. As a working-class lad from The Dales, I fit the bill.'

Anne just stared at him, not really grasping what he was saying.

'You've never stopped talking about your father. Daddy said this and Daddy sent me that and Daddy told me the other. I knew you were wrapped up with his memory, Anne, but I hadn't realised you're obsessed by it. I reckon the sooner you realise you are, the better.'

Her brain reeling, Anne said, 'I don't know whether what you're saying is true or not. But do you really think . . .' she struggled to control her voice, 'tonight is the moment to tell me, a few hours after I've been to the cemetery to see his grave?'

'I dunno. Maybe it is. It's the way it's happened, luv.'

'Things don't always just happen. People . . . can . . . make . . . them . . . happen . . .'

It was no good, despite her efforts not to break down she couldn't control her emotions any longer. Throwing herself on to the counterpane, Anne started to sob wildly, but it was several seconds before she felt the movement of the bedsprings as Ben shifted his legs and moved to stroke her hair. As he did so, he said, 'Come on, Anne, it's been a hell of a few days for us all. It was a wicked stroke of fate, your Dad being killed just before the Armistice, but he was one among millions, as you've observed only too frequently in the last few days. He was an exceptional man and you loved him dearly. But he's dead, you're alive and you're an exceptional woman. You can't go on living with the memory of what you think he was. From what I've heard of your Dad he wouldn't want you to.'

Still sobbing, though less wildly, Anne waited for Ben to take her into his arms, to comfort and cosset and then to make love to her, but he didn't oblige. Lifting her tear-stained face, she said, 'I think you're a shit at times, Ben Broughton.'

Before he spoke, from the expression in his eyes she knew she'd misjudged his mood, as she appeared to have been doing since entering the room. He said, 'Maybe I am. Maybe your Dad was at times too. But we're not the same kind of shits. So get that into your head.'

Anne hauled herself upright again and shouted breathily, 'Oh, I have. Your messages have been received loud and clear. I'm over-emotional. Julian's a homosexual, a species for which you have nothing but contempt. You're sorry you left the cosy nest provided by long-suffering Irene. And most importantly, I'm in love with my father, not you. Who are you in love with, apart from yourself?'

'With whom.' Ben corrected her grammar, as she some-times did his. 'And I don't care what Mr Kendle does in his private life. But it doesn't mean I have to like pansies.'

Anne lammed out at him with her right hand, he caught her wrist and held it tightly but their physical confrontation did not lead into passion, as it had on the past occasions when Anne had tried to pit her strength against his. Instead, overwhelmed by the feeling that Ben had chosen the worst possible moment to behave with appalling tactlessness, she spat her anguish at him, literally once or twice. He kept saying, 'Shut up', then they were both on their feet, shouting at each other. It all happened so suddenly, awfully, but Anne couldn't stop herself and she knew it was because she was exhausted, emotionally and physically, but Ben should know that too.

She heard herself bawling, 'I'm glad I found out what you're really like.'

'You can go to your nancy-boy, can't you? Much good he'll do you. You're a randy little bitch.'

'And you're a disgusting lout. Where do you intend to go?'

'I haven't the least notion. What's it to you, any road?'

'Are you going to crawl back to Irene?'

'If I were a disgusting lout, or if I believed in sexual equality, you'd be on the floor.'

Their verbal slugging match suddenly blew itself out. For several seconds they stood breathing heavily, silently staring at each other. From downstairs in the street came the sound of French revellers, arguing the toss about which café they should go to next. Part of Anne wanted to say, 'I love you, I truly do', part of her waited for Ben to say those words, but the rest of her was consumed by fury at the way he'd behaved and the terrible things he'd said to her on this journey of all journeys, in this place of all places, on this day of all days. Abruptly she turned away from him and walked towards the door, a part of her still waiting for, wanting, him to call her back or to catch her in his arms. At the door she paused but there was neither sound nor movement from Ben. Without looking at him, Anne opened the door and slammed it violently behind her.

The next morning Anne felt awful. She hadn't slept much, lying in bed with her mind churning like somebody mixing cement, sitting up at the slightest sound in the corridor, hoping it would be Ben, growing more desolate and angry with herself when it wasn't. Despite or because of her condition Anne dressed carefully, choosing her donkey-brown, hand-knitted jumper suit because later, when they drove out to the Sambre Canal, she could wear her matching brown beret. Berets suited her no end.

In the dining room Rebecca and Julian were already seated at the breakfast table but of Ben there was no sign. Her friends' mood was as subdued as Anne's own and while they ate their freshly baked rolls and croissants and drank the tea they'd ordered specially, nobody mentioned last night or Ben's absence. Until eventually, pouring herself another cup of tea, Rebecca said, 'How was Mr Broughton when you last saw him?'

'In a bloody awful mood.' Anne saw the slight frown crease Julian's head but Ben was old-fashioned in that respect too, he didn't approve of women swearing either.

'I presume he's skipping breakfast but will join us later?' Rebecca further enquired.

'I presume so, too,' Anne replied.

To which Rebecca responded, 'Let's hope he's in a less bloody mood.'

Julian made no comment whatsoever. They went on to

discuss the itinerary for their homeward journey, once they'd located the place where Tom Whitworth had been killed by a German sniper's bullet. Then the waiter came over and looking at Anne, asked, 'Mademoiselle Vitvort?' She nodded and he handed her an envelope, saying, '*Bien. Cette lettre est pour vous, mademoiselle.*'

As she took the envelope Anne's stomach heaved but even when she saw the words 'Miss Anne Whitworth' in Ben's stylish hand, she couldn't believe he had gone, without accompanying her on the last pilgrimage to the Sambre Canal, without a word of farewell. But he had. And what he'd written on the single sheet of paper inside was totally, shatteringly, stunningly, numbingly unbelievable, for his note read:

Dear Anne,
   I don't think we've anything left to say to each other, not at the moment anyway. You made it clear that my continuing presence will not improve the unshining hour, so I've decided the best thing is for me to leave without further ado and make my own way back home. Our relationship has been interesting, to say the least, and I wouldn't have missed it for the world. Perhaps one day we'll meet again, in less emotional circumstances. In the meantime, look after yourself.
Yours, Ben.

13

On her return from France, clutching desperately at Ben's statement that they had nothing further to say to each other *at the moment*, Anne went on believing he could not have walked out on her just like that, not after all they had been to each other, he simply could not. He too had been in an emotional state in Le Cateau and tomorrow when the bell of the Gower Street flat rang, she would open the door and he would be standing there, perhaps not holding a bouquet of flowers which wasn't his style, but full of apologies and declarations of love.

September passed into October and Ben did not turn up on the doorstep, nor did he telephone, nor write, and Anne felt as if there were a great hollow inside her. Her mood varying from the tearful to the furious, she spent countless night hours making cups of tea and smoking heavily, whilst re-reading his letters and gazing at the tangible proof of their liaison. The sketchbook from Frankfurt, crayon drawings of her at the typewriter, in the garden and down on the beach of the Dorset cottage, were all she had but there had been no reason to amass more when their love was going to last to their dying days.

Otherwise Anne tried to fill the hollow by writing, by campaigning for the Peace Pledge Union and the Women's Peace Party, by broadcasting, by blasting the Government for not taking steps to counteract the cancer of unemployment that was eating away the lives of so many of her fellow citizens, by going to the theatre and to concerts, and by accepting a ridiculous number of the invitations to parties and literary functions that thudded through the letter box. Anything to stop her mind longing and her body aching for Ben; too many things so that she could fall exhaustedly into her solitary bed and hope to sleep.

Rebecca was sympathetic but said, 'He's not worth all this hyperactivity and prowling around in the middle of the night, Anne. He's behaved . . .'

'I know how he's behaved. But I love him. And I need to understand why he went off like that.'

'Because he's like most men. He's selfish, he hasn't grown up, and he doesn't want to face the responsibility of a real relationship – that wife of his is content to be his nanny. And in Ben's case, everything's with knobs on because he has the selfishness of a genuine artistic talent.'

While some of what Rebecca cynically averred might be true, it wasn't the complete answer to his disappearance, Anne felt sure. Rebecca had never had an intimate relationship with a man and she didn't, couldn't, know the closeness and depth of hers with Ben.

Then, at the beginning of November, the parcel arrived and Anne's heart leapt when she saw Ben's calligraphy on the brown-paper wrapping. He hadn't forgotten her! He still loved her! The parcel contained a painting of rows of white crosses fanning out in long lines from fragments of dun-coloured skulls, helmets, shells, bayonets, water bottles – all the rotting stuff they'd seen – heaped in the right-hand corner. Poppies seeped blood over these remnants of war, providing a dramatic, riveting contrast to the pallor of the rest of the canvas. There was no letter inside the parcel but, turning over the painting which was signed B. D. Broughton, on its back Anne found he had written: 'To Anne from Ben. In memory of a visit to Picardy and Flanders' fields. Autumn 1934.'

With the help of a magnifying glass Anne deciphered the smudged postmark on the wrapping. The parcel had been posted in Upperdale! She sent off a telegram to Madge who alas, but of course, had no telephone. Madge responded promptly in her painstaking handwriting and inimitable style:

'Dear Anne, You-know-who was seen at own and parents' house. Before more could be learned he vanished. Don't know where to. Sorry not to be of more help. Why don't you forget the bugger? Yours most respectfully, M. Kearsley.'

Partly because she found some peace of mind in the estate's tranquil beauty, but mainly because her mother was her bedrock, Anne went to Chenneys frequently and this November she made a particular point of driving down for Armistice Day. Since the end of the war it had become the tradition for virtually everybody on the Chenneys estate and in the village of Marshall Minnis, including the schoolchildren, to take part in a simple service in the Norman church, starting with the two-minute silence as the clocks struck the eleventh hour of the eleventh day of the eleventh month. When the service was over, led by the vicar and Sir Philip and Lady Marchal, the congregation walked the few yards from the church to the village green, to lay their wreaths of Flanders' poppies on the war memorial. It was always an emotional occasion and Anne's mother was always greatly affected – what memories Armistice Day must evoke for her – but after she'd had a rest and they'd lunched, Mummy said, 'For once it's a nice day, so before the sun disappears, shall we have a walk to Dedman's Down?'

'Are you sure you feel up to it?'

'Don't start behaving like your stepfather, Anne. Quite sure. You can get "Norman" for me.'

'Norman' was the battery-operated bath-chair Philip had had designed for Tom Whitworth's widow when she first came to Chenneys to recuperate from her heart attack and although the contraption was now somewhat outdated Mummy remained deeply attached to it. Dedman's Down was one of their favourite places, a curiously-shaped hillock with a clump of trees on its summit, from where there was a splendid view of the estate. (In the old days a gibbet had stood there and 'Dedman' was a corruption of 'Dead Man'.) Walking by her mother's side as she trundled Norman through the parkland, Anne decided this was an appropriate moment to raise the spectre that had been haunting her since that hideous night in Le Cateau. She said, 'Am I obsessed by Daddy's memory? Ben said I am. He also informed me I loved him partly because of my obsession.'

'Did he now?'

When Anne had returned to Chenneys to sob her heart out about what had happened during their pilgrimage, Kessie had to admit she'd felt almost as much relief as sympathy. Not that she hadn't liked Ben and she admired him enormously as an artist but, morality apart, embarking on a liaison with a married man was a recipe for disaster. She had hoped Anne would soon realise she was well out of it, recover her spirits and find somebody else, though it was now only too obvious that her daughter had done none of those things.

Insistently Anne repeated the question, 'Am I obsessed with Daddy?'

Seeing she had brought up the subject, Kessie said yes, and moreover Anne had created Seth Pollard in her father's imagined image, though she was glad to say Seth was acquiring a life of his own. She had to confess that she too had wondered if part of the reason why Anne had been attracted to Ben in the first place was because, like her father, he came from a working-class background in The Dales.

'Did you?' Anne said in astonishment. 'You never said anything.'

No, well, Kessie thought, Philip kept insisting it was wiser not to and I went along with his judgement, but we won't mention that.

They were approaching the path that wound over the chalky downland to the summit of Dedman's Down and which Norman had difficulty in negotiating. After a minor argument, Kessie switched off the battery and allowed Anne to push her. While her daughter manfully – or womanfully? – manoeuvred the bath-chair up the incline, Kessie leant her head against Norman's back-rest and smiled at her. What an attractive young woman Anne was, her cheeks nicely flushed, her dark eyes sparkling with the exertion, her beret at a jaunty angle on her shining copper hair. How splendidly she had taken advantage of the opportunities presented to her genera-tion but . . . Kessie waited until they had reached the summit before she said, 'I wish you could sort out your love-life, Anne. A good marriage is to be highly recommended.'

'You've had two, so you should know.' Detecting the slightly bitter note in her daughter's voice, Kessie merely nod-ded. Silently she watched Anne brush a flutter of falling leaves from her shoulders and gaze across the misty November blur of field and copse towards the mauve mass of Chenneys. Eventually Anne said, 'Perhaps I have been obsessed by Daddy's memory but I shan't be any more. And I didn't fall in love with Ben as a father-figure. I loved him, I still love him, for himself. Unfortunately, he doesn't appear to love me, so I shall just have to forget him.'

Despite her brave words to her mother, Anne waited and waited for Ben to contact her but he didn't even send her a Christmas card. She couldn't send him one because she had no idea where he was. As usual she spent the festivities *en famille* at Chenneys. A year old at the end of March, baby Callum was a dear little soul, sweet-tempered like his mother. The sight of Con pushing him round the wintry gardens, dressed in his woollen coat with the velvet collar, his warm gaiters, and knitted hat with the pom-pom, or Callum toddling to show Aunty Kate and Uncle Mark his Christmas presents, or sitting on grandma's knee, stirred Anne's normally quiescent maternal instincts and did nothing to lessen her longing for Ben. Nor did the news that some time in August, if Con's calculations were correct, she hoped to produce a baby girl!

Anne and Con stayed on at Chenneys, Kate and Mark returned from London, for the great occasion of their mother's fiftieth birthday which fell on New Year's Day 1935. Mummy rested throughout the day of New Year's Eve and at midnight the family and close friends who had gathered to celebrate her half-century, raised their champagne glasses to toast her and the next half-century and to sing happy birthday, before joining hands for Auld Lang Syne. Considering the long years of ill-health, their mother really was wearing remarkably well, Anne thought, not too many strands of grey in her lovely chestnut hair, nor too many lines marking her face, her figure still slender, her hazel eyes still sparkling. Grudgingly, Anne admitted that Philip's devoted concern was partly responsible for this happy state of affairs.

Early in the New Year, unannounced as usual, Kate turned up at the flat. In her student days, with the Royal Academy of Dramatic Art being just down Gower Street, she'd been a constant visitor, but since she'd been allowed to leave RADA and had embarked on her theatrical career, Anne had seen considerably less of her little sister. In a brown costume with darker brown fur collar and cuffs and fur 'wings' on the shoulders, Kate was looking adorable. Once she was comfortably ensconced in the armchair in front of the blazing fire in the living room, sipping the tea Anne had brewed, she fluttered her lashes and said, 'Darling, I'm not sure how to tell you my wonderful news. But you must know before the official announcement because it may come as a teeny bit of a shock.'

What now? Anne thought, as she extracted a cigarette from her lacquered case. Kate asked, 'May I have a ciggy too, please, darling.'

After they had lit their cigarettes Kate said, 'Darling, it's about Sandy.'

He had cast Kate in several of his productions which had been helpful to her career, though she had a clear bell-like voice and was developing into a good radio actress. With a laugh, Anne enquired, 'What's he going to do? Shake the BBC and shatter the air-waves with an avant-garde production starring Kate Whitworth?'

'No, darling,' Kate coughed slightly before continuing, 'actually, Sandy's asked me to marry him and I've accepted. We're holding back the announcement of our engagement until I start work on my next film. It'll be good publicity and we all need that these days, don't we? But we felt we must tell you.' Puffing prettily on her cigarette, Kate looked a trifle anxiously at Anne. 'I do hope you're not upset or anything, darling. I mean, I know you were ever so fond of Sandy once but honestly, darling, it just happened. We just fell in love. Honestly we did.'

Was she upset? Anne asked herself. Pole-axed with amazement was the more accurate description of her condition, though now she came to think of it the last time she'd seen Sandy at Broadcasting House not long before Christmas, he had behaved rather strangely, not inviting her for a drink, dashing off with the excuse that he was fearfully busy. Yet later she'd seen him propping up the bar with a coven of Communist cronies. Although Sandy had always protested Anne was the only woman in the world for him, seeing she'd ditched him, there was absolutely no reason why he should not marry somebody else.

Yet to choose her little sister!

Kate's marrying Sandy was, even on brief reflection, par for the course. The roots of her action lay in sibling rivalry. She had never been able to keep her velvet paws with their sheathed claws off anything that is, or was, mine, Anne thought. Con married young and Kate never could bear to be left behind. While Sandy was not the eldest son and heir to Melkeith, he was a well-heeled sprig of the Scottish aristocracy, he was one of the young Turks of the BBC, and Kate believed his social and theatrical contacts would be useful in her career. It was doubtful that the matter of loving Sandy entered the equation, though honestly Kate was able to convince herself of anything at any given moment.

In the light of the flames, Kate's green eyes were regarding Anne even more anxiously, flashing the message: please stroke my fur and say I'm a nice pussy-cat really, even if I have just dumped a dead rat at your feet. Anne decided that unless it was a truly important matter, being angry with Kate was a waste of time. After saying the news had come as something of a shock and either Kate or Sandy might have forewarned her, she wished her sister every happiness. Kate kissed her affectionately and, that matter settled, she prattled about not having a long engagement but marrying soon after she'd finished her part in the film, and her and Sandy's intention of leasing a *pied à terre* in Mayfair and buying a country house somewhere in Kent, nice and near to Mummy and Chenneys.

Then Kate said, 'Will you be one of my bridesmaids, darling?'

'No,' Anne replied, thinking there's a limit to everything and you've just overstepped it, sister mine.

'Oh.' Kate pouted but she didn't press the issue.

In the following months Anne continued to work and play frenetically hard. Perhaps to prove she was an emancipated woman and if men could use and discard her, she could do the same to them, on three separate occasions she went back to their flats with men she met at parties and made love with them. Two of the young men she already vaguely knew but the third was a complete stranger. All three came from upper-class backgrounds and were as unlike her father and Ben as they possibly could be, which may have proved something else, but apart from feeling desperately miserable and sexually frustrated, Anne was never sure of her motives. In any case, after the third bout she decided she simply hadn't the temperament to treat sexual love as a physical need like quenching one's thirst or going to the lavatory. Until such time as she could stop yearning for Ben and met another man she truly cared for, hard work and celibacy were the solutions for her.

Travel, Anne thought, might provide another answer and this might be the appropriate moment to visit Aunty Sarah, Uncle Misha and Tamara in Russia. But her aunt's response to the letter suggesting the idea was guarded to say the least.

The Communists were holding 'treason trials' in Moscow, the traitorous activities including plotting with bourgeois imperialists to overthrow the government of the USSR. Among the accused were several of Uncle Misha's old Bolshevik colleagues, and presumably Aunty Sarah considered the arrival of his English niece-by-marriage might jeopardise his own position. Though surely Comrade Stalin could never indict so famous and well-loved a figure as Mikhail Muranov?

In the spring Anne's mother enquired if the brighter weather had improved her spirits and whether she had recovered from the effects of Ben Broughton's behaviour? Ruefully she said, 'Not really, no.'

'But you have got over the shock of Kate marrying Sandy Dalziel?'

'Absolutely, totally and utterly,' Anne replied, which was true.

The marriage was solemnised at Chenneys early in June. In a wedding gown designed by Theo Marvell in Elizabethan style, with a jewel-encrusted Juliet cap holding her veil in place, Kate looked ravishingly beautiful. Having chosen to marry in his full Scottish gear, kilt, velvet jacket and lace ruffles, Sandy didn't look bad either. The Whitworth/Marchal family were always newsworthy and with her first film recently released and the plaudits lavished on its beautiful ingénue, Kate's marriage to the Honourable A. J. I. Dalziel of BBC fame was particularly so. The happy couple emerged from the Norman church in Marshall Minnis to a large crowd of well-wishers and sightseers, an explosion of flash guns and an unseemly barrage of photographers' and reporters' cries: 'Look up at your husband, please, Mrs Dalziel', 'Give us another smile like that, Katie!', 'May we have a family group, Sir Philip?'

Sir Philip was not amused, or at least not until Lady Marchal developed the giggles. The mob was not of course allowed to the reception, only a couple of well-behaved agency photographers being permitted to circulate among the guests.

It was one of Chenney's enchanted afternoons, the gardens in their early summer glory, the scent of the roses heady, a slight heat haze shimmering over the lake and lawns. By the side of the lake, where Kate had first appeared in her husband's production of *Comus*, Anne had a brief conversation with Sandy, who said, 'Do you know one of the reasons I fell in love with darling nutkin?' Which was his pet name for Kate. 'She's so like you in so many ways.'

Oh, is she? Anne thought. I don't regard that as a compliment. Smiling sweetly at Sandy, she said, 'I'm sure you and Kate were made for each other.'

When the moment came to wave the newlyweds off to Folkestone en route for their honeymoon in Venice, everybody crowded round the Silver Ghost, its bonnet suitably draped by Mark with 'Just Hitched' and 'Don't do anything I wouldn't do' banners, tin cans and old boots tied to its rear. Anne suspected that Kate and Sandy had reserved their passion for their wedding night. Apart from the fact that she never gave until she'd got what she wanted, to go to her marriage bed virginally pure would please a certain romanticism in her little sister. To use the phrase Ben had hurled at her – oh Ben, where are you? why have you deserted me? – Anne also suspected Kate was a randy little bitch. Her nuptials could therefore prove a severe disappointment. Or maybe, Anne thought maliciously, Sandy would rise to the occasion more auspiciously than he had done with her.

14

Julian was of course among the wedding guests, as was Rebecca, who had been Anne's companion on the way down, but she was travelling to a Zionist conference in Holland. Anne therefore offered Julian a lift back to London which he accepted. It was a beautiful evening as they bowled along the Kent lanes, the blossom in the orchards luminous in the golden evening light, the wind soft on their faces as Bill climbed stoutly up Wrotham Hill. Julian enquired how *Murder in High Places* was progressing (the title of Anne's fourth Seth

Pollard novel had a double edge, the murder taking place on the summit of Helvellyn, the characters coming from the upper ranks of society).

Anne replied, 'Slowly. I've had rather a lot on my mind.' Julian was aware of her liaisons with both Sandy and Ben and made a sympathetic noise. 'But it is progressing. And I've decided to marry Seth and Lady Helena off.'

'That's not in the synopsis,' her agent said swiftly and, as usual when talking shop, without stammering. 'And is it a good idea? Better surely to keep your readers on tenterhooks. Will they-won't they get married?'

'I think *Murder in High Places* is going to be my last Seth Pollard book, so it seems a good idea to tie things up neatly.'

'What on earth do you mean?' Julian said in a tone of utter astonishment. 'Your last Seth Pollard book?'

'I'm bored with him and Lady Helena. And with inventing fiendish plots. And with the limitations of the detective novel.'

'Oh really, Anne! How wilful and contrary can you be? You've spent the last few years complaining bitterly, and in my opinion rightly, that your books have failed to gain the recognition they deserve. For the snobbish reason that you've chosen to write detective stories for a popular market. Just when your talent and your originality have begun to be recognised – not to mention the rapid rise in your sales – you calmly inform me you're thinking of giving up.' Emphatically Julian repeated, 'Oh really, Anne!'

Ironically, *And Hideous Things Were Done* which had caused her so much trouble, entailing so much reshaping and rewriting, had recently been published to a glowing set of reviews. Anne had been particularly chuffed when Siegfried Sassoon, to whom she'd sent a signed copy, had written back to say how much he had enjoyed reading the book. As its plot concerned not only vengeance but reconciliation, she had asked Mr Sassoon's permission to use the lines from his poem *Reconciliation* for her title.

Perhaps she was being perverse, Anne thought, but having belatedly achieved some of the recognition she'd sought, she wanted to enter fresh woods and pastures new. Or was her restless desire to chart new territory connected with Ben's disappearance from her life? Starting a clean sheet and all that? At least she had one thing to thank Mr Broughton for. If she had originally created Seth Pollard in her father's image, that ghost had been exorcised. Although she would love Daddy to her dying day, she was no longer obsessed by his memory.

In the gathering dusk Anne drove past the cosy suburban villas of Eltham and into the mean streets of the Old Kent Road. They crossed London Bridge with the filthiness of the River Thames hidden by the blanket of the night and the reflection of the lights dancing prettily on its surface. All the while, gently but remorselessly, Julian went on telling her she was being more than perverse, she was being stupid.

'Having broken new ground for the detective novel, it'd be a crime to abandon it.'

'Ho, ho,' Anne said as she swung Bill into Cannon Street.

'The pun was intentional. What about your readers? All those thousands of people to whom you've given not only a great deal of pleasure, but whose horizons you've extended? I seem to remember you telling me one of your reasons for writing detective stories was . . .'

'You are a persistent Percy!'

'Though I say it myself, that's what makes me a good literary agent.'

Anne laughed. 'All right, all right. You've convinced me I should think again. I'll see how I feel about things when I've finished *Murder in High Places.*'

'Good.'

When they reached Gower Street, her spirits raised by the discussion with Julian and the evidence of how very determined he could be, Anne said, 'I brought a bottle of champagne back with me. There was loads over. Do you feel like popping another cork?'

Slightly to her surprise because he wasn't a night-owl, nor a great drinker, and certainly not a womaniser, Julian accepted the invitation. Between them they drank the bottle of Bollinger and around midnight Anne collapsed happily on to the sofa. Kicking off her shoes, paddling the folds of her long dress with her legs, waving the sleeves above her head, she carolled, 'It's been a delightful day, a de-lovely evening and I feel delicious. But I don't think I'm in a fit state to drive you home, Mr Kendle, so you'll have to get a taxi.'

'I'm in a s-similar s-state myself,' Julian confessed, making no move to telephone the taxi rank but uncharacteristically settling himself on the floor by the sofa. After a companionable silence he said, 'Anne, m–may I t-talk to you?'

'Of course.' She ruffled the centre parting of his smooth brown hair and was surprised when he didn't pull his head away. 'What are friends for?'

'That's w-what I w-want t-to t-talk about. Our f-f-f-friendship.' Anne turned her head on the cushion, regarding the stuttering Julian with an owlish curiosity. He stared fixedly at the rose-patterned carpet before taking a very deep breath and speaking ultra-carefully in the effort not to stammer. 'You know how much I've always liked and admired you, Anne. I've always been attracted by you too, and you may have wondered why I never made any approaches. I think you're at a c-crossroads in your life, Anne, otherwise, happily squiffy or not, I wouldn't dream of speaking like this. I know I'm at a crossroads in mine. I shall be thirty-one next month and I have n-never made love to a w-woman.'

It was on the tip of Anne's tongue to say, What about a man? But she resisted the temptation. Astonished by the admission rather than by the failure itself, she pulled herself into a semi-sitting position on the sofa and gave Julian her full attention as, still staring at the carpet, he said, 'I'm going to tell you things I've n-never told anybody. They concern my m-mother whom I know you don't like, and she is a difficult woman, but my father treated her very badly. I'm sure that ex-exacerbated her emotional problems.'

From what Anne's mother had told her and from her own memories of Uncle Guy, there were two sides to that story. But Anne again held her tongue because Julian was obviously having immense difficulty in unburdening his soul, while trying to curb the wretched stammer induced by emotion. He told her that for as far back as he could remember, from time to time his mother would come into his bedroom when she thought he was asleep, to fondle and to kiss him. Julian said that as a child he'd found it baffling and upsetting because if he so much as touched his mother, she drew away from him and told him not to be a baby.

Then, speaking even more slowly and carefully, Julian said, 'I was thirteen when my father was killed, you know, and after that it was much w-worse. For about eighteen months, every night during the holidays when I was home from boarding school, my m-mother came into my bedroom. I would l-lie there sometimes until midnight, pretending to be asleep, d-dreading her entry, but knowing she would c-come. I grew to h-hate the touch of her fingers on my face, the feel of her lips b-brushing my skin, but above all I h-hated her smell. I don't mean she stank. My m-mother's fastidiously clean.'

Julian laughed slightly before continuing, 'It was her f-female body scent that overwhelmed me. I felt as if I w-were being chloroformed and I wanted to vomit. Just when I thought I c-couldn't stand it any longer, she stopped c-coming. Perhaps she realised I wasn't always asleep. Anyway, she's never entered my room or t-touched me since. But for a time I almost h-hated her. Later I realised it was the only way she could show her affection and how much she really l-loved me.'

Anne wanted to say 'Bollocks', a swear word she secretly cherished but never used publicly. She'd realised Mrs Kendle was a jealous, possessive mother but for what she had done to her son, she should be made to crawl on her hands and knees to all the Stations of the Cross, or whatever penance the Catholic Church imposed on its sinners, though on second thoughts her twisted, self-martyred soul would probably enjoy that. And Julian was now saying, 'You see, Anne, I haven't been able to overcome the r-revulsion for the female body my mother unwittingly instilled in me. Yet I want to m-marry, I want to have children, I want to m-make love to . . .'

'Me?'

'Yes.'

For the first time since starting to speak, Julian lifted his head. The beautiful brown eyes blinked at Anne, who suddenly remembered the drive to Le Cateau and said, 'Are you short-sighted?'

His eyes widening in astonishment, he replied, 'Yes. Why? D-does it affect your f-feelings towards . . .'

'No, no, no.' With a laugh, thinking, I bet it's your mother who disapproves of your wearing spectacles, even if you do need them, Anne stretched herself sinuously on the sofa and said, 'Let's make love.'

She waited about half a minute for Julian to move on to the sofa, or at least to kiss her, before realising this was a situation in which she would have to take the initiative. As if to underline the point, he murmured, 'I'm a t-total n-novice, Anne, I-I . . .'

Gently she took his face in her hands and gently she kissed him. She couldn't say Julian responded with anything that might be called passion but he did finish up with his arms round her, holding her quite tightly. Disengaging herself, examining him to see if her female scent was making him want to vomit – no, he didn't look sick, only nervous – banishing from her mind Ben's comments on the perfume of her body, Anne said gently, 'Shall we go to bed?' As he nodded, she added, 'You'll have to excuse me for a moment. Precautions you know.'

'Oh yes.' Julian blushed. 'Yes, of course.'

When she returned from the bathroom Anne held out her hand and led him into her bedroom. There she undressed without flaunting her body or looking at him, but once she had discarded her clothes she turned to face him. He had taken off the morning suit, waistcoat and starched shirt he'd worn for Kate's wedding, placed them neatly on a chair, and he was standing in his vest and underpants, with the suspenders round his calves still holding up his socks. Slowly Anne walked towards him, while Julian stared at her naked-ness like a weasel transfixed by a stoat, except he was far better looking than a weasel. She had heard that some couples never saw each other's naked bodies, which seemed to Anne extraordinary, but if Julian was going to be her lover he would have to get used to the sight of hers.

Approaching him, she smiled and tugged at his vest. His smile at its most deprecatory, he helped get rid of that garment, and Anne stroked the skin of his chest which was hairlessly, silkily smooth. Pausing again to make sure he wasn't recoiling in disgust from the touch of her fingers – no, he was still smiling faintly – she knelt to undo his suspenders, whereupon Julian bent down to pull off his socks which, with an air of bravado, he tossed into the air, allowing them to fall on to the carpet.

That left him in his underpants.

When they were both standing upright again, Anne started to undo the buttons and, the bottom one freed, the underpants slid to Julian's ankles. With an elegant movement of each leg he stepped out of them, whilst Anne stepped back to survey him. She could hear Sandy saying, 'It's not Kendle's clever mind H.V.X. is interested in, it's his beautiful body', or words to that effect. Julian was a young Apollo, the only flaw being his penis which was dangling limply like a piece of chewed gum.

The champagne and the thought of making love after several months' celibacy to a man who had always attracted her, had already roused Anne and the taste of his lips, the feel of his skin, the sight of his body, had increased her desire but she told herself: don't rush things, Whitworth, softly does it. To prove she was on the right lines, Julian actually said, 'You're beautiful, Anne,' and his voice was breathy, though that could be from sheer nerves.

She said, 'Would you like the light off?'

'Not if you wouldn't.'

Anne switched on the bedside lamp before switching off the centre light, and they both climbed into her bed. The warmth of Julian's body against hers strengthened her desire but she could feel him trembling and with the utmost difficulty she stopped herself doing the things she'd done with Ben, or with those dispiriting one-night stands, or even with Sandy come to that. As unvoraciously as she could, Anne twined her legs round Julian's, she stroked those limp private parts, and she kept saying, 'Relax, Julian, relax. I won't overwhelm you.'

Slowly he began to respond, kissing her, touching her breasts, sliding himself on top of her and panting. 'Anne, oh Anne, I do want to love you.' She felt his tumescence and eventually he was stiff enough for her hands to guide him inside her, but Anne could not then prevent her own body reacting, nor her voice from saying, 'That's it, Julian, keep going, my darling.'

Only he couldn't. After far too short a while he subsided. Rolling off her, burying his face in the pillow so that his voice was muffled, Julian said, 'I'm sorry, Anne, I'm sorry, I'm sorry.'

Breathing deeply to counteract her intense frustration, Anne replied, 'Don't worry. Lots of people don't succeed the first time.' Then she realised the bed was shaking and she turned to look at Julian. 'You're not crying, are you?' His face still in the pillow, he shook his head, but he was. 'Oh Julian, don't. It doesn't matter. Honestly it doesn't.' Anne felt like Kate as she said those last words. She asked, 'Would you like a cigarette?'

'Please.'

When Julian had recovered his composure and they were sitting like any old married couple, propped against the pillows smoking, Anne said, 'Did you find it awful?'

'No. I just wasn't very good at it. Was I?'

'Oh well, practice makes perfect. Somebody once told me love-making is an art that has to be learned like any other. Why human beings should imagine it's as easy as falling off a log was, he said, beyond his comprehension.'

The somebody had of course been Ben, commenting on his good fortune in having had an excellent tutor. 'Who was she?' 'Does it matter?' 'No, but I'm curious.' 'Women always are. If you must know, she was my Sunday School teacher', which had made Anne laugh, though Ben had added, 'She didn't seduce me until some time after I'd left her class.'

And she must stop thinking about Ben, Anne told herself. To Julian she said, 'Do you want to try again? Not now,' she added hastily, seeing the expression on his face, 'but some time?'

'Please.'

It had been very slow, heavy going, rather like driving Bill across muddy fields, Anne thought, all the time wondering if, when, they were going to get stuck. But Julian's piteous desire to overcome his revulsion, do the right thing and be a good lover, had stirred her tenderest feelings. Lighting another cigarette, Anne thought of Sandy asking if she saw it as another of her noble duties to rescue Kendle from himself and Ben saying she could go off with her nancy-boy. The answer to Sandy's snide query was now yes, except it would be a pleasure, not a duty, to help Julian conquer his mother-induced sexual fears so that – sucks to Ben – there was no longer any question of his being a nancy-boy.

A few weeks later Anne was walking down Bond Street when she saw the painting in the art gallery window. To say she stopped dead in her tracks and her heart ceased to beat, were only slight exaggerations. For the large canvas, displayed to maximum effect in a modern light-coloured frame against a backcloth of dark green velvet, was one of Ben's industrial Lancashire scenes. The gallery was owned by Derek Elmar-Smythe who was a friend of Theo Marvell's, an ex-boy friend, Anne suspected, though it was difficult to keep track of Theo's amours. Having recovered from her shock, she therefore marched straight inside.

Fortunately, Derek happened to be in the main body of the gallery, immaculately dressed in a charcoal-grey suit and waistcoat, gold cufflinks gleaming, blond hair sleek. Anne presumed this was his successful gallery owner *persona* because the last time she'd seen him with Theo, he'd been a tousled-haired lad in an open-necked shirt. Holding out his arms Derek glided towards Anne and having embraced her effusively, he said, 'Dear heart, how utterly divine to see you, looking too mouth-wateringly delectable for words. Nobody would suspect you're the authoress of such blood-curdling stories. Mine positively froze at times while I was reading *And Hideous Things Were Done*. To what do I owe the honour and pleasure of this visit?'

'Where did you get the painting in the window?' Anne couldn't be bothered pussyfooting around.

'Ah, I knew you would have eyes for the too fascinatingly, disturbingly original, dear heart.'

'Thank you, but where did you get the painting?'

'That's a long boring story. The artist is a simply frightful Scot who . . .'

'Scot!' Anne exclaimed. 'He came from Lancashire when I knew him.'

'You know him, dear heart?' Derek's baby-blue eyes gave her a sharp glance. 'Perhaps you can persuade our talented monster to let me exhibit his paintings then. He says he's not ready yet. Did you ever hear the like? I mean, here am I offering him an exhibition in Bond Street and . . .'

'Why do you think he's Scottish?'

'He lives on some remote Hebridean rock, he has this ghastly accent and he's a surly brute, so naturally I thought he was a Scot.'

'You've met him then?'

'He condescended to pay me a visit last week.'

'Last week. You mean here in London?'

'Sheep and heather, screaming gulls and swirling mists, are not my cup of tea, dear heart. Though having been shown several of his paintings, I would have made the hideous journey if absolutely necessary. Our ungracious Mr Brough-ton is your genuinely, stubbornly, original creative artist.'

'Yes.'

The mystery of Ben's whereabouts over the last ten months was solved. Presumably he'd found somebody to loan him a cottage on some remote Hebridean island, where he could paint without distraction. But the thought that he had been, still was for all Anne knew, in London, without so much as saying 'Hello' for auld lang syne, made her sick at heart. She heard the sharp businessman in Derek saying, 'At the moment Sir's painting is a real bargain. It may take time for him to become established because what he has to offer is so utterly different and the peasants are too devastatingly conservative. Apart from its artistic value, I feel sure an early B. D. Broughton will prove to be a marvellous long-term invest-ment. Are you interested in buying, dear heart?'

Was she? Anne damned B. D. Broughton to all eternity as she said, 'Yes.'

Not having expected to buy a painting, she had not driven into the West End this morning but wanting to resavour Ben's work, she rejected Derek's offer of prompt delivery and returned to Gower Street by taxi, clutching the wrapped canvas. The taxi driver was unusually unhelpful, refusing to carry the painting to their third-floor flat, so Anne mounted the stairs with the bulky package under her arm.

161

When she reached their landing, she saw Ben sitting on the floor outside their front door, his legs stretched in front of him, his arms folded over his chest, his eyes closed. In her disbelieving astonishment, Anne dropped the painting to the floor and at the noise he opened his eyes. Standing stockstill, she stared at him across the landing. Slowly he climbed to his feet and said, 'Hello. I was just about to give up and call it a day.'

Her emotions as tangled as a briar patch, quite incapable of speech, Anne just went on staring at Ben as lazily he picked up the fallen parcel. His eyes, those entrancing, sexy grey eyes with their apparently mascara-brushed lashes, smiled slightly as he said, 'Been buying a picture?'

Derek had insisted on the painting being properly packaged and wrapped in his fancy silver paper which had 'Carillon Gallery, Bond Street, London W1' printed all over it in an italic script, so it wasn't difficult to put two and two together. Feeling herself at a crushing disadvantage but finding her voice, Anne said, 'Yes, it's one of yours. I bought it from Derek Elmar-Smythe.'

'How is she?'

'Greatly admiring of your work.'

'Are you going to invite me in?'

'Why should I?'

'No reason. Except I fled to escape you, Anne, which I reckoned would be best for both of us. And here I am.'

Anne wanted to cry out, 'Oh Ben', and fling herself into his arms but she had a few tattered remnants of pride left so she strode towards the front door. With difficulty, because her hands were trembling, she found her key and inserted it in the lock. Over her shoulder she said, 'Come in then.'

It was while she was bustling round the kitchen, having insisted on making a cup of tea, that Ben came up behind her and slid his arms round her waist. Loudly Anne said, 'Don't.'

Ignoring her request and her feeble struggles, he swung her round. Giving her his sunburst smile, cupping her face in those strong stubby fingers, he kissed her and after that there was no point either her body or mind struggling against him. They stripped off in the kitchen and made love as they stood. Later, prancing around in the nude, Anne brewed the tea which they took into her bedroom, where they soon made love again. After they had respent themselves, lying in Ben's arms smoking, Anne felt too utterly, devastatingly, delectably happy for words, as Derek might say, or at least her body did. Putting out her cigarette, she rested her elbows on Ben's damp chest and looking straight into his grey eyes, she said, 'Right, Mr Broughton, you have some explaining to do.'

'I've explained.'

'If you think "I fled to escape you, but here I am" is sufficient explanation for walking out on me in Le Cateau, staying totally silent for ten months . . .'

'I sent you the painting for last Armistice Day.'

'Oh yes, so you did. Thank you. But if you think that was enough, you can think again.'

'Look, Anne,' Ben swung his right forefinger backwards and forwards like a pendulum, touching her still-extended nipples as he spoke, 'I've never . . .'

'Don't do that.' She rolled off his chest and snuggled against his side. 'Not at the moment, anyway. I want to talk to you.'

'I've never been able to abide post-mortems. I told you in Dorset you'd bewitched me and I couldn't live without you. In Le Cateau, for various reasons, I decided to try to break the spell. I've discovered I can't.'

'I see. How did you know I'd take you back, after all the anguish you've caused me?'

'I didn't. I do now.'

Anne hit him hard, an admonition he received passively, before she said, 'Do you expect me to live on some remote Hebridean island?'

'Hebridean?' Ben said. 'I've been living in the Shetlands.'

Anne started to laugh. 'Oh well, they'd all be the same to Derek. Shetlands, Orkneys, Hebrides. I expect he imagines they're somewhere off the coast of Lancashire. If he knows where that is. You can at least tell me how you came to go to the Shetlands, what you've painted there, and whether you're intending to go back.'

'The answer to the last question is no.'

They were still lying in bed talking when the front door slammed. 'Oh hell.' Anne glanced at her alarm clock. 'I didn't realise it was that time. It's Rebecca.'

Hastily she flung on a pair of slacks and a blouse, brushed her hair, and sauntered into the living room. Rebecca was slumped in the armchair and as Anne came in she said, 'What a day! Thank heaven it's the Bank Holiday weekend! If anybody else relates Mr Weizmann's picturesque metaphors about the Balfour Declaration providing an easy birth for the Jewish Homeland, the birth-pangs coming later, and our now being at the Bar Mitzvah stage, dearly as I love Chaim Weizmann, I shall scream.'

'Sorry you've had a bad day,' Anne said sympathetically before taking a deep breath and saying, 'Rebecca, Ben's here. He's in my bed actually.'

Rebecca looked up at her and said, 'You're a bloody fool. And what about Julian?'

15

There was nothing Anne could immediately do about Julian because he had already gone north to Ryby Hall to spend the Bank Holiday with his mother. She therefore did her best to put him from her mind which, with Rebecca's pre-arranged visit to a friend giving her and Ben three days to themselves, proved not too difficult a feat. First thing on the Tuesday morning, however, while Ben was in the bathroom shaving, Anne rang Julian's London number but there was no reply. Waiting until Ben had gone out to buy some brushes – she didn't want him to know anything about Julian – she rang the Clarges Street office but she was put through to Julian's personal secretary who said, 'I'm terribly sorry, Miss Whitworth, but Mr Kendle hasn't returned from Lancashire. He's telephoned to say his mother is unwell.' Surprise, surprise, Anne thought. 'Is there anything I can do to help?'

'Not really, no. Will you ask Mr Kendle to ring me the minute he returns, please.'

It wasn't until the following Monday that he did, which unsettled Anne considerably because she wanted to get the ghastly business over and done with. Moreover Rebecca wasn't at all keen on Ben's staying at the Gower Street flat and he was impatient to leave London. Over the telephone Julian's voice sounded so friendly and obviously unsuspecting that anything was amiss, Anne really felt as if her heart were sinking into her shoes. After she'd enquired how his mother was and he'd replied, much better, thank you, she said she wanted to see him urgently. Julian said how urgently because he was frightfully busy catching up after his unexpected absence. Anne said very urgently and it was agreed they would meet in the office at four-thirty.

When Anne entered the inner sanctum she noticed several copies of Doctor Martindale's biography of Queen Elizabeth sitting on Julian's desk. Working at a much slower, more academic pace than Anne, his book had only recently been published, to high praise and a literary award. Looking at the copies made her think of H.V.X.'s secret homosexuality and she felt even more wretched, for though on one occasion Julian had actually managed to finish, what she was about to tell him would doubtfully assist his endeavours to sort out his sexual problems.

Julian smiled, offered her a cup of tea which Anne politely refused, and a cigarette which she accepted. Once they were sitting down puffing away, he tilted his head to one side queryingly. It was a gesture inherited from his father who'd had a similarly long, slender neck. She had to stop her thoughts wandering, Anne told herself, and concentrate on the matter in hand.

'Julian, something's happened. Ben Broughton's come back into my life and . . .' her voice sounded alarmingly high-pitched and Anne tried to soften and lower it as she continued, '. . . and I'm going to live with him. We're driving up to Lancashire to look for a cottage on the moors. I'm sorry, Julian. You can't know how sorry I am and how dreadful I feel about you . . .'

Anne's voice tailed away and there was what seemed to her an interminable silence, during which she looked anxiously at Julian, trying to assess his reactions, while with an expressionless face he gazed at the tropical fish in the tank. Eventually he said, 'I see. Thank you for coming to tell me in person before driving off.'

'Oh Julian, I know it's feeble to say I couldn't help myself but . . .'

'You don't have to explain your emotions towards him, Anne. I've seen the two of you together. I only hope he treats you better this time than he did last. And I'm sorry that what seemed to me a happily developing relationship between us, should have been of such short duration. How long is it since Kate's wedding? Eight weeks?' His eyes swivelled from their survey of the fish to look directly at Anne, who wished she could disappear under the thick pile of the carpet. It was Julian who was in control of the situation, not she, his voice cool, not a stammer to be heard. Rightly, he was angry with her and that emotion appeared to be overcoming shock or hurt. He said, 'Have you told your mother of your decision?' Anne nodded. 'What does she feel about it?'

Having been told about Anne's deepening relationship with Julian, her mother had been pretty cross and had said, 'Oh Anne, you really must stop getting yourself, and dragging other people, into these emotional messes.' Later, being the marvellous mother she was, she'd said, 'You're nearly twenty-six which isn't a vast age but it's too old for me to start smacking your bottom. I don't know what you're going to say to poor Julian, nor how he's going to take it, but so long as you're now clear Ben isn't Daddy and the two of you understand what sort of future you're letting yourselves in for, I can only hope his wife will eventually divorce him and you may settle down.'

To Julian, Anne replied, 'Well, Mummy wasn't exactly pleased. But I think she feels I'm a big girl now and it's up to me to shape my own life, for better or for worse.'

'I see,' Julian again said, though he didn't sound as if he agreed with her mother's liberal viewpoint. After a pause he went on, 'I take it you will not be accompanying me to the United States?' Miserably Anne shook her head. 'Pity. Only this morning I was discussing the offer of a most interesting and lucrative lecture tour for you.'

'Would you like me to find another literary agent?'

'Not unless you're dissatisfied with my services.' This time she shook her head vigorously to show she was more than happy with them. 'You'll let me have your address once you've found your cottage in Lancashire.'

Julian rose to his feet, indicating he'd said all he had to say. Anne blurted out, 'Was I any help to you? You know in . . .'

'Oh yes.' With scathing politeness he added, 'Thank you.'

'You know I won't ever tell anybody . . .' by which she meant Ben, in case Julian was worried about bedtime confidences, '. . . anything.'

'Really, Anne, I wouldn't expect you to.'

There were times when he sounded just like his mother.

The next day Anne rushed up to Scotland to see Con's newborn baby and her new house. The latter had been bequeathed to Gavin, fully furnished in grand Edwardian style, by a recently deceased childless aunt whose favourite nephew he had been. It stood in acres of ground on the lower slopes of Ben-y-Vrackie, overlooking the sleepy Perthshire town of Pitlochry. Having inspected it, Anne said, 'It's a nice little pad.'

Propped up in the king-sized bed with its solid mahogany head and foot boards, Con laughed. 'One of Daddy's political platforms was rectifying the injustice of "To those who have shall be given, from those who have not shall be taken", wasn't it? I suppose in theory we should give it away, but we haven't got a house in the UK, Gavin will shortly be doing a spell at the Foreign Office and with two small children I need a base. Thus do we justify our actions!'

With a wry smile Anne crossed to the bedside, to take another look at the latest addition to the Campbell-Ross family who was fast asleep in his cradle. She asked, 'Were you disappointed to have another boy?'

'Not really. We can hope for a girl next time.'

How many children was her sister intending to have? Anne wondered. She said, 'What are you going to call him?'

'Gavin suggested "Hamish" but when I told Doctor McKenzie, he said, "Our old dog was called Hamish. Got the mange. Had to be put down. No, Robert's the name for this wee laddie." After that, I felt Robert it had to be!'

They both laughed and Con said, 'You're looking much

happier, Anne. I do hope things work out for you and Ben.'

Anne said she was sure they would.

She drove from Perthshire to Lancashire where she met Ben and within days they had found the ideal house. It stood at the end of a track leading up from the remote village of Slattocks, with the high moors rearing behind; it was called Rowan Tree Cottage – there was a fully grown rowan, or mountain ash, in the garden; it was solidly built in the local stone, compact yet spacious; it faced due south so when the sun shone it was filled with light, and from the front there was a splendid view over the Pennine hills towards the crags of Netherstone Edge. There was of course neither gas nor electricity in the village but Rowan Tree Cottage's owner had started to renovate before shortage of cash forced him to stop, and he was only too delighted to rent the property to recoup his losses.

Anne liked the house and its view just as much as Con's and before the end of August she had signed a year's lease. Fittingly, they took possession of Rowan Tree Cottage on her twenty-sixth birthday. Madge Kearsley came up from Mellordale to help give the place a thorough clean, Ben humped the furniture Anne had bought, only growing tetchy when she kept changing her mind about where she wanted certain pieces. After Madge had returned home, Anne enjoyed herself in the role of housewife in what, after all, was their first real home (the cottage in Dorset didn't count). She drove into Blackburn to shop – though she had to admit not too many housewives owned MGs, or cars of any sort – she read recipe books and wondered whether she could make jam from the laden plum tree outside the kitchen window. Ben said if she'd keep still for more than two seconds, he'd do what she'd been asking him to do ever since they'd met, paint her portrait. Delighted, Anne agreed to start sitting still tomorrow morning.

They rarely listened to the radio in the mornings, Anne preferring to make breakfast in silence and peruse her post while she ate it, Ben to read the *Manchester Guardian*. But on the morning of the 16th of September, after he'd read the inside lead page, in a sombre voice he said, 'You'd better have a look at this.'

Unbelievingly, Anne read that on the previous day, from

the city of Nuremberg which the Nazis had turned into their domain, Adolf Hitler had promulgated laws for 'the Protection of German Blood and German Honour'. Under the first Nuremberg Law, German citizenship belonged only to those of German or kindred blood, while under the second Law Jews were defined as possessing neither German nor kindred blood, whatever that meant. Lower down the list, Jews were forbidden to marry or to have sexual relations with German citizens and, ludicrously it seemed to Anne, to fly the German flag.

Throwing the newspaper down, she said, 'This means all their rights have been taken away from them and German Jews have become non-persons in their own country. Herr Hitler can't do that to any group of citizens.'

'He's done it.'

'He's got to be made to undo it.'

'How? Other than by the force you won't condone. There's nobody left in Germany'll do it.' Across the breakfast table Ben's grey eyes looked steadily at her. Anne thought of Count and Countess von Krannhals and almost certainly he was right. 'And world opinion isn't going to change Adolf Hitler's warped mind.'

Despite the widespread condemnation of the shameful Nuremberg Laws which had taken Germany back into the Dark Ages, it appeared that Ben was right about that too. Except Anne could not, would not, believe that force was the answer.

At the end of the week, she said, 'I think I ought to go to Frankfurt to see the Wolffs. Temporarily at least, I think they should leave Germany.'

'Yeah, I thought you might.'

'Do you want to come with me?'

Ben shook his head, 'I'll get on with my painting. Give the old doctor and his missus my regards, though.'

Anne stopped off in London to see Rebecca who couldn't accompany her to Frankfurt because of prior commitments. She had kept the Gower Street flat as her London base and knowing that her friend earned a far from princely sum at the Jewish Agency, Anne was continuing to pay her share of expenses. They sat up talking half the night and Rebecca said,

'The Nuremberg Laws are quite unbelievable. I suppose the best thing I can do is to fight even harder for our Homeland in Palestine. Once we have that, things must change for the better.'

Anne said she sincerely hoped so. In the morning Rebecca hugged her and said, 'Bless you for going. And good luck with your mission.'

As Anne drove through the centre of Frankfurt in Bill – she had deliberately chosen to return in her desecrated MG and if anything happened this time she would play merry hell – the buildings were ablaze with Nazi flags, the streets filled with groups of *Hitlerjugend*, boys and girls constantly raising their hands in the Nazi salute, and the air of excitement was almost tangible. When she arrived in Westend the streets were leafily peaceful and free of swastikas, though if Jews were banned from flying German flags, whether or not they wanted to, they obviously would be. The minute Anne entered the Wolffs' house, despite or perhaps because of the warmth of her greeting, she was conscious of the strained atmosphere. Even ebullient little Helga was subdued and the Aryan members of the staff, including Gretchen, had left.

Anne asked Kurt what all the flags were for and why all the excitement? He replied, 'The Reich Chancellor himself, Adolf Hitler in person, is due to open the newly constructed Reichsautobahn between Frankfurt and Darmstadt tomorrow.'

'Oh.' The enthusiasm with which Frankfurters were reacting to his visit underlined their acceptance of the Nuremberg Laws.

In the evening, once Herr Doktor and Frau Wolff and Luise had retired, Anne and Kurt sat in the lounge. She said, 'What's happened, Kurt? I thought you said things had improved.'

'They had. It depends which sector of the SS or the Nazi party at large is currently enjoying the Führer's favour. Whether it's the faction that believes Jews should be kept firmly in their place at the bottom of the heap but utilised for their talents. Or the faction to which Helmut Ohlendorf belongs, which believes we should be shipped off to Palestine. Or the out-and-out Jew-baiting, Jew-hating faction responsible for the Nuremberg Laws.'

'They're monstrous. You can't go on living on an unpredictable see-saw. And where's it going to end up?'

'God alone knows,' Kurt smiled wryly, though behind his spectacles his eyes were unsmiling. 'I say that as a Jew who long ago lost his faith.'

Anne said briskly, 'As non-Zionists, none of you wants to go and live in Palestine. I'm not sure Rebecca herself actually wants to live there. But I think you should come to England. Rebecca knows the ropes about immigration permits and if you need extra guarantors, I or my family will willingly stand them.'

'Thank you, Anne.'

'Are you going to apply for permits?' Her mind was already busy with plans for settling the Wolffs into England.

'No. And before you demand "Why not?", with your dear English forthrightness, let me tell you that Luise is being wooed by a Dutch diamond merchant. Mr van Doncke is a nice, if unexciting man. Wealthy, Jewish, willing to marry a divorced woman with two children and offer them safety and security in Holland. I think Luise will accept his offer of marriage for Helga and Herta's sake as much as her own. The little ones can't understand what's happening. The other day, Helga asked me, "Why am I a dirty Jewess, Uncle Kurt?" Why indeed should that be said to a lovely, lively six-year-old?'

'What did you tell her?'

'Oh, I sought refuge in our special relationship with God which makes others jealous of us. Helga's intelligence already understands that jealousy makes people do stupid things.' Kurt offered Anne another cigarette. He was smoking like a chimney. 'My parents will never leave Germany, not even to join their relations in England. Germany is where they were born, it's their home and they retain their belief in the essential decency of the German people which will shortly resurface. You know why I came back to Frankfurt? Because my mother and father needed me. Should the situation worsen, if Luise and the girls go, they will need me even more.'

'Oh Kurt!' With the tears gathering in her eyes, impulsively Anne embraced him.

Her mission a failure for the most touching reasons, promising to keep in close contact with the Wolffs, Anne returned to

Slattocks. With Signor Mussolini's invasion of Abyssinia following close on the heels of the Nuremberg Laws – why the Italians, a people she had always liked, had been the first Fascists was beyond Anne's comprehension – she was invited to join a group of kindred souls styling themselves Writers Against Fascism. This Anne promptly did and as one of that rare breed, the effective young lady speaker, she was much in demand to address meetings up and down the country. Ben had no objection to her spreading the message that Fascism was evil, the anti-Semitism of the Nazis particularly vile, and they had to be stopped. Though he said, 'You're on a hiding to nothing, luv. The only answer's going to be force.'

That Anne steadfastly refused to believe.

When she was at home friends like Rebecca who didn't care whether she was living with a married man, woman or dog, came to visit. There seemed to be quite a lot of them and grumpily Ben said, 'I didn't know we were running a hotel.'

Anne didn't think he really minded.

With the new year of 1936 came the snow. The wind from the high moors swept it into spectacularly shaped drifts and for ten days they were completely cut off at Rowan Tree Cottage, but they had plenty of food in the larder, paraffin for the lamps and coal in the cellar, and fortunately Ben regarded grate-cleaning, fire-lighting and tending as man's work. When the snow stopped falling and the sun came out, the scene was so serene, so pure, so lovely, the sky the palest blue, the moors a glittering ice-blue, the lines of their dry-stone walls snow-speckled smudges, it was almost impossible to believe there was any evil in the world. Anne thoroughly enjoyed the experience, being alone again with Ben, with time to talk, for him finally to start work on her portrait, and to make love whenever the urge overcame them which it did frequently.

One evening after they had made passionate love in front of the blazing fire, Anne lay on the rug, while Ben sat propped against the armchair sketching her naked body. He had pulled a sweater on but his genitals were visible squashed between his legs. Anne said, 'You do look funny.'

'Ta. If you want me to draw you, stop wriggling about.'

Lying still as a mouse, Anne decided to bring up a topic

that was never long absent from her mind – his wife. 'Can't you ask her again if she'll divorce you? Madge says she must know by now that I'm the scarlet woman in your life. Half the folks in The Dales do, according to Madge.'

'If they do, that'll be all the more reason for Irene not divorcing me. She's proud and she's religious which makes me doubly hers, in the sight of her pride and her God.'

'Are you sure that's the reason you won't ask her again?'

'Yes.' Momentarily, Ben stopped sketching. 'Why?'

'I just wondered.'

Actually it was Madge who'd done more than wonder, stating much the same as Rebecca had once averred. 'He's still hedging his bets, you know. Seeing he's not a conventional lad, nor overburdened with conscience, being married to Irene saves him a lot of bother.'

'He has a strong artistic conscience,' Anne had protested.

'Mebbe he has. You'd know more about that than me. But why should he ask his wife for a divorce when he's got you where he wants you.' Madge had laughed raucously, there were moments when she was rather coarse and Anne had not pursued the subject.

To Ben she now said, 'Would it be any use my going to talk to Irene?'

'No, it bloody well wouldn't. So get that idea out of that scheming head of yours.'

He rarely swore in the presence of ladies so for the time being Anne dropped the subject completely.

Even when Ben had dug a passage down the track, the road to Slattocks was reopened to single-line traffic and communications with the outside world were re-established, Anne had little inclination to rejoin it, preferring to savour his company and their silent winter wonderland. A letter came from Julian politely hoping she was well and had not suffered unduly from the inclement weather, before enquiring how *Murder in High Places* was progressing. It was signed in his now customary fashion 'Yours sincerely', not 'Ever Yours'. Anne wrote back to say the book was coming along nicely, which was untrue because she'd been too busy with her other activities to write more than a few chapters.

For the next couple of months, working furiously on the

logistics of murder on the summit of Helvellyn and the marriage of Seth Pollard and Lady Helena – lucky them! – provided a valid reason for remaining shut away from the world. Anne held to her intention to marry off her leading characters. If she decided to write further detective novels, perhaps Lady Helena could have a baby.

In March a letter arrived from Derek Elmar-Smythe which read:

> Dearest heart,
>   What a sweet address you have! I've tried to imagine what *Slattocks* can possibly be like but have failed. You were a naughty girl not telling me how well you knew B. D. Broughton that day you bought his painting, letting me call him a monster and a brute! I'm sure he's the most gorgeous brute once you get to know him. Now the reason for this note-ette is because I more than suspect you agree with me that he should exhibit. You are therefore to use your oodles of charm and feminine wiles to make him hold an exhibition, in the Carillon Gallery of course. If you don't or won't, I shall descend upon you and talk to the gorgeous brute myself. I trust that threat will spur you into action and, much as I would adore to see you, save me a frightful journey to the back of beyond.
>   Loads of love and trillions of kisses, Derek.

Apart from the fact that she agreed with him about Ben's holding an exhibition, the prospect of Derek mincing up the track from Slattocks and the thought of her beloved's reactions, were sufficient spur. But Anne proceeded slowly because Ben was a horse that had to be coaxed, not goaded. On and off for several days she examined his canvases and sorted through his sketches, setting them out against the studio walls and on the landing, commenting on their strengths and which ones she particularly liked, drawing comments from Ben in return. Eventually he said, 'Just what are you up to?'

'Trying to convince you that you are more than ready to exhibit.'

'For Madam at the Carillon Gallery, I presume.'

'Yes. Derek may be a camp Chloe but he does actually care about paintings.'

'Yeah.'

At that admission Anne swung round and asked, 'Will you exhibit?'

'I might.'

'If we can arrange it for May, will you come to Philip's first night with me, too?' Apart from being, in both Anne and her mother's opinion, the best thing Philip had ever done, his latest play was a family affair because he'd more or less written the juvenile lead for Kate. Ben again said he might, which meant he almost certainly would, and Anne danced across the room to hug him and say, 'I do love you.'

16

A delighted Derek agreed to organise the exhibition to open ten days before the first night of Philip's new play, the sole onus on Ben being to arrange for the selection of his paintings and drawings to arrive at the Carillon Gallery in good time. Anne and he enjoyed themselves arguing which to select, and Ben was like Mother Hen with her chicks about the packing, which he insisted on doing himself. He also thought his work could and should speak for itself and did not care for the publicity hand-outs which had a photograph of him looking plebeian, though highly attractive in Anne's opinion, with the text focusing on his being a young artist whose startling originality was rooted in his industrial working-class background, which Anne said was true.

When they drove down to London in Bill to have their private preview, she knew Ben was pleased with the way his paintings had been hung on the white walls of the main part of the gallery, and his drawings arranged in a side-section. He even said to Derek, 'You've done a good job.'

The campness in Derek – unsureness? urge to blow rasp-berries at the heterosexual world? – had to spoil the moment, by saying, 'Thanks, ducky.'

However, his sterling endeavours produced results and the early evening opening of the exhibition was well attended by art critics and possible patrons. Philip and Kate were unable to be there because they were rehearsing round the clock for *The Lie of Circumstance* which was not doing a pre-London tour but opening cold in the West End. With the first night coming up Mummy was resting at Chenneys, Con was still in Scotland, but Mark arrived with a beautiful blonde girl hanging on his arm, though naturally he had to say, 'We've only come for the booze, haven't we, Petronella?'

Was that really her name? Anne wondered, as the girl smiled at Mark and lisped, 'I came becauthe of you, darling.'

'Actually,' Mark drawled, 'I'm going to buy a couple of Ben's sketches.'

'What with?' Anne enquired, seeing her brother had done sweet Fanny Adams in the way of work since coming down from Oxford.

'Philip's money. What else? I'm sure you'll approve of it being spent on a deserving cause.'

Anne pulled a face at her brother and went over to Theo Marvell who was waving for her to join him. After he'd kissed her, Theo, who was himself garbed in a beautifully tailored white silk suit and an enormous white straw hat, said sibilantly, 'You're looking chic, even if it isn't one of mine.'

Surveying her short-sleeved blue dress which had gold buttons and a gold belt, with a chiffon scarf round the neck, Anne informed him, 'I bought it "off-the-peg" at Kendal Milne's in Manchester.'

'Good God!' Theo exclaimed. Tucking her arm into his, confidentially he said, 'I heard you'd gone in for "rough trade" . . .' Was that what people were saying about her? Anne thought furiously. '. . . which didn't sound to me like the Annie I know. Now I've met him, I absolutely understand. He's his own man and he's certainly got some-thing as a painter. Don't ask me what it is, sweetie, because all these chimneys and scurrying ants aren't for Uncle Theo. I like the sketches, though. I shall buy several of Flanders' fields. Of course, I only saw them from the ranks of the Pay Corps.' Then his voice changed and quietly he said, 'But my brother's buried at Tyne Cot and I wept like a baby when I saw all those white headstones.' Having momentarily revealed a part of his soul Theo hurried away, shrieking, 'Teddy-bear, I haven't seen you in simply ages . . .'

Anne did like Theo, in limited doses anyway. If one could use the masculine gender, Theo was his own man, whereas Derek was a made-up creature, much of him a carbon copy of his older ex-lover.

By the end of the evening Anne thought Ben had enjoyed himself and was convinced the exhibition was a huge success. Over the next ten days, however, the critics of such newspapers or magazines as deigned to review it, were either condescending, dismissive, or disgusted. B. D. Broughton might have a certain talent for drawing but as a painter his subject matters were morbidly uninteresting or aesthetically displeasing, he was a *faux-naïf* or an untalented primitive. One idiot even used the Nazis' favourite words, decadent and degenerate. A sole voice shared the view that here was a genuinely original talent with considerable technical skill, an innate sense of composition, an unusual use of colour, and a striking vision of the industrial society that Lancashire had spawned.

Just before Philip's first night Derek reported to Anne that though the sketches had sold well, only two of the canvases had been bought. He said, 'Still, it's early days. I told you they were a bunch of peasants and it would take time for our gorgeous brute to establish himself. Is Sir disappointed?'

'Yes, I think he is, actually.'

Ben was upset and when Anne tried to comfort him he said, 'What the hell? I can go on painting and living off you.'

He minded her paying most of the bills, did he, whatever Madge thought about his lack of conscience? Did the same apply to Irene's paying the bills? Anne said, 'I know you're restless. Do you want to go back to Slattocks? I can't obviously because of Philip's first night but if you . . .'

'No, I'm looking forward to it. Sounds an interesting play. I'll even hire an evening suit!'

For those closely involved, opening nights were always slightly nerve-racking and Anne felt the usual butterflies in her stomach as she took her seat in the royal box for the first night of *The Lie of Circumstance*. She surveyed the glittering audience in the front stalls and circle before her gaze travelled to the upper circle and the 'gods' packed with Philip's less expensively attired devotees, though quite a few of the women were wearing floral evening gowns and fox furs.

The first scene of the play, with its opulent country house setting just after the end of the Great War, was well received. Typical Philip dialogue was greeted with waves of laughter. Con laughed delightedly and dug Gavin in the ribs at the line, 'God is not necessarily an English gentleman. The Foreign Office was not therefore created in His image', before whispering, 'Or a Scottish gentleman!'

This was what was expected of Philip Marchal. Although the wit remained, with the introduction of the play's serious theme – the lunacy of war and what it did to people – the laughter lessened. The first-act curtain came down to more muted applause than usually greeted Philip's plays. During the interval, while friends visited the author and his wife in the royal box, Anne and Ben, Con and Gavin, Mark and another willowy blonde, though this one didn't lisp and answered to the name of Babs, stretched their legs in the direction of the bar. En route, all sorts of people called, waved, or came up to Anne, and Ben said, 'Is this normal for first nights? Is simply everybody who's anybody here?' He parodied upper-class speech patterns. 'And does simply everybody female drip diamonds?'

'I don't for one.' Anne was wearing one of Theo's slinkier creations, midnight blue in colour, cut low and straight across her bosom, held by slender shoulder straps, one decorated with silk roses. Her only jewellery was small pearl earrings. 'But Philip's first nights do tend to be snazzy affairs. You're not letting the side down, Mr Broughton.'

In his black tie and tails Ben looked anything but 'rough trade' – that remark had rankled – and with considerable pleasure Anne noticed several of the women who were dripping diamonds, casting appraising, appreciative glances. As they resettled themselves for the next act, Mummy said, 'I think it's going well, don't you?'

The second act switched to the front-line trenches on the

Western Front and to how Jeremy Anstruther-Cholmondley had behaved in the aftermath of a 'big push'. With his gammy leg Philip himself had not of course seen action, though he had visited the rear areas and support trenches as a writer for the War Propaganda Bureau. Anne knew he had devoured the works of Wilfrid Owen, Siegfried Sassoon, Isaac Rosenberg, Edmund Blunden, Robert Graves, Richard Aldington, Frederic Manning, to name but a few; that he had spoken to many of the survivors; and that Mummy had let him see Daddy's letters and war diaries. To Anne it seemed that Philip had caught the authentic, unsentimentalised reality to perfection, but she sensed the audience's growing surprise and resentment that Philip Marchal should be making them feel uncomfortable.

Then, after a dramatic but unedifying scene between Jeremy Anstruther-Cholmondley and a young 'agony', as unblooded subalterns had been known, from the back of the circle a woman's voice called out loudly and angrily, 'This is a slur on our boys. I was a VAD and I know.'

Anne felt sure she'd also been a suffragette, for it was a middle-class voice that sounded accustomed to heckling. More feebly other voices cried, 'Shame, shame.'

The shushing and counter-cries of 'Be quiet' sounded and the interruptions subsided, to be followed by an uneasy quiet. When it was revealed that Jeremy Anstruther-Cholmondley's behaviour had subsequently caused the death of the 'agony' and his entire platoon, the same voice again called out, 'It's a travesty, I tell you, a travesty. Our boys weren't cowards.'

Fortunately, the revelation brought the curtain down, but when the house lights came up, Anne felt everybody was looking at the royal box and its current occupants. Ben murmured, 'I take it this isn't normal.'

'Shut up,' she said.

Anne was feeling so angry she could have charged up to the circle and strangled the woman with her own hands, or at least given her a piece of her mind, but her main concern was the effect the reception of the second act was having on her mother. It was obviously Philip's too and he said, 'I think I should break my golden rule and go backstage before the end. Do you want to leave, my darling? It could get worse in act three.'

'Don't be silly, Philip. But somebody can get me a drink, please.'

Everybody except Babs leapt to their feet to offer their services and Mummy said she'd have a large gin and lime. Anxiously, Anne watched her mother while she sipped the drink but though her skin was pale – she wore little make-up, only light lipstick and a dab of powder – she looked composed and very lovely in the silver lamé gown and evening cloak Theo had designed.

It was with considerable apprehension that Anne watched the curtain rise on act three, which was again set in the Anstruther-Cholmondleys' country house in England. For the last act was Philip's most ambitious, the one in which he probed the circumstances that had driven Jeremy Anstruther-Cholmondley to belie his nature and to weave a tissue of deceit.

The third act also contained Kate's big scene.

Although the audience was restless and an awful lot of people were lighting cigarettes, their orange tips glowing in the darkness, initially there were no further interruptions. When some of the bitingly funny lines were greeted with laughter, Anne breathed a sigh of relief. Then Kate, as Jeremy's fiancée, came on to confront him. In a 1920s afternoon dress of white organdie trimmed with scarlet ribbons, she looked angelically beautiful and her performance was utterly believable. You wanted to hit 'Lucy Langton' for being such a shallow selfish creature, yet you pitied her bewilderment as her heroic image of Jeremy was shattered. Whatever mysterious ingredients made up 'star quality', Anne thought, her sister had them.

Kate exited to a storm of 'bravos' and clapping that halted the show for several minutes. Anne was uneasily unsure whether the applause was for her acting or for the content of Kate's final speech in which she rounded on Jeremy, fiercely upbraiding him for his despicable cowardice, and threw her engagement ring in his face. When in the next scene, Lady Anstruther-Cholmondley showed sympathetic understanding for her son's plight and tried to comfort him, Anne knew that for a section of the audience the latter was true. For the forceful voice from the circle shouted, 'Shame on you, Miss Maddern. You were there.' Mary Maddern who was playing

Lady Anstruther-Cholmondley, had served both as a VAD and in Lena Ashwell's concert parties entertaining the troops.

'Shut up, you old harridan.' That voice was unmistakably Theo Marvell's and Anne could have hugged him.

Alas, after that it was bedlam. People shouted and waved their programmes, from the back of the circle the voice launched into *Land of Hope and Glory* and all over the auditorium people rose to their feet to swell the chorus of '. . . Mother of the Free, How shall we extol thee, Who are born of thee? . . .' Other members of the audience, led, Anne thought, by Theo, burst into the more sardonic Great War songs, *Hanging on the Old Barbed Wire* and *We're here Because we're here Because we're here*, whilst on stage Mary Maddern and Donald Tyndale, who was playing Jeremy, sat frozen-faced.

'Jeez!' Ben said.

Rex McCorquodale, the young producer of *The Lie of Circumstance*, came rushing into the box to ask, 'Shall we bring the curtain down, Sir Philip?'

'Yes,' Philip snapped.

Anne and Con had their arms round their mother who, with shaking shoulders, had put her head into her hands. Brushing them aside, Philip lifted his wife gently to her feet and said softly, 'Let's get you out of this madhouse, Kessie.'

She looked up at him with tear-stained eyes and said chokily, 'It's the best play you've ever written, Philip. Its true worth will be recognised one day', before unprotestingly allowing him and Mark to assist her to the door.

With the rumpus continuing unabated below them, Philip paused to say directly to Anne, 'Please go backstage for me. If the audience doesn't disperse quickly, call the police. Ask the cast to wait until I return. Mark, will you stay with your mother at the flat until I get back there?'

Philip kept a service flat in Albemarle Street and Mark replied, 'Of course I'll stay with Mumkins.'

It took some time, but the audience finally dispersed without the need to call the police. Backstage, everybody except Kate appeared as shell-shocked as the victims of a Great War bombardment. After she had allowed her husband to kiss her and Sandy had expressed his sentiments which included his opinion that the disgusting scenes were proof, if proof were needed, that capitalism was in its terminal stage, Kate said to her sisters, 'Darlings, it was unbelievable, wasn't it? I was peering through the curtains on the OP side and I actually saw two men tugging at each others' shirts and a woman hitting another woman with her evening bag! Oh, poor Pip!' Uncle Pip had been their childhood name for Philip, now used without the 'Uncle'. Then Kate enquired, 'How's Mummy?'

'Desperately upset,' Con replied. 'What else would you expect?'

The cast and most of the stage-staff waited until Philip returned when, at his request, everybody gathered on stage in the country house set. There was, Anne thought, something peculiarly forlorn about empty theatres in the dimness of working lights, like houses without occupants. Philip always gave the cast lavish first-night presents before the show, carefully chosen to suit their individual personalities, but as they gathered on stage Anne saw that he was carrying a basket filled with violets. She assumed that on his way back from Albemarle Street, he had bought an entire basket from a late-night flower-seller in Piccadilly Circus. Assisted by Kate, Philip proceeded to give the posies to his cast and to the stage-staff. During this touching scene, his limp seemed more noticeable than ever.

After he had distributed the last bunch of violets, his right hand leaning on his stick, Philip stood downstage centre, facing his audience. In his most splintered accent, which Anne felt hid, or perhaps revealed, his emotion, he said, 'These are the only tokens of appreciation that I can at this late hour offer. I am not going to make a speech. I merely wish to thank all of you for your dedication and hard work, my cast for their remarkable performances in the face of finally unbeatable odds, and to say the show will go on, tomorrow at least. How long after that I would not care to predict.'

As he finished speaking and bowed his head, Kate jumped on to a chair and in her clearest stage voice called out, 'Three cheers for Sir Philip whose play we are proud to be part of!'

Everybody cheered lustily and as the sounds died away,

Kate said defiantly, 'We're going on to the first-night party, aren't we?' Philip was footing the bill at the favourite theatrical restaurant, The Ivy, for cast and friends, if not for the stage-hands (they got beer money). 'And the hell with 'em all – particularly that ghastly woman in the circle!'

Anne felt proud of her sister and knew why it was difficult to dislike Kate for long, whatever she did.

Philip himself did not go to The Ivy but straight to the flat to be with his wife; nor did Gavin and Con. Gavin had become increasingly po-faced as the evening's events had unfolded, and Anne suspected he would have preferred to be at the Foreign Office dealing with less personally riotous matters, such as the war in Abyssinia or the Nazis in Germany. But a good crowd trooped into the exclusivity of The Ivy, where Mark later joined them. The party verged on the hysterical as everybody waited for the early editions of the national dailies. When they arrived the hysteria mounted for the notices were worse than anybody could have imagined, apart from those for Kate.

'Just listen to this!' Rex McCorquodale said, '"There is only one sweet spot in this dunghill, only one rose blooms among the rusty barbed wire of Philip Marchal's putrid play."' As if the thought had only just occurred to him, he turned to Kate and added, 'Nice for you, of course, darling.'

Anne had noticed Kate lavishing a fair amount of attention on 'Corky' who was cleaner of limb and features than most of the leading men he directed, and *vice versa*. She wondered if Sandy had. Or was he too busy explaining Communism to 'Bunty', the impressionable ingénue?

With few exceptions, one notable one being James Agate who opined at considerable length that Philip Marchal had written the great play that would be his monument, the reviews in the Sunday papers and the weekly magazines were uniformly bad. Some of the attacks in the articles that appeared in the dailies were viciously, personally wounding, observing that Sir Philip himself had not fought in the war but had seen fit to involve his beautiful, talented stepdaughter, whose father had been a war hero, in his vile, unpatriotic play. Within the fortnight it didn't really matter what anybody said because *The Lie of Circumstance* was off. Neither the furore of the first night, nor the subsequent scurrilous press attention, nor James Agate's august opinion, persuaded the great British public to judge for themselves.

Despite Ben's dislike of London and disappointment over the failure of his exhibition – though compared to the way Philip had been slaughtered, he'd come off lightly – he remained stalwartly by Anne's side. In the circumstances, Rebecca said she had no objection to his staying at the Gower Street flat. In fact, she and Ben became quite matey. The day before they returned to Slattocks Anne drove down to Chenneys to see her mother.

It was a dark, drizzling June afternoon as the two of them sat in the drawing room at Chenneys. Through the mullioned windows that looked on to the terrace, Kessie could see the rivulets forming in the cracks of the flagstones and the rain dripping from the roses. The weather fitted her mood. She now felt unutterably weary and depressed, everything within her having suffered with Philip, whose sensitive soul had been cut to the quick. Did souls, like fingernails, have quicks? Why not? The only difference between her and Philip's reactions had been the temperature; his glacial, Kessie's boiling.

She refocused her attention on Anne's indignant voice which was saying, 'Why have they been so peculiarly horrible? Rebecca and I have come to all sorts of conclusions. One of them is that Philip could sue some of the newspapers for libel.'

'I agree, but he's not going to. Nothing would persuade him to subject me to the publicity and *angst* of court proceedings.'

Kessie smiled wryly and after a few seconds' consideration her daughter said firmly, 'He's quite right. They would be awful.'

'Why have they been so horrible?' Kessie repeated the question. 'Philip and I have discussed that, too. We've come to the following conclusions. People like tearing down those they've raised up, particularly if, like Philip, they were privileged to begin with. In England we like putting people in boxes. Philip's was marked "Sophisticated comedies". He had no business to pop out of his box. If he had to, he should have made it clear it was a serious play and not included funny

184

lines. Perhaps for once his timing was wrong. People don't want to think about war at the moment. Not for the right reasons, not to use every possible non-violent means to prevent another one, but because they hope Signor Mussolini and Herr Hitler and Fascists everywhere will quietly disappear. Which they won't, of course. I begin to wonder if we aren't deluding ourselves about the effect of the Peace Pledge Union and our dream of renouncing war.'

'Oh Mummy, you mustn't say that!'

'No, I mustn't, because I don't think I could bear to live through another war.'

'You're not going to, because there isn't going to be one. There isn't.'

Her voice ringing with passion, Anne jumped up to kiss her mother. Returning her daughter's warm embrace Kessie wondered when, if, Anne would have a child. Unlike Con, but like Kessie herself, Anne did not possess a deeply maternal instinct (it was Tom who'd wanted children so much) but nonetheless Kessie believed her daughter would miss a great deal if she remained childless. For even the last few weeks had had their compensations, proving, if she needed proof, how blessed she was in her family.

Following her train of thought about children, Kessie said, 'How are things between you and Ben?'

'Couldn't be better.'

'Apart from his wife.'

Anne inclined her head but said breezily, 'Oh, I intend to sort that out very soon.'

17

Anne was not certain how she was going to 'sort out' Ben's wife. Whatever he thought, she would probably have to go to Upperdale to see Irene personally. She imagined the scene in which she would express her deep regret for Mrs Broughton's unhappiness but point out that such things happened and Ben had not returned to her even when he'd temporarily separated from Anne, with a final appeal to Irene's good sense and her agreement to a divorce. But it was so nice to be back in their own dear little home at Rowan Tree Cottage, to breathe the pure moorland air of Slattocks, that Anne decided not to make any move for a week or two.

Three weeks after their return, Generals Sanjuro and Franco invaded southern Spain from Spanish Morocco, raising the standard against the Popular Front government which had been elected by a large majority. Avidly Anne listened to the wireless and read the newspaper reports and it was soon apparent that Spain was in the throes of a civil war. Ben said, 'You've got your classic battle between good and evil. What are you going to do about it, Anne? How are you going to stop the forces of darkness now?'

'I'm not sure,' she admitted. 'But I'm not giving up campaigning for the Peace Pledge Union. If we, as the mightiest empire in the world, renounce war, then other nations will have to follow suit.'

Ben kissed the top of her head. 'You're a romantic idealist, but I love you.'

The following week the weather was excessively dreary, with the rain clouds sitting on top of the moors day after day, but then summer returned and they awoke to the sun streaming through the windows. Anne enjoyed gardening, so after breakfast she donned her slacks and wellies and sallied forth to pull out the weeds that had shot up with the downpours. On the main road she saw the telegraph boy pedalling along but she continued to burrow away with her trowel, unearthing docks and dandelions and pestilential trails of ground elder. When the lad turned on to their track, pushing his bike up the steep slope, Anne stood stockstill clutching a clump of chickweed in her gardening gloves.

Ever since the day she had cheerfully handed her mother the telegram which regretted to inform them Major E. T. F. Whitworth had been killed in action, she'd had a horror of telegrams. There was no telephone at Rowan Tree Cottage but nobody who knew her ever sent a telegram, unless it was absolutely vital. Of course, people who didn't know her well sometimes did and the message could then be good news. Pulling off her gardening gloves, dropping them and the chickweed on to the path, Anne took the yellow envelope from the telegraph boy and tore it open. The telegram read: 'Your mother ill Stop Please come at once Stop Philip.'

'Any reply, missus?'

Devastated by the message, without thinking clearly, Anne shook her head. For a few seconds she stood clutching the telegram, watching the lad freewheel down the track, before she let out a howl. Ben's face appeared at the studio window and Anne sobbed up at him, 'Oh Ben, Ben, it's Mummy. She's ill and I've sent the boy away without telegraphing to say I'm on my way and . . .'

They met in the lobby as Ben raced down the stairs and she lurched through the front door. He took the telegram from her hand, read it, and said, 'You go and get changed, luv, and pack a few things. Leave a key and a note for Mrs Sutcliffe. She'll look after the cats. I'll go up to the Livesleys.' Mrs Sutcliffe was the woman who came in to 'do' for them and they had acquired two cats, a randy tabby tom and a fluffy tortoiseshell female they'd christened Romeo and Juliet. The Livesleys, with whom they'd become friendly, lived in the largest house in Slattocks and possessed a telephone.

By the time Ben returned from the Livesleys, Anne had scribbled a note for Mrs Sutcliffe, left the key under a flower pot, shut the windows and locked the doors. The case into which she'd shoved a few things for them both was standing by the gate, and she was pacing round the garden smoking furiously. She ran towards Ben but before she could speak, he put his finger to her lips and said gently, 'Your mother's had a heart attack. She's in hospital in Folkestone but she's holding her own. Would you like me to drive?'

Since they'd come to Slattocks Ben had learned to drive, at first climbing into Bill with the utmost suspicion, now taking the wheel with confidence but, unlike Julian, circum-spection. Over the twisting moorland roads and winding valleys of Lancashire and Derbyshire, along the miles of open roads in the Midlands, Ben drove faster than Anne had ever known. Through the sprawling suburbs of north London he

187

exceeded the speed limit, through central London he followed her instructions for short-cuts, once they had crossed the River Thames, cleared the equally sprawling southern suburbs and were into Kent, he again put his foot hard on the accelerator pedal. It was still the longest journey of Anne's life and the summer light was fading into twilight before they reached the hospital in Folkestone.

A nurse showed Anne into a private waiting room on the first floor where Mark was standing by the window and Kate was sitting bolt upright in a chintz-covered armchair. Both of them had cigarettes in their hands and Anne's brain registered the wreaths of smoke, the brown chrysanthemum pattern of the chintz, and the heavy make-up on her sister's face. Presumably she had come straight from the film studios at Denham. As Anne entered the room Kate stubbed out her cigarette, leapt to her feet and tripped towards her sister. With the tears trickling down her face, she threw her arms round Anne's neck and cried, 'Darling, I'm so glad you're here. Con's on her way down from Scotland. They're giving Mummy oxygen and all sorts of ghastly things. She's not going to . . . is she?'

Kate could not bring herself to say the word 'die' and in her own distress Anne had the urge to shout, 'How the hell do I know?', though Kate's distress was genuine enough, even if she still managed to trip daintily and, despite the make-up, to cry prettily. Over her sister's heaving shoulders, Anne looked towards her brother. In a flat voice Mark said, 'We're just waiting, Annie. Pip's with her at the moment.'

Anne became conscious that Ben was standing behind her. Softly he said, 'I'll leave you with your family. I'll get myself a cup of tea and a bite to eat. Can I get you anything?'

'They keep bringing us cups of tea and sandwiches,' Kate sobbed.

'I'll come back later then. All right?'

With a tremulous smile, Anne nodded. Poor Ben, he must be tired and hungry because they had only stopped for petrol on the three-hundred-odd-mile journey. After he had gone Kate returned to the armchair, Anne accepted a cigarette from Mark and joined him at the window. She asked her brother who'd been at Chenneys, how it had happened? He said their mother had been feeling under the weather for the last few days so she'd had her breakfast in bed, then she'd got up and Eileen, who was her personal maid, had found her collapsed on the bedroom floor. Doctor Stuart had come immediately and as immediately he'd called the ambulance and she'd been rushed to the hospital with the bell clanging all the way.

Then Kate started to chatter, to tell Anne what she had doubtless already told her twin brother. They had brought her the news on the set but fortunately she'd just finished a satisfactory take and 'Dobbin' – Kate was addicted to nick-names – had been simply marvellous and said she must go *tout de suite* and he'd rearrange his shooting schedule. Anne wished her sister would shut up, whilst accepting this was her way of relieving her tension. After the maddening recital about how marvellous everybody had been, how she'd been chauffeured to Folkestone at a hundred miles an hour in Alex's own Rolls-Royce ('Alex' being Alexander Korda, for whose London Films she was currently working) and how she'd cried all the way, Kate extracted copies of the London evening papers, *The Star, Evening News* and *Evening Standard* from a pile of magazines lying on the table.

'It was front-page news in the early editions,' she informed her sister. 'Lady Marchal suffers heart attack. Sir Philip at her hospital bedside. Her children dash to join the vigil. You know the sort of thing. We were on page three in the later editions.'

Kate handed the newspapers to Anne who gave them a cursory glance, noting that in the early editions there were photographs of Kate, Mark and herself, though not Con, who was the least newsworthy member of the family and merely referred to as Mrs G. Campbell-Ross, wife of the diplomat, as well as of Mummy and Philip. By the later editions the photographs had been reduced to Mummy and the rising star in the celluloid firmament, Miss Kate Whitworth.

Kate's prattling was brought to a merciful end by their stepfather's entry into the room. With his long hollowed face, sallow skin and melancholic expression, Mummy always said Philip was an El Greco figure. At the moment he looked like Saint Sebastian at the stake. Silently, tensely, the three of them gazed at him. He greeted Anne before saying in his most splintered accent, 'Your mother is sleeping. She is breathing slightly more easily and seems a little more comfortable. If you would like to see her, Anne?'

The large private room was already filled with flowers from friends and well-wishers. Anne sat by the bedside holding her mother's hand in which the veins were blue-ridged against the pallor of the skin, listening to the shallow, panting breathing that every so often rattled ominously. From time to time Mummy moved her head fretfully and the chestnut strands that were still visible among the spreading grey of her hair, gleamed in the subdued light. Any minute, Anne knew, her darling, best beloved mother could slip across that bourne whence no man, or woman, returned. Suddenly the rattling sound worsened and her mother was gasping for breath. Clutching her hand Anne cried out, 'Nurse, nurse.'

At the double two nurses were in the room and Anne was bundled out.

For the next couple of hours the family sat or prowled around. The flowers were ejected into the corridor and every time a doctor or nurse appeared through the blooms and foliage, Philip looked as if another arrow had been shot into his body and Anne felt as if her own heart had ceased to beat. Ben returned from wherever he'd been and she asked him to stay, which he did. Sandy turned up and Kate said, 'Oh, I'm glad you've come, darling.'

'You might have let me know, nutkin.'

'I knew you had a play going out this evening. And I knew you'd hear the news.' Which actually meant Kate hadn't considered him at all, Anne thought.

'How is your Mama?' Sandy asked gravely.

At that question Kate burst into tears and allowed her husband to comfort her. Some time after midnight Con arrived with Gavin who'd met the Perth train at King's Cross station and driven her down to Folkestone. With no need to express their emotions verbally, for several minutes Con and Anne just clung to each other. In the small hours of the morning, when the early August dawn chorus was sounding and the light breaking, Philip again conferred with the heart specialist who'd come post-haste from London. Their stepfather returned to inform them, 'They're doing everything known to modern medicine and . . .' he repeated the words used earlier by Ben, '. . . she's holding her own. If she can hold on for the next few hours . . .'

His voice faltered and putting his left hand to his face, Philip stumbled from the room. The sound of his stick echoed down the corridor. They stayed at the hospital, drinking tea, smoking, resuming their prowling, dozing fitfully as the seemingly endless hours ticked slowly away. To give herself something to do, Anne examined the cards attached to the flowers. One of the most beautiful baskets, containing long-stemmed red roses, was from Julian. Dear Julian. She had treated him rather badly and it was typical of him to have chosen the red rose of Lancashire, from one Lancastrian to another.

Anne recalled her childish terror when her mother had nearly died after the twins' birth just before the outbreak of war and again after her first heart attack, and how first Daddy, then Aunty Sarah, had comforted her. Now she had Ben, whose arm had come round her shoulder as she reseated herself in the waiting room, on whose chest her exhausted head was leaning. Gently stroking her hair he said, 'She must be holding on, Anne. You haven't been called in.'

Then Philip was summoned to his wife's side and Kate sobbed hysterically, 'Oh no, oh no.'

In a strangled voice it was Con who said, 'Do be quiet, Kate.'

When she saw Philip returning to the waiting room Anne couldn't bear the tension and she reburied her head on Ben's chest. As if from the North Pole she heard her stepfather's voice drawling, 'The doctors now consider your mother's condition to be tolerably stable.' His emotion again overcoming him, Philip started to laugh. 'She has defeated the grim reaper the third time round.'

Sandy and Gavin returned to London and within a couple of days, when it looked as if their mother's condition was stable, if fearfully weak, Kate was back on the film set. Con, Mark and Anne stayed on at Chenneys until the end of the week, taking it in turns to visit their mother in hospital. Then Mark said he had a fairly urgent matter to attend to in London – what that might be, Anne did not enquire, though from the several female voices that had been telephoning for him, she presumed it was the complications of his love-life – and Con said she must return to Scotland and her babies.

Before Gavin came to collect her, she and Anne went for a walk. They were wandering through the rose gardens when Con said, 'Philip thinks Mummy's heart attack was brought on by what happened over *The Lie of Circumstance*.'

'I suppose to an extent it probably was.'

'Yes, but Philip's blaming himself. If he hadn't written the play, Mummy wouldn't have been stricken.'

'That's a piece of deathless logic, if ever I heard one.'

'But he believes it, Anne. And he thinks we believe it, too. And he's torturing himself. Will you talk to him and tell him not to be such an ass?' Anne had an awareness of her stepfather's state, though she hadn't realised it was as bad as Con was indicating. She turned her head to look at her sister with a why-me? expression. Con answered the silent question. 'I've always loved stepdaddy. I know you think I love everybody, though I don't actually. Anyway, you and he have had a sparky relationship, though I think you're fond of him now, aren't you? So if you tell him not to be an idiot, that we all know how much he loves Mummy and we don't in the least blame him for writing the splendid play he had to write, I think it will help.'

After Con had left, Anne knocked on the door of Philip's study. This had always been his *sanctum sanctorum* where nobody except Mummy disturbed him when he was writing, into which he was now shutting himself during the hours when he was not at the hospital. His voice called out brusquely, 'Who is it?'

'Anne.'

There was a pause before the voice said slightly less brusquely, 'Is it important?'

'Yes.'

'Come in then.'

Of the many lovely rooms at Chenneys the study was one of the loveliest, the mullioned windows overlooking the flower gardens, the original ceiling with its entwined Tudor rose *motif* intact, panelled walls and bookcases, and the beautiful rosewood desk at which Philip handwrote his plays. He was at the desk as Anne entered but she saw no sign of work in progress. After he had ushered her to a chair, when they were both sitting down smoking, Anne decided there was no point beating about the bush so she said, 'I just want to tell you that Mummy would be furious if she thought you were blaming yourself for her heart attack. If you don't stop being stupid I shall tell her you are, which won't do her any good at all.'

Philip started to laugh, not in the wildly emotional way he had at the hospital, but with genuine amusement. He said, 'You won't take any such action, Anne, but am I to assume you don't blame me?'

'Of course I don't! None of us does. And I think the best thing you can do is to start writing another play.'

'Is that one writer speaking to another?'

'Yes. Though before I was speaking as your stepdaughter.'

'I see. Thank you, Anne.'

With a man of his perceptive sensitivity, there was no need to hammer your points. Philip smiled at her and his normally cold grey eyes were filled with the warmth usually reserved for Mummy. There was a moment's silence during which Anne felt closer to her stepfather than at any time since she'd first known him as 'Uncle Pip'. Then he said, 'Let's discuss what we're going to do about your mother. She wants to come home. Do you consider it a good idea?'

'Yes, I know she does. If the doctors agree, I think it's the best possible idea. Mummy loves Chenneys.'

'That's settled then. We'll organise a resident nurse for her, and an ambulance, and we'll bring her home as soon as possible. Will you stay until she comes?'

Anne nodded.

Kate was galloping her mare across the sweep of fields known as the Ridgeway, when she saw Ben Broughton's sturdy figure walking from the summer house towards the copse that led down to the rustic bridge spanning the stream. She had intended to go with Anne and Pip to collect Mummy from the hospital, honestly she had, but the studio photographer had wanted to take one more 'still', then another, and by the time she arrived at Chenneys they'd just left for Folkestone. There was nobody in particular around – she hadn't realised Ben was still here – but it was a beautiful afternoon so she'd decided to fill the waiting hours by having a good gallop. Bringing the mare to a trot, Kate rode her into the woods on the far side of the stream, calculating that she should arrive at the rustic bridge, accidentally on purpose, about the same time as Ben.

After fifteen months of marriage, she knew exactly why her sister had ditched Sandy. He could be fun but what a bore he was with his endless pontificating about Communism and what a lousy lover he'd turned out to be. Kate had suspected this ever since their unsatisfactory first night but now she'd slept with Rex McCorquodale she knew it to be a fact, for darling Corky was eminently satisfactory. When Anne had first taken up with Ben Broughton, Kate thought her sister had gone mad. With that accent, those clothes and surly manners, other than in the most broad-minded circles one simply couldn't be seen dead with him. Recently, however, several people whose opinion Kate respected had spoken highly of B. D. Broughton the artist. Having seen more of Ben himself because of Mummy's ghastly heart attack, she now appreciated why Anne had fallen for him. He had the most gorgeous bed-room eyes, he was obviously pretty hot stuff, and he was far from stupid; all in all a most intriguing man.

'Hello there.' Kate waved as, with perfect timing, she reached one end of the bridge, Ben the other.

'Oh hello,' he said, walking on to the bridge. 'When did you arrive? Anne and your stepfather waited the best part of an hour for you.'

'Did they? How awful. I simply couldn't get away. I shall be on the terrace for the triumphant homecoming, though.'

Ben watched as Anne's young sister slid gracefully from her horse and led it down the slope to the stream where it bent its glossy reddish-brown head and lapped eagerly at the water. Smiling up at him, Kate said, 'We've had a hard gallop but she's allowed to have a drink now she's cooled down. Her name's Sorrel. Isn't she beautiful?'

In her riding gear – velvet hat, tailored jacket, white silk shirt, well-cut breeches and polished leather boots – the same could be said of Sorrel's mistress. From the middle of the bridge, Ben surveyed Anne's sister as she took off her riding hat. Having placed it on the ground, she shook her shining black hair which was cut into the latest style, side parting, flat across the forehead, swinging just below the ears, *très chic*, but Ben reckoned to wear it you needed good features. Those Mrs Dalziel had in exquisite proportions.

With another smile Kate said, 'I'm going to follow Sorrel's example. 'Tis hot, isn't it?'

Unbuttoning her jacket she threw that on top of the riding hat. Still smiling up at him, she untied the ends of her collar, flapping them to ventilate herself, before bending down to cup water into her hands. Her movements were instinctively graceful and ineffably provocative, for as a result of her gallop the silk shirt was clinging to her body, outlining the shape of her lovely breasts, and the untying of her collar had revealed their cleavage. Ben stayed in the middle of the bridge, leaning his bare arms on the wooden rail for 'twas a hot day and he'd rolled up the sleeves of his check shirt. Looking down at Madame, he debated what her next move was likely to be.

Having quenched her own thirst and presumably decided her horse had lapped enough, Kate tethered it to one of the wooden struts of the bridge before climbing on to it herself. Her slim hips swinging in concert with her black hair, she started to walk towards Ben. They were a slim family, the Whitworths. At some five feet three inches tall, Kate was the smallest, but her figure was as exquisitely proportioned as her features. Her eyebrows were, Ben suspected, naturally thick but they'd been plucked into the fashionably thin line and Kate arched them as she walked towards him, a gesture which widened her cat-like eyes. Ben continued to lean his hands on the rail, she came right up to him and he could smell the perfume of her body and the faint odour of perspiration, a mixture he found decidedly sexy.

In her clear actress's voice Kate said, 'Alex has bought one of your paintings. Alexander Korda, that is. He has it on the wall of the lounge at his house in Avenue Road. I'd like to buy one of your Lancashire scenes to hang in my lounge. Which one would you suggest for me?'

'It's your lounge. You choose.'

Kate laughed. 'Why don't you come over to help me? My house is quite close, you know, this side of Ashford.'

Then, without looking at him, she ran her fingers, which were lacquered with green nail varnish, over the back of his left hand and up to his elbow, ruffling the fine brown hairs as she did so. When Ben made no response, her fingers traced the check patterns of his shirt up to its open neck where they twirled round the brown hairs below his throat. When that failed to produce a reaction, Kate ducked her head to gaze straight into his face and her rosebud lips were slightly open, her green eyes alight with invitation. Without doubt, Ben thought, she was one of the best bits of crackling he'd ever been offered on a plate.

Restraining his natural instincts, conversationally he said, 'Do you covet everything you think belongs to your sister? I don't belong to anybody but I do love your sister. So bugger off, luv.'

With his tone being so conversational, the intonations so strongly north country, it was several seconds before Kate absorbed what he had said. During this time she continued to gaze provocatively at him, whilst thinking, honestly, she simply must be back at the house and changed before darling Mummy came home, so they hadn't much time, though Ben looked the type who'd hurl you to the ground, tear off your clothes and . . . The full implication of Ben's words struck her hard. How dare he speak to her like that? Furiously, she slapped his face. Like her father, Kate was naturally left-handed, though, unlike him, she had not been beaten to use her right hand, and the impact of her wedding and engagement rings raised a red weal on Ben's right cheek. Seeing the anger spark in those sexy grey eyes, instinctively she backed away from him.

Ben said, 'Don't worry. I'm not going to hit you. But don't ever do that again, or I might.'

With that he turned on his heel and walked away from her.

'I don't think Mummy's ever going to walk again, do you? This time I don't think even her determination and courage will win that battle.'

'No,' Ben said.

Everybody else had retired for the night and Anne was sitting on the floor of the drawing room at Chenneys, her back between Ben's legs. He was in an armchair and he was massaging her shoulders and neck because he said she was like an overwound spring, ready to snap at any moment.

'Still, she's alive and back with us. Wasn't her homecoming marvellous.

'Yeah,' Ben said.

When they arrived at Chenneys late this afternoon, the entire staff was standing on the terrace and when Mummy's wheelchair was lifted from the ambulance – she'd refused to return on a stretcher – everybody cheered. Neither Anne nor Philip had organised them, they had turned out of their own volition. The ground-floor suite that had been Mummy's when she'd first come to Chenneys in 1919, as Tom Whitworth's sickly widow, had been redecorated and its living room was a mass of flowers, presents and cards. Mummy had cried tears of joy and gratitude but oh, how thin, pale and fragile she looked and the slightest exertion affected her breathing. She had been sedated and Anne had seen her sleeping peacefully in the house that had become her beloved home.

'I think Kate was deeply affected, too. I've never known her so quiet and preoccupied. She hardly said a word all evening. Mm, that's lovely.' Anne leant her head backwards as Ben's fingers soothed the muscles of her neck. She smiled up at him. 'She didn't even flirt with you!'

Recently, Anne had noticed her sister being flirtatious with Ben, as was her instinct with any man she considered attractive. Secretly she was pleased that Kate should have added him to her list. Gazing up into Ben's face, she registered the weal on his right cheek that she'd vaguely noticed earlier in the evening. Touching it with her finger she said, 'That's a nasty mark. How did you get it?'

Truthfully Ben said, 'Something hit me as I was walking through the woods.'

'Well, I should take care of it. It looks rather painful.'

Other than grunting his agreement Ben made no further comment on the subject. He considered it unlikely that Kate would ever flirt with him again and maybe one day he would tell Anne about her little minx of a sister throwing herself at him, but that day was not to hand. After several minutes' comfortable silence, during which he continued to massage her shoulders and she purred with pleasure, Anne said, 'Ben, it's my birthday the day after tomorrow. Just think, I shall be twenty-seven!'

'Yeah, I know, old lady. While you've been at the hospital with your mother, I've been doing a couple of different paintings of Chenneys. One for your birthday, one for her homecoming. Only they're not quite finished.'

'Oh Ben, I do love you.' Anne stretched up to kiss him and, with Kate's behaviour to the forefront of his mind, he responded with considerable passion. When they had uncoiled themselves from the embrace, breathlessly Anne said, 'That wasn't why I mentioned my birthday. I wasn't angling for a present, though I'd have been deeply hurt if you had forgotten! We signed a year's lease on Rowan Tree Cottage on the third of September last. Remember? I have been in touch with our landlord and he's happy for us to continue renting on an *ad hoc* basis for the time being but he's even keener for me to sign another year's lease. He considers me a model tenant, even if I am living in sin! Do you want to live in Slattocks for another year? Or what?'

Ben knew Anne had deliberately kept her tone light as she mentioned the lease. The renewal date had slipped his mind and its timing was lousy. With all that had been happening to her mother, he would have preferred to have kept Anne in happy ignorance of his decision for another few weeks but, in the circumstances, he had no option but to tell her.

He drew her back into his arms before he spoke. 'I know how you feel about the abomination of war. You know I respect your sincerity. But your views aren't mine, Anne. If we don't stop General Franco and his Fascists in Spain, my view is you don't need a crystal ball to forecast another full-scale European war, so we've got to stop them. You know an International Brigade's being formed to fight for the Popular Front. I reckon I should put my beliefs into practice and volunteer.'

Anne buried her head on his chest and in a muffled voice said, 'Oh Ben, I've been dreading this moment.'

Kissing her hair he said, 'Then you do understand why, much as I love you, my dearest darling Anne, I have to go.'

Her voice even more muffled, she said, 'Yes.'

198

18

They locked the door on an empty Rowan Tree Cottage. Most of the furniture and household goods had been given away to needy villagers, the cats had been found a home, Ben had been to The Dales to say farewell to his parents and, Anne suspected, his wife. No mention was made of Irene and raising the subject of divorce at the moment seemed an irrelevance. Anne felt certain that, despite the awfulness of Mummy's heart attack, the last twelve months at Slattocks would prove to be among the happiest of her life. Before she turned the ignition key and pulled out Bill's self-starter, she said, 'Goodbye, cottage. Goodbye, moors.'

'We'll find another cottage with another view of the moors,' Ben said.

Staring straight at the crags of Netherstone Edge, where in her mind's eye she could see her father's cairn, Anne said, 'Just promise me one thing. Don't tell me you're a born survivor. Daddy apparently believed he was.'

'I wasn't going to. Apart from something worth fighting for, I've somebody worth coming back to. And I'll do my damnedest to return in one piece.'

With the tears pricking her eyes, the lump in her throat making it difficult to swallow, Anne started the car and they set off for London. Ben didn't want to depart from Dover or Folkestone as he said that would inevitably entail a visit to Chenneys which might upset her mother. Anne therefore said goodbye to him on Victoria Station. She couldn't think of anything sensible to say – had Mummy been able to when she'd seen Daddy off so many times during the Great War? – before the guard was blowing his whistle, the engine was belching into action, and the boat-train was steaming from the platform. Ben leant from the window to give her one last kiss and to shout, 'I'll write as soon as I get there.'

Anne stood on the platform waving and then he was gone.

The only thing to do, she decided, was to pitchfork herself into activity the way she had the last time Ben disappeared from her life. This time she had the knowledge that he loved her, but she also had the gnawing fear that this time his beloved body might find its last resting place in some Spanish field. All she could do was to keep working and await the letter he would write when he finally reached Spain.

In December much of Britain, and other parts of the world, notably the United States, was transfixed by the question: will he–won't he marry Mrs Simpson?, though Anne considered the whole affair had become ridiculously overblown. She happened to be down at Chenneys when Edward VIII made his broadcast, informing the nation that he could not be their king without the support of the woman he loved and was therefore abdicating. After their uncrowned and now ex-monarch's emotion-filled voice had faded away, Philip, who might have been expected to have sympathy for those unable to function without the support of the woman they loved, said, 'He always sulked when he couldn't get his own way. We're well rid of him.'

Christmas Anne spent *en famille* at Chenneys, everybody making the effort to be with their mother who remained fearfully weak, as fragile-looking as the most delicate glass, her always husky voice breathier than ever. But she announced, 'I refuse to be a bedridden old hag. When I don't feel like operating dear old Norman, you can all perform your filial duty by pushing me around in my new chair.'

Con confided that she was expecting again, which yet again made Anne long desperately for Ben. Her siblings departed but she stayed at Chenneys to celebrate the New Year and her mother's fifty-second birthday and she was back at Gower Street before the long-awaited letter arrived. After an amusing description of his unamusing journey to Spain, Ben wrote:

I finally reached Figueras where a motley collection of volunteers from an assortment of European countries, Canada and the United States, was assembled. We were issued with uniforms. One of the problems about said uniforms, is that your average Spaniard is not a tall lad.

My trousers came to just below my knees and apart from making me look like an overgrown boy scout they were draughty, so I've reverted to my own gear plus forage cap to give the required military air.

From Figueras we were driven in lorries to Barcelona where, with a Spanish brass band at our head, we marched through the streets to a tumultuous welcome from the populace. That was something special, Anne, and whatever you read in the papers, it is 'the people' who have risen to oppose General Franco. There is a giddy atmosphere of exultation and freedom. How long it lasts we shall see.

We then moved on to Albacete, which is some twenty miles from Valencia, and it's the base camp for the International Brigade. At the camp there were some hundred of us true-born Britons, so we formed ourselves into the British Brigade. Many of the lads are Communists and as we're all equal in the sight of Karl Marx (not himself a great believer in the equality of human intelligence), we had fierce arguments about whether some should be more equal than others and be appointed officers. Strongly assisted by B. D. Broughton, inequality won the day. I am more than happy to be serving under a ferocious Great War survivor from the King's Own Scottish Borderers, who is teaching us how to use a machine-gun, though at the moment we have no ammunition.

Our subsequent move was to Madrigueras which is where I am penning these lines. However small and impoverished they are, and Madrigueras qualifies on both counts, every Spanish village has an enormous Catholic church. Speaking of Catholicism, an Irish lad who crossed the border with me, although a citizen of the Irish Free State, decided to join us in the British Brigade. His devoutly Catholic mother managed to say the right prayer to the postal authorities and get a parcel through to him for Christmas. It contained a fruit cake and a message your sense of humour should appreciate: 'I was that sad to learn you have joined forces with the Enemies of God. Hope the cake arrives fresh.'

If you can get a parcel through to me, I shall love you more than ever. [Ben gave a list of his various requirements which included warm underwear, for, as he went on] This part of sunny Spain in winter is, as they say, cold enough to freeze your balls off. Speaking of which . . . how I miss you, my dearest, darling witch.

Otherwise, I don't know whether or not you will be pleased to hear that the women of the Popular Front have been fighting alongside their menfolk. Which is the stronger in you? The pacifist or the feminist? Please send the requested parcel to the base camp at Albacete, though the rumours abound that we shall soon be on the move to assist in the defence of Madrid, by which time I trust we shall have been issued with ammunition.

I love you.

Yours aye, Ben.

Enfolded in the letter was a card with a delightful painting he had done of Madrigueras and its enormous, partially wrecked, Catholic church. On the back, in his beautiful script, he had written, 'From me to you. Everything we both wish ourselves and the world for 1937.'

Having put the painting in a frame by her bedside, Anne rushed out to buy pencils, hog-hair and sable brushes, tubes of Winsor and Newton paints, rolls of high-quality paper and . . . oh, everything Ben had requested, together with other things she thought he might need. After posting the parcels – the first one was overweight so she had to repack it into two – Anne slipped into a nearby church to offer up a prayer to the God she doubted existed. For if Ben and the British Brigade were now in Madrid, they would soon be in action.

Her association with Ben known to more people than she had imagined, Anne was approached to lend her name to or sit on the committees supporting the Popular Front and/or Spanish civilians suffering from the ever more ferocious air-raids. These of course were mainly the work of German aeroplanes piloted by Fascists flowing unimpeded to the aid of General Franco's Falangist forces. When her own Government unearthed the Foreign Enlistment Act which made it illegal for British citizens to join the International Brigade, Anne's fury knew no bounds.

She said to Rebecca, 'I don't think Mr Baldwin and his bloody gang want the democratically elected Spanish Government to triumph.'

'Personally,' Rebecca replied, 'I wouldn't credit them with any coherent policy about anything. But there are a lot of covert Fascist supporters among our powers-that-be who think Herr Hitler and General Franco have the right idea, slapping down Communists, Socialists, trade unionists and Jews. And you're going to have to make up your mind which side you're on, aren't you, Annie?' Just as she only called her friend 'Becky' in moments of stress or deep emotion, Rebecca likewise used 'Annie'. 'Campaigning for the Peace Pledge Union and aid for the Popular Front ain't logical, you know.'

Anne was only too aware that the question Ben had posed – which was the stronger, her feminism or her pacifism? – had already widened into the question: which was the stronger, her pacifism or her loathing of Fascism? At the moment, it was the latter. She felt so furious about the whole situation in Spain that she sat down and banged out an article, lambasting the attitude of the democracies in general, the British Government in particular, calling for their immediate intervention on humanitarian as well as political grounds. To her delighted surprise, because the article was not written from 'the woman's angle', the *News Chronicle* immediately accepted it.

Anne's delight swiftly changed to outrage. Within a week of the article's publication, the *Daily Mail* launched an attack on her. It printed a photograph taken in her Oxford days, which made her look absurdly young and rather raffish. It enquired what qualifications Miss Anne Whitworth, that well-known writer of detective stories, had to criticise the position taken by the British Government? It said everybody deplored the suffering of the Spanish people but those who opposed General Franco were being manipulated by the Communists. It warned its readers to be wary of Miss Whitworth's allegedly humanitarian concern for the plight of Spanish civilians. Her own close friendship with an obscure artist named B. D. Broughton was well known. Mr Broughton was currently fighting with the Communist International Brigade and one might presume that Miss Whitworth shared his political views.

Anne could only hope to heaven Irene Broughton didn't

read the ghastly rag, though she worked in a municipal library where newspapers were freely available, did she not? From what Anne had learned of Mrs Broughton's character, she would not take kindly to the public linking of her husband's name with Miss Anne Whitworth's.

The *Mail* kept up its attack, dragging Anne's name into its gossip columns at every possible opportunity and some improbable ones. She had sympathised deeply with Philip throughout the savaging of *The Lie of Circumstance* but she now knew exactly how he had felt; angry, sickened, hurt and, almost worst of all, impotent. Anne's instinct was to write a scathing letter to the editor of the *Daily Mail*, refuting the downright lies and half-truths. But both her mother and Philip advised against any such action.

'The editor always has the last word, Anne,' Philip said.

'You'll just have to grin and bear it, my darling,' her mother said. 'Until they get bored and find another quarry.'

Anne debated whether to mention the horrid saga in her bi-weekly letters to Ben, but eventually decided not to. When his next letter arrived, she was glad she had kept quiet because it made her mauling by the *Daily Mail* appear a very tame affair. He had written after he'd taken part in the fighting in the Jarama valley and he said, 'War, me luv, is hell. Until you've experienced them, you can't comprehend the confusion, the noise, the smells, the sights, the fear and, for our first taste, the cold eating into our marrows. What war does is to absolve you from everyday responsibility, though I know you don't think I'm noted for that. Your responsibility becomes centred on surviving yourself and helping your pals. Afterwards, there is the exhilaration of having survived.'

Which, thank you God if You exist, Ben had done. He was now apparently out of the front lines, nursing what he described as his good luck, i.e. somebody had dropped a Maxim gun on his foot.

The news from Russia soon took Anne's mind off her problems, though it provided the *Daily Mail* with the opportunity to remind its readers that Miss Anne Whitworth's aunt was married to the discredited Communist leader, Mikhail Muranov. Further state trials were underway in Moscow when suddenly the unbelievable happened. Uncle Misha himself was arrested.

Aunty Sarah's response to the frantic cables and letters from England told them virtually nothing they hadn't read in the newspapers. Misha was in prison alongside his old revolutionary comrades, Nikolai Bukharin and Alexei Rykov; she and Tamara were fine; Kessie was not to worry and she would keep them posted. Gavin made enquiries through the Foreign Office but gained little further information. Madame Muranov and her daughter were under virtual house-arrest in Moscow, but were as well as could be expected in the circumstances. One might, according to Gavin's sources, hope that Mikhail Muranov's immense popularity would save him from the earlier fate of his disgraced comrades-in-arms, which had been execution or twenty-five years in a Siberian labour camp. With that scant news Anne and her mother, who was desperately worried about her favourite sister-in-law's plight, · had to be content.

Anne's dejected mood was marginally cheered by the news from Germany that arrived in a letter from Kurt. He wrote, 'It is strange, Anne. Since the Nuremberg Laws were enacted, we have been subjected to fewer actual indignities and less harassment. Perhaps the less rabidly anti-Semitic cohorts are currently in command, or perhaps the Nazis feel, that having reduced us to nothing, they can afford to be generous, though I've given up trying to fathom how their minds work. The improvement in our situation is, of course, only comparative and Luise has accepted Mr van Doncke's proposal of marriage. He is in the process of paying the Nazis sufficient money to enable my sister and nieces to leave the Third Reich. As soon as he has done so, the wedding will take place in Amsterdam, which is Mr van Doncke's native city. This will mean my parents and I will be unable to attend but you will, of course, receive an invitation. Luise dearly hopes you will accept, not forgetting Helga who confided to me she wished her Mummy were marrying an Englishman, so she could live in England next door to Aunty Anne!'

The invitation to the wedding arrived hard on the heels of Kurt's letter. Feeling very much in need of a break, Anne accepted it eagerly. She and Rebecca duly crossed the North Sea to Holland. It was Anne's first visit to Amsterdam and in the spring sunshine the city was at its loveliest, the light dancing on the waters of the canals and reflecting the bridges, glowing on the wares of the flower-sellers and the ornately decorated hurdy-gurdies in the cobbled market squares, glancing over the intricate designs of the gabled houses.

The reception was held in Mr van Doncke's beautiful house overlooking one of the canals. He and his bride were an incongruous couple – in an ivory satin dress, a favoured floppy hat and high-heeled kid leather shoes, Luise overtopped her new husband's rotund figure by a couple of inches – but they seemed fond enough of each other.

Little Helga attached herself to Aunty Anne, announcing, 'I speak the English very good now. Uncle Kurt he teach me.'

'You speak *English very well* and Uncle Kurt *teaches* you,' gently, Anne corrected her.

Solemnly the little girl repeated the corrections before pulling a face at Anne and saying, 'Now I have the double-Dutch to learn.' Laughingly Anne explained that 'double-Dutch' in English meant nonsense and Helga laughed with her. Then she frowned and asked, 'Why have not my granny and grandpa and Uncle Kurt come? Mummy would not tell me.'

No, Anne thought, and how did she answer the question whose shadow lay over the joyful occasion. Briskly she said, 'Because the nasty old Nazis wouldn't let them come.'

'There will be no nasty Nazis in Holland, will there, Aunty Anne?' Helga asked anxiously.

'No, my sweetheart. You're going to be very happy here.'

Soon after Anne's return to London, Kate telephoned in a state of considerable excitement. She said, 'Darling, I don't suppose you ever read the gossip columns or film magazines . . .'

'Yes, I do sometimes.'

'Oh,' Kate sounded very surprised. 'Well, you'll know Samuel J. Sylberg's here then.'

'Yes.' The arrival in London of the most flamboyant,

publicity-conscious and currently successful of Hollywood's independent producers – he had a string of recent box-office 'smasheroos' to his credit – had been noted outside the columns of gossip-writers and film magazines because Mr Sylberg was also considered to be one of the more creative and literate of Hollywood moguls.

'Darling, he has the most fabulous proposition to put to you, us, and he wants to meet you, us, at noon today. You know what Americans are like. Everything has to happen five minutes ago. So please say you'll be at the Savoy on the dot of twelve. Please, please, please.'

'What's the proposition?'

'He'll explain. Will you come?'

'All right but . . .'

'Must dash and get changed. See you. 'Bye, darling.'

Anne changed into one of her, or rather Theo Marvell's smartest outfits, a patterned cream silk dress with a high neck and a green silk waistband that matched the fashionably wide-shouldered jacket, topped by a green and white slouch hat. She was glad she had dolled herself up because when she arrived at the Savoy Hotel, Kate was looking particularly ravishing in a boldly patterned floral dress and a cerise-coloured straw hat. They were conducted along the thick pile of the Savoy's hushed corridors to a suite overlooking the Embankment Gardens and the River Thames. The room they entered was full of people, two well-groomed secretaries clattering away on typewriters, clean-cut young men consulting lists and each other. The focal point was Samuel J. Sylberg who was on the telephone saying 'Yeah. No. Yeah. No. Absolutely not. Not a cent more than ten thousand. That's dollars, not your goddam English pound.'

He looked up as Kate and Anne were ushered in and waved a large cigar at them. In the flesh he had a pitted, sallow skin and was heavier jowled and wore thicker glasses than was apparent in photographs, though his comparative youth (he was thirty-six, Anne had checked) was also more evident. Slamming the telephone receiver into its slots – he obviously thrived on noise – Samuel J. Sylberg stood up and said, 'Hi, Kate. You must be Anne. Glad to meet you.'

Anne did not care for people she did not know addressing

her by her Christian name and she also considered Mr Sylberg should advance towards her, rather than holding out his hand for her to greet him. In the event she advanced and he had a flabby handshake. Then he shouted, 'Listen, guys and gals. We're going in there . . .' He waved his cigar towards one of the doors leading off the main room. 'I don't want any interruptions, and I mean any, for one quarter of an hour. If King George calls, tell him I'll call him back.'

At that sally everybody except Anne roared with obsequious laughter and Kate smiled prettily. The room they went into was in fact his bedroom which Anne found off-putting but she and Kate perched themselves on chairs, whilst Mr Sylberg roamed around, puffing clouds of smoke and spitting out his words like a machine-gun.

'Looked through your books coming over on the *Queen Mary*, Anne. That's some boat. The film options on the first two have lapsed, I can buy the third up cheap and you haven't sold the fourth. That's the one grabbed me, Anne. The marriage of your detective and Lady What's-it. You'll have to get off your English asses but my proposition is this: your stepfather writes the screenplay based on *Whatever Happened to Wordsworth?* which is the best storyline but a lousy title for a film. We'll change it. He'll incorporate the best bits of the other books, plus the marriage, which is why I'm prepared to do a deal for all four books. Kate's a natural for Lady . . . what is her goddam name?'

'Helena Brockenhurst,' Kate said.

'Yup. It's a publicist's dream. Book by one beautiful aristocratic English rose, starring another, her sister, screenplay by their stepfather, Sir Philip Marchal.' Mr Sylberg's voice was reverential as he uttered Philip's titled name. 'Saw a screening of one of your English movies, lousy, your moviemakers think small, but there was this guy in it, Colin Cornwell. He's right for . . . what's your detective called?'

'Seth Pollard.' This time it was Anne who tartly replied. Really, the great Mr Sylberg might have remembered the names of her characters, seeing he apparently wanted to buy them. Though Kate, if far from aristocratic by lineage, was ideal casting for Lady Helena and why hadn't the idea occurred to her? Anne asked herself. And she had to give Samuel J.

Sylberg full marks for casting ideas because Colin Cornwell, whom Anne had seen in an exciting season at the Old Vic, would indeed make a splendid Seth.

Having recovered from the explosion of Samuel J. Sylberg's words, Anne was about to make her rejoinders when there was a knock on the door. Mr Sylberg yelled about not being effing interrupted and Anne couldn't make up her mind whether he was deliberately trying to shock her by using words like 'asses' and 'fuck' or whether he liked to shock, period. The intruders were in any case two waiters who, absolutely po-faced in the best English tradition, ignoring the foul language and the fact that two young ladies were sitting in the master's bedroom, wheeled in trollies, one bearing alcoholic drinks, canapés and sandwiches, the other tea, coffee, more sandwiches and cakes. Anne had wondered if they were going to be watered and fed, and she accepted a cup of coffee, a pile of the Savoy's wafer-thin sandwiches and a squelchy cream cake.

While Samuel J. Sylberg was gulping his whisky, she said, 'I do have an agent, you know, Mr Sylberg. Mr Julian Kendle of the J. C. Kendle Literary Agency and I think you should be speaking to him and . . .'

Mr Sylberg pivoted round to face her and he was surprisingly light on his feet. Over his shoulder Anne saw a rainbow arching across the River Thames which might, or might not, be a good omen. He interrupted her to say, 'Agents are *schlemiels* who talk money. I like to deal with people in the first instance. What I wanna know is, are you interested in my proposition? If you're not, we're wasting our time.'

'Yes, I am interested.' Anne said briskly. 'However, I'd better tell you straight out, Mr Sylberg . . .'

'If you're interested, call me "Sam".'

Avoiding calling him anything, Anne continued, 'Unless Sir Philip . . .' she couldn't resist parodying the reverential tones '. . . is allowed to write the screenplay in England, he won't consider doing it. My mother is an invalid, she could not undertake the six-thousand-mile journey to Hollywood and my stepfather would not contemplate leaving her.'

'Sorry to hear about your mother.' Anne thought 'Sam' already knew and that was one of the reasons she was here.

'The situation you outline would be goddam unusual but in the circumstances I might consider it.'

In the end they had three-quarters of an hour of Mr Sylberg's precious time, or at least Anne did, for Kate knew when to keep quiet and mostly sat looking demurely beautiful. It was agreed that Anne would consider the proposals, consult with her agent and stepfather, and get back to 'Sam' within forty-eight hours. He kept insisting money came second, trust and respect were what mattered in the making of a good movie, which Anne did not altogether believe, but she liked Samuel J. Sylberg more when she left the bedroom than she had on entering it.

As her sister was not working the next day either, they drove down to Chenneys the same afternoon. Throughout the journey Kate was at her most charmingly solicitous, enquiring after Ben, saying how awful the Spanish Civil War was and how she was going to do her bit by taking part in a special charity matinée the Duchess of Atholl was organising, as part of her Foodships for Spain campaign. But her sister wanted something from her, didn't she? Anne's signature on a contract for Samuel J. Sylberg to produce a film in which Kate would star.

As usual, when Anne was feeling jaundiced about her sister, Kate upturned her emotions by confiding, 'Darling, my marriage is in a mess. I made a fearful mistake marrying Sandy. I suppose you'd say it serves me right. But if I could get away from him for a while and go to Hollywood, it might help clear my head one way or the other. But should I go? If anything happened to Mummy while I was there . . . I do love her so much and I wouldn't do anything to hurt or upset her. Honestly, I wouldn't.'

For once Anne almost believed her sister, though if it came to the crunch of Mummy or a Hollywood career, she wouldn't swear which Kate would choose. She said, 'Let's see what Mummy has to say.'

Their mother insisted it was a marvellous opportunity for her daughters to advance their careers and she would be furious if they rejected it on her account. To her husband she said, 'If our great Hollywood mogul will let you write the screenplay here and you can get a watertight clause about the extent of rewrites, and you never know, seeing you are a "sir" he might agree, I think you should accept the offer too, Philip.'

Philip professed to be amused that the great Samuel J. Sylberg should have chosen to approach him via his step-daughters but Anne believed her stepfather was intrigued by the idea of doing a screenplay from her Seth Pollard novels, in which Kate (who'd always been his pet) would star. She thought it would be good for Philip too, because he hadn't written a line since the débâcle of *The Lie of Circumstance* and Mummy's heart attack. After hard-nosed but swift bargaining with Samuel J. Sylberg, in which money loomed as large as trust and respect, contracts were signed.

At the end of July Con's third child was born, another boy, christened Ian. Early in October, amid a fanfare of Samuel J. Sylberg's best publicity, Kate sailed for New York. Philip had not yet completed a final draft of his script but Kate had signed a three-film deal with Mr Sylberg's company and she was to star in another of his films before embarking on her role as Lady Helena Brockenhurst. Anne's relationship with Julian was now politely formal which, recalling their old intimacy, she found sad, but he was elated by the deal he had struck with Mr Sylberg and not long after Kate's departure he invited Anne to lunch.

Halfway through the meal he finally mentioned the topic Anne suspected was the real reason for the lunch. 'You are going to write more Seth Pollard stories, aren't you? With the film in the offing, Stoddard and Simpson are panting for another. Which means I can get you a really good advance.'

It surprised Anne how interested Julian was in money or maybe, like Philip, he enjoyed the actual negotiations and upping the stakes for his authors. She said, 'Yes, I've decided to do one more at least. I'm working on a plot using the theme of Browning's poem, *Porphyria's Lover*. Do you know it?'

Julian said, ye-es, but he couldn't instantly recall the theme. Anne re-enlightened him. 'It's about a man who strangles the woman he loves "The moment she was mine, fair, Perfectly good and pure."'

'Sounds suitably grisly!' Julian said.

With the prospective film promising vastly increased sales of all the Seth Pollard books, Stoddard and Simpson were enthusiastic about the synopsis Anne proceeded to write. She duly signed another contract and began work on *The Moment of Murder*, the title she had chosen. Otherwise she was sitting on so many committees, Rebecca said she'd buy her a pair of roller skates. The sweetest moments of Anne's existence came with the erratic arrival of Ben's letters, and the information that he was managing to draw and paint provided some small consolation for the pain of his absence and the constant fear for his safety.

In one letter he mentioned the Russians who were fighting with them, though he told Anne she should discount the stories about the influx of Russian troops and arms to the Popular Front, and he wished to heaven Uncle Joe Stalin were supplying more of both, seeing the democracies weren't. Ben then enquired what was happening about her uncle, Mikhail Muranov, which was a good question.

Her mother remained deeply worried about Aunty Sarah's situation so Anne decided to approach Sandy, to see if he was any better informed than they were. He wasn't and he had the dyed-in-the-wool Communist *chutzpah*, as Rebecca would say, to observe, 'I realise what a shock it must have been to you, but your uncle can't have been arrested without good reason, Anne.'

'Oh bollocks!' Anne was so furious she actually used the word. 'Mikhail Muranov has been a dedicated Bolshevik all his adult life. He was one of Lenin's favoured young men. The notion that he's been working for the Nazis, or plotting to overthrow the Communist regime and restore bourgeois imperialism, or murder Stalin, or that he's been a secret British agent since the year dot, is absolute rubbish.'

Quite seriously Sandy then made a statement which left Anne momentarily speechless. He said, 'He is married to an Englishwoman, you know.'

PART IV

19

'You being English isn't helping him,' Tamara shouted at her mother. Gazing at her cousin's flushed face, Anne experienced the same feeling of speechless astonishment as she had with Sandy Dalziel. Tamara was bi-lingual, speaking English as fluently as Russian, but her accent was an idiosyncratic mixture of emphatic Russian 'zh' and Aunty Sarah's Lancashire vowel sounds. Rounding on Anne she almost screamed, 'And you being part of the English aristocracy isn't helping my father. I don't know why you came.'

Anne could cheerfully have hit her cousin but Aunty Sarah said quietly, 'And your ranting and raving isn't doing anybody any good, Tammy.'

'Don't call me "Tammy".' This had been her baby nickname in the postwar days when she and Aunty Sarah had lived at the Whitworths' house in London. 'You know I hate being called "Tammy".'

With that Tamara ran from the living room of the Moscow apartment, into the bedroom she was sharing with her mother (thus ungraciously allowing Anne to have hers), and slammed the door hard behind her. After a brief silence Aunty Sarah said, 'You'll have to forgive her. Remember how your world collapsed when your Dad was killed? Tamara's in a similar state. She's been brought up as a privileged member of the Communist élite and she's a good Communist herself. Suddenly her privileges are withdrawn, she's an outcast, and her father's being denounced as Public Enemy Number One. And she loves him as much as you loved your Dad.'

Anne made a sympathetically understanding noise, though she had been only nine years old at the time, whereas Tamara was nineteen. And why was Anne here, upsetting the cousin to whom she had *not* taken? Just before Christmas, out of the blue, the brief letter had arrived from Aunty Sarah. It read:

'Dear Kessie, I have been given permission to write to you. If you would allow Anne to come to Moscow, I should be most grateful. I understand there will be no difficulties about visas and I assure you she will be well looked after. I do hope your health is better. Tamara and I send our love to you all, Sarah.'

Gavin was immediately consulted and he said the Communist authorities were obviously willing to let Anne travel to her aunt's side, he doubted their motives were humanitarian, in the tyrannously unpredictable climate of spy mania, arrest and trial in Russia, he did not believe Anne's safety could be guaranteed and she should not, in his opinion, go. To that Mummy responded, 'Unless Sarah were desperate and believed Anne would be in no danger, wild horses wouldn't have persuaded her to write the letter.'

'They use more sophisticated methods than wild horses in Stalin's Russia,' Gavin observed dryly.

Mummy ignored his comment and said, 'You have my blessing, Anne, but it's up to you to decide.'

Anne's own instinct was to proceed hotfoot to her beleaguered aunt's side and her mother's blessing meant she'd go if she were in her eldest daughter's shoes, but Anne still hesitated. Like Kate she was worried that their mother's fragile health might suddenly deteriorate and for that reason she had resisted the temptation to visit Spain and Ben, despite both the *Manchester Guardian* and the *News Chronicle* intimating that though they wouldn't send her, a woman, as an accredited war correspondent, they would be interested in publishing any articles she might, as a woman on the spot, send them. Eventually, instinct and her mother's attitude had won the day and towards the end of January, documentation obtained, Gavin's rundown on the situation and warnings to make immediate contact with the British ambassador and to hold her tongue absorbed, Anne had made the long train journeys across Europe to Moscow.

Looking at her aunt as she sat hunched in her chair – a position Anne remembered of old – she appeared to be bearing up under the strain, though it had taken a severe physical toll. Her once jet-black hair was quite white, her sharp features were deeply lined, her small figure seemed to have shrunk and she looked older than Mummy despite her heart attack. Anne said, 'Was getting me here a nefarious plot? Have I harmed Uncle Misha's chances at his trial? Have I given them an extra opportunity to talk about his British imperialist links?'

'I don't think it matters one way or t'other, Anne luv.'

Having made that pronouncement in fairly broad Lancashire, her aunt jumped up from the chair and crossed towards the windows, and her movements remained sprightly. Another flurry of snow was drifting from the leaden sky and though it was only four o'clock in the afternoon, the light was fading with murky swiftness. Peering through the windows, down into the Kadesevskaya which ran alongside one of the frozen loops of the River Moskva, Aunty Sarah said, 'They must be perished, stuck out there night and day. And the lower ranks of the NKVD aren't well-paid. Still, power of any sort is its own reward for some folk.'

Realising her aunt was talking about the roster of Russia's not-so-secret servants which kept the Muranovs under constant surveillance – two enormous women, allegedly housekeepers, took it in turns to sit like Buddhas in the corridor outside the apartment – Anne said, 'I think you're wonderful and I am glad I came.'

Swishing the heavy curtains together, shutting out the greyness, Aunty Sarah replied, 'I can't tell you how glad I am that you came. Things have definitely improved for us since your arrival, not just the money and lovely things you were allowed to bring with you. Do you know what nearly broke me, Anne? Not having anybody to talk to, apart from Tammy of course, but you've seen the muddled state she's in. Our telephone's "tapped", tha knows.' With a wry smile, she again lapsed into Lancashire idiom. 'They put peg-things on the line and listen to our conversations. You can hear them doing it! So even the few courageous or desperate souls who ring the disgraced Muranovs can't say much.'

Although her mother had believed Sarah herself to be desperate, Anne found it hard to conceive of her aunt at breaking point, as briskly she went on, 'Knowing my daughter, she's going to sulk until she gets hungry which'll be in a couple of hours. So let's make a samovar of tea and now we've got some fuel, let's sit in front of the stove and have a good talk.'

While her aunt made the tea, Anne drew up the chairs which were of solid oak and handsomely carved. The remaining furniture in the apartment was similarly handsome – to survive since her husband's arrest, Aunty Sarah had been forced to sell many pieces at knockdown prices – but it had come from Mikhail Muranov's ancestral home in Odessa, had it not? If anybody was 'aristocratic', or at least decidedly upper class, it was Tamara's father, not Anne's. The stove was a black monster with a huge pipe, iron feet, and doors through which it ate fuel. Anne tried to imagine what it must have been like for Aunty Sarah and Tamara earlier in the freezing Moscow winter, without fuel. When they were comfortably seated, drinking their lemon tea, she asked her aunt, 'When did you last see Uncle Misha?'

'They don't have visiting days at the Lubyanka prison,' Aunty Sarah replied dryly. 'But they let me see him last September. Dunno why. He didn't look at all bad then, though God knows what they've done to him since, but six months off the vodka had done him no end of good. Your uncle always was a hard drinker but he'd been knocking it back by the gallon for the last few years. Attempting to drown the nightmares of how they'd allowed Joseph Stalin, the man your uncle used to patronise and never regarded as more than an efficient organiser, to outfox and outbox them all. And the even worse nightmare of what Comrade Stalin was doing to your uncle's beloved Russia and the brave new Bolshevik world. I saw it happening but then I'm not a Communist, as my daughter observed I am English, so they didn't take any notice of me.'

Whilst her aunt poured more tea from the samovar and dropped fresh slices of precious lemon into their cups, Anne thought those years couldn't have been easy for her either. Briskly Aunty Sarah said, 'That's all in the past. Future historians can enjoy themselves explaining the questions that tortured Misha. It's the immediate future that concerns us. Tammy can go on hoping for Uncle Joe's forgiveness but I know her father's doomed.'

The matter-of-fact way her aunt made this startling

announcement caused Anne to gasp but she continued even more briskly, 'So, I reckon, does Misha. He may be a romantic but he's a realistic one. It's therefore a question of getting the best deal we possibly can. I don't have any aces up my sleeve but, whatever Tammy thinks, my being English has helped in some ways and I have a possible trump card. It may turn out to be the two of clubs, but I'm going to play it. Shall we make an appointment to see his nibs the British ambassador and give my bodyguards some exercise?'

The British Embassy was not apparently situated in the heart of Moscow and they had to change trams on the journey from the Muranovs' apartment in the Kadesevskaya. Anne had never played rugby football but Mark had and he said it was a lethal game to be avoided by all sane people. She felt the same about travelling on Moscow's trams. To make matters worse Anne sensed a sullen hostility emanating from the hundreds of people packed on the trams and walking along the pavements, though not all the streets were paved. She was wearing a glossy mink coat and hat and real leather boots which probably didn't help matters, seeing that everybody else was so drably dressed, but it was bitterly cold with an icy wind blowing across the River Moskva and Anne wasn't going to freeze to death to placate anybody. When they alighted from the second tram she voiced her feelings to her aunt and asked, 'Is it envy? Or evidence of the class struggle? Or do they just hate foreigners?'

Aunty Sarah replied, 'Individually, Russians are lovely people. Well, not all of them, but lots of them. *En masse* they're a beleaguered nation, old in history, young in political ideology, in fearful internal turmoil, regarded with hate or suspicion by the outside world. If you're not for 'em, you're agin 'em. You don't look likely to be for 'em.'

Inside the British Embassy was different. There, Anne was obviously regarded as one of us but Madame Muranov was not. Anne personally had telephoned the ambassador who had immediately agreed to see them, but when they were ushered into his room, while she sat down in the proffered chair, Aunty Sarah ignored hers and walked to the window. After she had looked through the curtains, she said to the ambassador, 'Just checking to see if they've arrived safely. My NKVD men, you know. Wouldn't like to think they'd got lost, though they'd have been forewarned by my niece's telephone call.'

Tea and biscuits were brought in and the ambassador enquired after Mr and Mrs Campbell-Ross and their delightful children – actually Robert, or Rob as he was known, was a little devil – before asking in what way he could assist? In the opulence of the room, in contrast to the well-fed, well-dressed ambassador and to Anne herself, Aunty Sarah looked so small and shabbily clothed, like a bedraggled sparrow, but she sounded chirpy enough as she directed her words straight at the ambassador.

'You know who I am and you know who my husband is. Except he isn't legally my husband. Mikhail Muranov and I never married. Actually, Anne's mother floated the notion of our being married, to save my and the family's good name. Mikhail and I never bothered to contradict it or do anything to turn it into a reality. It couldn't matter less now if it becomes public knowledge. But I've never taken out Russian citizenship which means I'm a British citizen. My daughter's father is Russian but she was born in England, which means she has dual nationality. When her father comes to trial and is sentenced to be executed as he assuredly will be, I want to leave Russia with my daughter and return to England. I'm trying to get a personal interview with Comrade Stalin. He may grant me one. He used to quite like me, as much as he likes anybody that is, and he never had a high opinion of the female sex. Depends what sort of mood he's in.'

Aunty Sarah leaned forward in her chair and in a quietly insistent voice she continued, 'I'm going to be absolutely straight with you. I want to stop Mikhail doing a deal with Stalin which he thinks'll save us but will mean he has to stand up in court and accuse himself of every crime known to mankind, the way that some of the others have. It's too degrading and I couldn't bear it. But to be in any kind of bargaining position, I need to be able to tell Comrade Stalin that my daughter and I are both British citizens. What I want from you, sir, is the assurance that the British Embassy won't baulk me and say they'll have to investigate and eventually issue us with British passports some time next year. Because by then, on past form of what's happened to the disgraced men's families who haven't been shot, we'll be in a labour camp.'

Part of the recital astonished Anne almost as much as it had when her aunt had related it last night. The things that had gone on in the supposedly sedate days of her childhood; Aunty Alice having an affair with Julian's father, Aunty Sarah conceiving an illegitimate child and living in sin with Mikhail Muranov, and her mother a party to the proceedings! Watching the ambassador as her aunt finished speaking, Anne thought a faint smile twitched his lips which was a good sign because he couldn't be accustomed to being spoken to like that, certainly not by a woman. When he responded, however, his voice was dryly formal. 'Please believe me, Madame Mur . . .' He stopped himself completing the non-legal name. 'I have every sympathy with your current predicament. Your information will require substantiation but . . .'

Aunty Sarah interrupted him, 'There'll be no difficulty about our daughter. Her birth was registered at Ventnor on the Isle of Wight in June 1918. And you can't substantiate something that didn't happen, i.e. my marriage to Mikhail Muranov. So are you going to be difficult about my passport?'

'No, madam, I am not. In the circumstances, I shall do everything within my power to expedite matters. Once your citizenship is established and your passports are issued, you will come under the protection of His Britannic Majesty and his servants, including myself.' The tone remained formal, not to say pompous, but then the ambassador said, 'May I say how much I admire your courage? And I wish you well in the interview with General Secretary Stalin, which I most sincerely hope you will be granted.'

'Thank you.' The unexpected sympathy produced a tremor in Aunty Sarah's voice.

During the next few days the telephone rang several times in the Muranovs' apartment. Apart from Nikolai Bukharin's wife ringing to consult Aunty Sarah – in addition to the fears for her husband's fate, she had a baby son to worry about – the rest of the calls were from the British Embassy for

Anne. She presumed the ambassador was letting the NKVD telephone tappers know that an eye was being kept on Miss Whitworth and incidentally on Madame Muranov and her daughter too. But each time the call was for her cousin, Tamara exercised her furious disappointment and displeasure by rushing into the bedroom and slamming the door behind her.

Then, on the Sunday morning, the telephone rang again and it was not for Anne. Standing absolutely still, she listened to Aunty Sarah speaking rapidly in Russian and watched Tamara's face flush with excitement. When her aunt put the receiver into its hook, Tamara said, 'Oh Mum! I knew Uncle Joe would see you. I told you he would. When?'

'Tomorrow afternoon. The trials of ex-comrades Muranov, Bukharin, Rykov and sundry unfortunate smaller fry are to open on the second of March. That's official. Comrade Stalin wants to see you too, luv. I am instructed to bring my English niece with me.'

While Anne stared stupidly at her aunt, Tamara shouted, 'What about me?'

'I have no instructions for you, Tammy.'

'Oh . . .' Tamara let out a howl of fury and picked up the nearest object to hand, a figurine of a shepherd and shepherdess, which she hurled against the wall. The fragments scattered across the once thick, now threadbare, pile of the carpet.

Monday was a beautiful day, the sky a bright blue, the air crisp, the sun glistening on the snow, glancing across the water and the floating ice, as Anne and her aunt walked across the two bridges that lay between Kadesevskaya and the Kremlin. Perhaps the sudden beauty of the February day was a good omen, Anne thought, perhaps Tamara was right about 'Uncle Joe's' change of mind. Aunty Sarah had rubbed up the wool of her old astrakhan coat, polished her battered boots and agreed to wear one of Anne's tighter-fitting fur hats – unfortunately her niece's coats and boots were several sizes too large – and if she couldn't be called smart, she looked neat. Anne herself was wrapped in her mink coat and hat.

When they reached the massive yellow-and-white stonework of the Great Kremlin palace that was now the seat of the USSR's government, they were conducted through truly magnificent rooms. The intricacy of the gold-work, the richness of the artefacts, the brilliance of the frescoes, the mastery of the paintings, the sumptuous marble of the staircase, stunned Anne's eyes. On their journey into the heart of the palace, they were handed from minions to increasingly important Communist functionaries but without exception their attitudes were a curious mixture of severe distancing from the disgraced Madame Muranov and awe that she was proceeding into the presence of the infallible one, the almighty Stalin. What any of them made of her personally, Anne couldn't imagine.

Penultimately they were led into an ante-room where they were left in the charge of two stony-faced Red Army guards. Anne wondered if her aunt's heart was thumping, her stomach somersaulting, the same way as her own. Presumably they were because Aunty Sarah said, 'We shall be here for some time. This is the softening-up process. Get your nerves working at full stretch. Let's play a game. I spy with my little eye something beginning with . . . I.'

'I think you're a splendid lady,' Anne said. 'Ikon.'

'Right, let's play summat else.' By way of ignoring the compliment, Aunty Sarah lapsed into Lancashire. 'How about famous people?'

They took it in turns to identify characters whose surnames began with the letter W (William Wilberforce), T (Ellen Terry), B (Simon Bolivar) and F (Elizabeth Fry). Anne was trying to guess the identity of somebody whose surname began with H, when a door at the far end of the ante-room opened. A youngish man with an expressionless face entered and spoke to Aunty Sarah in Russian. She nodded at him before turning to Anne and saying, 'Right, we're under starter's orders. I needn't have bothered togging myself up because we're to leave our coats and hats here.'

Underneath her carefully brushed astrakhan coat she was wearing a plain grey skirt, its seat shiny with age, and a darned jumper, though Anne's high-necked, dark-brown two-piece was smart enough. After they had laid their outdoor clothes over the backs of the chairs, Aunty Sarah said,

'Just be your natural, charming self, luv. If Stalin asks if he can do anything for you – he likes being magnanimous occasionally – you ask if Aunty Sarah and Tamara can see Uncle Misha before he's shot. No, don't say anything about him being shot.' As they followed the young man, she added, 'The H I was thinking of was James Hargreaves. He came from Blackburn, you know. It was there he invented the Spinning Jenny. Be nice to be in Lancashire again, to walk through The Dales and see Netherstone Edge before I pop off.'

The room they were ushered into was small in comparison to those they had passed through and it was a masculine room, wooden chairs, a table, a desk, bookshelves, few ornaments. Through the windows Anne saw the sweep of the River Moskva below and in the open fireplace the flames were leaping. Joseph Stalin was standing in front of the fire, warming his backside. He looked exactly as he did in his photographs, heavily, squarely built, the dark hair brushed off his forehead, the eyebrows thickly arched, the eyes slightly slanting, the nose prominent, the moustache luxuriant, the broad features unsmiling. He was in a khaki uniform with gold epaulettes, red and gold tabs on the collar, medals pinned to the left breast. By his side but not too close, was another youngish man with another of those expressionless faces. Did they go on special courses, Anne wondered, to learn how to deaden their emotions? Even before the almighty one spoke to the young man, she presumed Aunty Sarah was not to be trusted to translate and he was here to act as interpreter.

Stalin's voice was monotonous in timbre, but unlike Leon Trotsky or Mikhail Muranov he had never been one of the orators of the Revolution. The interpreter said, 'General Secretary Stalin welcomes you to the Kremlin, Miss Whitworth. He trusts you are enjoying your visit to our beloved Russia.'

Anne couldn't think of a suitable response to that so she smiled and took Joseph Stalin's outstretched hand. He had a bearlike shake. To Aunty Sarah he gave the briefest of nods and they were invited to sit in the chairs ranged round the fire. These were placed so that Stalin was in the dominant position, able to fix them with his basilisk stare, the interpreter to his left, while Anne and her aunt were sitting level but a few feet apart, which meant they had to turn their heads to communicate and Stalin could watch their faces.

Then he said something in Russian, the interpreter rose to his feet, walked to the door and called out in a peremptory voice. To Anne's astonishment, two men pushed in trolleys laden with a silver samovar and platefuls of cakes. They were followed by a woman who proceeded to pour out the tea and hand round the plates. While Stalin spoke to the interpreter, Anne stole a glance at Aunty Sarah but her face was as inscrutable as the most dedicated *apparatchik*'s.

The interpreter announced, 'General Secretary Stalin would suggest you try these, Miss Whitworth. They are Russian honey cakes and they are entirely delectable.' He indicated one of the plates and Stalin himself smiled jovially at Anne and said, '*Da, da.*'

The honey cake was delicious but Anne had a sudden vision of Kate and herself munching away in Samuel J. Sylberg's bedroom at the Savoy. That had been a bizarre occasion but there was something macabre about this one and she didn't know what she was doing here, anyway. The three servants left the room and during the next quarter of an hour Anne had even less idea why she had been invited because the conversation was carried on entirely in Russian between Stalin and her aunt.

As a language it was richly melodic to listen to, but sitting there not understanding a word was an extraordinary experience, and Anne felt as if she were watching two unusually loquacious poker players. Just once she thought Aunty Sarah was about to lose her temper, when she sat bolt upright in her chair and emitted the curious mm . . . mm . . . mm noise which sounded as if the speaker had lost the thread of their argument, though lots of Russians made it so presumably it was a speech idiom. Just once Aunty Sarah interrupted the low-pitched monotony of Comrade Stalin's flow and momentarily he looked thunderous. Suddenly Anne realised that they had stopped speaking. She looked at her aunt but her face remained blankly uninformative.

Stalin said something to the interpreter who then addressed Anne. 'Secretary General Stalin enquires if you have enjoyed a night at the Bolshoi Theatre.' Anne shook her head and, unless his NKVD men had failed to make regular reports, he knew damned well she hadn't. The interpreter said, 'Then it will be his pleasure to see that two tickets are made available for you and a friend from the British Embassy.' The NKVD men obviously had been reporting. 'General Secretary Stalin trusts that during your visit you will explore the great achievements of our glorious revolution and learn why we were revolting.'

Anne liked that phraseology and said she certainly hoped to do so. Then Stalin spoke to the interpreter again and before the young man translated, she thought she saw a flicker of a smile cross Aunty Sarah's face. Solemnly the young man said, 'General Secretary Stalin will be interested to hear your first-hand impressions of the coronation of your King George and Queen Elizabeth in your Westminster Abbey. We, as you are aware, have abolished such anachronisms.'

Anne had been nowhere near Westminster Abbey during the coronation. Neither had any member of the family. Upper-class Philip might be, a peer of the realm he was not. Was it a genuine interest? Or was it a heavy-handed attempt to be friendly? Or was General Secretary Stalin slyly sending her up? Uncertain which was the correct answer, Anne hedged her bets by saying the coronation had been a fascinating experience, though she agreed that in the century of the people, royal families were anachronisms. Of any sort, she felt like adding, whether hereditary or self-appointed. It did not appear that the Communist fairy godfather was about to grant her dearest wish, so directing her most charming smile at Stalin, employing her softest voice, she said to the interpreter, 'Will you ask General Secretary Stalin if he could possibly allow my aunt and my cousin to see Mr Muranov?'

There was a pause before the interpreter translated the request, during which the crackle of the wood burning in the fire sounded to Anne like rifle shots and through the windows the glare of the setting sun spilled into the room like blood. Stalin's response was swift, though Anne had no idea whether it was for good or ill until the interpreter said, 'It is now understood that Mr Muranov and your aunt are not married.'

Aunty Sarah had patently done her stuff. 'In spite of this unfortunate circumstance, General Secretary Stalin will exercise beneficence and your aunt will be allowed to visit her . . . mm . . . mm . . . mm . . .'

The interpreter's considerable grasp of the English language failed him. Whether Tamara was to be embraced by the General Secretary's beneficence was unclear but Anne felt she had done her bit.

Once they were out of the palace Aunty Sarah said, 'I need to clear my head. Tammy'll be bursting to know what happened but it's bad news for her, so let's have a walk round the Kremlin before we break it to her.'

Anne herself was bursting to know what Stalin had said but she sympathised with her aunt's need to assemble her thoughts. Silently they walked up the snow-covered slopes of the citadel. The sunset was spectacularly lurid, in keeping with the threatening atmosphere of their lives, the crimson glare enveloping the helm and onion domes of the cathedrals of the Dormition, the Annunciation and the Archangel Michael, turning the gilt crosses to molten gold.

Eventually Aunty Sarah said, 'I now know why Stalin saw us. If the trials are to serve their purpose, which I take it is to establish his supremacy by proving to the Russian people at large that Uncle Joe, and only Uncle Joe, has their true interests at heart and all the rest are a pack of treacherous hounds, he needs to put the people's erstwhile favourite, Mikhail Muranov, in the dock. Your Uncle Misha always was unpredictable and Stalin's not sure they've broken him. Bless his courageous heart! *Ergo*, he wants a deal as much as I do. That's why he's going to let me see your uncle, so's I can spell it out and your uncle will behave himself in the courtroom.'

'What deal has Stalin agreed to?' Anne asked.

'He's accepted that Tammy and I are British citizens and that he could have problems if he tries to stop us leaving Russia, once your uncle's dead.'

Anne wondered if her aunt's insistence on making these statements about her common-law husband's death was to accustom herself to the idea and lessen the shock, if or when it happened. She asked, 'Why will that make Uncle Misha behave himself in court? I'd have thought it might . . .'

'Ah, that's where you come into the equation, Anne. That's why you were invited for tea and cakes. Our Joe reminded me of the British engineers from Metro-Vickers he put on trial. He could, he implied, if he chose to, hold you on a similar charge of spying.'

'Could he?' Anne's shiver was not entirely caused by the chillness of the air.

'Don't worry. He's not going to.' Aunty Sarah's voice was at its briskest. 'It's all part of the game. Providing Misha behaves himself in court, which does *not* mean he has to grovel publicly – I made it clear that's not part of the deal – we should emerge bloodied but unbowed.'

'I see.' Anne wasn't sure that she did. It sounded a dangerously uncertain 'game' to her. She didn't want to upset Aunty Sarah who seemed to have recovered her equilibrium but she felt she had to say, 'How do you know Stalin will keep his side of the bargain and let you and Tamara leave Russia once the trial is over?'

They were nearing the tower of Ivan Veliki, the dying sun's rays were striking the highest cupola like bloodshot arrows and at Anne's question about Stalin's honouring the bargain, her aunt stopped in her stride. She looked straight at Anne and her face was enveloped in the scarlet light as she said, 'I don't know whether or not he'll let us leave, luv. But Stalin's a devious devil and he has a certain respect for those who play him at his own game. I'm banking on that to make him keep his side of the deal. And as a further insurance, I'm banking on our being English and your "aristocratic" connections – I enjoyed the bit about the coronation – because General Secretary Stalin has enough problems on his plate at the moment without a full-scale diplomatic row with England.'

'Oh.' Anne could not say she felt wholly reassured. And had Aunty Sarah been as devious as Stalin? In her desperate desire to salvage as much from the wreck as possible, primarily for Uncle Misha and Tamara, incidentally for herself, had she used Anne as a pawn? What would happen if Aunty Sarah was wrong and Uncle Misha wasn't sentenced to death?

Would she and Tamara still want to leave Russia? Anne left these questions unasked. As they started to retrace their steps, instead she said, 'Isn't Tammy to be allowed to see her father?'

'No, poor lamb. She has no purpose to serve. Mebbe it's for the best. She'd probably break down if she did see her Dad. I don't reckon she'll want to go to England, so she might create a scene too.'

'When will you be allowed to see Uncle Misha?'

'No idea, luv, but it'll be before the second of March when the trial opens. And knowing the NKVD, it'll be without warning.'

20

After Tamara learned that she was not to be allowed to see her father, she stormed round the apartment shouting at her mother as if it were her fault. Then she went into a deep Russian gloom, shutting herself into the bedroom for twenty-four hours. When she finally emerged, her mother, whom Anne considered to be exhibiting remarkable patience, said briskly, 'General Secretary Stalin was right about one thing. Anne should see something of Moscow while she's here. Why don't you show her round, Tammy? If the NKVD men want to trot after you, that's their business.'

So the two of them toured the city which to Anne's eyes was astonishingly traffic-free, apart from the groaningly overburdened trams, some horses and carts, and the occasional limousine bearing Communist dignitaries who remained in favour. Tamara didn't talk to Anne, she lectured or hectored her. In Red Square, for example, she declaimed, 'In Russian the same word means "red" and "beautiful".'

'That's useful for the Communists, isn't it?'

Tamara did not deign to reply but the magnificent expanse of the snow-covered square, the swirling domes of St Basil's

Cathedral glinting in the pale winter sunshine, its rays illuminating the salmon-coloured walls of the Kremlin and the rhubarb-red walls of Lenin's mausoleum, fulfilled both meanings of the word. Tamara said of course Anne would wish to see Lenin's body, to which Anne replied of course. They joined the long line shuffling towards the entrance of the mausoleum, the watery sun disappeared, the snow started to swirl across Red Square, and by the time they eventually got inside Anne's feet felt like blocks of ice. But if Tamara could stand the discomfort, so could she. They mounted the stairs to file past Lenin's embalmed body under its canopy of plate-glass, and in the harsh glare of the electric light Anne blinked at the wax-like figure in the dun-coloured jacket. She exclaimed 'Goodness, wasn't he – isn't he – tiny?'

'Size has nothing to do with strength of purpose or achievement.' Tamara sounded just like her mother.

Staring at Lenin's neat brown moustache Anne whispered, 'I wonder what he'd have thought of his old comrades being put on trial and knocked down like a row of ninepins.'

To that comment Tamara did not reply but it made her frown.

Apart from the tourist sights which dated from Czarist days, her cousin took Anne for a ride on the Moscow underground system and showed her blocks of workers' apartments, she pointed out hospitals, clinics, schools and nurseries, all of which were Communist achievements, whilst spouting statistics and lauding the equality of the Communist system. When they passed yet another group of women wrapped in old overcoats, ill-fitting boots and headscarves, digging up a road, Anne said, 'Women don't seem to me to be any more equal here than at home. The only difference seems to be they're doing the sort of heavy manual labour that women in England haven't undertaken since the war. How many women are there in the Praesidium? Or in any high rank of Government.'

'Aleksandra Kollontai was on the Central Committee and she's now an ambassador. We have thousands of women doctors and . . .'

'We have a few women MPs and quite a lot of women doctors,' Anne observed.

Tamara sniped and argued about everything and Anne felt

that if she said, 'The moon isn't made of green cheese', Tamara would reply, 'Yes it is. In Communist Russia it is.' Her hostility was unrelenting and Anne could only presume it came, as Aunty Sarah had said, from the terrible dilemma her cousin found herself in, of having been brought up to believe in the Communism that appeared set on destroying her father. How nice it would be, she thought, if just for once her cousin would behave like a human being, open her heart and discuss things.

When the tickets for the Bolshoi Theatre arrived – Anne was surprised that General Secretary Stalin had remembered – Tamara accepted the invitation to accompany her, but even there she never stopped saying what a beautiful building it was and commenting on the brilliance of the ensemble acting Konstantin Stanislavsky had created from Communist principles, the like of which obviously could not be found in England. The only time she showed an interest in anything other than her own concerns, was after Anne had said she would like to buy presents for her friends and relations. Tamara took her to a second-hand bookshop stuffed with books printed by the old St Petersburg presses, which presumably were considered decadent because they were on sale at ludicrously low prices. After Anne had chosen an exquisite volume of aquatints of St Petersburg for her mother (they had visited that lovely city, by then renamed Leningrad, when the Muranovs were briefly living there); a sumptuous volume of the Complete Works of William Shakespeare – in English – for Philip; and Byzantine art books for Con and Rebecca, she spent a long time deciding which book to buy for Ben, before selecting a lavishly bound set of ikon paintings printed on the most gorgeous paper.

'Is that for somebody special?' When Anne nodded Tamara further enquired, 'You're not engaged, are you?'

'No. I have the misfortune to love a married man. He's fighting in Spain at the moment.'

Inevitably Tamara spoiled the moment by saying, 'On which side?'

Anne snapped, 'It won't fit your apparent image of me as a Fascist in bourgeois capitalist clothes, but he's fighting with the International Brigade.'

It wasn't until the end of the interesting but tense week – apart from the strain of Tamara's company, they were anxiously awaiting Aunty Sarah's summons to see Uncle Misha – that the third secretary from the British Embassy came to the Muranovs' apartment. He rejoiced in the name of Peregrine Dennett-Mardon, he was tall and thin with wispy brown hair, he sported a monocle and spoke as if he were either gargling or yawning. Anne couldn't make up her mind whether he was as big an idiot as he looked and sounded, or whether it was a great big act designed to baffle the Russians, or the natives of any other country in which he happened to be serving.

Looking uncommonly pleased with himself, Mr Dennett-Mardon stood in the living room and extracted two brand-new British passports from his briefcase. The gold of the lions and unicorns gleamed against the dark blue of the covers, and with a ceremonious bow, he handed one passport to Aunty Sarah, the other to Tamara, gargling, 'It is with the greatest pleasure I personally deliver these into your safe keeping.'

Aunty Sarah gave a heartfelt sigh of relief and said, 'Thank you.'

But Tamara's reaction was to throw her passport across the room and to shout, 'I am not English, I am Russian. I don't want to go to England. And I'm not going. I'm staying here where I belong.' With a furious look at her mother she yelled, 'You can do what you want.'

With that she made her usual storming exit into the bedroom. Allowing for the fearful circumstances, Anne still considered her cousin's behaviour childish, boring, and something her mother could live without. Aunty Sarah gave another sigh, moved to pick up the passport and said, 'Sorry about that, Mr Dennett-Mardon. But we all react differently to pressure.'

'True, true,' he murmured politely. When Anne was showing him out, he yawned, 'Corking-looking girl, your cousin. But a bit of a tartar, what?'

Anne agreed with both comments. Having inherited her father's broad features, wide-set eyes and platinum-blonde hair, but her mother's dark skin, Tamara was indeed a 'corker'.

Then, in the early evening of 27 February, there was a sudden hammering on the front door of the apartment. Aunty Sarah said to her daughter, 'They're here. Go and answer it, luv, while I put my coat and hat on.'

Tamara threw herself into her mother's arms and, the tears pouring down her face, she sobbed, 'Oh Mum, Mum, tell him I love him. And tell him I shall be in court every day. And I know he hasn't done anything really wrong and he's going to be all right. Ask Dad what he wants me to do and . . . oh Mum, I wish I could come with you . . . and tell him *vstretimsya snova uvidmsya* . . .'

While the hammering continued and voices shouted loudly, Tamara lapsed into her father's language and Aunty Sarah stroked her daughter's blonde hair. Feeling genuinely sorry for her cousin, Anne went to open the door to the NKVD men.

Pulling her astrakhan coat tightly around her, Sarah sat waiting on one side of the table in the small, cold, windowless room, dimly lit by a single blue bulb in the ceiling. All prisons were hateful places – she'd done a stretch in Strangeways Gaol during her suffragette days in Manchester – but the Lubyanka was notably, grimly hateful. They were assuredly not laying out the red carpet for what she was certain would be her last meeting with the man she had loved for twenty-one tumultuous years. Whatever she did, Sarah told herself, she was not to waste one second of these precious minutes by breaking down and crying.

When the door finally opened she was standing stamping her feet, folding and unfolding her arms, banging her shoulders hard, the way waiting cabmen did to keep themselves warm. In the brighter light of the corridor Sarah saw two men standing guard but in the dimness of the room she could initially only make out two figures entering, one of which barked at her in Russian to sit at the table where she'd been told, that she was to speak in Russian and under no circumstances was she to touch the prisoner.

Seating herself back in the chair, Sarah strained her eyes to focus on Misha's beloved figure. At least he was walking erect and unaided, but dear God – she saw him more clearly as the man shoved him towards the chair on the other side of the table – what had they done to him in the last six months? Misha's once-splendid frame was like a blasted oak tree, the once-shining blond hair was thin and grey, the once-leonine head a shrunken skull. When he sat down and looked directly at her, although his eyes were sunken in their sockets, Sarah saw them glint and his mouth cracked into its wide smile as he said hoarsely, '*Kak mne nekhvatalo tebya! Obezhayu tebya, moya dikaya angliiskaya roza.*'

How she had missed him! And 'I adore you, my wild English rose' had been the first words of love he had spoken, in those long-ago wartime days when she had been one of Doctor Elsie Inglis's nursing orderlies and he the thrilling Bolshevik orator. Sarah struggled hard to control the gathering lump in her throat.

Having seated himself on the chair placed at the end of the table, the NKVD man barked at Misha to cut the cackle and listen to what his mistress had to say. A flicker of contempt crossed Misha's face and Sarah suddenly realised the young man was none other than Alexei Kustov, Alexei Ivanovitch whom they'd semi-adopted as an orphan lad in the chaotic but heady days of the early 1920s, when the millennium had still been a beckoning mirage. Coming from Alexei, the 'mistress' gibe was singularly nasty and Sarah resisted the urge to lean across and slap his face. But he had always been ambitious and it was, she reckoned, quite clever to have somebody who knew Misha's strengths and weaknesses, somebody who because of the past association would bend over backwards to prove his zealous loyalty, as an interrogator. And she mustn't waste her emotional energy on a shit like Alexei Kustov.

Choosing her words with the utmost care for the shit's benefit, in Russian Sarah said to Misha, 'I have had a personal interview with Comrade Stalin. He is of the opinion that you must plead guilty to the generality of the serious charges laid against you, otherwise Comrade Stalin would not have allowed them to be laid in the first place. He does not, however, consider it will be necessary for you to plead guilty to each detailed charge. Comrade Stalin agrees that it would be best for Tamara and me to return to England once the trial is ended. We have our British passports. Anne is here in Moscow. The three of us will travel to England together.'

Anxiously Sarah gazed at Misha, to see if he had grasped the implications of her words. For the further months in the hands of the NKVD in the dungeons of the Lubyanka had taken as severe a mental as a physical toll. Overjoyed as he was to see her, Misha was finding it hard to concentrate his attention. An ineffably weary, distracted gaze kept clouding his eyes. He was a near-broken man. Sarah herself longed to shout at Alexei Ivanovitch, 'You've beaten me, too. I'm exhausted. I want to die with Misha. Can't you arrange to shoot us both?'

But she had a daughter she loved dearly who would need her in the years that lay ahead, Misha would not want her to give up and Whitworths were not quitters, any road. Sarah went on talking as clearly as she could, without suggesting the charges were a monstrous frame-up or insulting General Secretary Stalin. Then impatiently, Alexei Kustov interrupted, 'Do you understand, Muranov, what is expected of you at your trial, in return for the unprecedented clemency our beloved comrade is showing towards your mistress and daughter? They are as contaminated as you with the disease of filthy, lying, treacherous imperialism. Yet they are to go free.'

Slowly Misha turned his head to look directly at Comrade Kustov. In almost his old buoyant, ringing voice he swore loudly, using two favourite obscene, Russian expressions, 'Yob'tvoyu mat'! Da na khuya!', before he said, 'Of course, I understand. If I behave myself in court and go meekly, but not abjectly, to the slaughter, my wife and daughter will be allowed to leave the country for the safety of my wife's native land.'

Sarah could have laughed out loud and how right Comrade Stalin had been to send her here, for Mikhail Muranov, her beloved Misha who insisted on calling her his wife, was not a completely broken man. Still fixing Alexei with his old commanding gaze, in English he went on, 'Now I'm going to "cackle" to my wife in her language, which you understand anyway. Bozhe moi! Alexei Ivanovitch, we taught you!'

Peering at his watch and proceeding to light a cigarette to hide his confusion, their erstwhile house-guest – ah, the holidays Alexei had spent at their dacha outside Moscow – said, 'Five minutes.'

Five minutes! Just three hundred heartbeats, Sarah thought, *yolki-palki!* they were already thumping away. Misha asked after *dorogaya moya*, his precious Tamara. Sarah said she sent her dearest love, she would be in court, they all would, and she wanted to know if her father wished her to go to England.

'Tell Tamara, yes. Tell her all revolutions are betrayed. It's in the nature of the human animal. But tell her also never to lose faith, never to cease fighting the good fight. We have achieved great things. One day we shall achieve true Socialism with a human face and one day Tamara will return to Mother Russia.' Misha leaned as far towards Sarah as he could, tenderly asking, 'For you, *moya samaya dikaya izo vsekh angliis-kikh roz*, has it been worthwhile? Or do you rue the day you sailed with me from England's shores?'

In a whisper because she couldn't trust her vocal chords to operate at full volume, Sarah said, 'It's been worthwhile, *moi lyubimyi*, every good and bad, ecstatic and rotten minute. Oh Misha, recite some Milton for me.'

At this request he leaned right across the table to grasp Sarah's hands. Studiously ignoring the forbidden physical contact, Comrade Kustov blew out a cloud of smoke. Holding her hands tightly in his, the hoarse voice throbbing with the passion of the poet he revered and the woman he loved above all others, Misha went into the opening lines of *L'Allegro*: 'Hence, loath'd Melancholy, Of Cerberus and blackest Midnight born, In Stygian cave forlorn, 'Mongst horrid shapes, and shrieks, and sights unholy . . .'

Before he reached the lines, 'Haste thee, Nymph, and bring with thee Jest, and youthful Jollity, Quips and Cranks and wanton Wiles, Nods and Becks, and wreathed Smiles', the tears were trickling down Sarah's cheeks. Misha's voice soared as he said, 'Come, and trip it, as you go, On the light fantastic toe; And in thy right hand lead with thee . . .' Lifting her hands high, with his old fire and conviction he declaimed, 'The mountain-nymph, sweet Liberty.'

The echo of his voice rang round the dank room, the

memory of the first time she had heard him speak those lines flooded through Sarah and the contrast with Misha's present condition was well-nigh unbearable, but Comrade Kustov, or maybe it was the ghost of young Alexei Ivanovitch, allowed him to recite the whole of *L'Allegro*. As their last minutes together drew to their close, the tears were pouring down both Sarah's and Misha's faces.

'The trial of the Twenty-one', the number of the accused, duly opened on 2 March, Aunty Sarah, Tamara and Anne were rudely shown to the back of the packed courtroom, which was where the relatives were stuck. How drawn and defeated the wives and families looked, Anne thought, though as her aunt said, 'Unlike Tammy and me, they haven't got a bolt-hole they hope to squeeze into.'

Even though Aunty Sarah had warned Anne that her uncle's health and strength had suffered as a result of nearly twelve months' imprisonment, she was still shocked when she saw his shrunken frame shuffling into the dock. Her memory of Uncle Misha stemmed from the family visit to Leningrad when he had been a handsome, boisterous, extrovert, larger-than-life figure.

They were in court every minute of the next few days. Aunty Sarah whispered translations of the salient points, but there was no need to understand Russian to feel the hatred directed against the prisoners or to hear the blood-lust in Citizen Prosecutor Vishinsky's voice as it regularly screamed to a peroration which, according to her aunt's stony-faced translation, demanded, 'Shoot the mad dogs!'

In the evenings, when they returned to the apartment, Tamara either bolted into the bedroom, where her loud sobbing could be clearly heard, or stormed excitedly round the living room asking questions of nobody in particular. 'How can they be so gullible as to believe the rubbish that's being talked about Dad? I mean, there are people who know him sitting listening. If all the leading members of the party, except Comrade Stalin and Comrade Lenin, have always been in the pay of bourgeois imperialists or Fascists, how have we managed to survive at all, let alone thrive, as everybody knows we have?'

With a trace of her old spirit Aunty Sarah observed, 'If Lenin were alive today, I wouldn't put my money on his chances of survival.' Then wearily she said, 'Don't tear yourself to pieces, Tammy luv. People believe partly what they're told to believe and partly what they want or need to believe. Just occasionally, they think for themselves which is when we have upheavals or revolutions. But thinking for yourself is a tiring operation which not everyone is equipped to do, any road.'

Typically Tamara rounded on her mother and said, 'I don't think you're a genuine Socialist at all.'

Even more wearily Aunty Sarah replied, 'Put it down to me being English.'

Tamara retreated into the bedroom and while her aunt was preparing the supper, without knocking, Anne entered the room. Her cousin was lying on the bed and the look she gave Anne would have done credit to Philip when his study was invaded. Ignoring it, without preamble, Anne said, 'I think it's about time you started thinking about your mother. It may have escaped your notice, though it hasn't mine, but she really is near breaking point. She's known your father longer than you have, you know. What do you think she feels, seeing his broken figure pilloried as the arch-Satan day after day, listening to that ghastly prosecutor Vishinsky baying for his blood? Your parents made the deal about your going to England, not because they want to tear you away from Mother Russia, but to save your life, or at best to save you spending years in a labour camp. And I don't mind helping your mother around the house, but it wouldn't hurt and it might comfort her, if you stirred your stumps.'

Her cousin made no response so Anne marched to the door which she slammed hard behind her, in best Tamara fashion. The next morning, when she got up to make Aunty Sarah a cup of tea, Tamara was already in the kitchen preparing a tray for her mother to have breakfast in bed. But she didn't smile at Anne, she glowered, and part of Tamara's problem was that she couldn't bear to admit that she, or Communism in practice as opposed to theory, could ever be in the wrong.

On the seventh day of the trial, when Uncle Misha was

again being examined by Citizen Prosecutor Vishinsky, Anne suddenly heard the ringing note in his voice which soon caused a stir in the courtroom. She saw the judges shuffling their papers, looking distinctly discomfited, and she whispered to her aunt, 'What's he saying?'

In response Aunty Sarah murmured, 'Oh Misha, my love, don't let rip. It won't do any good.'

Tamara, however, hissed excitedly, 'Mr Vishinsky asked Dad about his confession. And Dad said, "To which one in particular are you referring, Citizen Prosecutor? I appear to have made hundreds of them." And he roared about Dad's secret visit to Finland in June 1927, to plot with British agents to dismember the USSR and restore bourgeois capitalism. Dad said, "Ah. I thought I spent June 1927 touring the Ukraine." Which of course he must have done! Dad always had a marvellous memory! Mr Vishinsky said it was a slip of the tongue and he'd meant 1929, not 1927. So Dad said for the whole of June 1929 he was in hospital recovering from an operation. Which he was. I remember that. And he's getting Mr Vishinsky in a terrible tangle. He's saying . . .' Her eyes shining, her dark skin flushed with pride, Tamara translated, '. . . he considers confessions and recantations . . . mm . . . mm . . . more worthy of the medieval Inquisition than twentieth-century Communism. Oh . . . he's wonderful.'

In her excitement Tamara made to stand up but Aunty Sarah said furiously in English, 'Sit still, Tammy, sit still', which she did.

Her father couldn't possibly have seen her but the following minute was an extraordinary, eerie experience which made Anne shiver. As if he had suddenly become aware of the dangerous excitement his challenge had induced not only in his daughter, but the entire courtroom, Uncle Misha stopped in mid-sentence. When he answered the Citizen Prosecutor's next barked question, the ringing note had gone from his voice and he was once more the uninterested spectator at his own trial.

As they left the courthouse that evening several people jostled them and a woman spat at Aunty Sarah. Anne did not know whether this was because they too had been discomfited by Mikhail Muranov's refutation of the more absurd charges, or because they were demonstrating their conviction that Citizen Prosecutor Vishinsky could not have failed to do his homework properly. But she knew it was all hateful and the fear that enveloped the relatives' lowly corner of the courtroom had penetrated Anne's confident soul. Much as her heart bled for Uncle Misha and Aunty Sarah and even Tamara, she longed for the trials to be over, she longed to be back home in England, and she longed to have news of Ben.

On the eleventh day the trials ended. The verdicts were swiftly pronounced. Anne hardly needed to ask what the sentence on Mikhail Muranov was because Tamara let out an anguished gasp and started to sob quietly, while Aunty Sarah put her face in her hands. Almost immediately she looked up, staring intently as the prisoners were led from the dock, not speaking until Uncle Misha's figure had vanished from sight.

In a flat voice she then said, 'He is guilty as charged. He is to be shot.'

Just before midnight of 15 March, two days after his trial ended, two guards entered Mikhail Muranov's cell and they had to shake him hard to waken him. Misha was sleeping soundly because there was no point bothering any more. The mystery of life would soon be revealed, or more likely not. The guards told him to get dressed and to be sharp about it. Pulling on the rough prison shirt and trousers, Misha thought perhaps he was being summoned for a final interrogation but when he saw Comrade Kustov in the corridor he knew his last minutes had come. There were no firing squads for the likes of himself. The despatch was swift and secret. As ordered, his heart beating faster but his head held high, Misha set off walking along the corridor, down the twisting stone steps into the lower labyrinths of the Lubyanka. Alexei Ivanovitch had not looked happy and Misha wondered if he had been delegated to pull the trigger. He was thinking about the first time he had met Sarah, his Sarochka, his Sabrina fair, in that smoke-filled room in Reni in those euphoric days of 1917, he was hearing her dear English voice saying, 'Go on, tell me all about yourself. Where do you come from? Those are real leather boots, aren't they? Are you rich? Why aren't you in the army? Why . . .' when the bullet exploded in the back of his head, killing him instantly.

21

'I can't tell you how glad I am to be back in dear old England! The forty-eight hours after Uncle Misha's trial ended were a living nightmare. The second night I dreamed I was standing on the terrace here at Chenneys. You were there, Mummy, and Uncle Guy and Aunty Alice were smiling at each other. There was this thundering noise and I asked Daddy what it was and he replied, "It's the guns firing on the Somme, Anny-Panny." Then I woke up, Aunty Sarah was standing by my bed, and there was a thundering noise. I said, "What's that? What time is it?" and she said, "Three o'clock in the morning, NKVD time and it's them hammering on the door."

'Our bags were more or less packed but they gave us no time to collect our wits, nor for Aunty Sarah and Tamara to have a last look round. They drove us to the station and then of course we sat around waiting for hours and all the while I kept expecting something awful to happen. When we finally boarded the train, the journey seemed endless. The Ukraine just went on and on and the train kept grinding to a halt, and I don't think I stopped trembling until we crossed the frontier and were safely in Poland.

'We missed our connection in Warsaw and crossing Germany seemed to go on for ever, too. The trains were full of swaggering Nazis and we saw Jewish people being harassed and things have obviously worsened for them again. I didn't begin to perk up until we reached Calais. Then, as we sailed across the Channel, the sun was shining on the white cliffs of Dover. That was a sight for sore eyes!'

Anne had not stopped talking since entering her mother's bedroom but as she paused for breath, her mother said, 'I gather there was a mob of photographers and reporters waiting for you at Dover.'

'Wasn't there just! I suppose we were – are – news, Madame Muranov fleeing to England with her daughter, in the company of her detective authoress niece. I suppose we should have been prepared for them but we weren't. The questions they fired at Aunty Sarah, really, they were disgusting! Tamara bristled at the reporters but fortunately she was pretty exhausted by then, so she didn't put her foot into things unduly. The strange thing is the NKVD haven't spread the news that Aunty Sarah and Uncle Misha never actually married. They didn't use it at the trial and they obviously haven't leaked it in the West either. But as Kurt Wolff says of Herr Hitler and the Nazis, I've given up wondering how Stalin and his minions' minds work.'

With a sympathetic smile her mother said, 'I'm glad I sent Philip to meet you.'

'So am I! He was simply splendid. At his haughtiest and iciest, you know! But it worked and he got us through the press scrummage and into the car. Aunty Sarah was superb too. She kept absolute control of herself until we arrived at Chenneys.'

Maybe it was Aunty Sarah's finally reaching the security of Chenneys, Anne thought, or seeing her sister-in-law for the first time in a decade, or the sight of her fragility, or a bit of all three emotions, but she had broken down and wept uncontrollably in Mummy's arms. The Muranovs were now in bed, soundly asleep Anne hoped, but she herself felt wide awake. She went on talking nineteen to the dozen, pouring out her heart to her mother, relating her experiences in Russia.

'And Tamara's ferociously Russian. I don't know how she's going to make out in England.'

'Given time I'm sure she'll adapt, though I gather she can be difficult. Aunty Sarah told me when they first returned to Russia, Tamara was very wary of her father. Perhaps as a consequence he spoiled her abominably and Sarah let him.' Anne was glad to hear her aunt was aware of her daughter's shortcomings. Her mother continued, 'Anyway, for the moment they'll both stay here. After what she's been through, a little cosseting and pampering won't hurt Aunty Sarah, though, knowing her, it will only be a little. And don't you think you should go to bed and get some sleep, my darling?'

'Why? Are you tired?'

As her mother laughed and shook her head, the telephone extension in the bedroom rang. Her mother picked it up, smiled and said, 'It's for you.'

Anne expected it would be Rebecca whom she'd already 'phoned, with more news to impart or perhaps to confirm that she'd posted on the three precious letters from Ben that had arrived during her absence. Cheerfully, Anne said, 'Hello. What's new?'

'Quite a lot since I last saw you.'

'Ben!' At the sound of his voice Anne didn't know whether she was coming or going, standing or sitting. 'Oh Ben! Where are you?'

'In London.'

'Oh hell. I'm at Chenneys.'

'I know you are. That's why I'm phoning you.'

Her mother took the receiver from Anne's hand and said into the mouthpiece, 'Hello, Ben, Kessie Marchal here. Welcome home. Anne's only just returned from Moscow herself. Whatever she says, she's exhausted and in no fit state to travel anywhere tonight. So make arrangements to meet tomorrow, will you?'

Her mother handed the receiver back and slightly to Anne's disappointment – she would have preferred him to say he'd come hotfoot to Chenneys – Ben said he'd waited fourteen months to see her so he reckoned he could wait a further fourteen hours. Apparently he was telephoning from the Gower Street flat where he'd arrived unannounced, fortunately to find Rebecca at home and she'd offered him Anne's bed for the night. With the Muranovs here it was probably more sensible to have their reunion in London and Anne arranged to travel up to Town first thing tomorrow morning.

When she arrived at Gower Street, Rebecca was still there. Feeling constrained by her friend's presence and absurdly shy in Ben's, Anne just gazed at him. He was wearing one of his old check shirts, a sleeveless pullover with a hole in it, and a pair of baggy corduroy trousers. His skin was weather-beaten, he'd lost weight and the grey eyes were even more watchful, but when the sunburst smile spread across his face and he said 'How do', Anne knew he loved her as much as she loved him.

After Rebecca had embraced her warmly and said how lovely it was to have Anne back safe and sound, she informed them, 'I'm going to be ever so tactful and leave you two alone. Actually,' her voice sharpened, 'I'm going to Berlin to try to ascertain what the latest policy of Section 11 112 of the *Sichererheitsdienst*, otherwise known as the SD, is with regard to what is known to them as the Jewish Problem.'

'Oh,' Anne said. 'The best of luck.'

'I shall need it. The Nazis marching into Austria and Herr Hitler's rapturous welcome in Vienna have altered the situation. Not for the better either. Oh well, Berlin here I come.'

Once Rebecca had departed, for several seconds Anne and Ben stood looking at each other, then slowly he moved towards her and for several more seconds they held each other tightly. Anne started to weep and he said, 'I didn't used to have that effect on you.'

'I'm just so happy to see you,' she snuffled, ignoring his bad grammar.

His tongue licked the trickling tears from her cheeks, travelling down to her mouth, and then both their tongues were entwined. When their mouths parted without a word Ben picked Anne up and carried her into the bedroom. They threw their discarded clothes across the carpet, their naked flesh touched, wound and unwound, his lips now kissing her breasts, his stubby but still well-tended fingers caressing her skin, her nails scratching, her teeth biting. When Anne stretched on the bed, her legs wide apart inviting his entry, and Ben thrust himself inside her, she knew that the kingdom of their conjoined bodies remained a very heaven.

A good hour later, lying languorously in Ben's arms, Anne started to talk. She wanted to know why in particular he had come home and he said, 'I needed some leave and I bumped into somebody you know well. Jenny Macdonald. I didn't realise our great woman war photographer is Canadian. Any road, she organised the free trip home for me.'

'Darling Aunty Jenny, bless her! She isn't Canadian and don't dare say she is. She hails from Newfoundland. I presume she's still a convinced Communist? Her photographs of the Spanish conflict are very popular in Russia. They are strikingly good, aren't they? Is Aunty Jenny back in England? Aunty Sarah would love to meet her again. They were both nurses in Russia during the Great War, you know.

'You haven't changed, have you? Can't you let a fellow answer before you fire off your next question?'

Anne laid her head on Ben's chest and murmured, 'I shan't say another word, while you tell me all about the Spanish Civil War.'

Ruffling her hair he gave a mock groan and said, 'Rather than that, you can go on firing your questions.' Seriously he went on, 'The answer to the question whether your "Aunty" Jenny is a convinced Communist is, she supports the Stalinist line, which is part of our problem in Spain, me luv. We have Stalinites, Trotskyites and various satellites revolving around them. Instead of concentrating their energies on fighting the Fascists, they're at each other's throats. At the moment, I've had a bellyful of their political shenanigans.'

Anne lifted up her head and looking straight into his grey eyes she said, 'You say you've had enough at the moment . . . are you thinking of going back then?'

'Dunno. Depends.'

Anne decided not to pursue the topic of Ben's returning to Spain, particularly as he was running his hands up and down her back, pressing her body against his and she could feel him hardening again. When they had slaked their passion once more, Anne said, 'I'm going to make a cup of tea and read my letters, starting with yours.'

Propped up in bed sipping her tea, she embarked on the enjoyable task of reading the small mountain of mail that had accumulated during her absence in Russia. 'You do write well,' she told Ben after she had absorbed the contents of his epistles. He said, 'Thanks, miss. Shall I go to the top of the class?' Anne hit him on the head with a wodge of envelopes and asked, 'Where are your paintings? I'm dying to see them.'

'Courtesy of Miss Jenny Macdonald, they came home in a beautiful leather holder.'

'That reminds me. I've a beautiful Russian art book for you.'

'Ta. And you can put off dying until tomorrow. My energies are concentrated on one channel only today.'

Ben's fingers stroked the hairs in her crotch and Anne said, 'Stop it. For the moment, anyway. I'm reading a letter from Kate. She's still in Hollywood, you know.' Anne continued to peruse her sister's neat handwriting.

Everybody thinks I'm awfully good in *Farewell Yesterday* which will shortly be released. So do I! Sam's already pulling out all the publicity stops. He finally managed to sign Colin Cornwell to play Seth, and we start shooting on *A Dangerous Affair* at the end of next month. [Which was the title Philip had given the Seth Pollard script, approved by both Anne and Samuel J. Sylberg.] Sam's peeved with you, darling. He says if you can go to god-damned Russia, you can accept his invitation to visit the good old US of A. You must come out to California soon. It is the most heavenly place.

As a doyen of the English colony in Hollywood, Johnny Conway's been doing his avuncular act looking after little me, his dear dead wife's English suffragette friend's daughter. He goes in for explanations like that. Was he always a pompous ass? I find Margaret-Jane Conway a pain in the neck too, but you can make up your own mind because you're going to have the pleasure of her company soon. She's bored at the moment – she usually is – so she's decided to pay a solo, grown-up visit to little old London, where her dear dead Momma lived for so many years.

After she'd glanced through her sister's next paragraph, with a laugh Anne exclaimed, 'Do listen to this, Ben!' She read out:

I went to a party last week and I was wandering around a house twice as large as Chenneys, looking for a lav actually, and I put my head round this door and this hideous little man grabbed me. I don't know what he was doing lurking

246

there and you won't believe it, darling, but he unbuttoned his flies and took his thingummy out. Honestly, apart from anything else, stuck out like that they're not a pretty sight, are they? So I wrinkled my nose and said, 'Do put it away.' He shouted, 'Who the f..k do you think you are, you f..king Limey bitch?' I said sweetly, 'I'm Kate Whitworth. Who the f..k are you?' That finished him. Because I have an English accent and look like an English lady, none of them expects me to say anything stronger than 'Oh blow it'. Do you know who he was? Hyman Goldsmith, the boss of Stellar Studios. Even more sweetly, I told him *le droit de seigneur* went out in Europe years ago but of course he had no idea what I was talking about.

Having finished reading, Anne said, 'There are moments when I love Kate dearly.' She turned towards Ben to see if he agreed with her sentiments, in a platonic fashion of course, but he was fast asleep. The exhaustion, the strain of what he had been through during the fighting in the Ebro valley, somehow seemed more apparent when he was asleep.

When he woke, she insisted Ben show her the paintings and drawings he'd done in Spain. Silently, but not too slowly, so that she could gain an impression of the whole, Anne examined them. The style of the paintings was the same as in his industrial Lancashire scenes, hundreds of ant-like figures with bandoleers round their shoulders, berets on heads, makeshift uniforms on backs, scrambling up sun-scorched hillsides or huddled in snow-covered dug-outs; dehumanised but recognisable figures of men, women and children fleeing from air-raids in the streets of Madrid; all overwhelmed, not by many-windowed factories and mill chimneys but by field- and machine-guns, aeroplanes and bombs. Ben's charcoal and pencil drawings were poignantly simple, children playing games among the rubble of a house, stray animals, peasant women pushing handcarts laden with their possessions, a little girl sitting by a roadside Calvary, pals from the International Brigade and Spaniards who had attracted his artist's eye.

When she had finished her inspection Anne looked up and said, 'No wonder you're tired, fighting, painting and drawing. They're brilliant, Ben, they really are. You've captured the Spanish Civil War on canvas and paper. You must exhibit, you simply must.'

'Yeah, they're good,' he agreed. 'If you want to get on to Miss Derek Elmar-Smythe, you can. But not yet. These days are for thee and me.'

For the rest of the week they made love, they slept in each other's arms, they talked, and very occasionally they went out. Anne told Mrs Guppy not to bother cleaning the bedrooms, for Miss Lawson was away and her own was strewn with half-unpacked cases. She thought Mrs Guppy knew damned well there was a man in her bedroom but preferred not to acknowledge the fact. The telephone rang frequently and Anne let Ben answer it because many of the callers were reporters, wanting Miss Whitworth's view on the execution of Mikhail Muranov and the situation in Russia. Ben enjoyed himself answering the calls with variations on the lines, 'This is Miss Whitworth's butler speaking. She is not at 'ome at the moment and I 'ave no idea when she will return.'

From time to time he would say, 'Oh hello, Lady Marchal. Yeah, it's me. What? You don't think I'm cut out to be a butler', or make similar cracks to Con and other personal friends. When Julian telephoned he merely said, 'Yeah, she's here. It's your literary agent.'

Julian had called to welcome Anne back, to inform her he had received several offers for her to write about her experiences in Russia, and to enquire whether she was interested in accepting any of them, or whether she preferred to finish *The Moment of Murder*, which was an oblique way of asking how her fifth Seth Pollard book was progressing. Anne said she was keeping her head down because she was too personally involved to write a good book about Russia, she would therefore finish the detective novel and maybe synthesise her Russian experiences later. All the while she was speaking to Julian she was fending off Ben's advances with her free hand, for they were lying naked in bed and because the caller was Julian, Anne felt sure, Ben kept stroking her nipples and other erogenous zones.

When she put the receiver back in its hook she said, 'You are a bugger at times, Ben Broughton.' Much later, after they had made love again, she said, 'I suppose I should get on with *The Moment of Murder.*'

'Yeah, magic time's over. I must go up to The Dales to see my folks.'

'And Irene?' Anne nestled against his warmly damp body. 'You know what I often say as we're finishing? I shall be twenty-nine in September. All of thirty next year. I'd like our baby to be legitimate, not just because it's supposed to be moral and it definitely makes things much easier, but because I want to be your wife. Do you want to be my husband? Do you want us to have a baby? Or don't you care?'

'I care, Anne, otherwise I wouldn't be here.'

'Will you talk to Irene then? I mean she must realise by now that I'm not a passing affair. She must know you're not going to return to her.'

Ben said he'd see his wife while he was in The Dales and do his best to persuade her to divorce him. A couple of days later he took off north, as usual he was vague about his movements but he reckoned he'd be back in London in about ten days, when he agreed they could have one of those serious talks Anne loved so much, depending on what Irene had to say.

A few hours after he had left, a weary-looking Rebecca returned from Berlin. Anne stopped typing Chapter 18 of *The Moment of Murder* to listen to her friend unburdening her soul about the situation in Germany which had definitely changed for the worse again. Then she said, 'Becky, I've had a bright idea. Let's have a party. We haven't had one for ages and I think it'll do us both good. I'm certain it'll do you no end of good to forget about the Nazis, their self-created Jewish Problem, and Palestine for a few hours. Agreed?'

After a pause for thought, Rebecca agreed.

Virtually everybody Anne invited at short notice accepted, for, though she said it herself, she was a good hostess and her parties were noted for their excellence. By nine o'clock on the Saturday evening the Gower Street flat was already flowing with guests, the conversations were animated, the atmosphere inspiriting. 'Aunty' Jenny Macdonald arrived, flamboyant as ever in a bright-yellow silk pyjama suit decorated with a beaded serpent that wriggled across her bosom as she moved. Her short red hair was still flaming, courtesy of henna powder Anne suspected, and she had a long cigarette-holder in her hand.

'Sarah!' she shrieked as she entered the living room. Waving her cigarette-holder, she rushed towards Aunty Sarah who had come up from Chenneys with Tamara. After Jenny had hugged her she said, 'Gosh! Is this Tamara? I stayed with you a few years back when I was on a photographic assignment in Russia. Remember? Gosh, you've grown into a beauty. I'd like to photograph you. Marvellous bone structure. Just like your father's. Oh double-gosh, I've put my foot right in it. I am sorry. But I don't understand what's been happening in Moscow. I mean, I know Misha wasn't a British agent and all those things they said he was. Can you bear to talk about it, Sarah?'

Sarah said, not really, but Tamara said she could. Anne excused herself as her cousin and Aunty Jenny embarked on a voluble conversation. Much as she enjoyed the role of hostess, one of the drawbacks of being a good one was that you had to circulate. Derek Elmar-Smythe was cooeeing at her and Anne definitely wanted to speak to him. He asked, 'Where is Sir? I can't see the gorgeous brute anywhere.' When she said Ben didn't much like parties and he was up north anyway, Derek snorted, 'Well, you can tell him. I've looked at his Spanish *oeuvres* and I absolutely agree, dear heart, they're masterly. If you have to drag him by the short and curlies, you're to arrange for us to meet the instant he returns to London, so that we can set up an exhibition.'

Anne promised that she would. Pushing her way through the throng, urging people to start eating – a cold buffet table was laid out by the windows and Mrs Guppy and her daughters were carrying the hot food from the kitchen – she walked towards Margaret-Jane Conway who had recently arrived in London and whom she'd invited as a matter of courtesy. For, though Kate's censure of persons or things was not necessarily endorsed by Anne, from her brief acquaintance with Margaret-Jane she agreed with her sister's verdict. If you could have a beautiful pain in the neck, la Conway was its personification.

She was holding court near the fireplace and she had the same regular features, rosebud mouth and corn-coloured hair as her dead mother, though her eyes were a velvety brown, not the cornflower blue of Aunty Alice's. Even slimmer than her mother had been, Margaret-Jane had an elegantly graceful neck, shown to best advantage in a strapless oyster-pink evening gown, and from somewhere in her parents' genes she had inherited a touch of undoubted class. The classy beauty was marred by a spoiled child, marshmallow softness, and as Anne approached, in a breathy Californian accent she was saying to Sandy Dalziel, 'You're Kate Whitworth's husband, are you?'

Anne had bumped into Sandy at Broadcasting House, after she'd taken part in a discussion programme. She'd invited him because once upon a time she had been fond of him and with Kate in Hollywood and their marriage apparently in a rocky state, she felt a teeny bit sorry for him. Sandy did his devoted, understanding, liberated husband act as he said to Margaret-Jane, 'Kate's career is immensely important to us both. Hollywood is the Mecca and Kate obviously has to go there to establish herself as an international film star. I shall be joining her soon. Taking a sabbatical from the BBC, you know.'

'I wonder if Katie knows that?' Mark murmured.

It did not surprise Anne that her brother was among Margaret-Jane's courtiers because he had a penchant for beautiful blondes, though he said it was a myth that men liked only one type of woman and he'd known some agreeable redheads and brunettes. With Mark, Anne took it he meant 'known' in the biblical sense. She was, however, faintly astonished to see Julian among the adoring male circle. Fluttering her long lashes, la Conway asked for another cigarette. Julian was quickest on the draw, extracting a cigarette-case from the pocket of his dinner suit and proffering it to Miss Conway, while Mark leapt to ignite Anne's portable gas lighter. As he held the snaking flame to the cigarette, Margaret-Jane said breathily to Anne, 'It's such a cute little apartment you have. I'm thinking of leasing one myself. Hotels are so boring. I just love London and I'm aiming to stay a while and get to know it really well, if somebody will show me round.'

The assembled males all said they'd be delighted to but her eyelashes were working overtime in Julian's direction. He blushed slightly but looked far from displeased and Anne thought, well, what do you know? Then Aunty Sarah trotted up and said briskly, 'Hello, are you Margaret-Jane? I'm Sarah Muranov.'

'Hi.' La Conway waved her cigarette-holder.

'I reckon I should say "Hello". I brought you into the world.'

That information momentarily attracted Margaret-Jane's interest but Anne again excused herself. After she had chatted to several friends and checked that all was well with Mrs Guppy and daughters' waitress service, she piled her own plate with food and walked towards Rebecca who was deep in conversation with Gavin. Standing behind the two of them, tucking into her salmon mousse, she listened to Rebecca saying, 'Yes, we are demanding the Homeland in Palestine we were promised twenty years ago. We are also demanding that pro tem Jewish immigration quotas be radically increased. You served in Berlin, Gavin, you know what the situation is for German Jews. You're going to Vienna and you'll see what it's like there. We're fighting an uphill battle at the moment. The Foreign Office is stuffed with Arabists, not to mention anti-Semites.'

'Palestine isn't my patch, but I consider that a little unfair.'

'It isn't the least unfair.'

'Come, Rebecca, you are well aware how complicated the situation is. There are Zionists deliberately working to build a Jewish state which will overwhelm the indigenous Arabs, whom it is our duty, as the mandated power in Palestine, to protect.'

Rebecca replied, 'I'm not one of them. And complicated situations are unlikely to be resolved by constant prevarication on the part of the British Government which is the mandated power.'

With mock severity Anne leaned over the back of Rebecca's chair and said, 'You're supposed to be having a night off, so shut up about Palestine.' Seeing his sister-in-law, Gavin immediately made to rise from his chair but Anne waved at him to stay put and said, 'Con 'phoned last night. I gather

252

the Vienna posting is another rung up the ladder for you. Congratulations.'

Nodding at her, Gavin allowed himself a brief smile of satisfaction.

By midnight, though some guests had departed, the reception rooms remained well filled, with the overspill in the hall. Having been butterfly-skimming round the place, making sure nobody was being left out, it was only then that Anne realised the largest groupings had congregated round Margaret-Jane, who had transferred her court to Rebecca's partially cleared bedroom, and Tamara, who was ensconced in the living room. The former's group was all-male, the latter's of both sexes. Anne considered drawing the groups together but decided against any such action. The two beautiful blondes, spoiled daughters of famous men and ex-suffragette mothers, could not be less alike in background, upbringing or beliefs, that was if Margaret-Jane had any beliefs beyond her own pleasure. If she brought the two of them together, the sparks were liable to fly from Tamara, and Margaret-Jane would collapse gracefully into the nearest man's arms, preferably from the way she was flirting with him, into Julian's.

Anne then heard Tamara's voice saying loudly, 'You are an idiot. You have no idea what you're talking about.'

The object of her cousin's scorn turned out to be Sandy who had transferred his allegiance from Margaret-Jane's court, so it didn't really matter, but was Tamara aware quite how rude she could sound? Or, despite her fluency in English, was there a slight language barrier? The minute Tamara saw Anne she said excitedly, 'This has been a most important evening. Fate has spoken to me. I have met Jenny Macdonald who is a wonderful person and I am going to Spain with her.'

Nonplussed, all Anne could think of saying was, 'Are you? What as?'

'I shall be a nurse like my mother.'

'Do you think you'll be any use as a nurse? And what does your mother have to say?'

'I can be most unemotional when I choose. And my mother says yes.'

253

Oh can you? Anne thought and went off to find Aunty Sarah whom she located having forty winks among the coats and cloaks in her bedroom. As Anne entered, her aunt opened her eyes and with a yawn said, 'I'm getting old, luv, and it's past my bedtime. But the party's done me good. Taken my mind off . . . you know. And it's been nice meeting old pals and seeing new faces. Alice's daughter is a spoiled little madam, isn't she? Mind you, so was her mother. It was only meeting your Mam saved Alice. Her daughter doesn't appear to have found a cause to occupy her energies.'

'I gather Tammy has. She says she's going to Spain with Aunty Jenny. Is she? Are you going to let her?'

'I reckon so. She's all at sixes and sevens here. By the time she gets back the newspapers'll have lost interest in us. She has a valid British passport and Jenny'll look after her.'

'Won't you miss her?' Aunty Sarah inclined her head in a gesture which said, yes, and Anne asked, 'What are you going to do?'

'Your Mam's galloped to the rescue as usual. The present occupants are moving out of her house in Milnrow and she's letting me have it. I lived there for a while when Tammy was little, you know, so it'll be like going home. With the unemployment situation being what it is and the poverty levels what they are, I reckon I'll find plenty to do in The Dales.'

Anne was glad her aunt was 'going home'. At that moment a friend came into the room to collect her coat, Anne accompanied her towards the door and as they reached it, the bell rang. Thinking it was a returning guest, she opened the door and said, 'What have you forgotten? Or do you want another drink or . . .'

Her voice trailed away because standing on the doorstep was Ben. As she smiled delightedly at him, a roar of laughter came from the direction of Rebecca's bedroom, doubtless induced by a hilarious Hollywood story from la Conway, and a group of friends swept noisily across the hall, calling for Anne to join them. Ben's eyes scanned the scene and then to her utter astonishment, he said, 'It's Liberty Hall here tonight, is it?'

Ben's visit to The Dales had not been a happy one and the

last thing he'd wanted to return to was a flat filled with Anne's yapping friends. In his irritation he swung on his heels and strode towards the stairhead. Anne ran after him and catching his arm, she said, 'Ben, don't be silly. Where on earth are you going?'

Where was he going? He hadn't the least idea but it was a clear starlit night, at least for London, so he reckoned he'd walk off his displeasure and maybe clarify his thoughts. He shook her arm away, adjusted his rucksack on his back and, without looking at Anne, continued down the stairs.

Anne knew Ben disliked parties, but really! Part of her wanted to chase after him but she was the hostess and he was behaving ridiculously so she merely called out, 'You might have let me know when you were coming back. Ben, don't be stupid. Come and have a drink. Everybody'll be gone soon.'

Ben went on walking steadily down until his sturdy figure disappeared round the bend of the staircase. Furious with him, Anne marched back into the flat.

22

Ben looked at Anne, propped up on the pillow beside him, and wondered tiredly what her present ominous silence and rigid avoidance of bodily contact heralded. After his tramp through the streets of London he'd returned to the flat to find her still up and they'd had a right old barney. In the course of it, in none too tactful a fashion, he had given her the results of his visit to The Dales.

'My Mam says Tom Whitworth and his family have always been held in the highest regard by Herbert Broughton and his family and she doesn't know what his daughter, that's you, is playing at. There's never been a divorce in the Brough-ton family and they'd all die of the shame if there were. Mam doesn't have to worry about that. I promised you I'd see Irene and I did. But I didn't know what I was letting myself in for. Why the hell didn't you tell me about that stuff in the *Daily Mail*?'

'Because I didn't want to bother you, stuck in the fighting lines in Spain,' Anne had yelled back at him. 'Since "that stuff" appeared I have had other things to occupy my mind. Like going to Russia.'

'Yeah well, Irene hasn't. When she said, "Will you please ask your mistress, who apparently can't keep her name out of the newspapers, at least to keep yours out?" I knew I was on a hiding to nothing. But I did my best. I told Irene I respected and admired her but I didn't love her and I couldn't live with her. I begged her to divorce me. She said, "You know I cannot do that." I said, "For God's sake, Irene . . ." and she said, "It is for His sake. We were married in the sight of God." Game, set and match to Irene.'

Conscious of his gaze, Anne was now slowly turning her head towards him. The expression in her eyes was less angry than it had been, but Ben recognised that she was about to make one of her pronouncements. Glancing at the bedside clock, she said, 'It's half past six. We're both exhausted and I suggest we get some sleep. Before we do, I'd like to clarify the situation as I see it. If Irene's absolutely adamant she won't divorce you, we'll just have to live together, won't we? You'll want to live in Lancashire, I presume. I'm happy to and I earn more than enough to buy a house, though I'm sure you're going to be in the money once you've held your Spanish exhibition.'

During their altercations, Anne had informed him that Derek Elmar-Smythe had been at the party and was more than enthusiastic about his Spanish *oeuvre*. Her voice at its clearest she went on, 'Then I'd like to have a baby. I can always adopt your name by deed poll, so I can be addressed as Broughton, even if I'm not legally your wife, which will make life easier for us and our babe.' She paused to let him respond. When he did not immediately do so, exasperatedly she said, 'Oh Ben, for heaven's sake, say something, anything.'

While he had been in The Dales, apart from his Mam going on at him and encountering Irene at her most righteous, Ben

256

approached by dozens of lads. They were all eager to do their bit in the fight against Fascism, anxious to know the best way of getting to Spain without passports and in the face of the Foreign Enlistment Act that forbade them to join the International Brigade. The lads had reminded him of the pals he'd left behind on the Ebro and that the job was not yet finished. Slowly, Ben said, 'Before we set up home together and think about having a kid, I reckon I should go back to Spain, to see it through to the end.'

Inhaling deeply on her cigarette, Anne thought, Well, I asked for it and I got it. I guessed that was the decision he'd reached, didn't I? And that's one of the reasons he's in such a foul mood. She said, 'Are you going back partly to escape from the complications of Irene and me and your mother's nagging?'

Momentarily, as Ben unwound his arms from behind his head, Anne thought he was going to hit her. She half-wished she hadn't asked the question, though – sod Irene and the *Daily Mail* – it seemed to her a perfectly valid one. However, Ben merely leaned over to take a cigarette from her case. After he'd lit it, he blew out several smoke rings with a cool ferocity before he said, 'There are times and circumstances when personal relationships have to come second.'

True, Anne thought, but you haven't actually answered my question, have you? Still there's no point pressing it and I can't stop you, and Daddy went back to see the Great War through to the end, didn't he? Oh God, I mustn't think like that, lightning doesn't strike twice, history never repeats itself exactly. She said, 'When do you propose to go back?'

'I'll stay for my exhibition. Then . . .' Ben left the sentence uncompleted.

'Where do you propose to stay until then?'

Anne turned to look at him and there was a faintly surprised expression in his beautiful grey eyes as he replied, 'With you, here at Gower Street, if that's okay.'

'It isn't wildly convenient, though you get on well enough with Rebecca now. But we do have Mrs Guppy around the place and at least one set of nosey, highly virtuous neighbours.'

'I'll push off somewhere else then.'

Turning her head away, in a muffled voice, because she

was close to tears, Anne said, 'Ben, don't, please. Of course you can stay here, but you do take things for granted.'

During the next few days Ben rose early and disappeared before Mrs Guppy arrived. When he returned, often quite late at night, he was in uncommunicative mood, though Anne gathered he was helping to set up the exhibition at the Carillon Gallery. She was unsure whether his absences were because he had taken note of her chiding, because he wanted to give her peace to write the last chapters of *The Moment of Murder*, or because he was a cussed individual. At the end of the week, Anne was typing a page of Chapter 21, assuredly destined for the wastepaper basket, when the telephone rang.

'Am I speaking to Anne Whitworth?' the caller asked before Anne could make her usual identifying announcement. Immediately recognising Margaret-Jane Conway's breathily girlish voice, dryly she said, 'Yes.'

'Darling, it's happened! Wham! Zap! We're in love! I just had to let you know, seeing we met at your party!'

Margaret-Jane's voice was ecstatically exclamatory but she had omitted the vital information, so even more dryly Anne enquired, 'With whom have you fallen in love?'

'Darling, didn't I tell you? Silly little me! I'm just too excited! Julian, of course! My Momma wasn't a Roman Catholic but Popsky comes from an Irish Catholic family. They weren't very devout but soon after we arrived in Hollywood, Popsky passed through a religious phase so I was baptised in the Faith. Isn't that lucky? Because Julian tells me his Momma is just too devout. He's going to tell his mother all about me, then he's taking me to meet her. I guess you know Ryby Hall. Is it as gloriously oldie-worldie as it looks in photographs? Once we're officially engaged you'll be guest-of-honour at our engagement party . . .'

The thoughts splashing through her own head like a waterfall, Anne half-listened as the breathy voice cascaded on. It sounded as if that old black magic known as love had cast its spell because Julian, though presumably not Margaret-Jane otherwise she would assuredly have mentioned it, was aware that her mother and his father had enjoyed a passionate wartime romance. Again presumably, that was why Julian

258

was initially going to Ryby Hall by himself, to break the news to his mother. However tactful he was, it was difficult to imagine Mrs Kendle reacting favourably to her darling son marrying the daughter of the woman who had stolen her husband. Should Julian succeed in persuading his Mama to meet Margaret-Jane, it was equally difficult to see her approving of la Conway as a suitable bride for her only son and the heir to Ryby Hall.

After Margaret-Jane had finally rung off, Anne lit a cigarette and paced round the living room for several minutes. Then, unable to resist the temptation, she telephoned the J. C. Kendle Literary Agency and asked to speak to Mr Kendle. As usual, assuming Julian was in the office and not urgently engaged, she was put straight through to him. Having disposed of her pretext for 'phoning – a query about a book club contract – Anne mentioned that Margaret-Jane had recently been on the line.

'Ah,' said Julian.

'Are congratulations in order?'

'I h-hope so, Anne. There are certain p-problems to overcome b-before our engagement c-can be announced.'

'Mm.' Having ascertained that Margaret-Jane was not aware of them, Anne said, 'I hope your mother won't be upset by the idea. And I do hope she likes Margaret-Jane.'

Julian's stammer disappeared and his voice had its note of asperity as he replied, 'Of course she'll like her. Who would not? I hope my mother will see our union as the healing of old scars.'

After that there wasn't anything Anne could think of saying. When Ben returned in the evening, with a certain satisfaction she informed him that Julian Kendle whom he considered to be a nancy-boy and Margaret-Jane Conway who was a dishy, sexy, American blonde, had fallen head-over-heels in love. Sexy la Conway undoubtedly was and Anne wondered how she and Julian would fare in the physical stakes, but she'd never told Ben about her brief, unsuccessful fling with Mr Kendle so she didn't mention that. In any case, Ben's only response to the news was, 'Bully for them.'

Anne then asked if he wanted to go to Chenneys for the weekend. 'It's Philip's fifty-eighth birthday on Saturday. Just a quiet celebration. I'm driving down on Friday morning. You'll be very welcome.'

After due consideration Ben said, 'Yeah, all right. I quite like the old geezer. I'll give him one of my Spanish paintings for his present. Do you reckon he'd like that?'

Anne said she was sure Philip would be delighted to add to his collection of B. D. Broughtons. In many ways Ben was arrogant about his painting but at times he was nicely humble.

It was a beautiful early May morning as they drove to Chenneys in Bill, with whom – Anne tended to regard her motor car as semi-human – she refused to part. Rounding the bend of the long drive and drawing to a halt on the gravel area below the terrace, Anne saw her mother returning from a walk, or more accurately from being pushed in her wheel-chair by Muriel, her devoted nurse. Philip was limping by their side. After they had greeted each other warmly, Anne said, 'I have news for you. Julian Kendle and Margaret-Jane Conway have fallen madly in love and . . .'

'Oh God!' Mummy rarely swore or blasphemed and Anne looked at her in surprise as she went on, 'Oh Philip, what are we going to do?'

Gently Philip told his wife not to get excited, before asking Anne if she would come to her mother's room as soon as she had settled in. He smiled briefly at Ben. 'If you will excuse us for a short while?'

'Sure,' said Ben.

Trying to fathom why her announcement about Julian and Margaret-Jane had so disturbed her mother, unable to find a satisfactory answer, Anne shot up to her bedroom and back down to Mummy's room as fast as she could. Her mother was still looking upset and Philip was standing by the window smoking. He offered Anne a cigarette which she accepted and, once she'd sat down, Mummy said huskily, 'What we've decided we should tell you, Anne, is known for certain only to a few people, though Aunty Alice wasn't noted for keeping her mouth shut and other people guessed, including Mrs Kendle. Once Aunty Alice met Uncle Guy here at Chenneys in August 1916, that was it. She no longer cohabited with her husband. Margaret-Jane, you may recall, was born at our house in The Grove in December 1917.'

Her mother paused to let this information sink in. Dumbfounded, Anne finally stuttered, 'You m-mean . . .'

'Yes,' Philip drawled. 'Guy Kendle was the father of Alice's child. Of that there is no doubt. Julian and Margaret-Jane are therefore half-brother and sister.'

'Oh God!' Anne echoed her mother's initial response. Once Mummy had told her about the Alice – Guy affair, how could she have been so stupid as not to have worked out the time-scale and put two and two together to make the blindingly obvious four? It was from Uncle Guy that Margaret-Jane had inherited that long graceful neck, those velvety brown eyes, and her classiness. Why on earth hadn't she noticed the physical resemblances? Because she wasn't expecting to find them, was the answer, and Julian hadn't put two and two together or noticed either.

'Oh God!' Anne said again. 'Poor Julian. The news is going to devastate him. And Margaret-Jane too.' Though she was more worried about him than her. 'And Julian's supposed to be going to Ryby Hall to tell his mother. Oh, he mustn't. That would be too awful. We've got to tell him, haven't we?'

'Yes,' her mother said. 'I think the best thing . . .'

Gently as ever, Philip interrupted, ' . . . is for me to undertake the task. The unhappy news will, I believe, best be broken to Julian by another man. And from our brief acquaintance with the young lady . . .' Margaret-Jane had visited Chenneys soon after her arrival in England '. . . I suspect she will prefer a man's shoulder to weep upon. Is she still at Claridge's?' Anne nodded. 'I shall go up to Town and give them the unpleasant information personally, but individually, I think, not together.'

After Philip had limped away to make his telephone calls in private, Anne looked at her mother who said, 'It's partly my fault, you know. I did nothing to stop Johnny Conway registering Margaret-Jane as his child. At the time it seemed the best thing and . . .'

Alarmed by her mother's husky breathlessness, Anne jumped from the armchair and knelt down in front of her, saying firmly, 'Mummy, stop it! You might just as well say it's my fault for inviting Margaret-Jane and Julian to the same party. And if you're castigating yourself for not being honest, what about Mrs Kendle and Jonathon Conway?'

Anne went on talking and thankfully her mother calmed down. Philip returned to say he'd been in luck and had managed to contact both Julian and Margaret-Jane. He'd arranged to see each of them and Dickinson was driving him up to Town after lunch, which news cheered Mummy slightly.

Rebecca had as usual been invited to celebrate Sir Philip's birthday and for once she was able to accept the invitation. She was looking forward to a relaxing weekend in the comfort and beauty of Chenneys but when she arrived on the Friday evening, it was to be greeted by uproar. Sir Philip and Margaret-Jane Conway – what on earth was she doing here? – were standing in the panelled entrance hall. They were both dressed in outdoor clothes so obviously they'd just arrived from somewhere. Margaret-Jane was bawling her eyes out and Anne and Lady Marchal were trying to comfort her.

She howled at Mark, 'You're not my brother too, are you?'

Running his hand through his thick black hair, Mark drawled, 'No. One look at my father's photograph and then at me will convince you my mother's virtue is intact.'

With the tears pouring down her face, Margaret-Jane pivoted round to Ben, who said laconically, 'I'm definitely not your brother.'

It sounded like the dialogue from one of Sir Philip's plays but having missed the first act, as it were, Rebecca found the plot incomprehensible. It continued to thicken, with Lady Marchal's nurse being summoned to calm Margaret-Jane's hysteria, her being put to bed sedated, and Anne saying, 'Sorry, Becky, I'll explain later.' It was nearly midnight and Rebecca was performing her ablutions, before Anne finally explained.

Sprawled on the bed, she said, 'And apparently Julian kept repeating over and over again that despite knowing about his father's affair with Alice Conway, the notion that he and Margaret-Jane might be half-brother and sister never entered his head. But he remained in control of himself and thanked

Philip for coming up to Town personally to give him the shattering news.

'It was an entirely different story at Claridge's. Margaret-Jane rampaged around her suite, screaming at Philip and when poor Julian telephoned, she said she never wanted to speak to him again and slammed the receiver down. Mummy gave Philip strict instructions that if either Margaret-Jane or Julian, or both of them, couldn't cope with the news, he was to bring them here. Which is why we're stuck with Madam. It must have been a fearful shock – I can imagine how I'd have felt if somebody had told me Ben was my half-brother – and I do feel sorry for Margaret-Jane, but she is a pain in the neck, isn't she?'

Rebecca nodded and Anne observed, 'Of course, Ben says only the rich can afford the luxury of indulging their emotions the way she's doing.'

He would, wouldn't he? Rebecca thought, though perhaps he had a point. Having brushed her teeth, she asked Anne to toss over her pyjamas. Anne frequently stripped off in front of her, or pranced round the flat in the nude, but she was not sexually inhibited and moreover she had a sylph-like figure. Not wanting to seem prudish, Rebecca took off her bra, panties and corset but as she did so, in the long mirror she saw the reflection of the spare tyres round her middle and the bulges of fat everywhere. That was one good reason, she thought sadly, why Julian Kendle was never attracted to me. To compound her misery and her self-consciousness Anne said cheerfully, 'You're getting fat, Lawson.'

Rebecca replied shortly, 'I've always been fat.'

'You could stop eating chocolates and gooey cakes by the hundredweight, couldn't you?'

'You could stop smoking.'

Having just lit a cigarette, Anne laughed. Then she sighed and said, 'Poor Julian, I feel so sorry for him. I think he really had fallen in love with Margaret-Jane, you know.'

How Rebecca wished Anne would shut up about Julian.

Some time ago her mother had informed her that the way she was going, she was destined to be an old maid. Mummy hadn't entirely given up hope. She kept trying to introduce her baffling daughter to good Jewish boys, several of whom

263

were decidedly long in the tooth. Rebecca herself had come to the conclusion that, unlike Anne, she was not cut out to have a tempestuous love-life and be a successful career woman. It was better to do one thing well than to fail at several, Rebecca believed, and her mission on earth was to live long enough to see the establishment of the Jewish Homeland in Palestine.

On her return to Gower Street, what she could or should do to help Julian through a trauma that would affect his sensitive, introverted soul, bothered Anne considerably. Ben said, 'Send him some flowers', which wasn't helpful. Rebecca suggested a letter rather than a 'phone call because Anne wrote such good letters. That was what she did, tearing up several long-winded epistles, before completing a single page which she finished with the words, 'If there is any way I can be of help to you, Julian, please, please, don't hesitate to get in touch with me' and the signature 'Yours aye, Anne'.

Julian did not contact her, at least not for three weeks, during which time Anne fretted that she should telephone or go round to see him or suggest they dine together or something, but Rebecca said, 'Let him be. He's a proud man.' When Julian finally telephoned it was a business call and his voice was politely, unstutteringly formal but just before he rang off, he stammered, 'I – I received your n-note, Anne. Thank you.'

That presumably was all the help he wanted or needed from her. By then, Anne's attention was in any case focused on the exhibition of Ben's paintings, due to open at the Carillon Gallery in June. This time she endured a double anguish over the outcome, the fervent desire that the exhibition be accorded the success it deserved and the fear that it might not be, and the dread that once it had opened, Ben would return to Spain. As before, Derek Elmar-Smythe organised and publicised the exhibition extremely well and Ben was more amenable than he had been last time.

From the start of the opening junket, even before Derek rushed up to her at an early stage of the proceedings, Anne smelled success in the air, which his news confirmed. Waving his hands noisily at her – he'd taken to wearing gold bracelets which jangled on his wrists – Derek said, 'Darling heart, the gorgeous brute's en route to the hall of fame. We've sold six paintings already! I espy a buyer's gleam in Lord Crossley's eye. See you anon, duckie.'

'Hello, duckie,' a mock-Cockney voice said in her ear.

Anne turned to see Mark, with Margaret-Jane hanging on his arm. She was resplendent in one of the trouser suits she favoured, a turquoise-green shot-silk affair with exaggeratedly padded shoulders and a plunging neckline that showed off her graceful neck. Having kissed Anne effusively, in her little girl tones she simpered, 'I just don't know how I'd have survived without your marvellous mother. What a wonderful person she is. Or without your brother.' She fluttered her eyelashes at Mark, before squeaking, 'Oo, there's Theo Marvell. I must arrange my next fitting. Fetch me a drinkie, darling.'

The flares of Margaret-Jane's trousers were exceptionally wide, they swished and male heads turned as she trotted on her high heels towards Theo, who greeted her with a shriek and open arms. To her brother Anne observed, 'Madam appears to have recovered. I'm still surprised she's elected to stay in London. Despite her aversion to Jonathon Conway, in the circumstances I'd have thought she'd have wanted to get the hell out of England.'

Margaret-Jane had been particularly vitriolic about the man who not so long ago she'd thought of as 'Popsky' and who had after all brought her up in the luxury of Hollywood film stardom. How dare he pretend to be her father, she'd raged at Chenneys, when her real father was an English gentleman? He'd been a lousy father anyway and she never wanted to see Jonathon Conway again. Anne's mother had, however, persuaded her that illegitimacy was not the most highly-prized of attributes and seeing that the secret of her birth had, rightly or wrongly, been hidden for years, it might be wiser to keep it that way.

Mark drawled, 'She's talking of settling here. She's taken to the idea of secretly being a daughter of the English landed gentry in a big way. Which is very American of her, of course. Rather sweet, though.'

Anne looked at Mark as he brushed a lock of black hair from his forehead, and said, 'You're not getting serious about Margaret-Jane, are you?'

'Depends what you mean by serious, sis.'

'Don't call me "sis". I mean marriage.'

'No,' Mark grinned. 'Madam's strictly for fun. And I have a piece of staggering news for you.'

'Not another one,' Anne groaned.

Casually he announced, 'I have a job.'

'I don't believe it.'

'I knew you wouldn't.'

'What as?'

'Well, remember Humph?' Mark was obviously enjoying himself, intending to tease out the story. Playing the game, Anne said yes, she remembered Humphrey Lakeman-Greaves, who had been prominent in Mark's set at Oxford. 'Well, several moons ago, having learned to fly and got his pilot's licence, Humph bought himself a couple of kites with the money his old man left him and set up the Lakeman-Greaves aeroplane charter company. Definitely the coming thing, air travel. Humph's doing nicely, thank you. Always was a secret swot. Actually enjoys wrestling with accountants and bank managers and turning in profits. Anyway, recently he asked if I'd like to join the thriving concern.'

'What and learn to fly, you mean?'

His inflections at their most casual, her brother drawled, 'I got my pilot's licence last week.'

'Mark!' Anne gasped in amazement. Then she frowned, 'Does Mummy know?'

'Not yet. But Mumkins has always been an enterprising woman. She'd have flown but for her dicky heart. I aim to persuade her, or Pip, to put some money into the company. Humph's looking for a partner, actually, so's he can expand. Pip enjoys the money business, doesn't he? All those grasping, country gentleman ancestors of his.'

From across the other side of the gallery, Margaret-Jane called, 'Where's my drinkie, you naughty boy?'

'Coming instantly,' Mark called back. Grinning at his sister, he collected a glass of freshly-poured champagne and walked towards la Conway.

You could, as they said, have knocked Anne down with a feather. She'd always known Mark had hidden depths but she hadn't expected them to be exercised in the clouds.

266

She decided to restrict her assessments of people, and her predictions about their behaviour, to the characters in her novels. And she sent up a prayer to God if He existed, or to The Fates, that Ben would behave unpredictably and decide not to return to Spain.

The exhibition was a huge success, the reviews for Mr B. D. Broughton's Spanish paintings and drawings being almost as unanimous in their praise as they had been damning for his scenes of industrial Lancashire, though the style, the approach, the technique were the same. Carried away by their rapture, several critics compared his depiction of the Spanish Civil War to Goya's paintings of the Peninsular War, and only a few Tory newspapers carped about Mr Broughton's political views. Apart from the serious reviews, Ben himself suddenly became a figure of interest which, in Anne's opinion, he always had been. Why hadn't the good-looking, intelligent, working-class lad from The Dales who'd won a scholarship to Ruskin College, Oxford, been thrown out of night-classes at art school and developed his own startlingly original talent, been of interest two years ago? Ben's irritation with his sudden fame, as opposed to his genuine pleasure that his paintings had been recognised, was manifest. With a sinking heart, Anne awaited his announcement.

It came on a sultry evening at the beginning of July. Standing by the open window, staring down into Gower Street, he said, 'I reckon the next months in Spain will be the crucial ones, luv. So I reckon I should go back now.'

Anne had already decided not to argue, so she just nodded.

23

'Come on, Annie, snap out of it! Cheer up!'

Frowning at Mark, who was sprawled on the sofa in the living room of the Gower Street flat, smoking and sipping whisky, she asked, 'What is there to be cheerful about? The man I love is somewhere in the fighting zone outside Barcelona. Kurt Wolff says the situation has deteriorated again in Germany. Adolf Hitler's snarling about Czechoslovakia and . . .'

Blowing a smoke ring up to the ceiling, Mark interrupted, 'Look, it's your birthday next week. Let me take you for a joy-ride.'

'A joy-ride where?'

'Into the blue, blue yonder, up above the world so high, like a tea-tray in the sky. It's great fun, provided it isn't sheeting with rain.'

The sun appeared for Anne's birthday – 3 September usually was a nice day – and early in the morning she drove to Croydon airport on the southern outskirts of London, which was where the Lakeman-Greaves charter company had its headquarters. It was interesting to observe Mark in his role as pilot, wrapped in a flying jacket, leather helmet and goggles in hand, for, though his attitude was flippantly casual, there was an underlying air of assured authority. Her brother led her into a large hut a short distance from the main airport buildings, where he introduced her to several young pilots who answered to such names as 'Puffin' and 'Porky' and had a wizard slang of their own. In the hut Anne was kitted out with a flying jacket, helmet and goggles and after she'd been helped into them, everybody agreed Miss Whitworth looked abso-bally-lutely ace.

Feeling more like a stuffed penguin and in the gathering warmth of the sun rather hot, Anne followed Mark across the grass to the corner of the airfield from which the Lakeman-Greaves company operated. After she'd removed her helmet so she could hear properly, her brother introduced her to 'Ginger' whose curly hair was the appropriate colour and without whose brilliant ingenuity as a mechanic the company could not survive. With considerable pride Mark then showed Anne the bi-plane in which he was taking her up. He said, 'She's a handy kite. DH Hornet Moth. Nicely sociable side-by-side seating. Give my sister a leg-up, will you, Ginger?'

Mark himself had leapt on to the lower wing and into the

268

cockpit. Assisted by Ginger, Anne climbed in beside her brother. Before she redonned her helmet and goggles, she said, 'Why do men call inanimate objects like ships and motor cars and aircraft "she"?'

'Dunno.' Mark pulled on his own headgear. 'Why do you call your old bus "Bill"? I have no doubt it's all deeply Freudian.'

'The Nazis have thrown Sigmund Freud out of Vienna, you know, as another piece of Jewish vermin. We've given him sanctuary here in London.'

'Three cheers for us. Give it a rest, Annie, for Pete's sake.'

She had no choice but to obey her brother's exasperated request because he waved his heavily gloved hand at Ginger who proceeded to give the propeller a swing to get it going. Mark then started the engine and the noise put a stop to further conversation. A few minutes later he gave the thumbs-up sign to Ginger who pulled the chocks from the wheels, before returning the sign. With less juddering than Anne expected the 'plane began to move, they were taxiing across the grass, they were gathering speed, the wind was rushing past her face, the Hornet Moth's nose was rising upwards, and they were airborne!

Mark flew her back over London, over the neat lines of suburban houses and gardens, over the regimented rows of terraced houses, over the crowded wharves of dockland, up the River Thames and over Tower Bridge to Westminster. Anne found herself shrieking and pointing excitedly as she recognised the Houses of Parliament and Nelson's Column in Trafalgar Square and it was like a map come to life, with the expanses of the London parks and the smaller areas of the city's squares providing a brilliant green relief. Mark then piloted the 'plane over the loops and bends of the Thames towards its wide estuary, along the Kent coastline, over the white cliffs of Dover and the even whiter stretch of the Seven Sisters gleaming in the sunshine, before turning inland. They flew over the patchwork quilt landscape of southern England and at certain moments when the strong sunlight was behind them, the shadow of the Hornet Moth moved clearly below.

Tapping her brother's arm, Anne shouted intoxicatedly, 'It's fabulous, Mark, it's fabulous.'

Her brother grinned at her. Suddenly she saw the trees on top of a chalky hillside and Anne knew that curiously-shaped clump. It was the summit of Dedman's Down! They were flying low over the stubble of the cornfields, over the stream winding through the wood, over the immemorial elms of the parkland, she could see the summer house nestling in the trees, and the elegant chimney stacks and the mellow Tudor brickwork of Chenneys! Anne screamed with ecstatic delight as Mark banked the Hornet Moth and there on the terrace was her mother waving from her wheelchair, and Philip circling his stick above his head. On the lawn by the lake, the entire staff and the workers on the estate appeared to have assembled and as the 'plane swept over their heads, they lifted an enormous banner which read, 'Happy birthday, Miss Anne!'

The Hornet Moth was descending, the treetops and the grass were rushing up to meet them, momentarily Anne closed her eyes, then with a bumpity-bump she felt the 'plane hit the ground, and as she opened her eyes Mark brought it to a standstill in the long meadow. When they had climbed from 'the kite' and removed their helmets and goggles, her brother crooked his arm and said, 'Lunch awaits you, madame.'

'Whose idea was all this?'

'Once I mentioned taking you for a joy-ride, everybody pitched in.'

Stretching up, Anne kissed her brother on the cheek and said, 'Thank you, thank you a million times, for the most thrilling birthday treat of my twenty-nine years on earth.'

'Don't mention it, old lady.'

In aural memory Anne heard Ben's deep Lancashire-accented voice using the same mocking expression, when she'd joked about her age to him. Oh God, keep him safe, bring him back safely, soon, soon, she prayed.

But the birthday treat lifted the depression from her shoulders and at the end of the month, despite the Czechoslo-vakian crisis, Anne's mood was more buoyant as she arrived in Canterbury for a peace rally. The meeting at which she was a principal, and the sole woman, speaker was in the evening but she drove down early because she loved

Canterbury and it was an ambrosial autumn day. After a saunter through the splendours of the cathedral, which provided a soothing balm even for her agnostic soul, Anne went into the walled garden consecrated to the memory of the dead of the Great War.

Vaguely she noticed the two men sitting on the bench by the memorial cross, but she didn't pay any attention to them. The chrysanthemums and Michaelmas daisies were in bloom, the browns, golds, auburns, whites, purples, massed in the borders, and Anne was soaking in the colours and the tranquillity of this garden in the shadow of the cathedral, when she heard her name called. Glancing towards the men, she realised with astonishment that one of them was Julian, the other Doctor H. V. X. Martindale. They had both risen to their feet and as they walked towards her Doctor Martindale held out his hand, smiled and said smoothly, 'This is an unexpected pleasure, Miss Whitworth, though we were expecting to see you this evening. We are visiting my mother who lives just outside Canterbury and obviously we would not miss a rally in support of that greatest and currently most threatened of all causes, peace.'

With a smile Anne shook his hand and Julian said, 'You're looking most attractive, if I may so, Anne.'

'Thank you.' Whenever she appeared on public platforms she always took pains with her attire, partly for her own satisfaction, partly to dispel the persistent myth that feminism equalled frumpishness. For this evening's meeting Anne had chosen to wear a pale-green silk blouse, a tailored bottle-green costume and a matching straw hat anchored at a jaunty angle. Kid gloves, a crocodile-skin handbag and court shoes completed her outfit.

'We are about to have tea,' H.V.X. said. 'Will you join us?'

Anne said she would be pleased to and they walked towards the nearby teashop. When they were seated at a window table overlooking the cathedral precincts, after Doctor Martindale had ordered toasted teacakes, a selection of fancy cakes and China tea, he informed Anne, 'We are taking a short holiday. Julian needed a break. We're spending a few days with my Mama, before driving north to see Julian's.'

Since Anne had last seen him Doctor Martindale had put on weight, he now had a rather puffy appearance like an overcooked eclair and his manner had become more precious. The suave precision of his speech was slightly more sibilant, he steepled his fingers in a more exaggerated gesture, frequently resting his chin on their immaculately manicured tips. The waitress arrived with their order and after H.V.X. had asked Anne to be 'mother' and she had poured out the China tea, he said, 'I gather one of your "whodunnits", to employ the vulgar American expression . . .'

'Don't be such a pedantic snob, Victor,' Julian smiled as he interrupted. 'It's a vivid expression and languages l-languish if they aren't watered with new words and phrases.'

Briefly returning the smile 'Victor' continued, '. . . that a film has just been made from your detective novels.' Wiping the butter that had dripped from her toasted teacake from her mouth with the napkin, Anne acknowledged that *A Dangerous Affair* had finished shooting and would soon be released. Victor said, 'We are both devotees of your books and we look forward to seeing the film.'

His conversation continued to be peppered with what 'we' were doing or thinking. It was deliberate, Anne knew, but really there was no necessity for the emphasis. Munching an iced cake, she listened to H.V.X. holding forth about the prospects for peace in our time, but her mind wasn't with Adolf Hitler and Neville Chamberlain and Czechoslovakia. It was contemplating the decision Julian had so swiftly but assuredly reached, namely to enter into a relationship with Hector Victor Xerxes Martindale, and her mind felt sadly confused. Unless you chose to flaunt your proclivities like Theo Marvell or Derek Elmar-Smythe, disarming the hostile world by ostentatiously amusing it, the homosexual's own world was shadowy and secretive. Apart from the criminality of the act, a legal state Anne personally considered to be ridiculous, how would the knowledge that his religion said he was committing a mortal sin, weigh on Julian's sensitive shoulders?

Had she failed him as lover and friend, she asked herself, forced him, despite himself, into Victor's only too willing arms? Then, with the slightest of smiles, she thought: at least one person will be happy, his mother, who will not now lose her darling son to some harpy of a female. Julian wouldn't have to worry about his mother's reactions to his friendship with the well-bred Oxford academic, for Anne very much doubted homosexuality was a subject within Mrs Kendle's ken. If she were aware of its existence, it would be as something practised by depraved creatures in the depths of the underworld.

'May I tempt you to another cake, Miss Whitworth?'

'No, thank you. They're delicious but not good for my waistline.'

'With a figure like yours, I shouldn't have thought you needed to bother about such things.'

Victor had decided to be gallant, Julian thought. Ah well, he could afford to be, could he not? Julian had noticed the faint smile flicker across Anne's expressive face and wondered what notion, or observation of Victor's, had induced it, despite her being obviously upset by their encounter. Victor had been tiresome, putting on a special performance for Miss Whitworth's benefit, though Anne would have found out one day soon. Julian wanted to tell her that she had done her very best to 'help' him, that she and Margaret-Jane who, thank God, had proved to be his half-sister, had finally forced him to be honest with himself; to come to terms with the long-suppressed knowledge that he had always been attracted to members of his own sex and that his mother's nocturnal embraces had not retarded his heterosexual development. He knew he would never say any of those things to Anne, but he hoped their friendship would continue because he was fond of her, emotional, impulsive, vulnerable woman that she was. Although her passion for Ben Broughton was beyond Julian's comprehension – boorish, ill-bred creature that he was – if that was what she wanted, he also hoped Ben would return safely from Spain and the path for their marriage would eventually be cleared.

Julian said, 'Should we not be returning to your Mama's, Victor, if we want to bathe and change before the meeting?'

As Victor agreed that we should, it occurred to Anne that Julian had hardly stammered throughout a good hour's conversation unconnected with business affairs. And Ben's instinct about his sexual inclinations had proved correct.

Ben's letters from Spain grew increasingly bitter. He said the pictures of Neville Chamberlain descending from the 'plane at Heston airport, waving that bit of paper and babbling about 'peace in our time', had made him ashamed to be an Englishman. Czechoslovakia had been sold down the river and if Anne or anybody imagined the Führer's territorial claims and vaulting ambition would be halted by the so-called Munich Agreement, they were out of their minds. Anne could continue to be a pacifist but she could no longer realistically expect to check the Nazis because the only thing they understood was force. Anne's intelligence told her Ben was right but her heart clung to the belief that somehow a peaceful solution could yet be found.

In his next letter he wrote: 'The rumour that the Spanish Government is disbanding the International Brigade appears to be true. They say it's a gesture of good faith and belief in the strength of their cause but I believe it's a desperate, last-ditch attempt to stir the conscience of the democracies. Doing down the opposing brands of Communism and Socialism has become infinitely more important for Stalin than defeating the Fascists, and the Russians are consequently withdrawing their support for the Government. Without Russian aid, with the Fascists pouring in aid for General Franco, unless our lot intervenes in Spain's "internal problems" at the eleventh hour, I fear Franco must triumph.'

His next letter confirmed that his company was being withdrawn from the lines outside Barcelona and it had a scribbled postscript which made Anne laugh: 'The other day I went to see a pal from The Dales who's in the nearby hospital at Murcia-Denia. You didn't tell me your cousin Tamara is working there. She's a character and a half. Twice as bossy as you, me beloved witch, and three times as mixed-up. The lads call her "the blonde bombshell", with the emphasis on the "bombshell", because you need to duck when Tamara roars into action, but I gather she's a damned good nurse.'

Although in the wider context she knew they should not,

both letters made Anne's heart thump with joy. For the disbanding of the International Brigade meant Ben would soon be home!

The telegram arrived early the next morning. When Anne opened the door of the flat to see the telegraph boy standing outside, momentarily her whole body trembled. It could not be about Ben, he could not have been killed at the very last minute as his company was being withdrawn from the lines, history did not repeat itself. The boy said, 'Miss Lawson?' and looked curiously at Anne as she started to laugh with relief. Rebecca was up in Manchester but Anne accepted the telegram on her behalf and immediately put through a telephone call to the Lawsons' house. Fortunately, Rebecca had not left for her meeting and she asked Anne to open the telegram and read it out.

'It's in German.'

'Do your best.'

Over the telephone line Anne read the message. '*Kurt verhaftet Stop Gefangensetzt in Konsentrationslager Dachau Stop Helfst du bitte Stop Aaron Wolff.*' Anne did not need to understand German to grasp its import and as she finished she gasped, 'Oh God, Becky! How are we going to get Kurt out of Dachau?'

'By the bribery and corruption in which the Nazis are only too willing to indulge. I've got this damned meeting today and it is important but I'll come back this evening and I'll go straight to Frankfurt tomorrow morning.'

'I'm coming with you. Because I know who we might be able to bribe and corrupt. Helmut Ohlendorf.' Helmut had sent Anne a card at the Christmas of 1933 and Rebecca had said, 'Oh, send him one back. You never know when we might need him.' Since then they had exchanged cards and news each Christmas. Anne therefore knew that he was still living in Frankfurt and was still involved in 'the Jewish problem', that he had been promoted to *SS-Hauptsturmführer* and had recently married. She went on, 'You said Captain Ohlendorf might come in useful one day. Don't worry, Becky. You go to your meeting and get back as quickly as you can. I'll make all the arrangements.'

24

The next morning Mark flew them to Frankfurt as he had promised Anne he would, provided the weather wasn't too foggy. Thank heaven, when the alarm clock went off at six-thirty and she ran to the window, the lights on the other side of Gower Street were visible. Kitted out in sheepskin jackets and the rest of the paraphernalia, they left Croydon airport at nine o'clock in a Percival Gull, which was a mono-plane with seating for three passengers. According to Mark it had a cruising speed of 168 m.p.h. but the journey still seemed inordinately long to Anne and bore little resemblance to the heavenly jaunt in the Hornet Moth. It started to rain, they kept flying into banks of cloud which Anne found frightening, and the 'plane kept lurching which made her feel sick. When they were once more on *terra firma*, standing in the airport building at Frankfurt, she was astonished to see it was only one o'clock.

'Look, are you two sure you'll be all right on your own?' Mark asked.

'Quite sure. You and Humph have a business to run and I know flying us here today was a special favour. So get back to London as soon as possible and Mark . . . thank you.'

'Don't mention it, sis.'

'Let me mention it,' Rebecca said. 'I can't tell you how grateful I am, Mark.'

'I hope you get your cousin out of that bloody concentration camp. And Rebecca . . .' Mark looked towards Anne '. . . see she doesn't do anything stupid.'

Rebecca smiled slightly and replied, 'I'll do my best to make her count ten before she dashes into action.'

They hired a taxi from the Rebstock district in which the airfield was situated. Although the journey to Westend did not take them into the centre of the city, where Anne gathered the worst excesses of *Kristallnacht* had occurred, even in these suburban areas there was evidence of that horrific night; piles of broken glass lying in gutters, houses daubed with swastikas, the charred remains of bonfires. Grimly Rebecca said, 'We could hardly have arrived in Germany at a worse moment to secure Kurt's release, could we?'

'No,' Anne agreed. 'But we're going to do it, Becky.'

When they reached the Wolffs' house off the Bockenheimer Landstrasse, that did not appear to have been molested. But as Rebecca rang the bell, Anne noticed the curtains in the front window twitching, she heard the sound of heavy bolts being drawn back, before the door opened and was swiftly re-bolted behind them. Herr Doktor and Frau Wolff's greeting was emotional and Anne was conducted to the bedroom that had been Ben's, the one in which they had first made love. All her energies must for the moment be concentrated on Kurt, not Ben. During a belated lunch, served by the one elderly Jewish maid who remained in the Wolffs' service, Rebecca told Anne that Kurt had in fact been arrested three weeks ago. Cousins Aaron and Sophia had no idea why, other than the obvious fact that he was a Jew and their efforts to gain further information had met with a brutal lack of concern. In the wake of *Kristallnacht* it seemed useless to pursue them further, which was why they had appealed to Rebecca for help.

After lunch she and Anne had yet another discussion about the best way to go about things. Rebecca agreed they should first approach *SS-Haupsturmführer* Ohlendorf, though she said if necessary she was prepared to go to Berlin or Munich where she had contacts. Convinced that Helmut Ohlendorf could secure Kurt's release, Anne said she was going to telephone his home number.

'He's not likely to be there in the middle of the afternoon,' Rebecca said. 'How do you know his wife speaks English?'

Anne had no idea whether or not Frau Ohlendorf spoke English but she insisted on telephoning. To her astonishment the call was answered by Wanda Ohlendorf who said, 'What a top-hole surprise, Anne, to hear your dear English voice and to learn you are once more with us in Frankfurt.'

Wanda was in voluble mood and full of top-hole surprises. She was staying with her dear brother and her sister-in-law Lili who was in a happily expectant state. Unhappily, and from the tone of Wanda's voice un-Teutonically, Lili was having a bad pregnancy. Today was Helmut's birthday, this evening they were having a party and Wanda was organising things because Lili was in no state to do so.

The second she heard about the birthday party, the idea struck Anne. Fortunately it also occurred to Wanda who said excitedly, 'Anne, why would you not join us? Dear Helmut would be as overjoyous to see you as I myself. Please say you would not be engaged this evening.'

Anne said she would be delighted to join the Ohlendorfs' celebration and she looked forward to seeing them at eight o'clock this evening. She rushed to give the news to Rebecca who said, 'I thought all good Nazis were supposed to be in deep mourning for the death of Ernst vom Rath.'

It was the shooting of the Third Secretary at the German Embassy in Paris, by a German-Jewish student half-crazed at the fate that had befallen thousands of Jews, including his own father, summarily expelled by the Nazis and dumped on the Polish border, that had precipitated last week's nightmare; *Kristallnacht*; the night of the broken glass; the night of systematic attacks on Jewish property and people throughout Germany.

'Apparently not all Nazis are in mourning,' Anne replied.

'Seeing it's a social occasion, be tactful in your approach to Helmut Ohlendorf, won't you?' Rebecca urged. 'And seeing you've been up since the crack of dawn and had a pretty gruesome flight, I suggest you have a nap.'

Bridling slightly, Anne said of course she would be tactful. She supposed she'd better buy Helmut a birthday present but after that she agreed a nap would be a good idea.

The Ohlendorfs lived in a spacious apartment in a handsome, neo-classical house in the Krögerstrasse, close by the Eschenheim Gardens. Thanking Anne for her so gracious gift – she'd bought him a leather wallet – Helmut greeted her with as much enthusiasm as his robot-like personality allowed. As he lifted his head from kissing her hand, she saw a flicker in those cold blue eyes which said Captain Ohlendorf still found her attractive. It was an attraction she hoped to use for Kurt's sake. His wife was quite pretty in a washed-out way but did not speak English, nor appear to have much to say for herself in any language. Wanda was only too obviously in charge of the household and Anne's curiosity was stirred, but she told herself she was not here to probe into the tripartite relationship between the beplaited bossy Rhine-maiden sister, the wan Rhine-matron wife, and the ramrod specimen of Nazi manhood.

Apart from the plethora of SS uniforms, Anne thought it could be a well-heeled, fairly crass party anywhere in Europe. Wanda kept swooping on her to introduce people who were dying to meet the famous English detective authoress. (Her Seth Pollard books had now been translated into German, though when the offer had been made Anne had wrestled with her conscience. She'd finally decided to accept it and to give all the money to anti-Fascist organisations.) After an English-speaking mouthpiece for a coven of SS officers had told her how much he had enjoyed reading her books, which did not please Anne, he went on to say, 'Like our beloved Führer, we in the *Schutzstaffel* believe our two great Anglo-Saxon nations have so much in common. What a wise statesman your Mr Neville Chamberlain is, with so true an understanding of Germany's legitimate territorial claims.'

Biting her tongue hard, Anne smiled sweetly at him and his ghastly colleagues.

Helmut seemed to be permanently surrounded by back-slapping cronies and fawning Frankfurters of both sexes but somehow during the course of the evening she had to get him on his own. At nine-thirty Wanda shooed everybody into the dining room where a lavish buffet supper was laid but before they ate, Helmut proposed the toast to their beloved Führer and the Thousand Year Reich. Standing close by him, Anne compromised by raising her glass to her lips but not drinking. When she had finished eating and was about to enjoy a cigarette, a hand holding a lighter came up to her mouth. Before he spoke, Anne knew it was Helmut's hand.

Flicking the lighter he said, 'Still smoking, I see.' He had a cigarette in his own mouth but Anne recalled reading that the Führer did not approve of women smoking. She had noticed that Wanda had given up and Lili Ohlendorf did not indulge. 'And to what do we owe the great pleasure and honour of your company in Frankfurt, Anne?'

Breathily she replied, 'My brother's a pilot and he had to fly to Frankfurt today. I thought it would be nice to see old friends.'

'Including the Wolffs?' Helmut enquired.

Utterly pompous he might be, altogether stupid he was not. Anne looked straight into his pale blue eyes and said, 'Yes, I am staying with them and Herr Doktor and Frau Wolff have told me about Kurt being arrested, though they don't know why he was. Some time ago Kurt wrote to tell me how helpful you'd been and how grateful he was to you.'

What Kurt had actually written was that he'd been walking across the Römerberg one day, when he'd bumped into Helmut Ohlendorf who had not only deigned to speak to him but had enquired if he was still giving private tuition. Banned as a Jew from lecturing or teaching in any public place, Ohlendorf knew damned well this was the only way Kurt could earn his living but he said he'd metaphorically tugged his Jewish forelock and agreed he was. Whereupon Ohlendorf had given him the names and addresses of two young men who required coaching for university entrance and told him to mention his, Ohlendorf's, name. Both young men had come from impeccably Aryan families and Kurt said he'd definitely abandoned the effort to analyse the Nazi mentality!

Even more breathily Anne said, 'Can you help Kurt now? Perhaps there has been a mistake. They do occur even in the most efficient, best-organised States, don't they? I can't believe Kurt has done anything really wrong, can you? I mean, he's not the sort of person who gets involved in things, is he?'

Anne's voice trailed away. Pleadingly, willing him to be helpful, she gazed at Helmut. It seemed an eternity before he spoke, during which the chink of glasses, the clatter of plates, the guttural chatter of the guests, sounded like distant echoes.

Eventually Helmut said, 'The repercussions of the martyr-dom of Ernst vom Rath could be prolonged and serious.' Anne's heart sank because his tone suggested – against that background, of what concern to an SS officer were the problems of one miserable Jew? Then he smiled at her, or rather he gave her the same sort of smirk his Führer employed before he said, 'You English gravely underestimate the threat of the worldwide Jewish conspiracy. However, I agree there are individual Jews who are not detestable. I always found Wolff pleasant enough, although as you rightly observe, Anne, he is a lazily uninvolved person. I would not know whether his arrest was wholly justified. But I shall make enquiries.'

For the next few days, while they anxiously awaited the results of Helmut Ohlendorf's enquiries, Anne and Rebecca did a lot of walking through the streets of Frankfurt. They went to the Börneplatz where the blackened, burned-out shell of the synagogue, destroyed on the night of 9/10 November, was etched against the grey sky. Overcome by emotion, Rebecca put her face in her hands. As Anne slipped a comfor-ting arm round her friend's trembling shoulders, she thought of the sketches Ben had made of the Jewish traders in front of the synagogue. They would now be historic documents.

Elsewhere, apart from the boarded-up Jewish shops and the anti-Semitic slogans scrawled on walls, the bustling life of the city proceeded as if the events of *Kristallnacht* had never happened. When they were walking through the hothouses of the Palmengarten, Rebecca suddenly said, 'You know I've been asked to work for the Anglo-Jewish Refugee Agency in London. After what I've seen in the last few days, I'm going to accept the offer.'

'What, and give up your work for Palestine?' Anne looked at her in astonishment.

Staring at the sunlight filtering through the glass roof on to the lush tropical vegetation, Rebecca nodded fiercely. 'For the time being, yes. Germany and Austria are in the grip of a hideous madness and we've got to get as many Jews as possible out of "Greater Germany" before it's too late.'

Anne did not enquire what she meant by 'too late' but said,

'Will Doctor Wolff and his wife come to England now, do you think?'

'No. Cousin Aaron may not be permitted to desecrate Aryan flesh with his filthy Jewish hands, but the Nazis have nobly decided to license some Jewish doctors to treat their own kind. Cousin Aaron has just learned he's been licensed. Apart from his sentimental attachment to his native land, he won't dream of leaving his patients and Cousin Sophia won't dream of leaving him.'

At the end of the week, when they had heard nothing from Helmut Ohlendorf, Rebecca said, 'I'm not waiting any longer. I've already made enquiries in other directions and I'm going to . . .'

Anne interrupted, 'Have your enquiries produced any results as yet?'

'Not really,' Rebecca admitted. She realised Anne desperately wanted to be the person who, via Helmut Ohlendorf, secured Kurt's release. Perhaps she was suffering from an attack of Gentile guilt, Rebecca thought, and needed to expiate it in this way.

Then, on the Sunday evening, he telephoned and Anne came off the line in a state of high excitement. She began by parodying his sister's English. 'Dear Helmut is anxious to be of jolly old help. He thinks he may be able to effect Kurt's release, which means he can, and he has to go to Heidelberg tomorrow. He asked if I'd been there and I said, no, and in his pompous way he suggested we rectify that omission. So he's picking me up at half past eight tomorrow morning and we'll discuss things while he shows me the beauties of Heidelberg.'

'Why can't he discuss things in Frankfurt?' was Rebecca's immediate reaction.

Anne didn't see anything peculiar in Helmut's inviting her to accompany him to Heidelberg, in fact she became rather hoity-toity. Rebecca was worried about her friend's impulsive nature and highly conscious of Mark's plea to keep an eye on his sister. In the circumstances the only thing she felt she could do was to remind Anne that two thousand Reichsmarks was a good sum to pay for Kurt's release but if Captain Ohlendorf preferred gold or jewellery they would obtain it, to beg her to remember she was in Nazi Germany and urge her to have an early night.

The following morning, on the dot of eight-thirty, the swastika flags hanging limply from its bonnet, the huge Mercedes-Benz drew up outside the Wolffs' house. Helmut Ohlendorf stood on the pavement in his SS uniform and as Anne walked to meet him, she wondered how many nearby Jewish hearts were palpitating. Actually, her own was beating fairly fast. The SS chauffeur drove through the centre of Frankfurt, southwards over the River Main, and politely Anne asked Helmut how Frau Ohlendorf was. Frostily, he said she was very well, thank you, and implying that his wife was other than in the pink of expectant health had not been a good idea. Soon they were bowling along the carriageway of the Reichsautobahn to Darmstadt, which provided Helmut with the opportunity to extol the Führer's magnificent achievements.

When they reached Heidelberg, Helmut regretted that the weather was so gloomy and Anne was not seeing the town in the full glory of the sun. Looking at the fairy-tale castle perched above the red rooftops, with the wooded sweep of the Königstuhl behind, she exclaimed, 'Oh no, Helmut, even today it's lovely! Sometimes famous beauty spots are a disappointment, but not this one.'

Those comments went down a treat. They proceeded into the Kornmarkt where the Mercedes-Benz drew up outside the Town Hall. Anne was conducted into the mayor's parlour and Helmut said he would be back as soon as he had finished his business. She had only just finished her coffee and cakes, when he returned. They then drove through the narrow streets and squares of the old town – everything got out of the way of the SS vehicle – and Anne said, 'Oh, it's just like a stage set for *The Student Prince*.'

That remark did not go down so well. They finished their tour in front of an ornately baroque hotel and once they were inside, Helmut introduced Anne to several of the local burghers. It was obvious he enjoyed showing off his famous, aristocratic (ha!) English friend and Anne had in fact taken pains to look the part to Nazi perfection. Early this morning she had shampooed and set her hair into a softly feminine style, parted in the centre, framing her face and curling into her neck. Aware of Herr Hitler's dislike of 'painted women' and corresponding penchant for rosy-cheeked maidens, she had merely applied a dab of powder and a light lipstick. She was wearing her glossiest mink coat and hat, one of Theo Marvell's expensively simple, jersey wool dresses in a pastel green that complemented the copper of her hair, and high-heeled leather boots.

When was Helmut going to discuss the matter that had brought her to Heidelberg? Anne wondered. Not over the five-course lunch, but she felt she must restrain her impatience and let him get round to the subject in his own good, or bad, time. After lunch he announced that he was taking her to the castle and as the Mercedes-Benz drove them up the hill, Helmut started to talk about the Jewish Problem in general, rather than the fate of one specific Jew in Dachau.

'The solution is emigration, Anne.' She refrained from observing that if he truly believed in a worldwide Jewish conspiracy, expelling thousands of Jews, deeply hostile to the Third Reich, would not seem a good idea. He went on, 'In Vienna, *Untersturmführer* Eichmann has had considerable success in encouraging Jews to emigrate.'

Encouraging them! With the utmost difficulty Anne held her tongue. From the Austrian capital, where she had joined her husband, Con had written describing the terrible public humiliations and pressures being heaped on Austrian Jewry which had driven some, not to emigrate, but to commit suicide.

While Helmut showed Anne round the castle's romantic ruins and impressive remains, through the gardens, past the fountain of Father Rhine, he continued to hold forth about the Jews and racial purity and the glorious future of the Thousand Year Reich. Why only a thousand? Anne thought, though heaven forbid it should last one more year. Time was passing, the light was fading, and how much more of his bilge had she to endure? Then he led her on to the Altan, the great terrace of the castle, and as sometimes happens towards the end of the greyest of days, the sun suddenly broke through the clouds. For several minutes they stood silently looking

284

down on the rooftops of old Heidelberg and the placidly flowing River Neckar, bathed in bands of platinum light.

Helmut broke the silence by saying, 'It is so beautiful, is it not? You are so beautiful, Anne. Why is one so lovely as you not married? Why are you still a maiden, when you should be tasting the pleasures of love in the arms of a strong man?'

God save me from this pathetic attempt at seduction, was Anne's first thought, to be swiftly followed by more worrying ones. Did Helmut imagine she was aching to lose her long-lost virginity in his strong arms? Was he under the impression that was why she had accepted his invitation? He couldn't seriously believe she would go to bed with him in exchange for Kurt's release. Could he? Could she do such a thing? No, she could not.

As she turned her head to look at him, Helmut moved towards her, a slant of the dying sun illuminated his face and the smugly lascivious expression said he did believe she was his for the taking. Oh God! Anne felt panicky and she babbled, 'Actually, I'm in love with an Englishman but he's already married, though we're hoping his wife will soon agree to a divorce, and you must come to our wedding, you and your wife, and . . .'

'Ach, so you are telling me you are not a maiden.'

'No, I'm telling you I love my . . . my . . . lover and . . . um . . .'

There was a smirk on Helmut's lips and like a rabbit hypnotised by a cobra, Anne stared into his pale blue eyes. As she stood transfixed, Rebecca and Mark's warnings thumped in her head and she became fearfully aware, using 'fearfully' in its correct meaning, that the man standing a few inches away from her was an SS officer, who believed absolutely in Adolf Hitler and the creed of the Order of the Death's Head, who was accustomed to exercising a virtually unbridled power, unaccustomed to being thwarted. There wasn't a soul to be seen on the terrace and in truth they had encountered few people on their tour of the castle. If he chose to do so, *SS-Haupsturmführer* Ohlendorf could rape her among the ruins of Heidelberg Castle and who in Nazi Germany would accept her account? What was Fraulein Whitworth doing with an SS officer in Heidelberg Castle late on a November afternoon, anyway?

Roughly Helmut pulled her towards him, holding her hard against his body. Instinctively, Anne closed her eyes. Then, from the recesses of her memory, she recalled Kate's words to that Hollywood mogul, 'Oh, do put it away'. If her little sister could handle an amorous predator, so could she. Opening her eyes, giving a theatrical shiver, Anne smiled up into *SS-Haupsturmführer* Ohlendorf's face. As if he had taken her in his arms to keep her warm, she said, 'It is getting cold, isn't it? Actually, I'd love a cup of tea and we can discuss the matter of Kurt Wolff's release from Dachau in comfort.'

For a few seconds Helmut stared down at Anne and she wasn't sure which way he would jump; on her, or towards the patiently waiting Mercedes-Benz. Abruptly he released her and with a tremendous effort she continued to smile at him because she still needed him. To avoid ruffling his feathers even more, she must act as if nothing untoward had occurred. On the walk from the Altan, Anne chattered away nineteen to the dozen and in return Helmut was once again the politely correct German officer. He apologised for keeping her out in the cold, saying his only excuse was that he tended to be overwhelmed by the beauty of Heidelberg.

Over coffee and luscious German cakes in another pictur-esquely baroque building, Captain Ohlendorf became ex-tremely businesslike. Indeed, they could have been discussing the sale of a motor car, or the purchase of a tin of beans, rather than the life of a human being. He said, 'If Wolff should be released, the sooner the better. You will understand that a justified arrest and imprisonment costs the State money. It is a question of how much the Jews are prepared to pay in recompense for the inconvenience they have caused the Third Reich.'

Anne said she fully understood and what sum would the State have in mind? Helmut gave the impression that he was making a rapid mental calculation how much food Wolff would have eaten during his incarceration in Dachau, the cost of the SS guards' wages, etcetera, etcetera, before he said, 'Four thousand Reichsmarks.' How much? Anne thought. Oh, you are being a greedily vindictive sod. Before she could reply, he added, 'The value of money rises and falls. Jews know this and they always have gold and jewellery hidden away. Some such recompense would also be required.'

'Yes.'

Before Rebecca had mentioned the Wolff family's willingness to pay in kind as well as cash, if required, Anne had already decided to make her own personal contribution to Kurt's release, if required. Over the years she had amassed a nice collection of jewellery, from which she had selected the most expensive and lovely items, a pair of sapphire and diamond earrings and matching necklace which she had brought with her to Frankfurt. Unsure about customs regulations and declarations, she had carried them hidden in the boots she was wearing at the moment. Actually the jewels had been a present from her mother and Philip when *Whatever Happened to Wordsworth?* was first published but Anne was certain they wouldn't mind them going to help Kurt's release.

From the handbag in which they were now hidden, she extracted the necklace and earrings, wrapped in a velvet cloth which she laid on the tea-table under the lamp. Unfolding the corners, Anne revealed the blue glow of the sapphires and the sparkle of the diamonds. After a quick, expert glance at them Helmut refolded the velvet but Anne had seen the avarice in his eyes. He smirked as he observed, 'I would expect the Wolffs to have good taste.'

That the jewellery belonged to Anne had obviously not crossed his mind, but the notion that she was willing to make a sacrifice for Kurt was almost certainly beyond his comprehension. Helmut then said Wolff's release would be on the strict understanding that he emigrated from Germany forthwith. Once Anne had obtained his entry visa for England, it would merely be a question of arranging payment and the hand-over of the prisoner.

On the mostly silent journey back to Frankfurt, Anne wondered how much of the money would go into the coffers of the Third Reich and how much into Captain Ohlendorf's personal account. She felt damned sure he would keep the jewellery, though whether or not it would be presented to his wife was a moot point. Despite the warmth of the Mercedes-Benz which had some sort of internal heating system, she kept shivering and Helmut trusted she had not caught a chill.

An anxious Rebecca was waiting up for Anne's return to the house off the Bockenheimer Landstrasse. Taking one look at her friend's pale face and shivering body, she propelled Anne into the lounge, sat her down in front of the fire and went to make some cocoa. When they were sitting comfortably on the rug in front of the fire, drinking the cocoa, Anne related the day's events. She finished by saying, 'And you were quite right. He is a pig and I was an idiot to go with him.'

'Never mind about that now. All that matters is you're safe and you've done a marvellous job.' Rebecca wondered whether, in the circumstances, to leave her news until tomorrow morning but Anne would undoubtedly be furious if she did. Slowly she said, 'Your mother telephoned earlier this evening.'

'Ah, I suppose Mark finally decided he should tell her where I am and what I'm doing. Was Mummy upset? You reassured her, didn't you? You didn't say I was in Heidelberg with an SS officer?'

'She was upset that you'd rushed off without saying anything to her. Yes, I said you were fine and no, I didn't mention Heidelberg.' Anne was obviously unsuspecting that her mother might have had another reason for telephoning and even more slowly Rebecca said, 'That wasn't really why your mother rang, Anne. They've had a cable . . .'

Anne's head shot round to look at Rebecca who saw the fear spark in her tired eyes, as she said, 'Not Ben. He's not . . . oh Becky, no, no, he can't be . . .'

Shaking her own head furiously, taking Anne's hands in hers, Rebecca said, 'No, he's not. But they've had a cable from Tamara. Apparently Ben was brought wounded into her hospital.'

'Wounded?' Anne cried out. 'How badly? What else did Tamara's cable say?'

'Only that she was nursing him and not to worry.'

PART V

25

Anne stood at the bedroom window and it was a beautifully still, clear night. The snow-covered slopes of Ben-y-Vrackie shone like polished silver, and the stars sparkling in the deep blue of the sky reminded Anne of the diamonds and sapphires that had, despite Rebecca's protests, been handed over to *SS-Haupsturmführer* Ohlendorf. The jewels had helped secure Kurt's release and he was safe in England, if still shattered by his experiences in Dachau. Leaning her head against the window jamb, Anne looked at Ben, who was still shattered by what had happened to him in Spain.

Literally on the day his company was due to be withdrawn from the lines, a shell had exploded in the shallow trench in which Ben and three other men had found refuge. The other three had been killed outright, including the Irish lad who had initially crossed the Spanish border with Ben and whose mother had sent him the cake. He himself had been half-buried under a mound of earth. When Ben had recovered sufficient consciousness to scrabble his way out, scarcely aware of where he was or what he was doing, he had stood up in the trench. That was when he had actually been wounded, a sniper's bullet hitting him in the right arm. Ben had been rescued and taken first to a field hospital where a doctor had cleaned and stitched the gaping wound in his arm, then to the hospital in Murcia-Denia where Tamara had nursed him. She was still in Spain but Ben had been brought back to England.

They had spent Christmas at Chenneys, Con had been there with the boys, and during a walk on Boxing Day morning Anne and her sister had had a long talk. After Con had given her the news that she was expecting again and this time she was definitely producing a baby girl, she'd said, 'I'm not going back to Vienna, Anne. I don't have to tell you what it's like, though people who've been in Berlin recently say the atmosphere there isn't as hideously anti-Semitic as it is in Vienna. Anyway, I simply can't take any more. Or at least not without blowing my top and doing Gavin's diplomatic career no good at all. So I'm going to Pitlochry with the boys. If you and Ben would like to come up, I'll be only too delighted to see you. There's a bothy on the estate where you can live without anybody bothering you. It's an ideal place for Ben to recuperate, and perhaps you'll be able to sort out your future, too.'

Anne had hugged her sister and said she would suggest the idea to Ben. Ungraciously he'd said, much as he liked her mother he certainly didn't want to stay at Chenneys, nor live in London, and he reckoned Scotland would do for the time being. For two months they had now been living in the bothy, which Gavin's aunt had used as an overflow guest house and in which electricity, indoor sanitation, and an Aga cooker that provided one always warm focal point, had therefore been installed. A dour individual named McTavish with whom Ben got on better than Anne did, chopped wood and performed odd jobs for them, while his only slightly less taciturn wife came in three times a week to do the cleaning, washing and ironing.

Ben was at the moment propped against the pillows of the double bed, his right arm lying stiffly across the counterpane, and Anne watched him turn a page of *The Moment of Murder*, awkwardly with his left hand. Her last Seth Pollard detective story had been published in time for the Christmas market but Ben had only just got round to reading it, though she supposed that was a minor step forward. Drawing the curtains tightly together, Anne crossed towards the bed where she discarded her thick woollen dressing-gown, jumped in beside him and snuggled against the warmth of his body. Ben continued to read her book and after a while she said, 'Are you enjoying it?'

'Yeah.'

'*A Dangerous Affair* is on in Perth next week. Shall we go and see it?'

'You've seen it.'

Anne had attended the film's première in London, a charity

gala whose proceeds had gone to the Anglo-Jewish Refugee Fund. She said to Ben, 'You haven't seen it. Despite what Kate has to say about William Warburg . . .' he was the director, himself a refugee from Hitler's Germany who had found fame and fortune in Hollywood. In Kate's opinion, if he hadn't been a Jew, he'd have been a Nazi '. . . it really is a most entertaining and stylish film. Kate and Colin Cornwell are as romantic and exciting a partnership on screen as we gather they are off.'

Kate's letters were filled with her overwhelming, undying love for Colin, and his for her, and what a pig Sandy was, being difficult about giving her a divorce. Currently, with the huge success of *A Dangerous Affair*, she and Colin were making another film for Samuel J. Sylberg in Hollywood.

Ben said, 'It's a long way into Perth. The roads can be treacherous at night. I can't drive.'

'We can go to an afternoon showing of the film. You know I like driving.'

He made no response whatsoever. When Ben was in one of his moods – these days they came in several varieties – there was little to be done. Anne was in any case feeling tired so she said, 'I'm going to sleep.'

''Night,' he grunted.

Despite her tiredness, long after he had finally switched off the light above the bed, she lay awake listening to his regular breathing. Thank God, tonight he was breathing with sleep-laden regularity. The wound in his right forearm was not a pretty sight and though it appeared to have healed, some days it had a livid, festering look. During those days – and nights – Ben almost cried out with the pain. Overall he found immense difficulty in using his right arm, his painting arm. Anne encouraged him to do exercises, to try to get his fingers and wrist supple, his tendons working again. Some days he would practise willingly, on others he flatly refused. Yesterday had been one of the negative days and Anne had said, 'Why not try using your left hand?'

'It's taken me thirty-two years to learn to paint halfway decently with my right hand. I'm not spending another thirty-two bloody years relearning with my left one.'

'Ben, if your arm isn't getting better, why don't you see

another doctor? "Stephen" Abbott treated enough ghastly injuries during the Great War. She might be able to . . .'

'I'm not seeing any more bloody doctors.' He now swore frequently. 'I don't like women doctors, any road.'

'Oh Ben, for heaven's sake!'

If Anne wasn't careful, or let her temper get the better of her, they ended up having a row, or with him stamping out. Ben spent hours walking across the estate in the foulest, coldest weather and if it was a bright, snow-shining morning he would frequently disappear after breakfast and not return until nightfall. If Anne asked where he'd been, he usually said nowhere in particular, but she wanted to get on with her writing, didn't she? She didn't want him under her feet all the time, did she?

The success of *A Dangerous Affair* had consolidated Anne's position as the Crown Princess of the detective story and she had succumbed to Julian and Stoddard and Simpson's pleas to write at least one more Seth Pollard novel. In fact she'd enjoyed working out a plot with a theatrical background, using the inside knowledge learned from Kate and Philip's involvement in that world. The story concerned a Shakespearian company's visit to an eccentric millionaire's Highland castle, to perform *Macbeth*, and Anne had entitled it *The Way to Dusty Death*. But she was not progressing particularly well, perhaps because she suspected Ben resented the fact that she could write, whilst he could not paint.

There were good days when they would sit around the fire talking, or go out for a walk together, or up to what the McTavishes and others on the estate referred to as 'the big hoos'. Ben particularly enjoyed the company of Con's son Rob who was far more of an original and a daredevil than Callum or Ian – he was usually to be found trying to climb a tree or on a glittering hoar-frost morning precociously asking, 'Who put de icing on de grass?' How Anne longed to have a child of her, their, own but there was absolutely no point raising the subject at the moment. The best she could do in that direction was to make Lady Helena have a baby in *The Way to Dusty Death*. It was but small compensation for the real thing.

On the bad days Ben fell into a silent depression, either

refusing to get up at all, or sitting staring into space. Anne would then try to coax him into a visit to 'the big hoos' because he and Con had established a deep rapport. In the evenings after the boys had gone to bed, in the warmth and comfort of the music room, she would play the piano and Ben's tension would visibly lessen. Without her sister to talk to, Anne herself sometimes felt the sense of helpless despair about Ben would overwhelm her.

Con put things into perspective. 'It is only three months since he was wounded. His arm's obviously Ben's major concern but I'm sure he's suffering from the psychological effects of his experiences in Spain, too.'

Anne agreed he was. Being half-buried in a mound of earth had induced a partial claustrophobia, manifest in the days when Ben had to be in the open air whatever the weather, and in the occasional nightmares when he woke gasping for breath, shouting, 'Get me out, get me out.'

She said to Con, 'The trouble is he won't discuss "psychological effects". He has this peculiar idea they're effete and effeminate. I suppose that is his working-class background.'

Her sister smiled sympathetically and said, 'Yes, I know. I've tried but he won't listen to me either. He does need you desperately, Anne, so you'll have to be patient and help him by just being here.'

Anne's mother said much the same thing. There was no telephone at the bothy but they wrote to each other regularly and every Sunday afternoon she rang 'the big hoos' specifically to speak to her eldest daughter. On one occasion Mummy said, 'I think you have a vague memory, Anne, of your father's volatile moods when he came home wounded from Passchendaele. Actually, he was in a terrible state and at times I was driven to despair, not knowing how to help him. But he, we, fought through eventually. I'm sure you and Ben will. Spring will soon be with us. New life, new hope, they do work their spell.'

'Rebecca, what on earth are you doing here?'

Before Julian stopped to see why the crowd had gathered on the pavement outside the Home Office, Rebecca had noticed his elegant figure approaching along Whitehall.

Momentarily she wondered whether he would acknowledge that he knew her, or whether Mr Kendle's dislike of dramatic behaviour would cause him to hurry on, pretending he hadn't recognised her. Politely saying 'Excuse me, please', he pushed his way through the throng and stood by her side.

Shifting her weight on her camp-stool, Rebecca looked up at him and in answer to his question what she was doing here, she waved her right hand at the collage of photographs and the placards surrounding her. The photographs were of Jews being beaten by Stormtroopers in German streets, of Jewesses being forced to scrub the pavements in beautiful Vienna, of Jewish children standing with *Juden* notices round their necks, of Jewish inmates of concentration camps with humiliatingly shorn heads and degradingly striped uniforms, and of the results of *Kristallnacht*. Most of the photographs had been taken over the last six years by Jenny Macdonald and were therefore of a vividly arresting quality.

The placards stated that six hundred thousand Jews remained condemned to a living death in Greater Germany and demanded that His Majesty's Government, specifically His Majesty's Secretary of State for Home Affairs, uphold Britain's long-hallowed tradition of providing a haven for the victims of racial, religious and political persecution, by an immediate increase in entry visas for these victims of Nazi persecution. In bold type the placards also stated that Jewish refugees would not be allowed to take jobs from British citizens, nor receive unemployment benefit, but would be supported by their sponsors.

Rebecca was unable to gesture with her left hand because that was chained to the railings of the Home Office, an idea she had pinched from the suffragettes. Anne's mother said very few of them had actually chained themselves to railings but she admitted the action had caught the public attention and fired its interest. By chaining herself in this very public position in the middle of Whitehall, Rebecca hoped to do likewise.

Having inspected the photographs and perused the placards, Julian said, 'How long have you been here?'

'Only since this morning. But I've already been photographed and interviewed by half Fleet Street.'

'How long do you intend to stay?'

'As long as it takes for the Home Secretary to stop dragging his heels and do what he should. Which specifically, at the moment, is to admit hundreds of Jewish children the Nazis have agreed to let go – they've been well paid of course. We've got the sponsors but not the entry permits.'

'It's a lovely day today but what if it starts to rain?'

Rebecca nodded towards an umbrella and a bulging canvas holdall which were propped against the railings and said, 'I was never a Girl Guide but I've come prepared.'

'I must say, I have to admire your . . .'

As Julian paused, searching for the right word, with a slight smile Rebecca suggested, '*Chutzpah?*'

In return he gave her his charming smile which still made Rebecca's inside wobble, even though Anne had told her about his shacking up with the distinguished Oxford historian, Doctor H. V. X. Martindale. That had been a tremendous shock and to begin with Rebecca had been convinced Anne had got the wrong end of the stick. Why should she have done? On the whole, despite her never suspecting Rebecca's passion for Mr Kendle, she was a perceptive person. The only unedifying consolation the astonishing news had given Rebecca, was that if she couldn't have Julian, neither could any other woman.

Rebecca handed out leaflets to several interested spectators and then, seeing she was in a forthright frame of mind, she decided to beard Julian about a proposal Anne had made and forgotten in the plethora of problems she was apparently having with Ben Broughton. Looking directly up at Julian she said, 'Anne told you about my cousin, Kurt Wolff, I believe. Before Adolf Hitler decreed he was a non-person, Kurt was considered one of the brightest of young German historians. During the last few years, he's had plenty of time to think about German history. He is slowly recovering from his traumatic experiences in Dachau and I think it would do him no end of good if he could get back to academic work. Do you think your friend Doctor Martindale could help?'

Julian blinked slightly at the open mention of his 'friend' before he said, 'I'm sure he'll be delighted to do whatever he can. The academic freedom on which the Nazis have trampled is of the utmost importance to Doctor Martindale. I'll give him a ring and perhaps we can arrange for your cousin to meet him in Oxford.'

'Thank you.'

Hesitantly, Julian said, 'Is there anything you want, or I can do? Food or . . .'

'No thanks. I'm being well supplied and . . .' Rebecca could not resist being naughty and adding, 'I have several stand-bys for when I need to spend a penny.'

That remark made Julian blink rapidly.

In the early evening, while Rebecca was tucking the rugs round her, preparing for a long cold night, a taxi drew up outside the Home Office, and two waiters descended on to the pavement. Informing Rebecca they were from the Savoy Hotel, from inside the taxi they produced a folding table, covered silver dishes, a bottle of wine, cutlery, crockery, a glass, and an oil-lamp, with the compliments of Mr. J. C. Kendle. Once they had finished laying out the meal, Rebecca asked the stand-by sympathiser currently on duty, temporarily to unlock the padlock of her chained left hand so that she could savour the meal to the full. Sitting in the chill darkness, with the huge bouquet of spring flowers Anne had telegraphed to be delivered to Miss Rebecca Lawson, outside the Home Office, Whitehall, London SW1, shining in the light of the oil-lamp, Rebecca thoroughly enjoyed the splendid repast. Whatever his sexual inclinations which, she supposed, were his own business, Julian Kendle was a nice man and this was the nicest thing he had ever done for her. And Anne Whitworth was a friend in a million.

At the beginning of March the condition of Ben's arm improved and his whole attitude changed as slowly, gingerly, he began to sketch again. Despite the fall of Madrid and the triumphal entry of General Franco's troops into the Spanish capital, Ben's mood remained buoyant, though Anne thought he had reached the nadir of bitterness in January when, even though he had predicted the collapse of the Popular Front, Barcelona had fallen to Franco's forces. With Ben in increasingly good spirits, the snow gone from all but the tips of the

Perthshire mountains and the scent of spring in the air, Anne's own spirits soared.

In the middle of the month, after her success in twisting the arm of the Home Secretary and obtaining entry permits for the Jewish children, Rebecca came up to Pitlochry, ostensibly for a brief well-earned holiday. At Anne's suggestion, with Ben's agreement, she was accompanied by Kurt Wolff, who was currently living with her family in Manchester and who could certainly do with a holiday.

Anne hugged her friend and said, 'Who's a clever girl?'

'I have my moments. Look, I must go over and see Con.'

'Oh yes? I thought you were here for a rest.'

'I am,' Rebecca protested. 'And I can already feel the pure Highland air doing me a power of good.'

To Anne's absolute lack of surprise she continued to go over to 'the big hoos', to discuss the affairs of the Scottish branch of the Anglo-Jewish Refugee Agency, for which organisation Con was working voluntarily. While his cousin was in conference with her sister, Anne drove Kurt round the countryside in Bill. She showed him the dramatically wooded defile at Killiecrankie where, after the battle in 1689, a fleeing soldier had allegedly leapt his horse across the rushing River Garry. Kurt's comment was, 'A remarkable horseman and an even more remarkable horse.'

Anne drove him across the wildness of Rannoch Moor to see the perfect triangular peak of Schiehallion reflected in the tranquil waters of Loch Rannoch, and on a glorious afternoon of vividly blue sky and slowly sailing white clouds, she took him up to Queen's View. As they sat in Bill surveying the scene, which was supposed to have been Queen Victoria's favourite Highland view, Kurt said, 'I hadn't realised Scotland was such a beautiful country.'

'I hope your few days here will do you good, Kurt. You are looking better.'

'Thank you,' he said politely.

On hearing the news of Ben's injury, Anne had rushed back home, leaving Rebecca to arrange the final negotiations with Helmut Ohlendorf, and she had not seen Kurt until he reached England. What he must have looked like when he first came out of Dachau she could not imagine, because several weeks later he was still a pitiful wreck of the man she had known in Frankfurt, unable to stop shaking, his gait shambling, his head downcast. When he finally looked up at Anne, his skin was a haggard grey and his eyes, the brown eyes which had regarded the world with sardonic amusement, were those of a dead man.

After they'd been sitting peacefully surveying Queen's View for quite a while, Anne posed the question she had not until now felt she could or should ask. 'What was it like in Dachau, Kurt?'

For several more minutes he stared intently at the panorama of lake and wood and mountain which appeared to have been designed by a landscape artist. Then with a hint of his wry smile, he said, 'Like something out of Hieronymus Bosch or Dante's Inferno. An enclosed world in which those who have previously been denied power, are given absolute power to indulge every bestial and brutal fantasy that enters their heads. If I say that one of the sights I had to stand in line to witness, in my striped pyjama suit, with the bitter November wind blowing across the compound, was a naked prisoner – a young man I knew, one of my ex-students – having a hose thrust into his anus and the water turned on at full pressure, will that suffice?'

Staring at Kurt, Anne whispered, 'What happened to the man?'

'Eventually he burst, Anne, like an overblown balloon. But in the still of the night, I hear his screams.'

In the still loveliness of Queen's View, Anne's imagination heard the screams and she shivered violently. Kurt put his arm lightly round her shoulder and said, 'I'm sorry. One shouldn't. But you did ask. Man's inhumanity to man has always been of a high order. The Nazis are merely bringing it to a new peak of perfection as a state-run concern. I've never thanked you for what you did to get me out of Dachau, have I? Do you know why not? Because when I first emerged I wasn't at all thankful. Why should I survive? To what purpose?

'However, I learn that my sister, like your sister, will soon bring forth new life. In Holland, Luise is allowed to be her elegant Jewish self. In England I, another Jew, am next week to see Doctor Martindale. I shall do my best not to have the shivers which, as you will have noticed, occasionally overtake me. Even though I am a quasi-Cambridge man, I find the thought of working at Oxford desirable. So thank you, Anne.'

Impulsively, she kissed him and said, 'Bless you, Kurt, for finding the courage to survive. And shall we track down a teashop and have a nice cup of tea?'

'Yes please, Anne.'

It was the first time she had heard Kurt laugh since he arrived in Britain.

After Rebecca and Kurt had gone Mark dropped in, more or less literally. Having flown his 'kite' on a business trip to Edinburgh, he decided to continue on to Perthshire, landing the 'plane on the one flat piece of ground in front of 'the big hoos'. As always, he provided a welcome relief to the gloomy news and the war Anne accepted was now inevitable. Ben was not overfond of Mark and he declined the invitation to dine with Con but after they'd had their meal, while they drank their coffee in front of the fire, Mark brought his sisters up to date with the latest news from London.

After he'd regaled them with stories of who was doing what to whom and why, Anne said, 'You're as big a gossip as Kate, you know.'

'And you know your problem, Annie. You take life far too seriously. And you don't have to listen to the next spicy bit, if you don't want to.'

'Oh but I do,' Anne laughed.

'Margaret-Jane has her sights set on Bunny Huntingford.'

'Bunny Huntingford!' Anne exclaimed. 'But isn't he . . .?'

'AC-DC. Yes. La Conway seems to fall for them, does she not?'

'Not altogether,' Con murmured. 'I'd never accuse you of being other than wholly DC.'

Giving his sister a grin, Mark went on, 'Once Madam came of age last December and inherited the vast fortune her dear dead Momma left in trust for her, she lost interest in a lowly wart like yours truly. And as the actual daughter of the heroic soldier-poet, English country gentleman, Guy Kendle,

Margaret-Jane fancies herself as the future Marchioness of Huntingford. I fancy she'll make it, because Bunny's always short of cash and having her as his wife will provide a smokescreen for his other activities.'

When Mark was escorting her back to the bothy, Anne said, 'Have you been to Chenneys recently? I'm a bit worried about Mummy. Her handwriting's become awfully spidery and she didn't ring last Sunday. When I rang Philip he said she was a bit under the weather again.'

'She hasn't been too good. But it's been a long winter. I'm sure she'll perk up again now spring's here.'

'I think I'll go down to see her.'

26

On her arrival at Chenneys Anne was deeply shocked by the deterioration in her mother's condition since Christmas, when she had seemed in better health and spirits than for years. The glossy thickness of her hair had become thin and brittle, and she was spending much of her time in bed which had caused her to put on weight and given her an unhealthy puffy appearance. When Mummy insisted on getting dressed and being helped into her wheelchair, the effort left her breathless. Whether propped up in bed, or sitting in the wheelchair, the glazed look suddenly came into her eyes, her concentration wandered and in the middle of a conversation she frequently fell asleep.

'How long has she been like this?' Anne demanded of Philip. 'Why didn't you let me know?'

In the viperish tone that had in its day reduced actresses to tears and theatrical producers to silence, though Anne more than suspected his own anxiety was partly responsible, Philip replied, 'Since you first spread your wings and flew the nest, this is by no means the first time your mother has been in a poor state of health. Had I summoned you here each time it happened, you would not have thanked me. When there was real cause for alarm, you were immediately informed. You have recently had problems of your own, I gather, which have kept you in Scotland.'

Ruffled by the response, though recognising its validity, Anne snapped, 'What does Doctor Stuart have to say? I presume he has been called in.'

'Yes, Anne, he has. Doctor Stuart believes there is little we can do, except let your mother have the rest her system obviously needs and trust she will rebuild her strength in the process. Do you have other suggestions?'

Anne admitted she had not.

Then they had a week of beautiful spring weather. Outside her mother's bedroom window, the brilliant yellow of the daffodils splashed over the tender green of the resprouting grass, the camellias shone silkily pink and white against the evergreen of their leaves. At the end of the week, when Anne brought back a posy of wild violets and primroses from the woods, with a sparkle in her eyes, her smile at its most delightful, Mummy said, 'Oh thank you, Anne, they're lovely.'

With the same rapidity as she had sunk into it, spring and hope anew (and maybe Doctor Stuart's prescription of rest) appeared to have hauled her from her nether world. Anne left Chenneys in a considerably more cheerful frame of mind than her arrival had induced, though before she set off on the five-hundred-and-fifty-mile drive to Pitlochry, she said to Philip, 'You will let me know if Mummy has another bad spell, won't you? Please.'

With a hint of a smile, responding to the 'please', her stepfather assured Anne he would.

Within seconds of coming through the front door of the bothy, which opened into the one largest downstairs room, Anne knew Ben's problems – which meant her problems – were not in the past tense. He was sitting in front of a miserable fire and did not respond to her cheerful, 'Hello, I'm back. I had a splendid drive from York today. The roads were beautifully clear. How are things? How are you?'

Crossing to the armchair, Anne leant over to kiss him but as she did so, he winced and drew away. Anxiously, she said, 'What's the matter? It's not your arm again, is it?'

'Yes, it bloody well is.'

With that, he stood up and strode towards the front door which he slammed violently behind him as he disappeared. Ben was gone for several hours and when he finally returned, Anne realised that though he appreciated the reason why she had stayed on at Chenneys, he also resented the fact that she had not been here when the festering and the pain had suddenly restruck his arm.

'Why didn't you tell Con?'

'Because she's six months gone, she has a damned great mansion to run, and three boys of her own and two stray German-Jewish kids running around the place. If I were her husband, I'd make her slow down. But I'm not. I'm her sister's lover and in that capacity I have no intention of burdening her with my troubles.'

In the following weeks, at times it seemed to Anne that it was only as lovers, in the strictly sexual interpretation of the word, that she and Ben now functioned. The intensity of their desire was as strong as ever, and sometimes in the mornings Ben looked at her body and with a frown asked, 'Did I do that?'

'You know how easily I bruise.'

'I don't want to hurt you.'

'Don't worry. I'll let you know if you do.'

The dividing line between sexual pain and pleasure was thin and at times Anne thought he was working his anguish off on her. At other times his strangled, non-sexual cries of pain brought the pleasure of their love-making to an abrupt halt. Cursing his bloody arm, Ben then refused to be mollified by her protestations that it didn't matter, or amused by the tangle of their bodies which always seemed ridiculous to Anne, once passion subsided. To begin with they also talked, both about the darkening European situation and the one Ben found himself in. He admitted he was feeling particularly savage because he had thought the worst was over. Hope thwarted was a bugger to overcome, he said, and to be faced with renewed pain and the renewed inability to paint was doubly depressing. But he still flatly refused to see any more doctors.

'They don't know what's wrong with my arm and why it keeps breaking out, any more than we do.'

One mild spring evening at the end of April, after Ben had been in a good mood all day, doing his exercises and trying to sketch, they went for a walk. A nearly full moon was gliding swiftly across the sky, its rays silvering the summit of Ben-y-Vrackie, glistening on the slate roofs of sleepy Pitlochry, glinting on the dark waters of the Tummel, its light marbling the clouds as it passed behind them. In her desperation Anne had consulted 'Stephen' Abbott and the beauty of the night having worked its spell on Ben, she decided to give her own doctor's opinion and damn the consequences.

'Stephen wonders if perhaps your wound has "false-healed". In the chaos of the campaigns she was involved in during the war, she says it was often days before the wounded got to her, and she noticed that sometimes the wounds that had been left open healed better than those that had been stitched straightaway. She says she meant to follow up this interesting phenomenon, but never got round to it. She also says there is now a body of medical opinion she respects, which believes wounds can sometimes be "false-healed" and cause all manner of problems if they are.'

They were climbing up the steep path towards the bothy and Ben listened in silence to Anne's speech which emerged breathily, partly from the exertion of the climb, partly from nervousness. Then he said, 'If you want me to traipse down to London to see your Doctor Abbott, the answer's no. For your information, one of the specialists you made me consult wondered the same thing. He came to the conclusion that in my case, false-healing was not the answer. His prescription was – give the arm time.' Ben turned towards her and said savagely, 'How long, Anne? How long? Until I'm in my grave?'

From that moment he sank into a fearsome depression and Anne cursed herself for mentioning Stephen's opinion, though she had to keep trying, had she not? Refusing to shave with his left hand, Ben grew a beard which Anne hated, though Con said it made him look biblical, and he spoke more to her and McTavish than he did to Anne. Towards the end of May, after a notably bad day during which Ben had lain in bed until three o'clock in the afternoon, shambled around the bothy in his pyjamas and dressing-gown, his beard untrimmed, and was now sprawled in the armchair staring into space, Anne knelt down in front of him. Resting her arms and her chin on his knees, she gazed up at him and said, 'Ben, you can't go on like this. I can't go on like this. We can't go on like this.'

'No.' The beautiful grey eyes actually looked straight at her but their expression simultaneously tore at Anne's heart and infuriated her by its despairing inertia. Then he made an astounding remark. 'I reckon we're being punished. Or I am, any road.'

'What do you mean? Punished? By whom?'

'God mebbe.'

'You don't believe in God.'

As she spoke the words Anne thought: at the back of his mind, Ben does believe in the dour English Nonconformist God in Whose creed he was reared. His next words convinced her she was right, for he said, 'I've come to believe in some sort of retribution, divine or haphazard. What other explanation is there?' His normally laconic voice vibrating with emotion, his Lancashire accent thickening, he went on, 'I was given a talent, Anne, a talent as an artist. Your talent as a writer is understandable but I don't know where mine came from. Nobody in our family's ever been artistic. But it was there from me being a bairn. I allus had to draw and paint, to show folks how I saw things, my special vision.'

Wincing, Ben slowly lifted his right arm and held it aloft. Staring at its outstretched length, with the same throbbing passion he said, 'The means of exercising my talent has been taken away from me. My arm, my hand, my fingers, they're useless. I reckon I'm being punished for leaving Irene, who was the first person to encourage me and slogged her guts out to enable me to paint.'

Swallowing hard to stop herself shouting 'Bollocks!', trying to keep the incredulity from her voice, Anne said, 'Do you think if you go back to Irene, your talent will return?'

Slowly Ben lowered his arm and slowly the quasi-religious frenzy which had been heightened by the biblical appearance of his wildly luxuriant beard, seeped from him. With a half-smile, in his normal voice, he said, 'I dunno, Anne. I love you, you know. I want to spend the rest of my life with you, but I must get things straightened out . . . do you reckon I'm going mad?'

'No, I don't,' Anne said sharply but she reckoned she had better do something, and quickly, to get things straightened out.

Aunty Sarah had already invited Anne to be one of the speakers at an unemployment rally she had organised in the Free Trade Hall in Manchester. The Free Trade Hall had a particular significance for Anne because it was there her father had made his last speech before returning to France in the autumn of 1918. Everybody said it had been his greatest. In addition, deeply as she cared about the plight of the Jews in Greater Germany and now in Nazi-dominated Czechoslovakia, Anne accepted the argument that the plight of the millions of unemployed Britons remained desperate too. Ben's extraordinary belief in the wrathful Judaic/Christian God of Retribution gave Anne another reason for travelling post-haste to Lancashire.

Fortunately, he appeared to have no suspicion of an ulterior motive and considered the unemployment rally a good thing. Con said she would keep an eye on him and Ben himself agreed he would seek her sister's help if the glooms overcame him. It was only when she reached Mellordale and was sitting in the little terraced house at the end of Milnrow, laughing her head off at Aunty Sarah and Madge Kearsley's stories, that Anne realised how strained she had grown and what a relief it was, to be temporarily away from the tense, unpredictable atmosphere of the last few months at the bothy.

Madge and Aunty Sarah had of course known each other as children. In their late middle-aged widowhood, they had resurrected their friendship to form the most splendid double act, constantly arguing and contradicting each other – 'It was the day our Tom hit three sixes in a row . . .', 'It never was. It was the day them bulls got loose in the marketplace'; 'We called the strike meeting in the women's bog at Bank Top Mill in the summer of 1897', 'Get on with you, you weren't working at Bank Top in 1897'; 'She was a Crowther before she wed', 'No, she wasn't. She was a Sutcliffe.' Anne felt if they went on the music halls as Kearsley and Whitworth, the one large, blowzy and raucous, the other tiny, sharp and contained, they would bring the house down. But she was delighted to see that her aunt had plunged back into the life of The Dales, as if she had never been away.

After Madge had finally gone home and they were having another cup of tea before climbing 'up the stairs to Bedfordshire', Uncle Misha's name came into the conversation and Aunty Sarah confessed, 'I have my little weep for him from time to time. But I reckon Tammy's over the worst. And she's taken to The Dales.' It was obvious that the inhabitants had similarly taken to her; she was 'our Tamara', our very own strikingly, startlingly, different Russian/Lancashire lass. Aunty Sarah added, 'And Tammy's in love, or imagines she is, with this lad she met in Spain, tha knows.'

Anne did know. Her cousin was out this evening but before her departure she had held forth in typical Tamara fashion. 'Leslie is now an organiser with the Transport Workers Union. The workers certainly need organising. They are a lot of sheep. There is so much to be done here. I had not realised how backwards advanced England is in so many ways. I shall work with Leslie to change the social order. I liked your Ben. How is he?' When Anne told her, she said, 'He must pull himself together. Leslie was wounded, too. That is how we met. He has not given in to self-pity.'

The Free Trade Hall was packed and the unemployment rally was accounted a big success. Anne's speech was singled out for special praise which especially pleased her because it meant she had not disgraced her father's memory.

Early the next evening she drove to Upperdale. Not wishing to advertise her visit to Mrs B. D. Broughton – Bill was quite well known in The Dales – she parked the car in a side street lower down Longden Lane and covered the remaining distance on foot. She had no idea whether Irene would be at home but taking a deep breath, she climbed the steps leading up from Nether Brow, walked briskly along Gladstone Terrace, opened the painted brown gate of number seven, noticed that there wasn't a weed to be seen among the neat flower borders of the small garden, and rang the front door bell.

Within a few seconds the door opened. Irene's brown hair still waved in uncompromising fashion and she was wearing the same sort of grey skirt, crisply ironed blouse and woolly cardigan that Anne remembered from their sole previous encounter in the Mellordale Municipal Library. When she realised who the caller was, Irene made to shut the door but Anne put out her hand to hold it ajar and said, 'I apologise for calling unannounced like this. But I need to talk to you. Please.'

Momentarily, Anne thought they might have a tussle with the front door and forcing her way into Irene's house would make a dreadful start to what was undoubtedly going to be one of the most difficult conversations of her life. Her face impassive, her voice flat, Irene eventually said, 'Come in, if you must.'

She led Anne along the small hall and opened the door that led off to the right, into a room which had the faintly musty smell of the seldom used. Everything within the front parlour – the darkly patterned carpet, the polished surrounds, the small table with the bowl of china flowers on the crocheted mat, the oak sideboard, the glass-fronted bookcase, the inevitable three-piece suite, the lace curtains, the embossed beige wallpaper, the ornaments on the mantelpiece, the embroidered firescreen covering the grate – was in immaculate, apparently pristine condition. Standing waiting for Irene to invite her to sit down, Anne tried to keep her gaze away from Ben's paintings hanging on the picture-rails, and from the gilt-framed photographs of him and Irene which rested either side of an empty fruit dish, on the linen runner of the sideboard.

'Do you wish to sit down?'

'Thank you.' Anne walked towards the armchair Irene was indicating and sat down. She held her tongue until Mrs

Broughton had seated herself in the armchair placed on the other side of the fireplace.

With a seething, mounting fury Irene listened to Anne Whitworth explaining why she had come. How dare she knock on the door without an appointment and sit here looking as if she had stepped out of Vogue magazine, smart panama hat, glossy red hair cut in pageboy style, pleated cream shantung summer suit, sheerest silk stockings, high-heeled cream leather shoes. (Anne had taken pains to dress with what she considered to be subdued simplicity.) Though on close-range inspection, Irene was pleased to observe that Anne Whitworth could not be called beautiful, or even pretty. It was the money she reeked of that made her appear attractive.

'I know how you must feel about me but . . .'

Do you? Irene thought. Since her promotion at the library, she spent less time than before answering queries about Anne Whitworth's detective novels – Irene suspected some people deliberately came in to test her reactions or humiliate her in this fashion – or in date-stamping *And Hideous Things Were Done* and the rest of them. One of the less hideous things she would gladly do to Anne Whitworth was to date-stamp her lipsticked mouth, from which the words were issuing in honeyed fashion, though the deliberate softness of her voice failed to disguise the confident clarity of her Oxford accent. And she would enjoy applying extra pressure to stamping the bridge of Anne Whitworth's aquiline nose, right between the big brown eyes that were gazing pleadingly at her.

'Ben has a terrible conscience about you, you see, and . . .'

Has he indeed? Irene thought. He has shown few signs of it in the last six years.

Anne Whitworth was the incarnation of everything she detested; alleged Socialists shouting about injustice from the opulence of their Tudor manor houses and smart flats in London; women born with silver spoons in their mouths – in Anne Whitworth's case transmuted to gold by her mother's second marriage – vociferously urging other women to fight for their rights; show-offs always holding forth in magazines and on the wireless, handing out their opinions like mashed potatoes. In Irene's opinion it was people like her, women who knew from bitter personal experience how unfair life was, women battling daily with sexual inequalities, who would effect real change, through getting on with their jobs and their lives and proving how efficient they were.

'I can't tell you how sorry I am that it happened. I would not have fallen in love with Ben if I could have stopped myself, but I couldn't. His painting really does matter, doesn't it? To both of us. We both love him and . . .'

Irene had only been half-listening to Anne Whitworth's fluent flow but at those words her self-control suddenly snapped. Jumping up from the armchair, she shouted breathily, 'You have absolutely no right to love him. He's my husband. Of course you could have stopped yourself. What are you? Some sort of animal? But you've always had everything you wanted, haven't you? Well, you're not having Ben. You can go on living with him in sin. That is if he'll have you any longer. That's what you're frightened of, that's why you're here, isn't it? It's not his painting you're worried about. Ben'll start painting again in God's good time. You think you're going to lose him, don't you? Well, I hope you do . . . I hope you suffer . . . I hope you go through what I . . .'

The long-suppressed rage, the long-festering jealousy, the humiliated pride, the years of loneliness – though she had her mother and her friends, Brenda and Sheila, who agreed entirely about Anne Whitworth's despicable, disgraceful, immoral conduct – overwhelmed Irene like an avalanche. Advancing on the . . . the bitch, she heard herself shouting, 'I hate you, I hate you, I hate you . . .'

She was looking down on the crown of the straw hat which was decorated with silk flowers, and Irene was filled with hatred for them, the symbols of the harlot's spoiled, heedless, selfish wealth. Tearing the hat from Anne Whitworth's head, she hurled it across the room. The hat landed on top of the china flower bowl Ben had given her as a present before he was bewitched by the hussy, and the sight of it sitting there stoked Irene's rage. Beside herself with fury, screaming at the top of her voice, she tugged at Anne Whitworth's silky red hair and flailed at her with her fists.

'Oh God!' Pushing hard at her, Anne Whitworth blasphemed as she struggled to stand up and babbled, 'I'm sorry, I'm sorry, I shouldn't have come. I'm sorry.'

Anne Whitworth was on her feet, shoving Irene and she half-fell to the carpet but she managed to hold on to the pleats of the cream shantung suit. Anne Whitworth started to kick her with those cream shoes which naturally were of the softest leather. One of the high heels caught Irene on the chin and enraged beyond measure by the blow, she dug her nails into the sheer-silk-stockinged leg. Anne Whitworth screamed. Perhaps it was the scream, or the sight of the blood seeping down the leg, that made Irene let go. Sinking on to the carpet, she put her face into her hands and she could hear Anne Whitworth's sobbing breath sounding as loudly as her own in the sudden stillness of the room. Irene's head was whirling, but in as controlled a voice as she could muster she said, 'Just get out of my house. And don't ever come back.'

Without stopping, or caring about the curious glances of passers-by, Anne ran along Gladstone Terrace, down the stone steps into Nether Brow, over the cobblestones into Longden Lane, and when she reached the side street in which Bill was parked she had an aching 'stitch' in her side. As fast as she could Anne drove the car on to the moors, where she bathed her leg in the clear waters of the rindle trickling down the hillside. For a couple of hours she then sat smoking and watching a splendid auburn and gold sunset sink behind the rim of the hills, while she tried to recover some composure.

Anne had witnessed the effects of impersonal mass hatred in Germany, but the accumulated venom, the actual violence, of Irene's personal hatred had shattered her. Half-laughing, half-crying, she thought of the scene as she'd imagined it so many times, she begging Irene to accept the realities of the situation, while showing the utmost sympathy for her predicament, Irene responding with noble resignation, their parting perhaps not good friends but with mutual understanding. The actuality had been awful beyond belief. Should she have left Irene in such a terrible state? Should she not have called someone to help her? Who, for example? Ben had certainly known what he was doing when he advised her not to approach his wife, though did even he realise the extent of the bitterness that had corroded Irene's soul? Anne supposed she would have to tell Ben about her visit to 7 Gladstone

Terrace and she would not care to predict his reactions, but at least she now knew that what he had long averred was true.

Irene would never, ever, divorce him.

It was dark before Anne returned to Milnrow. She had only just parked Bill at the bottom of the steps that led up to its terraced houses, when Tamara came flying down them, shouting, 'Is that you, Anne?'

'Yes.'

'Where the dickens have you been? We have been searching for you all over the place. It is not good news, Anne. Your stepfather has telegraphed. Your mother is ill again. You are to go at once.'

27

Throughout the long night hours Anne slept fitfully in the armchair on one side of her mother's bed, while Philip kept vigil on the other side. When the swish of the curtains woke her with a start, Anne realised she must have fallen into a deeper sleep. It was Philip who had drawn the curtains back. His darling Kessie loved the sun, and her view of the flowers and bushes especially planted and cherished by the gardeners at Chenneys so that something was in bloom for her at all times of the year. Mummy was here, rather than in hospital, because it was only too heartbreakingly apparent that the rallying of her spirit in the spring had been her last effort and it was now a question of time before . . . but though he had sent for her children, Philip was keeping up the pretence that his adored wife would yet again defeat the Grim Reaper.

It was 'the glorious first of June' and the day gave promise of being equally glorious, a pink glow spreading across the sky, the sunlight already sparkling on the light dew beading the lawn. Anne glanced towards the bed but her mother was oblivious of the light dancing through the mullioned windows and of the flowers massed in the herbaceous borders, visible through the elegant picture window Philip had long ago had installed for her pleasure. The puffy weight of recent months had disappeared, the bones of her face protruded, her outstretched arms were matchstick thin, her skin transparent. She was moving her head restlessly but at least her breathing was less rasping and more regular.

'Why don't you have a wash and some breakfast, Anne?' Philip's voice was at its most clipped.

'What about you?'

'Don't worry about me.'

There was no point arguing with him, so Anne just nodded. She was drinking her second cup of tea and nibbling a piece of toast, when she heard the drone of the aeroplane's engine. With considerable difficulty, because Mark appeared to have girl-friends in every airport and nobody was sure which one he was staying with on this flight, late last night he had been located in Paris. Gulping down her tea, Anne ran to meet her brother as he landed the Hornet Moth in the long meadow. Jumping from the cockpit, pulling off his goggles and flying helmet, with a grin he started to speak but looking into Anne's face he stopped. Then he murmured, 'Oh Annie, she's not . . .?'

'Yes, she's dying, Mark.'

When they reached the bedroom Con was up and dressed, sitting by the bedside with Philip. With her sister having undertaken the long train journey from Pitlochry and due to give birth any moment now, Anne had insisted she try to have a night's rest. The sound of the bedroom door opening penetrated their mother's semi-consciousness, she opened her eyes, turned her head and stared at Mark who moved towards her, saying softly, 'Hello, Mumkins. How's yourself?'

The lovely smile spread across Mummy's face, she held out her hand to Mark and said, 'Oh Tom, I knew you'd come.'

Momentarily her voice had its youthful huskiness, in the dawn light her hair regained its auburn tints, and her face was that of the girl who'd met Tom Whitworth some thirty years ago. Anne heard the intake of Con's breath, she herself felt unutterably chokey and she couldn't bear to look at Philip. What must he be feeling, as he witnessed the regression of the woman he loved so deeply, into her love for her first husband? Mark clasped the painfully thin hand. Mummy smiled up at him and said, 'Aren't you going to kiss me, Tom?'

Bending down to kiss her lightly on the cheek, her son, who so much resembled his dead father, said, 'Of course I am, Kessie.'

When Mark straightened up their mother frowned, she moved her head fretfully and made several little moaning noises, before the clouded look came into her eyes and she closed them again. Nobody spoke but the four of them stayed in the bedroom. Muriel came in to see how her patient was and if anybody wanted anything, but none of them did. To Anne's intense surprise, Philip said quietly, 'How long do you think she has?'

'I wouldn't like to say, but . . .' There was a slight tremor in Muriel's brisk voice as she answered the direct question, without the customary optimism of her profession. '. . . but not long, I don't think, Sir Philip.'

'Thank you.'

'Oh . . .' With the deepest of sighs, Con buried her face in her hands and sobbed quietly.

The tears blurring her vision, the constriction of her throat painful, Anne prayed: Don't leave us yet, Mummy darling. Hold on until Kate gets here. Hold on until Con's baby is born. Hold on to see your first grand-daughter. She's positive she's going to have a girl this time.

The only sounds in the room were the soughing and occasional rattle of their mother's breathing and the birdsong outside, and time lost any meaning. It could have been half an hour or twelve hours later that Mummy opened her eyes. Their again-clear gaze travelled from Anne to Con to Mark, and with rasping difficulty she asked, 'Where's Kate?'

Anne was unable to speak, so she suspected was her sister, and it was Mark who replied, 'On her way from the film studios.'

Mummy nodded, then she looked at Philip and holding

out her hand to him, she gasped, 'Will . . . you . . . open . . . the . . . windows . . . darling . . . it's stuffy . . . in here.'

They were the last words she spoke.

Mark and Anne opened the windows wide, the heavenly scents from the herbaceous borders and the orange blossom that was in full bloom drifted into the room and the song of the birds was like a choral symphony. Philip sat holding Mummy's hand on one side of the bed, Anne and Con on the other, and Mark stood behind them. The expression on her face was calm, her restlessness had gone, but her breathing was becoming shallower and shallower. Anne knew her beloved mother was slipping away from them but the shock and exhaustion acted as an anaesthetic, numbing the pain. She was dying gently, peacefully, in the house she loved, surrounded by the people she loved.

Quite suddenly, her breathing stopped. On the warm summer air the sound of the church clock in Marshall Minnis striking ten, carried into the heartbreaking stillness of the room.

Later in the morning, as Con was dreadfully upset, Anne telephoned 'the big hoos' in Pitlochry. She gave Con's housekeeper the news, told her Mrs Campbell-Ross would be staying until the funeral but would be in touch soon, and asked her to contact Mr Broughton. Within the hour Ben was on the line. Having kept reasonably calm with the housekeeper, Anne broke down on him and he said, 'Do you want me to come to Chenneys?'

'Please . . . Ben . . . please.'

'I'm on my way.'

Anne then had to deal with the members of the household outraged by Sir Philip's refusal to allow them to draw the curtains, in the customary mark of respect for the dead. Mrs Delve, the Chenneys housekeeper, led the deputation of weeping housemaids and kitchen staff. She said, 'All the blinds were drawn in Marshall Minnis, Miss Anne, the minute they heard the sad news. Your mother was the nicest lady it's been our privilege to serve, we're all very distressed and it doesn't seem right to us to be walking around in broad daylight, when Lady Marchal's lying there . . .'

With a loud sob Mrs Delve tailed off and Anne said, 'I quite understand your feelings. But you see my mother loved the light. *Not* drawing the blinds is Sir Philip's way of showing his devoted respect.'

Not entirely mollified but accepting that Sir Philip had his reasons, however peculiar they might be, the deputation withdrew from the sun-filled drawing room.

In the late afternoon Anne walked up to the summit of Dedman's Down. In the glory of the early summer's day, with the estate basking in its beauty, she wept as she had wept in the bedroom, though the full impact of her mother's death was still cushioned by the shock. Then she drove to Marshall Minnis Halt to meet Ben. When his train drew in and she saw him striding along the platform, Anne ran towards him and cried out, 'Oh, you've shaved your beard. I am glad.'

Putting his left arm round her shoulder, Ben said, 'I'm glad to have gladdened your heart in any way today.'

'How's your arm?'

'So-so. Let's not bother about it at the moment.'

Ben was a tower of strength and one thing at least her mother's death appeared to have done, was to have reminded him that other people had their problems too and drawn them close together again. Anne decided not to mention her visit to Irene which at the moment anyway, seemed totally irrelevant. With the news of the death of the ex-suffragette, formerly Mrs Tom Whitworth, latterly Lady Marchal prominent in all the newspapers, the telephone never stopped ringing, the condolence cards and letters poured in to Chenneys, and there was of course the funeral to be arranged. Mummy had said she wanted to be buried in the churchyard at Marshall Minnis but it was agreed the funeral would be held back until Kate arrived from Hollywood.

Within twenty-four hours Gavin was with them from Vienna and though he had to report to the Foreign Office in London, he was able to take the worry about Con's highly pregnant condition from Anne's shoulders. Her worry about Philip was another matter and she said to Ben, 'He's bottling his feelings up. Con and Mark and I all broke down and Chenneys was a positive vale of tears. But you can see what

Philip's like. Absolutely glacial. You know what he does at night? He sits by Mummy's coffin.'

'How do you know?'

'I couldn't sleep last night. I was prowling about. I went to Mummy's room and there he was keeping vigil by her coffin, hands clasped, head bowed, like one of those medieval statues in the church. I said, "Oh, Philip", and he looked up at me and said, "Yes, Anne?" The pain in his eyes . . . I mean, have you looked into his eyes? I said, "Come away, Philip." He said, "I prefer to stay here, thank you." I know what he's suffering because I know how much he loved Mummy and I know what I'm . . . but at least I'm able to cry and to talk . . .'

Anne's ability to talk trembled into tears. Ben took her in his arms and said, 'You are a worrier, aren't you? You've kept telling me we all have to come to terms with life's problems and tragedies. The same applies to your stepfather. He'll have to work his own way through his grief.' Gently, Ben added, 'Your mother has only been gone a few days. She's not even buried yet. So give him a chance.'

Clad in black from head to foot, looking ethereally beautiful, Kate finally arrived. Colin Cornwell supported her as she tottered gracefully from the limousine that had driven the two of them from Southampton, up the steps to the terrace and into the house. She held her arms out wide to her waiting siblings and stepfather and burst into tears.

Ben murmured, 'What an entrance!'

Anne knew what he meant but it was Kate's instinct to be dramatic and her grief was genuine enough. She was devastated at being unable to reach her mother's side before she died. Between sobs she later told her sisters, 'People can say what they like about Sam Sylberg, but he behaved marvellously to me. We had finished shooting, of course. I was actually in his office, with my American agent, and we were actually discussing the sequel to *A Dangerous Affair* . . .' Kate's interest in her career momentarily overcame her grief and she said to Anne, 'You are up-to-date with all that, aren't you? Julian has kept you informed, hasn't he? You do think it's a good idea, don't you?'

Frankly, with Ben's problems consuming most of her energies, Anne had not given much thought to another Seth Pollard/Lady Helena film, but she nodded and said yes.

'Anyway, there we were in Sam's plush office, when Pip's cable was brought in. Sam just roared into action, picking up telephones and shouting into them. Americans are wonderful in that way. He arranged for me to fly in private 'planes from Los Angeles to New York, though that was simply fearful, darlings. We kept landing and taking off and I was frightfully sick and if it hadn't been for Mummy . . .' There was a pause whilst Kate cried. Drying her eyes she went on with her story, 'Well, if it hadn't been for Mummy, I'd have given up at Chicago or some other ghastly place. They held the *Queen Mary* for me, you know. But we'd only just sailed when I got the radio message telling me Mummy was . . . and crossing the Atlantic I just felt so awful and helpless and . . .'

Kate burst into tears again. Colin Cornwell was, however, on hand to comfort her and their mutual passion was only too evident. In his late twenties, about the same height as Ben, five feet ten inches, which was less tall than he appeared on stage, Colin's darkly brooding personality had the same magnetic impact, his richly melodic voice the same singular inflections, as had thrilled Anne across the footlights of the Old Vic. From the brief conversations she had with him, in the few moments he could spare from comforting her little sister, Colin also seemed more intelligent than most actors Anne had met. Lucky Kate!

The weather the following day was as glorious as the first of June. As the cortège drove slowly through the main gates of Chenneys and along the leafy, sun-dappled road into Marshall Minnis, Anne was unsurprised to see villagers lining the route and the children standing in front of the schoolhouse, but the crowd outside the Norman church astounded her. When Colin Cornwell hurried to assist Kate from the leading limousine and there was a considerable stirring among the crowd, she realised some were here to catch a glimpse of the famous film stars. Walking behind the coffin, under the lych-gate, up the path through the churchyard, Anne also realised the church itself must be packed to capacity, for there was a smaller crowd outside the entrance. It included faces she recognised and even some of those who had personally known Kessie Thorpe/Whitworth/Marchal and had come to pay their last respects had obviously been unable to get inside.

The service in the church was intensely moving. Her north country voice suffused with emotion, Aunty Sarah read part of the lesson, 'O death, where is thy sting? O grave, where is thy victory?' Anne remembered her aunt reading a lesson at Daddy's memorial service and bowed her head to hide her tears. When they were in the churchyard and her mother's coffin was slowly lowered into the freshly dug grave, with one simple family wreath of her favourite flowers from the gardens at Chenneys resting on its polished surface, and the vicar intoned the words of the Elizabethan burial service, 'We therefore commit her body to the ground; earth to earth; ashes to ashes; dust to dust . . .' Anne heard Con's soft sobs and Kate's louder ones. Her own face crumpled, she felt Ben's arm coming round her shoulder and crying helplessly, she dropped her head on to his chest.

Once they were back at Chenneys, Anne stepped into the role of hostess for the funeral tea, though that was a misnomer for the spread of potted meats, honey-roasted hams, salads, freshly baked breads, pyramids of summer fruits, jugs of Chenneys' cream, biscuits and cakes prepared by cook and Mrs Delve and laid out to Philip's instructions, under parasol-shaded tables on the terrace. In a way Anne was grateful because being social kept the mind occupied and those invited to the house were of course close friends.

Circulating among the tables she saw Rebecca sitting with Kurt Wolff and Julian. Her dearest friend held out her hand as Anne approached and said, 'I once heard somebody up north say, "Ee, it was a luvly funeral", which in my impressionable 'teens seemed to me a highly inappropriate remark. But I know what the old biddy meant now. You couldn't have had a more beautiful day, Anne, and you couldn't have given your mother a nicer departure.'

Squeezing Rebecca's hand, with a slight smile Anne replied, 'Mm. Mummy always said that, apart from disposing of the body, funerals are for the living. I know what she meant now. I was enormously touched by all those people turning up. Do you know, there were several old suffragette and Socialist friends who came down from Lancashire? One elderly lady came all the way from Newcastle. I invited them back for tea, of course.'

Having naturally, like Julian, risen to his feet as Anne approached, Kurt said, 'I only met your mother once, Anne, so I feel somewhat of an intruder. But she was a very special lady whom it was my privilege to know, however briefly.'

'Thank you. How are things with you, Kurt?'

'Greatly improved, thank you, Anne.'

Julian said, 'Doctor Martindale has been able to arrange tutoring for Kurt next term.' Then, with the charmingly deprecatory smile that once upon a time had turned her stomach over, he went on, 'Anne, may I suggest you have lunch with me soon? I'd love to know how *The Way to Dusty Death* is progressing and I want to discuss the film sequel to *A Dangerous Affair*, in more detail. Keeping working is a good idea, you know.'

'Hear, hear!' said Rebecca, casting a quick glance in Ben's direction.

When they had eaten and drunk their fill, people wandered through the gardens in the shimmering heat of the afternoon. As she herself left the terrace, Anne saw Mark who was doing his fair share of the social rounds. With his charm, very good he was at it too. She asked her brother, 'Have you seen Philip recently?'

'When last seen he was showing that posse of Lancastrians you invited back, round the rose gardens. They were well into the stories of the good old days and what a wonderful person young Kessie Thorpe was. I think it was doing Pip good, actually. He seemed almost animated.'

'Thank heaven,' Anne said. 'Do you know who didn't come to the funeral? Margaret-Jane. I think la Conway might have put in an appearance, considering all Mummy did for her.'

'She probably had a dress-fitting today. That reminds me, what's happened to Theo Marvell? I thought his sobs were going to drown the organ.'

'Mark! He had to dash back to Town. He was genuinely fond of Mummy, you know.'

'Yeah, I know. Only he gets more and more of a theatrical old queen as the years go by.'

By the lake which appeared to be their favourite meeting place, Anne encountered Sandy Dalziel. Seeing he was Kate's husband and he had known her mother a long time, she had invited him, but aware that his wife and Colin Cornwell were in England – who, as so much as glanced at a newspaper, was not? – Anne had not actually expected Sandy to come to the funeral tea. But then the thickness of his skin was one of his characteristics, was it not?

After making the expected remarks about how greatly her lovely mother would be missed Sandy's next remark was totally unexpected. He said, 'I have decided to give Kate a divorce.'

'Oh. Have you? That's noble of you.'

'Isn't it? Particularly when you consider how I have been treated by the younger Whitworth women.' Ouch, Anne thought. 'I see no point in adopting a dog-in-the-manger attitude and hanging on when it's useless.'

Lucky, lucky Kate! How Anne wished Irene Broughton shared Sandy's viewpoint.

In the shade of a horse-chestnut tree she saw Ben with Tamara and Aunty Jenny. Tamara was poking her finger into his chest, Jenny was waving her cigarette-holder at him and bearing down upon them were Stephen Abbott and 'Aunty' Dorothy Devonald. They had lived together since the end of the war and recently Anne had wondered if theirs was a Lesbian relationship, though it was none of her business, and indubitably they were a happily ill-assorted couple, bossy little Dorothy ordering big booming Stephen around. With that formidable female quartet now surrounding him, Anne thought Ben might need help. Bidding au revoir to Sandy, she walked towards them.

'Anne, old girl!' Stephen gathered her in a bear hug. 'I still can't believe she's gone. Not Kessie. Your mother was a fighter if ever there was one.'

Tamara said, 'Jenny and I have just been telling Ben, it's about time he started fighting back and painting again.'

Anne was thinking, oh have you? that's not the best way to encourage him, when Stephen released her, swivelled her own bulk round to face him and boomed, 'So you're Ben, are you?'

'Sorry,' Anne said, 'I'd forgotten you don't know each other. May I introduce the well-known London County Councillor, Miss Dorothy Devonald . . .'

'Well-known to her male colleagues as "Alaric the Goth",' Stephen interposed.

After everybody, except Ben, had laughed, Anne introduced Stephen who said, 'From what I hear, meladdo, you're behaving rather stupidly. Doctors aren't magicians but we're not all idiots either. If you keep trying, one of us might be able to help. Why don't you come and see me about that arm of yours?'

'Depression will get you nowhere,' Tamara said.

'Think of Anne,' Jenny urged. 'She wants you fighting fit.'

'Now more than ever,' Dorothy said in her clarinet-clear voice. 'Stephen chose to return to General Practice but she is a surgeon. She knows something about wounds caused by bullet, shell and bayonet. I can't begin to describe the kinds of wounds she operated on, nor the conditions she operated in, during our wartime days in Roumania and Russia.'

Ben's face was growing more and more impassive, and Anne was wondering how to halt the well-intentioned but undoubtedly disastrous feminine onslaught, when she saw Gavin leaping down the terrace steps, racing across the driveway and over the lawn towards them. She had never previously seen her brother-in-law proceed at much faster than snail's pace, Anne reflected, before her emotionally drained brain realised it must be something to do with Con.

It was. Reaching Anne's side, Gavin panted, 'Con's gone into labour. She wants you, Anne. We must get her . . .'

Before Anne could react, Stephen said to Gavin, 'Calm down, laddie. I'm a doctor. Jenny, Dorothy and Tamara are ex-nurses. Ditto Aunty Sarah over there. Between us we've delivered tons of babies. I think we can manage to bring your latest offspring into the world.'

28

Anne peered into the double bassinet by the bedside, in which Con's daughters were sleeping peacefully. Newborn babies were not the prettiest of creatures but their tiny vulnerability was heart-catching and to have a baby of one's own, or rather of her and Ben's own . . . suppressing a sigh, Anne said, 'I must admit I was surprised how much you'd expanded this time, but I thought they were supposed to be able to detect twins these days.'

'Stephen says they can usually but sometimes one of the babies gets hidden. Either Kirsty or Fiona did.' Con had chosen 'Fiona' for the little girl she was convinced she would have and the unexpected arrival was to be called 'Kirsty', a good Scots name that resembled 'Kessie'. She went on, 'I couldn't be more delighted to have two baby girls but actually having them was no fun. I've told Gavin that's my lot. Actually, I think he agrees five Campbell-Rosses are enough. I can't tell you how glad I am Stephen was here to see me through it.' Slowly the tears started to trickle down Con's cheeks and in a trembling voice she said, 'I wish Mummy could have been here too. I wish she could have seen Fiona and Kirsty.'

Anne knew exactly how her sister felt because the fact that their mother was dead, that everything she had meant to them was now memory, had started to overwhelm her. Putting her arm comfortingly round Con she said, 'You believe in God and an after-life. If you're right, somewhere, somehow, Mummy knows you've followed in her footsteps and produced twins.'

Con smiled tremulously and after a pause she said, 'Having totally disrupted the day of the funeral . . .'

'Oh, your going into labour provided tremendous excitement!'

'Not for me, it didn't! Now I just want to get back home to Scotland. I want to see the boys and show them their new sisters.'

'Gavin's all ready to take you the minute you're fit to travel.' Anne sighed and said, 'I suppose I'd better go down for the reading of the will.'

'I shan't be sorry to miss that,' Con replied.

Philip had insisted on his late wife's will being formally read by the family solicitor and when Anne entered the drawing room he, Kate, Mark and Aunty Sarah, who presumably was a beneficiary, were already seated. Wearing an old-fashioned wing collar, black coat and striped pants, Mr Thundercliff was standing in front of the beautiful Adam fireplace. Why did solicitors have such peculiar names? Anne wondered. Was it a prerequisite for entering the profession? She focused her wandering attention as Mr Thundercliff adjusted his pince-nez, cleared his throat and started to read out the Last Will and Testament of Kessie Martha Marchal.

'To my beloved husband Philip Gerald Delamere Marchal, as is his wish, I leave no money but the following personal mementos.' Mr Thundercliff enumerated them before clearing his throat again and continuing, 'My four beloved children, Anne, Kate and Mark Whitworth, and Constance Campbell-Ross, are in comfortable circumstances and to each of them I leave the further comfortable sum of fifteen thousand pounds.'

Bless you, Mummy. Anne noted that her mother had not used Kate's married name, Dalziel, so either the will had been drawn up before the marriage and she hadn't bothered to change it, or she'd regarded Kate as a Whitworth.

Mr Thundercliff was intoning, 'To the Tom Whitworth Memorial Trust, to assist the upkeep of the Memorial Hall in Mellordale and the provision of the annual scholarship to Ruskin College, Oxford, I leave twenty-five thousand pounds. To my dear sister-in-law Sarah Whitworth Muranov, I leave the house in Milnrow, Mellordale, and ten thousand pounds . . .'

'Oh Kessie, you bugger!' Aunty Sarah's exclamation made Mark, Kate and Anne splutter, the faintest smile twitch Philip's lips and a frown cloud Mr Thundercliff's brow. She

325

looked at him and said, 'Sorry, but she really can't leave me all that.'

'The late Lady Marchal has done so, madam,' Mr Thunder-cliff replied.

Anne had always known her mother was a wealthy woman in her own right; the only child and heir to the Thorpe Mill in Mellordale who had sold out in the boom days of cotton at the end of the war; herself a beneficiary under several wills; the money invested by Philip who, as Mark said, was interested in that sort of thing. But as Mr Thundercliff continued to read out smaller bequests and Anne did her mental arithmetic, she realised her mother had left nearly a hundred thousand pounds! Apart, that was, from the jewellery Philip had delighted in giving her over the years, which Mr Thundercliff was dealing with now.

'I wish my daughters Anne, Constance and Kate to have my jewellery. I trust them not to quarrel over the division of the spoils, but because Anne disposed of certain jewels in the way she did, I specifically leave my sapphire necklace, earrings and bracelet to her.'

Anne thought of Helmut Ohlendorf and the café in Heidelberg and the tears pricked her eyes. Without doubt Mummy had been among the nicest people and the best mothers in the world. There was a further specific bequest which Mr Thundercliff proceeded to read out. 'As the literary member of the family, I leave to Anne the diaries her father wrote during the Great War, together with the diaries I have kept over the years, which in part provide a first-hand account of a tumultuous period in women's history, for her to do with as she sees fit.'

The summer dawn had long since broken when a bleary-eyed Anne decided she couldn't read any more and she must have a few hours' sleep, In a covering note, her mother had said she'd always intended to edit Daddy's diaries, including correcting his spelling, which was idiosyncratic to say the least, but had never got around to it. Although Anne had not read them all, from her perusal of selected pages, she wholeheartedly agreed her father's war diaries should be edited and published. Shining through his sardonic entries –

'Usual wellcome in Boulogne, Hordes of little boys gesticer-
lating with their thumbs and hissing "You want jig-a-jag?"' –
and his savage descriptions of the Somme and Passchendaele,
was his love for his darling Kessie and his children. This was
just as well, because in a covering letter to her own diaries,
Mummy had warned that some of the pages might shock
Anne. She had not read through thirty-odd years of assiduous
diary-keeping but the relevant entries were well sign-posted,
for her mother had had a habit of underlining or penning
'BLACK DAY!!!', 'SPECIAL DAY!!!'

The Special Days often referred to suffragette events such
as the first time she was arrested or the Midsummer Day
demonstration in Hyde Park in 1908, but they also included
descriptions of her and Daddy's love-making. Somehow you
never thought of your parents indulging, though your presence made it obvious they had, and Anne was astonished by
her mother's frankness. She and Philip had been passionate
lovers too, which was another shock. But the real shocks
concerned Daddy. That he had been 'a bit of a lad' in his
bachelor days did not surprise Anne, but the revelation that
he had been unfaithful after his marriage was shattering. And
as for the women with whom he'd betrayed Mummy . . .

The first person Anne met after she'd had a few hours'
sleep, washed and dressed, was Philip. Unable to contain
herself, she burst out, 'Have you read Mummy's diaries?'

Coldly he shook his head and said, 'They were entrusted
to you, Anne.'

'Yes, yes, of course. I'm sorry.'

Then, slightly less coldly, he said, 'I should wait until you
have read your mother's diaries in their entirety before you
come to conclusions about your father.'

So Philip did know, Anne thought. Aloud she said, 'Yes,
I will.'

She found Ben sitting on the terrace, staring at a butterfly
fluttering among the Sweet Williams in one of the flower-
filled urns. Pulling up a rustic chair, Anne sat down and
unburdened her heart to him. '. . . and do you know who
my good Socialist father had an affair with? Lady Louise
Claremont. And do you know who she was? One of Edward
VII's ex-mistresses! But what really takes the biscuit is his

other *amour*. I gather it was a moment of madness but it was Aunty Alice! You know, my mother's dear friend, the one who had the affair with Julian's father. She was obviously a raver! And how Mummy ever forgave her is beyond me.'

'Yeah, well,' Ben echoed Kurt's words, 'your Mam was a very special lady. I doubt your Dad's infidelities made him love her less.'

'No, I don't think they did. In the end I think they made him love her more. But he shouldn't have betrayed Mummy like that.'

'Your Dad was a human being, Anne, not a plaster saint.'

'Mm. You know what I'm going to do? I shall edit Daddy's wartime diaries eventually. But first, as soon as I've finished *The Way to Dusty Death*, I'm going to write Mummy's biography because you're quite right. She was a very special lady. And she was quite right too. She lived through tumultuous years in women's history and her vivid account of them needs to be recorded.'

'Good. That'll keep you occupied. I'm thinking of going up to London to see Doctor Abbott.'

This information was conveyed in Ben's most laconic tones and it was several seconds before its impact exploded in Anne's brain. Then delightedly, she put her hand on his good left arm and said, 'Oh Ben. I am so glad. Stephen really does know what she's talking about and . . .'

'If I didn't reckon the old battleaxe was a good doctor, I wouldn't be thinking of going to see her.' The female onslaught had worked! But shut up, don't over-enthuse, Anne told herself, or he'll change his mind. Then Ben said, 'Oh Jeez.'

Following his gaze Anne saw that Kate and Colin Cornwell were climbing arm-in-arm up the terrace steps. Ben was one of the few men who seemed not only impervious to her little sister's beauty but actually to dislike her. Colin drew up two more chairs and Kate called for cool drinks to be brought out, before she started chattering away. 'The new Seth Pollard script is a marvellous one, even if Pip didn't write it. And we want to do it, don't we, darling?' Colin nodded and Kate went on, 'But we hate the thought of being thousands of miles from dear old England, in case anything awful happens, don't we, darling?' He nodded again. 'But I'm sure Gavin's right and the situation is better in Europe because horrid old Adolf Hitler has calmed down. Aren't you?'

'No,' said Ben.

'Oh.' Kate gave him a look which said she considered him as horrid as Herr Hitler. Her love of England was genuine, her patriotism deep, but Anne suspected her sister's fear of being trapped in Hollywood should anything awful happen, was rooted in not reaching their mother's deathbed in time. Turning to Anne she pouted prettily and asked, 'Do you think we should turn down the film and stay here then, waiting for a war which Gavin says won't happen?'

Although more optimistic than of late, their brother-in-law had made no such categoric statement. Surprisingly, Ben spoke again, 'You can always come home when war breaks out.'

'That's what I've been telling you, isn't it, sweetheart?' Colin stroked Kate's hand.

Having nibbled his ear, she replied, 'Yes, of course we can come home *if* war is declared.' Kate gave Ben another scathing look, though paradoxically his endorsement of her beloved's view had swayed her because she said, 'That's settled then. We're going back to Hollywood. Though when my divorce comes through, we'll have to return home, darling. I couldn't possibly marry you anywhere but in England.'

'Nor me you, darling,' Colin murmured in his richly melodic voice.

After several cloudy, showery English summer days the sun reappeared and in the afternoon Anne took the year 1914 of her mother's diaries on to the terrace. Everybody had gone now; Aunty Sarah and Tamara back to The Dales, to decide what to do with the huge sum of money Mummy had left them; Con and her baby daughters to Pitlochry; Kate and Colin en route to America; Mark to London. Soon, Anne knew, she and Ben would have to make a decision about their future, though she did not yet feel Philip should be left by himself. He had resisted all their efforts to break through the barrier he had erected since Mummy's death, and was spending much of his time shut in his study. Anne believed that before she left Chenneys, she should and could persuade him to talk, to unburden his soul, to share his anguish. The future also depended on what happened today, though Anne had resisted the temptation to accompany Ben up to Town for his consultation with Stephen.

It was beautifully peaceful on the terrace, only the somnolent buzz of the bees, the chirruping of the birds and the distant sound of the church clock striking the half-hour, to disturb the calm. Anne settled herself in the *chaise-longue* with pencil and pad, to annotate her line-by-line read-through of the 1914 diary. Tea appeared, but engrossed in her work she only nibbled at the food and let the cup she poured grow cold. How poignantly her mother's record read; of those glorious July days on the Isle of Wight, when she was recovering from Kate and Mark's birth, while little Anne bossed little Con about as they played in the garden, dug sandcastles and splashed in the sea; all of them blissfully unaware of the imminence of the Great War that was to shatter their lives.

The threat of a second world war was only too evident and having read her mother's last entry in December 1914, when the casualties were already in their hundreds of thousands and the entrenched positions that were to claim millions more lives already stretched from Champagne to Flanders, Anne prayed: Please God, if You exist, rid us of Fascism and somehow stop another bloody conflict.

The light was turning golden, it was going to be a beautiful evening, and before dinner Anne decided to have a spin in Bill. Driving brought her some solace, the changing patterns of the lanes, the wind on her face, the scent of the honeysuckle in the hedgerows, and she could call in at Marshall Minnis Halt to see if Ben was on the seven o'clock train. Anne followed the road that wound round the edge of the estate towards the far side of Dedman's Down. What prompted her to stop Bill, to make the second decision to climb up to its summit, she never knew.

As she walked over the tussocky, chalky downland, Anne noticed the carrion crows wheeling above the clump of trees on the top but it was harvest time and the birds were in search of the gleanings. Rounding the edge of the trees, she saw the body lying on the grass in their favourite spot, with its panoramic view of Chenneys. Momentarily she thought somebody had fallen asleep in the sun, then her eyes registered

330

the peculiar position in which the man was lying, then a couple of the more venturesome crows swooped down, and with mounting horror Anne realised it was a dead body. She couldn't leave it here, like that, with those menacing birds hovering above. Slowly she moved towards the man. Before she reached the body, she knew whose it was.

Philip had blown his head off.

Anne stared at the golden light burnishing the shotgun and the mess of blood and . . . she put her hands to her face and cried, 'Oh God! Oh God!'

Then she vomited violently.

For minutes thereafter she crouched on the ground retching and weeping, and high above her she could hear the sweet song of a lark. Oh Philip, Philip, how could you have done this terrible thing? I'd grown to love you, with your kindness, your passion, your depression hidden beneath your cold exterior and sarcastic tongue. I could have helped you, if only you'd let me, we could have helped each other.

Eventually Anne stood up. She looked at Chenneys drowsing peacefully in the sunlight, she had no need to look at Philip's body because its image was branded in her mind, and the thought raced pell-mell through her head. Suicide . . . scandal . . . refusal to allow burial in hallowed ground . . . she had to do something . . . for Mummy's sake . . . for Philip's sake . . . for everybody's sake. The first thing was to get his body out of the way of those carrion crows.

Focusing her eyes on Philip's feet, Anne bent down, took off his shoes, grasped his ankles and keeping her gaze fixed on the sky, on the deepening gold of the light, she started to haul his body towards the clump of trees. By the time she reached their shade, her arms were aching and the sweat was pouring down her face. Her eyes wandered and she saw the trail of blood and pulp stretching from his shoes, sitting drunkenly on the grass, to the edge of the trees. After she had finished retching again, Anne ran down the chalky hillside. From the dicky-seat of the car she took the rug she carried in the MG and scrambled up to the summit of Dedman's Down. Avoiding looking at the ghastly mess that had been Philip's El Greco face, she draped the rug over his body. Then she drove back to Chenneys, parking Bill by the west wing.

Making sure nobody had seen her, Anne crept along the corridor to Philip's study. She presumed he would have left the door unlocked and he had. Once inside the beautiful room, she leant against the door and took long, slow breaths in the effort to calm her trembling body. Knowing Philip for the meticulous man he had been, she again presumed he would have left everything in order. Slowly Anne walked to the rosewood desk and on the virgin blotting pad, propped against his paperweight, were his will and four letters. Picking them up, she saw they were addressed to Mrs A. J. I. Dalziel – ah yes, Philip would use Kate's legal married name – Mrs Gavin Campbell-Ross, Mark Whitworth Esq., and Miss Anne Whitworth. She slit open the envelope addressed to her and inside was a single page penned in Philip's flowing hand, in his favoured green ink, which read:

My Dear Anne,
    Optimism about the behaviour of my fellow-man has never been one of my characteristics. Your mother was the light of my life, and with her gone, I prefer not to live through the darkness of another war. I was of little use in the last conflict. I should be of even less use in the one that is now inevitable.
    I have given thought to the effect my decision may have upon you, my beloved Kessie's firstborn child, whose initial hostility I fully understood. I believe your dislike of me lessened over the years and I loved you, Anne, as if you were my own. I thank you for the gaiety and the pleasure you brought into my life. You have followed your chosen path with singular success and you will survive well enough without me.
    My writing of this letter will, I hope, convince you that I have of my own free will – if there is such a thing – chosen to take this step.
My blessings upon you, Philip.

With the tears blurring her eyes and thickening her throat, Anne opened the drawer of Philip's desk and put his will neatly among a folder of papers. Having blown her nose hard, she stuffed the letters addressed to her siblings, together with her own, into the pocket of her print dress. Carefully she proceeded round the study, to make sure there was nothing to indicate Philip had done other than go out for a walk. Satisfied that there wasn't, she crept into the corridor and walked quickly towards her mother's old quarters. In the bathroom there, Anne had a wash and tidied herself up, before running back to Bill and driving the car round to the front of the house.

In the hall she met Mrs Delve who asked what time Mr Broughton would be back and whether dinner should be held for him. Oh Ben, I've forgotten you, oh God, I wish you were here. Then Mrs Delve said, 'You look upset, Miss Anne. Is there anything wrong?'

'Yes. Something dreadful has happened. I'm just going to 'phone Doctor Stuart. I'll tell you about it after I've spoken to him.'

Anne was surprised how calm her voice sounded but if she was to see her plan through, she had to keep in control of herself. Her voice remained calm when she was connected to Doctor Stuart's surgery and asked to speak to him urgently. 'Doctor Stuart? It's Anne Whitworth. I've just been out for a walk and I'm afraid my stepfather's met with a terrible accident. He must have been out shooting . . .' Philip's distaste for the huntin', shootin', fishin' brigade was well known but never mind and make it sound plausible. 'Since Mummy's death, he had taken to shooting, you know. It gave him a sort of solace, I suppose, and . . .'

'Had?' Doctor Stuart pounced on her use of the past tense. 'Are you telling me Sir Philip is dead, Anne?'

'Yes. His body's on the top of Dedman's Down. I moved it under the trees because there were carrion crows around. I've covered it with a rug and . . .'

'Are you telephoning from Chenneys?'

'Yes.'

'Stay there, lassie.' The kindly Scottish voice was brisk. 'Get them to make you a cup of hot strong tea with plenty of sugar. Have a cigarette to calm your nerves. Wrap yourself up if you feel cold. I'll go straight to Dedman's Down.'

After she had put the receiver back into its hook, Anne realised she was shivering. She went into the hall where Mrs Delve was waiting anxiously. Briefly Anne told her what had happened, or at least her version of what had occurred on Dedman's Down. Her eyes wide with horrified shock, Mrs Delve cried, 'Oh Miss Anne, I don't believe it. Not both of them within . . . oh, you poor lamb.'

Still shivering slightly despite the sweaters and blanket Mrs Delve had summoned, Anne was sipping her cup of hot sweet tea and lighting another cigarette, when Ben came striding into the drawing room.

His arms wide open, the sunburst smile spreading across his face, he walked towards her. 'My arm may never be one hundred percent again but my troubles are over and I'll be back painting soon. I didn't tell you, luv, because you've had enough on your plate the last few weeks but the last few days my arm's been festering badly again. Our Stephen took one look and prodded away and eureka!' Between the thumb and forefinger of his right hand, numbly Anne registered that Ben was holding something. 'I reckon I might frame it. It's a tiny bit of cloth from the jacket I was wearing when I was hit. Stephen says my arm was stitched too fast and the cloth's been trying to work its way out ever since and . . .'

Abruptly Ben stopped, his realisation that something was wrong with Anne penetrating his euphoria. Sitting down beside her on the sofa, gently he said, 'What's up?'

'Philip's shot himself. I found his body. Oh God, it was awful, Ben. But I don't want him to be labelled a suicide. I want him to be buried by Mummy's side. I'm waiting for Doctor Stuart. That sounds like his car now.'

Stubbing her cigarette into the ashtray, Anne raced into the corridor, across the entrance hall and out on to the terrace where she met Doctor Stuart at the top of the steps. He said, 'Don't worry, Anne. Everything's under control. The men are bringing Sir Philip's body down. There'll have to be an inquest but I'll get on to Colonel Gaunt and he'll arrange things.' Colonel Gaunt was the Chief Constable. Anne stared at Doctor Stuart as he looked over her head and said, 'Are you the boy friend?'

Becoming conscious that Ben was behind her, Anne heard him murmur, 'Yeah.'

'I presume you know Anne found her stepfather's body whilst she was out walking. She's in an obvious state of shock

334

and I am going to sedate her. In the days ahead, she will need comforting.'

'Doctor Stuart . . .'

'I told you not to worry, lassie. It was a dreadful *accident*. Understandable in your stepfather's bereaved state, as I'm sure Colonel Gaunt will agree.'

The slight emphasis on 'accident' told Anne that Doctor Stuart knew Philip had committed suicide but was prepared to assist in the cover-up. She whispered, 'Thank you.'

29

'What on earth was he doing messing about with a gun?' Sarah Muranov demanded of Ben.

They were standing in the drawing room at Chenneys, staring at the rain as it slanted across the mullioned windows, sploshed into the puddles on the terrace, and shrouded the gardens. The weather for the funeral of Sir Philip Gerald Delamere Marchal could not have been in greater contrast to that for his wife's. It had not, however, deterred the crowds who had huddled under a forest of umbrellas outside the church built by his Norman ancestors, peering at the members of a famous family afflicted by a double tragedy. Anne's version of the events on Dedman's Down had gone unchallenged, surprisingly so in Ben's opinion. Or could folk not believe somebody with Sir Philip Marchal's advantages would commit suicide even in the wake of his beloved wife's death, which had hardly been unexpected any road?

Sarah appeared to have her suspicions. After she'd taken a cup of tea from a circulating maid, gulped several mouthfuls and said she'd needed that, she went on, 'I don't understand what Sir Philip was doing up there with a gun. Do you?'

Ben made a non-committal noise. He knew Anne had told Con the truth but she had decided not to tell Kate, who had been stopped as she was about to board the Atlantic liner and who, according to Anne, leaked confidences like a sieve. Which was no surprise with that little madam. Because she was withholding the truth from Kate, Anne had not revealed it to Mark either. She'd said, 'They are twins. Though they always quarrelled and latterly they've gone their own ways, there is that special bond. Mark might feel he should tell Kate.' If Anne had kept the suicide a secret from dear Aunty Sarah too, Ben wasn't going to enlighten her.

There was a commotion on the far side of the room. Turning his head, Ben saw that with her usual clumsiness, Rebecca had managed to send a plateful of cakes crashing to the floor. Nearby him, one of the long-faced, crimson-mouthed Marchal relations raised her pencilled brows and drawled, 'Damned Jews! They get everywhere.'

Pushing rudely past the cow, Ben strode towards Rebecca who was apologising profusely. The minute he reached her side she broke off to whisper, 'I don't know what that Basil Goodwin-Lamburne creature said to Anne . . .' He was the eldest son of Philip's eldest sister '. . . but she's in a right old state.'

As he entered Anne's bedroom with Rebecca, Ben saw the half-packed cases on the bed. Palely elegant in her mourning clothes, simple black dress, black silk stockings, black leather court shoes, the copper of her hair providing a burnished contrast, cigarette in hand, Anne was pacing up and down like a caged animal. She continued to pace and between furious puffs of the cigarette the words cascaded from her.

'I've given up on the packing. They'll just have to send the rest of my things on. I'm leaving now. This minute. The Marchal family seem to think we're plotting to stay on at Chenneys and claim all sorts of things that don't belong to us. We're not. We've always known the estate was entailed and personally I wouldn't touch anything that isn't mine with a barge pole. Neither would Con, nor Kate, nor Mark. Personally I shall never set foot here ever again. You know why they're so furious? They've seen Philip's will. He remade it after Mummy died of course and apparently he's left all his personal things down to his cuff-links, and his personal fortune including every penny he earned as a playwright and the copyright in his plays, to us. Kate and Mark and Con and

336

me. Why shouldn't he? We were his family. Philip loathed his relations and they loathed him. And I can't stand the beastly atmosphere any longer. I want to leave now and . . .'

Deciding she'd gone on quite long enough, and he couldn't wait to leave the place either, Ben caught Anne firmly in his arms. Taking the cigarette from her fingers, he handed it to Rebecca who stubbed it in an ashtray already filled with butts. Gently, he said, 'So you shall, me luv. Rebecca and I'll take you to London this very minute.'

After Anne had bade Kate and Colin a second, tearful farewell before they reset off for the United States; after Mark had driven the Silver Ghost up to Gower Street packed with everything she had left at Chenneys; after she had agreed her brother could have the Rolls-Royce, temporarily anyway, Ben more than suggested they go to Pitlochry. All his belongings, not that he possessed many but what he had, were in the bothy. More importantly, he wanted to get Anne away from London, from the sandbags that were appearing outside official buildings, from the air-raid shelters that were being erected in public places and back gardens, from the hundred and one signs that the British Government was finally facing the probability of war with Nazi Germany. The war preparations were doing Anne's state of mind no good at all and Ben hoped the peace and beauty of the Perthshire countryside, the soothing proximity of her sister Con, would have a beneficial effect.

In the days after her stepfather's suicide she talked incessantly to Ben. Listening to her accounts of how she'd found the body and what she'd done, his admiration for the woman he'd lived with on and off for six years now, rose no end. But then Anne started to berate herself. 'I failed Philip. I mean, I knew that underneath his cold exterior there was a passionate man subject to depression. I knew the state he was in. I should have made sure I got through to him.'

'You can't get through to people if they won't let you. Your stepfather had made up his mind. He didn't want to live any more.'

That response only made Anne start to question her actions. She said, 'No, he didn't, did he? What right had I to interfere with a decision he made of his own free will? If, as Philip

337

said, there is such a thing as free will. Though we mostly behave as if there is, don't we? What right had I to keep his suicide notes from Kate and Mark? I've let Con have hers, of course, but what business have I to hold on to letters that rightfully belong to the twins? Should I let Kate and Mark have them, do you think?'

Firmly Ben said, no, he didn't. Anne's reasons for *not* handing them over seemed perfectly valid to him and to reveal the truth now would shock them to the core and serve no useful purpose.

Next Anne said she had a confession to make and she told him about going to see Irene, what a hideous scene that had been, and how it had been her fault. In other circumstances Ben reckoned this information would have angered him but with Anne in her weepy, hair-shirt, breast-beating condition he said, 'Sod Irene. You needn't worry about her. She's as tough as old boots.'

Those comments didn't raise a smile and nothing he said convinced Anne she was torturing herself for no good reason.

When they reached Pitlochry, the peaceful beauty of the Perthshire countryside did not have the desired effect. Anne rose early, she washed, she dressed, during the days she kept busy about the bothy, she shopped in the little town, and she went over to 'the big hoos' to help Con. In the evenings, if it wasn't raining, sometimes when it was, she disappeared for a solitary walk, or she sat with the little tortoiseshell cat she'd adopted purring on her lap, or she read and played records on the ancient portable gramophone her father had carried with him from the Somme to the Sambre Canal. Day or night she lapsed into a silence, speaking to Ben with the utmost politeness only when spoken to.

A silent, ultra-polite Anne, never raising her voice, never growing excited or outraged, never swearing, showing only a passing interest in the fact that he was painting again, doing no writing at all, an Anne who allowed him to stroke her hair or massage her shoulders but lay rigidly, unresponsively by his side in bed, was more than Ben could bear. After they'd been back ten days he said, 'Why don't you go and see Con's doctor, luv? What's-his-name . . .'

'Mackenzie,' Anne said politely.

'Yeah. He's a nice old cove and maybe he can give you something that'll . . .'

Even more politely she said, 'I don't want to see him, thank you.'

Beginning to appreciate the problems Anne had faced when he'd presented a brick wall, Ben smiled and said, 'You know what you told me when I wouldn't see a doctor?'

'Yes, but I haven't a bullet wound in my arm.' Anne sounded eminently reasonable. 'Doctor Mackenzie would only prescribe a bromide of some sort.'

Trying to control his mounting irritation, holding his smile with difficulty, Ben said, 'They can help.'

'Drugs don't solve anything though, do they?' Anne asked in the same reasonable tone.

'What is it you want solving?' Ben did his best to keep the impatience from his voice.

'Oh . . . everything.'

In the early days of their affair he had been amazed by the open way Anne's family and friends discussed matters folk in The Dales kept quiet about – intimate relationships, childbirth, nervous breakdowns, that kind of thing – and by the way he as Anne's lover, had been received into the fold. Normally he had little time for the psychiatric and psychoanalytic soul-searching rich folk indulged in, for it seemed to Ben to unearth as many problems as it resolved. But Anne's clamming up was unnatural and she badly needed to unburden her soul.

'Let's make a start on everything then,' he said cheerfully. There was no response. After he'd followed Rebecca's customary advice and counted ten, he went on, 'You know what you said about getting through to your stepfather? I can't help you, luv, if you won't let me.'

With deadly politeness Anne said, 'I'm not feeling talkative at the moment. But please don't worry. I'm not going to commit suicide.'

Jeez! She was in a worse state than Ben had imagined. He gave an unaccustomed amount of consideration to her state of mind.

In the last six months Anne had been clobbered by his injury and ensuing depression, by her mother's death, by reading her diaries and adjusting to the portrait of her father contained in its pages. She had surmounted those traumas and though she was distressed by the behaviour of the bloody Marchal family and the loss of Chenneys, which had been her home for best part of two decades, it was the event that had led to those circumstances, her stepfather's suicide, that had thrown her so completely off-balance. In the unlikely event of his re-encountering Sir Philip Marchal in some other world it would, Ben decided, give him the greatest pleasure to thump his well-bred face, as he'd known it before the gentleman had chosen to blow his head off. Life could be a bugger but it was here to be lived until your allotted time-span was up and Philip Marchal had no business to kill himself. He couldn't have known Anne would find his shotgun-blasted corpse but by committing suicide he had caused the step-daughter he had allegedly loved as his own, the anguish that had led to her current condition.

Seeing her reduced to these silent, haunted straits had made one thing absolutely clear to Ben. He loved Anne deeply. It was up to him to see her through the dark days of her soul, as she had seen him through his. Action rather than words might help.

'Come in,' Anne responded to the knock on the bedroom door. Ben had taken off for a few days – she hadn't enquired where – and in his absence she had agreed to be cosseted at 'the big hoos'. The knock heralded the arrival of the maid with her breakfast.

'Good morning, madame, I trust you slept better than you've been sleeping of late. No prowling around in the middle of the night.'

'When did you get back?'

'Late last night.'

Ben placed the breakfast tray, with the single red rose in the slender vase, flat on the eiderdown in front of her. Looking at the tray, Anne said, 'It has legs. You open them out.'

He gave her a look which said it was some time since she had opened hers out, to which Anne failed to respond. After she had helped him to undo the legs of the tray, Ben said, 'You can pour me a cup of tea.' When she had done so, he sat on the end of the bed drinking the tea, his watchful grey eyes regarding her steadily. Then he said, 'I reckoned it'd be a good idea to be with you today.'

'Oh. Yes. Thank you.'

Today was 4 August, 1939, the twenty-fifth anniversary of the outbreak of the war to end wars, and this month, next month, some time very, very soon there was going to be another war and those millions of lives, including her father's, would have been sacrificed in vain. The world was a hateful place filled with a mankind which learned nothing, in which evil flourished like the green bay tree. And it was a beautiful place filled with individuals like Con and Rebecca and . . . Ben, who remembered what day it was and how she might be feeling. But the Nemesis she had always known was lying in wait, had finally ambushed her. Anne's centre had ceased to hold. How arrogant she had been to imagine she had the answers to the world's problems. Whose honesty? Whose truth? Whose evil? How could she know when she had failed so dismally and hurt so many people in her own life?

'Was I absolutely objectionable when we first met in Oxford?'

'Eh?' Ben shot her a startled glance. Then the sunburst smile spread across his face as he said, 'Only moderately so. I always fancied you, you know. Give us a piece of toast.'

'Haven't you had your breakfast?'

'Yeah. I'm still hungry though.' Anne buttered a piece of toast, spread it with the delicious home-made marmalade and handed it to him. With his mouth half-full Ben said, 'Aren't you going to ask me where I've been?'

'If you want me to, yes. Where have you been?'

'To The Dales. To see Irene. I told her it was all over between us and I wouldn't be seeing her again. The cheques are rolling in from our Derek, you know. My genius is being recognised! They're even buying my Lancashire stuff. So I offered to buy Irene a nice house in a refined district away from all those vulgar folk round Gladstone Terrace. Go on, say, "Did she accept?"'

'Did she accept?'

'Yeah. She won't divorce me but the slate's clean.'

Ben had taken the positive action Anne had been longing for, willing him to take for six years, but she didn't feel anything. With an effort, mainly because she had to say something, she sighed, 'I'm only too aware I've become a pain in the neck, which I suppose is what happens to people like me when we collapse. How are those who thought they were mighty fallen. I haven't anything left to offer you, Ben.'

'You haven't changed, have you, me luv? You don't let me decide for myself what you have to offer.' Despite herself Anne smiled and Ben said, 'That's the first real smile I've seen in ages.'

The weather was awful – it had hardly stopped raining since Philip's funeral at the beginning of July – but later in the week Anne suggested she and Ben have a drive. Bill not being the ideal vehicle for swirling Scottish mists and squalls of rain, they borrowed Con's Sunbeam and drove along the deserted roads to Loch Tay. Ben parked the car by a sodden sandy reach and everywhere was grey, seen through a veil of grey rain, the stones on the edge of the loch, the stretch of the water, the blurred folds of the mountains, the brumal outlines of the trees. Yet suddenly, sitting in the car on this most depressing of August afternoons, Anne had the urge to talk, to try to explain the emotions, or the lack of emotion, that had overtaken her and the images that haunted her.

'I keep seeing Philip's face. And it keeps changing into that mess of blood and pulp.'

Ben put his arm round her shoulder and slowly he said, 'For months I saw the face of the first dead soldier I encountered in Spain. And I didn't even know him. So what do you expect, me luvly Anne, when in the tranquillity of the Kent countryside you stumble across your stepfather with his head blown off?'

With her head on Ben's chest, Anne wept with a relief she had not felt in weeks. When he was driving back through a deluge, his voice rising above the thwack of the windscreen wipers, Ben told her exactly what he thought about her stepfather's selfishness in committing suicide. Anne said, 'Is it selfish not to be able to endure life any longer? That's the one absolute choice we have. We don't choose to be born, or where we're born, or the circumstances that will shape our lives. We do have the choice of death, if we want to take it.'

Leaning over to kiss her, Ben said, 'That sounds more like the Anne I know and love.'

She said, 'Keep your eyes on the road.'

After dinner Ben said to Con, 'Thanks for the meal. We'll be off then.'

'You're not going back to the bothy, are you? It's a foul evening. There are beds made up for you both.' Tongues might wag about what Mrs Campbell-Ross's sister was doing in the bothy with that man who was not apparently her husband, but their sleeping together in 'the big hoos' was out of the question. Giving Anne an impish smile, her sister said, 'If you're determined to brave the elements, have a good night's . . . sleep.'

Anne felt herself blushing slightly, though something other than sleep was undoubtedly what Ben had in mind. After weeks of abstinence, in her still confused state, she wondered whether she would be able to respond. At least the night was not as foul as Con had thought. The rain had stopped, the mist had lifted, a few stars were visible in the clearing sky and by the time they reached the bothy the moon was gliding behind jagged clouds. They went into the kitchen and to postpone the moment of physical reckoning she wanted but was afraid of spoiling, Anne said, 'Would you like a cup of cocoa?'

'Yeah, why not?'

They drank the cocoa by the warmth of the Aga, then Ben lifted her to her feet and they walked up the stairs to the front bedroom. The curtains were open but as Anne made to draw them, Ben checked her. Silently he undid the buttons of her dress, compliantly Anne allowed him to take off her clothes and to lift her into the shaft of moonlight striking the bed. She watched as Ben undressed himself and lowered his own naked body on to the bed beside her. Still silently, Ben ran his stubby, well-tended fingers from the stretch of her toes, along her feet, over her ankles, up her legs to her thighs, over the flatness of her belly to the swell of her breasts. Stroking the extended nipples, his fingers moved to caress her neck, the outlines of her jaw and cheekbones, her eyebrows, her hair. It was a moon-silvered ritual of wondrous delight in her body, the most erotic experience of Anne's life.

'Oh, Ben.'

'Yes, me luv.'

Twining her legs and arms around his compact muscularity, she pressed her open mouth on to his. Their bodies

343

were so hot Anne felt as if she were in a furnace and when he entered her channel the images of golden-red metals burning to melting point, filled her mind. If only she could remain in this ecstatic inferno for ever and ever, isolated and insulated from the world outside, but inexorably, inevitably, the un-controllable moans of approaching orgasm overwhelmed her and she cried out, 'Ben, give me a baby, give me a baby, now, now, now.'

He cried back, 'Yes, yes, yes.'

With a final thrust he poured himself into her and then with a long sated sigh his weight sagged on to her. After a while Anne said, 'You're heavy. Get off.'

Ben rolled on to his side and for a longer while they lay blissfully in each other's arms in the moonlight. Eventually they snuggled under the blankets, Anne lit a cigarette and Ben said, 'You can give me one, too. That was something special.'

Puffing out a cloud of smoke she observed, 'I didn't use my thing. I could be pregnant.'

'Yeah, I suppose you could be.'

'We brought the sun with us.' Typically Tamara added, 'I had no idea English summers were so dreadful.'

'This is Scotland,' Con observed mildly. 'I shouldn't go around talking about "English" this and that here.'

Tamara gave her a blank look but Jenny Macdonald said, 'I'd no idea Scottish nationalism was so strong. Seeing my forebears were all good Scots I suppose I should have had, but I hadn't.'

Aunty Sarah and Tamara had arrived for a brief holiday in Pitlochry. Jenny had been taking photographs for a *Picture Post* feature about the growing demand for Home Rule for Scotland and she'd dropped in to see them all. After the dismal weeks of mist and rain, the weather gods had suddenly remembered it was summer and the last few days had been glorious. They were sitting in deckchairs on the lawn in front of 'the big hoos', below them Pitlochry drowsed in the heat, above them the slopes of Ben-y-Vrackie basked in the sunshine.

Fiona and Kirsty were sleeping under the tasselled sunshade of their double pram, Aunty Sarah had fallen asleep too, and

Ben was hunched on the grass sketching. On the flat stretch of ground where Mark had landed his 'kite', Rob was organising his older brother Callum, little Ian and assorted friends into two teams. He was the most precocious four-year-old, Anne thought, though with one of her impish smiles Con had said Rob reminded her of his Aunty Anne when she was a child!

It was an afternoon when all was right with the world, and if there was a God He was sitting benignly in His heaven. The conversation had been pleasantly desultory but Jenny was now asking Con, 'Have you heard from Gavin? What does he think about the Nazi–Soviet Pact?'

With a sigh Con replied, 'Yes, he telephoned last night. It was a fearful connection but I gathered he thinks it means war.'

'Of course it does.' Aunty Sarah opened her eyes. 'With no threat from the Russians, Hitler's free to march into Poland whenever he feels like it.'

'Why did Stalin do it? How could he sign a pact with the Nazis?' Jenny cried out with the anguish of the betrayed Communist.

'If he could murder my father, he can do anything,' Tamara said fiercely.

'It's finished me. I've resigned my membership of the Communist party.' Jenny turned towards Anne and said, 'I bumped into Sandy Dalziel before I left London. It's not finished him. He was parroting the excuses that Stalin has to protect Russia because the Western powers want to destroy Communism. The ends justify the means. If Britain and France decide to act, it will be another capitalist war. All that rubbish.'

'He is that ginger-haired idiot from the BBC who married your sister, is he not?' Tamara flapped the neck of her dress in disgust.

Poor old Sandy, Anne thought, what an epitaph!

Gazing at the cottonwool balls of cloud drifting slowly across the sky, Aunty Sarah said, 'Ah Jenny, where are the dreams of yesteryear?'

'Where did it all go wrong, Sarah? How did it happen?' Jenny wailed. 'How did we come to this pass?'

There was a silence as they considered these questions, broken only by the excited, high-pitched voices of the children. Wearily Anne could only think, how indeed? But Tamara said sharply, 'Will there be a war? Will Britain fight when the Nazis march into Poland? That is the real question.'

Looking up from his sketching Ben said, 'If we and the French don't honour our obligations to the Poles – not that we're likely to be of the slightest use to the poor buggers – but if we don't act this time, we might as well shut up shop.'

Anne noticed that he was flexing the fingers of his right hand, gently massaging the scar visible below the rolled-up sleeves of his check shirt. Ben's arm was never going to be one hundred percent which meant it was never going to be fit enough to fire a gun. When war came, there could be no 'if' now, it would save him from combat duty. A similar thought must have occurred to dear Con because softly she said, 'Ben will make a very good war artist.'

Anne looked at her sister and nodded thankfully. After a pause she asked, 'Will Gavin want to fight?'

'Oh yes. I can only hope the Foreign Office will require his services in a non-combatant field. Though if he insists on joining up, I expect I shall be like Mummy and accept his decision.'

The children had flopped exhaustedly on to the grass and the sound of their voices was momentarily stilled. Into the slumbering silence Anne said, 'In a way, I'm glad Mummy didn't live to see another war. It would have broken her heart.'

Even more softly Con said, 'Philip's too. Always remember that, Anne.'

30

They travelled to London by train in the early morning of Friday, 1 September. The big end had suddenly gone on Bill but Ben had arranged to see Derek Elmar-Smythe and Anne wanted to start picking up the threads of her life, so train it had to be. Just as they were leaving Pitlochry they heard the news that German troops had rolled across the Polish border at dawn. Kissing Anne goodbye, with tears in her eyes Con said, 'This is it then. It can only be a matter of hours before we're at war.'

When they changed on to the *Flying Scotsman* in Edinburgh, the numbers of uniformed men on board, reservists answering their call-up, underlined the point. As the crack express steamed southward the passengers were unusually, though quietly, loquacious. There was general agreement that Herr Hitler and his gang had to be stopped once and for all and we'd soon give them the bloody nose they deserved.

King's Cross station was a bedlam of schoolchildren, card-board gas-mask-holders slung round their necks, suitcases clutched in hands, labels stating their names, schools and religion pinned to their coats. Anxious, tearful parents were kissing their offspring goodbye, harassed teachers were shout-ing, 'Come here this instant, Billy Murgatroyd,' railway officials were marshalling the groups on to trains. The great evacuation of Britain's city-dwelling children was well under way, bound for their unknown destinations in the safety of the countryside. Fingering her own gas-mask in its leather holder, snuffling back her tears, Anne said, 'Oh Ben, what a sight.'

'It's the best thing for the kids, luv. I've lived through air-raids in Madrid and Barcelona.'

'I lived through them in the last war – oh God, the last war – I'm already saying it. We didn't leave London.'

'Yeah well, they've improved their techniques since then.'

Saturday was another lovely day but one during which Anne felt suspended in space. Ben took off for his appointment with Derek but she and Rebecca stayed glued to the wireless set in the living room of the Gower Street flat. Warsaw and other Polish cities were being heavily bombed, the Poles were fighting gallantly but against overwhelming odds, it was inferred. A sort of ultimatum had been handed to Herr von Ribbentrop, the Nazi Foreign Minister, to the effect that unless German troops withdrew forthwith from Poland, the

British Government would be forced to take action. Parliament was in emergency session but by the evening, no action had actually been taken.

'They can't be not going to do anything this time,' Anne cried out to Ben when he returned. 'Tamara can't have been right about our not fighting when the Nazis invaded Poland.'

Giving her a sardonic smile, Ben said, 'No, me little pacifist, I don't reckon she was. Chamberlain's hanging on to the last gasp of appeasement but I don't reckon even he can back down this time. Are we going out for your birthday tomorrow?'

Oh God, September 3, 1939, was her thirtieth birthday. Anne said, 'I don't know. Let's see what happens tomorrow.'

After a restless night she rose early and, seeing it was her birthday, Anne selected a sunflower-yellow dress Theo had designed. It was knee-length, it had padded shoulders, puffy three-quarter-length sleeves, a v-neck with large lapels, and a tight waistband with the skirt gathered into folds, all of which suited Anne's tall slim figure to perfection. Over breakfast they did their best to be festive. Rebecca presented Anne with a copy of *Finnegan's Wake*, saying, 'That'll keep you quiet. I've had a glance through it and I understand one page in three of what James Joyce is saying. At least I think I do.'

Ben gave Anne a new portable typewriter and, kissing him, she said, 'You shouldn't have.'

'That thing of yours is clapped out. You've no excuse for not getting back to work now.'

In the background they kept the wireless switched on low. Just before 11.15 Rebecca turned up the volume for the Prime Minister's broadcast to the nation. She joined Anne on the sofa, Ben stood in front of the fireplace, and tensely they listened to Neville Chamberlain's sadly throbbing voice. It informed his fellow-countrymen that the British Government had sought the assurance that German forces would withdraw from Poland but by eleven o'clock just gone, the hour the final ultimatum expired, no satisfactory assurance had been received.

'Consequently this country is now at war with Germany.'

Mr Chamberlain's plangent tones had barely faded away when the soaring and swooping wail of the air-raid siren sounded. Jumping up from the sofa Rebecca ran to the windows, saying, 'The buggers must have set off before the ultimatum expired.'

As Anne ran after Rebecca, Ben shouted, 'Get away from the windows, you bloody fools.'

Down in Gower Street Anne saw an air-raid warden in his tin hat, waving his hands at the few pedestrians around. Through the open window she heard him bawling, 'Take cover, take cover', and giving directions to the nearest public shelter. Ben had his arm around her, he was dragging her and Rebecca away from their vulnerable position, pushing them on to the floor behind the sofa. For several minutes they crouched on the carpet, Anne's stomach churned as she waited for the drone of enemy aircraft, for the reverberating thuds and thumps of exploding bombs that she remembered from her childhood days, in what was now definitely the last war. Nothing happened. Apart from a distant shout and blast of a police whistle, it was in fact eerily quiet.

Anne started to giggle and Ben snapped, 'It's not funny.'

Raising herself on to her knees and putting her head over the back of the sofa, she said, 'No, I know it's not, but I think it may have been a false alarm.'

It had been. The long steady wail of the 'All Clear' sounded and slowly they stood up. Ben looked mortified that his efforts to knock air-raid sense into them had been unnecessary and Rebecca said, 'Let's have a cup of tea.'

'Let's have something stronger,' Anne said.

While they were sipping their drinks Rebecca heaved the deepest of sighs. Anne said, 'Are you thinking about Cousin Aaron and Sophia in Frankfurt?' Rebecca nodded and Anne put a sympathetic arm round her friend's shoulder. 'They wouldn't leave. There was no way anybody could persuade them to. At least Kurt's safe in England. And Helga and Herta, and Luise and baby Jacob . . .' Luise had recently given birth to a son '. . . are safe in Holland.'

'I'm thinking about all the Jews trapped under the Nazis' jackboots.'

'You helped get hundreds away, Rebecca,' Ben said.

'Mm. But when you think what the Nazis did to Jews in peacetime while the newspapers of the world were reporting their behaviour, what are they going to do in wartime when there's nobody to report what's going on?'

Ben said maybe the Nazis would start realising what a talented lot Jews were and utilise them in the war effort. Rebecca gave him a sceptical look and Anne asked, 'Hasn't Poland got the largest Jewish population in Europe?'

Rebecca replied, 'No, Russia has. But there are nearly three and half million Jews in Poland. Why?'

'Well, Poland is alas going to be overrun. Cavalry charges won't halt the Panzer divisions. But isn't there safety in numbers? Not even the Nazis can shoot or beat up millions of Jews.'

Encouragingly Ben said, 'That's true. To round them all up would be a colossal exercise. Even the most dedicated Nazis aren't going to waste their energies like that.'

Rebecca frowned, then she smiled slightly and nodded her agreement. She was about to say something when the front door bell rang. Anne went to answer. For a couple of seconds she didn't recognise the figure in the air force blue uniform, standing in the shadows of the landing. Then the figure saluted smartly and said, 'Pilot Officer Whitworth reporting, ma'am.'

'Mark!' Anne exclaimed. 'What are you doing in that uniform?'

'I've been called up. Didn't I tell you I'd joined the auxiliary RAF?'

'You know damned well you didn't.'

'Stop sounding so cross and invite me in.'

Once Mark was in the living room, Anne's heart fluttered as she looked at him with his cap off, the sunlight full on him. His uniform was grey-blue, their father's had been khaki, but with his six-foot loose-limbed frame, the black hair neat and short, grinning at Rebecca as she admired the cut of his jib, the resemblance to Daddy was uncanny. Giving Anne her present – a huge bottle of Chanel Number Five – Mark said, 'Why you had to choose the day the balloon goes up, I dunno, but happy birthday, sis!'

Handing her brother a glass of Scotch, Anne prayed: keep him safe, don't let Mark be killed. The possibility that he might be did not appear to have entered her brother's head, or if it had he was keeping it firmly at bay. He was in the highest of spirits and enthusiastically he informed them, 'I'm hoping to be posted to a Spitfire squadron. I've done a bit of training on fighters and they let me take a Spit up last week. They're streets ahead of the Messerschmitt 109E, which is the best fighter the Jerrys have. Absolutely wizard kites. They handle like a dream, eight Oerlikon guns, four in each wing, and they can do 285 m.p.h. How about that!'

'Glad to hear it,' Ben said dourly. 'I reckon we're going to need all the "Spits" we can make.'

Giving him a momentarily serious glance, Mark put his arm round Anne's shoulder and said, 'Come on, Annie, it is your birthday. Cheer up. I know it's beastly and all that but it had to happen. We can't let those Nazi bastards stamp their way round Europe. And I fear I cannot stay. I'm meeting Penny for lunch and she'll slay me if I'm late.'

'Penny Southern?' Anne asked in astonishment. Her brother grinned and nodded. 'I thought she threw you over as an irresponsible wart.'

'Ah well, I'm a reformed character. We met up again in Paris. Penny's been working over there. Who knows, I may be following in the footsteps of Margaret-Jane. Did you see the announcement of la Conway's engagement to Bunny Huntingford?'

'Yes,' said Rebecca.

'Penny is a sensible, highly intelligent lass and I can't think why she should take up with you again.' Anne hugged her brother. 'I am glad, and give her my love.'

After Mark had gone, with elaborate salutes to each of them in turn, Ben said, 'I suggest we go out for lunch too. How about the Savoy Grill, ladies? As your brother says, war or no war, it is your birthday, Anne.'

While Rebecca went to don a dress suitable for the Savoy Grill, Anne sat on the bed watching Ben change into his best white shirt and one good suit. She said, 'Do you think it will be as terrible a war as last time?'

'Nobody's ever denied the Huns are bonny fighters and they've been rearming fast. This time they're fighting for a creed dedicated to death and destruction. So – if you want a straight answer – Yes. It'll be a terrible war. And I'm not going to discuss it any more today. Okay?'

'Okay.'

Anne rose from the bed and walked across the room to adjust his tie. Then she slipped her arms round his waist, looked up at him and said, 'I feel this is the appropriate, cataclysmic moment to tell you. I'm pregnant, Ben.'

His beautiful grey eyes with their smudgy lashes looked down at her. He said, 'You can't know yet.'

'Yes, I can. We haven't taken any precautions for the last month. And I'm a week late. I've sometimes been early but I've never, ever, been late before. I just know I am.'

Ben slid his arms round her and held her close. 'We'd better start looking for a house then, hadn't we?'

In a muffled voice because, though she presumed that statement meant he was pleased, she didn't know how he would react to her next proposal, Anne said, 'I'd quite like to stay in the south. I mean, I am a Londoner and . . .'

'If you are expecting, you're not staying in London.' Ben's tone was emphatic.

'And you hate the place anyway.' Anne lifted her head from his chest. 'Can we compromise on a country cottage, not too far away from what will undoubtedly be the hub of things?'

'Yeah, all right.'

'Oh Ben, I do love you.'

'I love you, very much, you witch.'

After he had kissed her, Anne said, 'You are glad, aren't you?'

'Yeah, of course I am. Are you?'

Despite everything, the terrible day her thirtieth birthday had fallen upon, the fact that she could not marry Ben, that her darling mother had not lived to see the little girl she was sure she would have, life had to go on. Anne whispered, 'Yes, I'm very glad.'